"Guy Jerald sits speechless and is visited by his old friend, psychiatrist James Meyer. As Jerald faces his past, the faulty choices he made, and considers the things he values, his old friend Meyer is forced to reevaluate his own choices, the things he really holds dear. . . .

"Few will not be totally engrossed with this tale of a man in midlife crisis who has come close to destroying himself. . . . "

—*Publishers Weekly*

"IMMENSELY FASCINATING."
—*Colorado Springs Gazette Telegraph*

Bright Flows
the River

Taylor Caldwell

FAWCETT CREST • NEW YORK

BRIGHT FLOWS THE RIVER

Published by Fawcett Crest Books, a unit of CBS Publications, the Consumer Publishing Division of CBS Inc., by arrangement with Doubleday and Company, Inc.

ISBN: 0-449-24149-1

THIS BOOK CONTAINS THE COMPLETE TEXT OF THE ORIGINAL HARDCOVER EDITION.

Alternate Selection of the Doubleday Book Club

Alternate Selection of the Literary Guild of America

Printed in the United States of America

First Fawcett Crest printing: December 1979

10   9   8   7   6   5   4   3   2   1

For Rita Smith,
of the Buffalo *Courier-Express*

"In the dark night of the soul,
Bright flows the river of God."

Prologue

The wet black road twisted and flowed before him, a rippling black river, glittering in the bouncing headlights of his car. He could hear the roaring shout of the awesome summer storm; lightning sprang back from the gushing windshield, glared in blue-white mirrors on the pavement. Water scrambled on the roof of the car, thunder made the whole vehicle shudder. He could feel the explosions in his very teeth, against the top of his head. Occasionally, as his car rushed in lunatic flight towards destruction, the lights flared on twisting trees, on marching steel rods of rain. The windshield wipers squealed shrilly: "Stop it, stop it, stop it!" Wind bawled against the shut windows.

But he was running, running away from his tranquil maniac life, his sweet life, his serene and terrible life, his secure and fulfilled and unbearable life, his life which was now a huge and untenable sickness in him, an agony too murderous to be borne even for another hour. His head rang with the groans and screams of his own pain which seemed to blast up from his very viscera, all clamoring for death, for surcease, for escape into nothingness, for an end—and sleep, and silent eternity without thought or memory.

He cried out, "Beth! Beth!" With each cry the pain twisted in him, wrenching him apart, snatching at his throat, echoing back into the vault of his skull, into shivering caverns filled with hot torment and exquisite anguish, into abysses that were in himself yet into which he was falling. His suffering climbed pointed mountains of flame, only to hurtle again down to crevices of burning darkness which vomited him up once more. His arms swung from side to side in his half-blindness on that running and

7

spurting black river which appeared to want to engulf him; his hands clung to the wheel and would not release it for all his blasphemous prayers. Death, death—but his hands gripped the wheel and would not let go in spite of his cursing. The will to live fought with the will to die, and it was losing.

He had one sudden cold and lucid thought: You are mad, you know.

He answered it aloud, through his clenched teeth and from his gasping throat. "Yes, of course. I always was. I was a coward, and mad cowards deserve to die. I should have done this before," and he laughed over and over and the awful sound beat against the thrumming walls of his car.

Thunder answered him, too—or was it his heart?— thunder that was not divided from his pain. Lightning dazzled him. It lit up the whole black and streaming and chaotic night of storm, and he did not know, for several moments, if he was within his car or joined to the yelling elements outside. A savage joy seized him, and he shouted again, "Yes, yes, yes!"

The car, like a sentient thing pleading for its life with all its resistance against ruin, was sliding here and there, rocking on its wheels, and again the lightning created a chaos of light, and he saw before him a copse of trees which was leaping at him with an insane speed. He saw the trunks, pouring with water, the embracing wild branches, and, in one second, the seething leaves blazing with white torn fire.

He closed his eyes and whispered, "Now, now!"

He did not feel the impact. He merely saw a redness and felt a bursting in himself, a rising, a floating, a soaring. He did not hear the trees crushing his car. He heard, at blessed last, only silence. A great white star, expanding and throbbing, and brighter than any sun, swarmed toward him with enormous velocity and he smiled and held his eyes upon it, waiting.

PART ONE

1

"He had—has—all the reason in the world to live," said Guy Jerald's wife. "Of course, I've heard of the male climacteric—Guy is fifty-five, you know. I understand, at that age, that men begin to 'reevaluate' their lives—or something."

Or "something," thought her visitor. I wonder if she knows what she is talking about. A stupid woman, really. She quotes all the jargon and all the clichés but without comprehension. That is true of almost everyone, though; she is certainly handsome for a woman of—fifty-six? I shouldn't be too critical; perhaps cynicism has become my way of life. Occupational hazard. He murmured, "True. There does come a time in a man's life when he thinks over the past and what, if anything, he has accomplished, and dreads the future, and ruts, and monotony and old age. He wonders where his life has gone, and what remains for him, and if day after day will only follow in dreary procession, until he dies. Then, he becomes desperate—"

"I know," said Jerald's wife very brightly. " 'The search for identity,' I believe it is called."

Oh, God, thought her visitor. He ached to ask her what the hell she meant by that, but he was certain it would only embarrass her as she fumbled among her other platitudes. Intrinsically, though he was a psychiatrist, he was a kind man, this in spite of all the fools he was constantly encountering, all the dangerous, pathetic, bewildered, stumbling, egotistic, maundering, self-pitying, wretched, hysterical fools. I am losing the virtue of compassion, he said to himself, but—my God! There are so few whom life has ruthlessly and genuinely persecuted, so few who have known authentic tragedy and despair and pain and awful disillusion. These are the ones who show a complacent and easy face to the world, who are rarely serious and apparently always interested, and laugh often. The others—my God!

They sat in the library of this great shadowy Georgian house, with its rosy brick walls, its white shutters and ivy and gardens covering four acres of ordered lawns, its fountains and grottoes and slate paths under stretching oaks and maples whose leaves were now brilliant crimson and scarlet on this autumn day in Cranston, Pennsylvania, within sight of the royal purple Poconos. As if Lucy Jerald had heard her visitor's admiration of this house and its grounds, she said, in her fluting voice—well bred—"This house belonged to my grandfather, you know, and my father enlarged it. Guy bought it for me. I was born here, and so was my brother. It was one of the happiest days of my life, when we bought my home. It had been in the hands of a very grubby person—" She never fully ended most of her sentences. Her voice would rise on a mellifluous note, as of inquiry, and as though assuming that everyone understood her immediately. Dr. James Meyer found himself, to his annoyance, nodding his head as if he, indeed, understood all the nuances she thought she was implying.

Grubby person! he said in himself. And what was your grandfather, lady? An ironmonger, as we say in England, and a very sharp one. Didn't he steal a very valuable invention from his brother and claim it as his own? Yes. Jerry once wrote me about it. A machine for coal mining. I understand Grandpa couldn't do much more than write his name—and keep his greedy accounts. Dr. Meyer nodded his head again and said, "Jerry told me in a letter over twenty years ago."

"Jerry? Oh. Is that what you call Guy?"

Dr. Meyer smiled. "Well, in England 'guy' refers to Guy Fawkes. You know, 'gunpowder treason and plot—please to remember the fifth of November.' " He stopped when he saw her blank expression. He added, "Also, in England, 'guy' means a fool of sorts, a simpleton, a mean fellow, or someone to ridicule."

"Oh. So that's why you call Guy 'Jerry.' I see." Her

11

voice was vague. She's one of those who can't follow a conversation, thought Dr. Meyer. Why do gifted men like Jerry invariably marry such stupid women? Their appearance? She has been a beauty in her time. Still—Jerry. He had thought better of his old friend. "A man who marries a woman for her beauty is like a man who buys a house for its paint." Chinese proverb. Very astute, the old Chinese. When the paint wears off you've got only faded lumber underneath, and worm holes and rusting nails and mildew. Yes, I thought better of Jerry.

Again, as if sensing his thoughts, Lucy Jerald said with some uneasiness, "You and Guy were in the war together, weren't you? He often spoke of it—and you. Didn't he invite you to our wedding twenty-seven years ago? I think I remember." But he saw that she was not really interested. Fools are concentrated on themselves; all the rest of the world is only a reflection in the mirror of their profound self-absorption and belief in their own importance. Nothing authentic exists for them; they have no values, no dedications beyond their own walls, no meditations. They aren't alive, and I suppose I should feel pity for them. I don't. Very reprehensible of me. The woman is so infernally boring, as are all the shallow conceited, all the wearisome pretenders, all, in short, the stupid. Jerry—what the hell! Or, were you, like most very young men, interested only in her genitals? Believe me, mate, one set of genitals is as cloying as another, and without imagination one female is a duplicate of millions like her. But how many women do possess imagination, delicacy, zest, and fire? Very few. These precious females often become concubines or interesting mistresses. Not often wives. If wives, they become bored and off they go, and can't say I blame them.

Jerry hadn't married for money. His wife, for all her finishing school, was the daughter of a bankrupt, whereas Jerry had been rapidly rising, and even extremely solvent, at that time, the time of his marriage. James Meyer said, "Yes, we were in the war together, especially at the Battle of the Bulge. I wasn't a physician then, but Jerry's
12

enthusiasm for medicine inspired me. Did he tell you that?"

Lucy was looking bored. Anything not completely related to herself inspired ennui and acute uninterest. "Guy? He wanted to be a doctor?" She smiled a tolerant and superior smile. "He never said anything about *that!* I suppose it was only a passing idea of his; Guy is very even-tempered, though, very much in control of himself, and he usually got what he wanted."

Did he? Dr. Meyer thought.

"That's why, knowing Guy, I can't understand—"

But I am beginning to, thought James. Even-tempered, is he? Not the Jerry I remember! Controlled? If ever there was a wild lad, Jerry was it. What in God's name happened to him? I should have been alerted by his dull and pedestrian letters which began years ago, and finally ended.

"Jerry saved my life," said James.

"Oh?"

"It was a long time ago. He had been given some medical training in the Army; he had a genius for medicine. That's why I often wondered why he didn't go on with it."

"Medicine?" Her voice was again vague and superior. "What on earth? Of course, there wasn't any money, and he had a mother to support— He's done much better than ever he would have done as a mere doctor."

She doesn't mean to be insulting, thought Dr. Meyer. It takes intelligence to be insulting. With all the advances in psychiatry we still haven't been able extensively to probe the primitive mind. We call it "animalistic," or "infantile" and "limited." It should be a profound study, so we can, perhaps someday, practice the science of eugenics, and control the births of such people—if you can call them people. The old Jews, and the present Continentals, were quite right in arranging the marriages of their children. In America, and England, now, all is haphazard, based on the spasms in the groin, God help us, and never on distinguished family and sound success, and intelligence, and compatibility and suitability. It is quite true, though the Socialists deny it, that the level of intellect in America and

13

England is definitely declining in the general populace, due to indiscriminate and heedless breeding. No wonder we have children who disappoint us. We should be better at choosing their mothers. I must talk of this at the medical meeting in New York, though probably I will be howled down by the professional brotherly-lovers who believe environment, not genes, is all.

James could see, through the windows which were flooded with golden autumn light, the carnival colors of the trees and the gardens, the scarlet and red and crimson, the last burning calla lilies and tawny chrysanthemums, the brilliant green of the grass, the hollow blue shadows under the trees—so lonely—and a distant elm fluttering its yellow rags in a bright and nimble wind. The royal purple of the mountains far beyond had turned a dull plum, and a round red sun stood, rayless, over them. Pale gilt fingers still lay on the mahogany-paneled walls of the library, seeking through the heavy green draperies of an involved pattern. Rows of books lined the shelves, and many of them appeared well worn—Jerry's books. A light green oriental rug, figured in mute rose and gold, lay on the pegwood floor. The furniture was comfortable and masculine, deep red and brown leather, and a fire hissed and crackled reflectively on the black marble hearth, exploding amber sparks occasionally up the chimney. From somewhere—records probably—came a meditation from Brahms, which seemed part of the warm and fragrant stillness, part of the scent of China tea and pastries, part of the blue and white English china on the silver tray on the tea table near Lucy Jerald, part of the antique glimmer of polished teapot, pitcher, sugar bowl, and jug of hot water, and the patina of old wood tables. James had no doubt that this was Jerry's particular room. Lucy appeared an intruder here. Had she received and fed him here in memory of her husband—the husband now in the genteel madhouse—or had she, in her vague way, known that the room was a masculine refuge?

Why hadn't Jerry taken a fine mistress, who might have saved his sanity and given him a reason for living, and
14

some joy and laughter, and some hope? Dimly, James recalled something. Wasn't there a girl in Germany? Had she been already married? He, James, must think about this. There might be a clue there. Suddenly he was overwhelmed with an unfamiliar grief. Had he, too, failed Jerry sometime? But we were both very young then, he thought, and the future seemed endless and eternal to us, with no horizon except brightness, no threat of age and ending, no cul-de-sacs, no dusty alleyways, no dryness, no dead bones, no fear. Someone should teach the young that youth quickly ends and middle age and old age come swiftly, and if a man is to endure life with some tranquillity he must prepare for all this. And, in middle age, he should violently change his course, for he is then rich with maturity and understanding and still capable of dreams, and wonderment. And the hell with "duty" and "responsibility" and "what is owed"! A man owes it to himself to live. And to love again, with the richness of comprehension and vitality which only a man in his middle years can know, and with renewed passion of the soul. At the last, thought James Meyer, the cynic, there does need to be a woman, preferably one to whom one is not married.

He looked at Lucy Jerald again. Yes, a handsome woman, slender in her gray silk dress with the mannish collar so favored by dieting women, who are usually breastless, as was Lucy. But her rump, her bum, as he had earlier perceived, was very substantial, and was blatant even under the pleated silk. "Superior" or not, a woman's rump betrayed her breeding, and a mare's fat bottom was not indicative of refined or patrician breeding.

Lucy gave the impression of being dainty, though she was a tall woman. This was due to the immaculate, and expensive, ministrations of expert hairdressers and masseuses, manicurists and exotic practitioners of "facials." Alas, these could do nothing for short thick hands, wide coarse feet, and heavy legs. From the waist up, however, she projected the illusion of fragility, for her face was narrow, with a good if low brow, fair thin skin with a frail

15

brushing of rouge, a small colorful mouth, small ears and chin, and a flippant nose. The smoothness of her complexion, the lack of lines and wrinkles, made James suspect very clever plastic surgeons. Her eyes were large and pale blue and wide with absolutely no expression and inclined to be somewhat watery. This was all topped by artfully tinted ash-gold hair and brows. James's first thought of her had been "colorless," for her long curled hair, eyes, and complexion were without vital luster. Yet she was obviously a healthy woman, in spite of the hesitant fluting voice and the long tendoned neck with its string of rosy pearls. She sat in practiced repose, ankles crossed, hands in lap, back straight, all with an air of courteous attention. James was beginning to dislike her intensely. The woman was apparently incapable of deep emotion or feeling. He doubted she had ever been in an honest rage or had ever uttered an expletive. Doubtless she had many friends and practically no enemies. Who could hate a woman so completely correct? Except himself, of course. She was as interesting as a slice of white flabby bread, and as tasteless. Why in God's Holy Name had Jerry ever married her? But young men were often seduced by an appearance of total virginity. Lucy had two children, twins, a married daughter and a son who was in the School of Business Administration at Harvard and unmarried. This he had learned from Lucy, earlier in the afternoon. She had announced, with pride, that she and Jerry had two grandchildren now, and she had preened. I wonder what her children, and grandchildren, are like, James asked himself. With all this, she still appeared virginal. He doubted that passion had ever stirred her. Correct as always, she had probably lain under her husband's feverish body mentally making out the list of persons to invite to her next dinner party, while politely heeding her "duty."

James would have liked to call her "a farce, a fraud," but he knew this was untrue. She was simply her inane self, witless and obtuse, as unaware of hectic life as a carrot. If she lacked any passion at all, she also lacked malice. Many would call her "a perfect lady," and she probably cultivated that aspect of herself with all the feeble sedulousness of which she was capable. To James, she was not a "lady" at all, in the true meaning of the word. Ladies had fire and wit and a quick intelligence, temper and humor and a slight touch of vulgarity when the situation seemed ludicrous. They could tell lewd stories with grace and aplomb and style. Lucy would not recognize lewdness if she heard it, and she certainly lacked élan and verve.

Lucy leaned forward from her slender waist to pour fresh tea into James's cup, and to offer him the silver tray of fine pastries.

"Dr. Meyer, when did you last hear from Guy?"

"Five years ago, I believe it was. I wrote him several letters after that, but he never replied. And then when I heard from an American colleague—concerning Jerry—I was alarmed, shall we say? We had been closer than brothers, to coin a cliché, for many years. I knew I was going to New York and came a day or two earlier to inquire about Jerry in person."

She hesitated. "Did you know that he attempted suicide four months ago?"

"Yes. So I was informed."

No expression on that composed face, no distress in those empty eyes, but only a slight pursing of lips and a small shake of the head.

"We—let it be thought it was an accident. But, you see, Doctor, Guy had been very strange for at least three years. Not himself, actually. At my insistence he consulted our family physician, who said Guy was only depressed. I believe he gave my husband amphetamines, and tranquilizers. I thought at first it was business, but it was not. Things could not have been better for Guy, in every way. But he became stranger and stranger all the time. He brooded. He began to refuse invitations. He was never a very good conversationalist; he was always too impatient with our nice friends. But he began to subside into long silences that went on for days. For days. It was as if he were deaf, and did not hear anyone speaking."

She hesitated again, and dropped the white lids of her eyes. "Three years ago he moved into one of the guest rooms. I would hear him walking the floor at night, for hours—"

And you never went into his room and tried to understand his despair, thought James. You never gave him the consolation or the hope he needed. But then, you never knew the terrors in the human soul. You never impulsively embraced him and let him see your anguished tears, for you were never anguished. You never comforted him because you never understood that most of us need comforting in this appalling world. To you the world was never appalling. It was just a measured dancing in the best refined manner. What do you call shit, woman? What do you know of agony? I bet you never sweated once in your life! While Jerry was walking in his private Gethsemane you sought your beauty sleep, and wondered why he did not go to sleep himself. That he was in torment you never knew.

She was speaking again in her automaton's voice. "The male climacteric, our doctor said. It would pass. So, I did not worry too much. Then, one night— It was raining very hard— He was out somewhere and was coming home— And then, on a very sharp bend, he went off the road and crashed into trees. He must have been driving very fast. It was a miracle he was not killed, only badly concussed and with a broken wrist. He was in the hospital for several weeks, and never spoke. Our doctor called in a psychiatrist. A very nice man, and understanding. When Guy was discharged from the hospital, he was taken to Mountain Valleys, a beautiful sanitarium, a mental hospital. He has been there ever since. I visit him once a week. They advised that. He never seems to know me or hear me. Billy, our son, and Marcy, our daughter, have visited him. Marcy lives in Philadelphia, I believe I told you. Her husband is a lawyer, a very lovely boy. But Guy ignores them, or something. He doesn't even speak to his private nurses. It is as if—Billy says—he was dead though his body was still alive."

18

Ah, then we have some perceptiveness on the scene, thought James. I'd like to meet that young man.

"And, your daughter?"

"She was so hurt at her father not speaking to her or acknowledging her visits that she cried for hours. She had been Guy's favorite, you know. She looks exactly like him. She was a great comfort to me in this trial. She sympathizes with me, the dear girl. This is all very hard, you know, Doctor."

"But you thought it was suicide, or an attempt at it, Mrs. Jerald?"

That curious hesitation of hers, lifeless, without emphasis. "I—thought so. So did our doctor, and the psychiatrist. Marcy consulted them over and over, and persuaded them to—not to believe it, really, and to hush it up. After all, it would have been very bad for Guy's business, you see. There would have been all sorts of inquiries—so embarrassing, you know, for the family."

"Who is taking care of his banks and his business?"

"Oh, we have excellent and trustworthy managers." For the first time there was a hint of enthusiasm in her voice. "One of them is my brother, Hugh Lippincott. Guy always liked him. Hugh's wife, Louise, is one of the Crosleys, you know, a very prominent family in Philadelphia. They live only two miles from this suburb. In a town house in the city. And Billy, in June, will be with Hugh, after he is graduated. At least, he will be in charge of the land development business which Guy established."

How lovely all this is, thought James. How creamy and mannered and serene and rich and secure. But I feel there is something else.

"What is the present prognosis, Mrs. Jerald?"

She lifted her pale eyebrows at him. "I'm not sure I know what you mean, Dr. Meyer."

"Is Jerry getting any better? What do his doctors say?"

"They have every hope. It's true that Guy has lost a lot of weight, which he could not afford. He was always very lean. But intrinsically he is physically well, they say, even if they have to force food on him. He gets a little—violent

19

—when they insist on him eating his very good meals. But one experience with the nasty pipe they pushed down his throat, and he began to eat a little himself again. The doctors are much encouraged."

She looked at him, waiting for soothing words. But James sat in stolid silence and stared at his cup. He was a man of fifty-five himself, but as he was large and deplorably fat he appeared older, and he was massive and somewhat crumpled. His brown tweeds were authentically shabby, but his boots were polished. His thick neck seemed to be fighting his school tie. His fine white shirt was wrinkled. He had a big round head, bald on top with a fringe of reddish-gray curls all about it, which gave him a deceptively jovial appearance. His stout and florid face added to this look of geniality, and inspired confidence in his patients, who often referred to him affectionately as Father Christmas. His red cheeks were dimpled, his nose not aristocratic, but solid and broad. Some said he resembled Winston Churchill, and called him Old Cherub. But there was nothing genial about his vivid small blue eyes, all-seeing, disillusioned, and radiant with intellect and awareness. He kept his fat and dimpled hands very still, and indeed there was a great stillness about him, like a contemplative beast. He was, thankfully, a bachelor, though he had a very brisk and beguiling mistress, who had been his loving and lighthearted companion for twenty years. Neither wanted matrimony. Emma was a rich widow, plump and merry and amusing, and, though charming, she was often considered to be ugly. They adored each other in a teasing way, and understood each other with remarkable and comforting precision. Emma had had a very tragic life, and therefore seldom seemed sad.

Lucy was speaking again. "We have every hope that Guy will be home, permanently, for Christmas. We always had such gay Christmases, all the family here. Such fun."

"Did Jerry's psychiatrist give you any hint as to what is troubling him?"

Lucy stared at him, her blue eyes slightly bulging.

"Why, he thought, perhaps, that Guy has something on his mind— Something that obsesses him. That is what the doctor said. But Guy isn't—communicating, though he has daily sessions with the doctor. He doesn't—respond. He doesn't speak at all. The doctor says, though, that he hears well enough, and apparently understands. But he won't answer questions. He ignores them. He just sits and looks at his hands, and turns them over and over— As if he didn't understand what they were. They are talking about electric-shock treatments. What do you think of them, Dr. Meyer?"

"I heartily disapprove of them in the majority of cases! Did Jerry's psychiatrist say he is psychotic?"

"No, indeed. The only time he became—violent—was when they first insisted he eat his meals. He is no trouble at all, his nurses say. Of course, they shave him themselves—precautions, you know. He even walks around those beautiful grounds lately, and seems to be thinking. They find that most encouraging. They are sure he knows where he is, though he doesn't talk to any of the other patients or go into the lounges where there is television. Guy was always an omnivorous reader. We take him books and magazines and there is a well-stocked library. But he doesn't read any longer. He walks in his room at night, as he did at home, in spite of sedatives. He doesn't sleep very much. One of the nurses said he appears to be—making some sort of decision for himself. They say he is really in a state of—abeyance, whatever that means."

A mauve twilight was filling the library, and the fire had become very red and glowing. James looked briefly at his watch. Lucy said, "Will you stay for dinner, Dr. Meyer? I would be very pleased."

"Thank you, no, Mrs. Jerald. I am expecting some calls." He studied her acutely. "I am due in New York in three days. Medical conferences, you know. You have an excellent hotel here, the Cranston." He paused. "I should like to meet Jerry's psychiatrist, and the family doctor. After all, I have known Jerry many years. So, I will return

21

to Cranston three days from now, and will consult those doctors and see Jerry for myself, with their permission."

"My brother, Hugh Lippincott, and Louise, will so like to meet you, Dr. Meyer. I don't know what I'd do without my family. Such a distressing time. Would you like to stay in this house when you return?"

"Very kind of you, I am sure. We'll see. I'm a bachelor, you know, with a bachelor's ways, and so am a difficult guest." He smiled rosily at her and stood up. She stood also and gave him her hand. He touched it quickly, then withdrew it. He could not abide the woman. A harmless poor fool, but he could not abide her.

"Guy will be so happy to see you," she said. "I'm sure he will talk to you, if he talks to anyone."

A maid in a very neat black-and-white uniform entered the room at some unknown signal Lucy had given, and brought his shabby coat and hat and British scarf. He looks like a butcher, Lucy thought, with mild distaste. A very poor butcher, at that. He probably has no money at all. How Guy could ever have been fond of him is quite beyond me. Two such personalities could have had very little in common, except during the war.

One of the Jerald cars was waiting for James to take him to his hotel. He looked back at the huge and solid Georgian house, and saw the muted light in almost every window. A fine house. Pity that its mistress was such a dolt. James sighed. He began to think of Guy Jerald and the war days, when both were young and excited and certain that the world was a wondrous place, in spite of all the slaughter and ruin they saw about them. To the young men even the war was an adventure, part of turbulent life. Guy had been the more naïve of the two.

What had happened to the handsome youth with his intense dark eyes, quick and eager expectations, joy in living and wild free laughing hope?

2

Dr. Henry Parkinson looked at James Meyer more completely, as the latter talked with Guy Jerald's psychiatrist, Dr. Emil Grassner. Meyer? Meyer? Is he a Jew? Dr. Parkinson asked himself with considerable distaste. Of course, there was a foreign and too emphatic way about him, a too sharp and swift a manner of speaking; he was too acute and probing, too impatient with hesitant speech and cautious wording. His eyes flashed with impatience also, and though he did not use his hands he gave the impression of speaking a different language, and with too insistent an underscoring. But Dr. Grassner, a "sound" German, of old stock, did not seem revolted.

The three physicians were sitting in the large comfortable visitors' lounge of the Cranston Memorial Hospital, and it was raining outside, a cold dark rain persistent and unrelenting. Though it was only three o'clock in the afternoon there was a duskiness in the air, a chill in spite of the warm fire and the hot radiators. Wind prowled about the long windows and rattled them, and the nearly bare trees outside responded with creakings and lashings. Lamps had been lighted here and there on the broad and polished tables, and there was a scent of fern about and a muted quiet. Drinks had been served by a very competent young lady attached to the hospital, and there were no others present during this consultation.

"Again," said James, in his strong and very certain voice, "you understand, both of you, that I am not intruding. I am not Jerry's physician. I am only his friend and am deeply concerned about him." (Dr. Parkinson resented the British accent. Affected?)

"Of course I understand," said Dr. Grassner. "Guy is fortunate to have you as his friend. Lucy Jerald has told me all about you both." He smiled. "Balliol College, at Oxford?"

"No. Magdalen."

"I lectured there once," said Dr. Grassner. "Then I was thrown out during the war. Suspected German spy." They both laughed. "I come of Amish stock, you know, and we are the least warlike of people, and never concern ourselves with 'worldly' matters. I'm a renegade."

They sipped their drinks comfortably. I might just as well not be here, thought Dr. Parkinson with sullenness. Psychiatrists! What do they know of anything? I'm now convinced Guy has had a small stroke, which would account for his aphasia, and his sudden change in personality. And there is his hypertension, a causative agent. I've known him for years. His attempt at suicide; not unusual in a man in his middle years when he decides he needs a change of scene. Yet Lucy is a delightful woman, very devoted and solicitous. Good family, too, which is more than you can say of Guy, who came from the lowest working class. A real entrepreneur. What else does he want? Good children, wealth, a lovely wife, position, established reputation, health, fine prospects, no worries, no pressures that I know of. What else does a man want or need? Perhaps Guy had too much, thought Dr. Parkinson with growing resentment. He couldn't take it in his stride. One must remember his background—too much too soon.

Dr. Parkinson was a thin man in his late fifties, and excessively neat and contained, and an internist. His small white mustache was precise in his long narrow face, and his brown eyes blinked constantly behind thick glasses. He had a nervous way of wringing his hands, which he did not know was the result of his unsatisfactory marriage, though he never admitted to himself that his marriage was unsatisfactory. He greatly esteemed his wife, a rigorous and upright woman of many small prejudices, and anti-sexual. She had convinced her husband that he owed much to her. He had, after all, been only an intern when she had married him, a poor intern, and it had been her family's money which had rescued his career and had made comfort possible even before he had set up offices for himself, thirty years ago. He had no children. He took a sip of his
24

very weak gin and tonic water, while the other two men drank lavishly of scotch. Maria did not believe in "strong drink." Dr. Parkinson was again resentful though he did not question why.

"I've read all your textbooks," said Dr. Grassner, who looked like a hearty farmer, all sun-browned face, hard large flesh and unusual height and muscles, and big square hands. He had a merry look about him, gray eyes, and coarse white hair, though he was barely fifty-nine. His red nose was evidence that he did not disdain the bottle. In fact, he had a joyful fondness for it. "You're not mad about Freud."

"I never was. A sex-obsessed man with an Oedipus complex. I think he blinded himself. I prefer Jung, and some others. But we are all searching, and none of us knows bloody much about the psyche, including our own. The human mind is the dark continent, unexplored, and I doubt it will ever be explored. But we psychiatrists are cataloguing animals. We like to put everybody in trim categories. If they don't fit, we call them psychotics or say they are noncooperative or stubborn, or evasive. We do like to keep our files tidy, don't we? Yet all the time we have a justified suspicion that psychiatry is an imprecise science, if a science at all. Candidly, an intelligent clergyman could do as well as we, and with less harm." He chuckled.

"Clergymen are too busy these days with raising funds or involving themselves in what they call social justice, and carrying on crusades for some eclectic cause or another, and being 'concerned.' They have no time for the agonies which devour the human spirit and alienate one man from another." Dr. Grassner smiled, and added, "In short, they have no time for God."

"Sad," said James. "I remember my mother's pet priest, a rough old boy with a rougher tongue. But he understood humanity to a great extent, and had a gloomy outlook, which also was justified."

"Your mother was Lady Mary Drummond, wasn't she?" asked Dr. Grassner.

25

"Yes. Related to the Norfolks. A very gentle woman and very pious. All she asked of life was to be let alone—an impossible request. Antisocial, too." He grimaced comically.

Dr. Parkinson came to attention. Lady Mary Drummond? Then he wasn't a Jew!

"My father," said James, "found her endearing. He owned three shops, finally, on Savile Row. It was a good thing for the Drummonds. He rescued his father-in-law from bankruptcy. A profligate fella, Lord Humphrey. He wasn't grateful to Papa, because my father came from Austria and could never learn English to any extent. But he kept diaries in pungent Yiddish, and I found them very enlightening. He had a healthy appetite for the ladies, which I consider admirable."

Dr. Parkinson winced. He wondered what Maria would think of this conversation. So Meyer was a Jew after all, in spite of his mother. That accounted for his coarseness, and his apparent approval of immorality. Jews were very carnal people. For some reason Dr. Parkinson thought of that pretty young nurse he had known before his prudent marriage. She, too, had been "healthy." For an instant there was a misty softening of his eyes, then he shook the memory away. He sometimes prayed for her soul. That she was now happily married was something he tried to forget.

However, as a physical diagnostician he was very capable, and had he not married his Maria he would have evolved into being a pleasant and venal man, full of sin and sympathy, and irreverent and compassionate.

He glanced furtively at his watch. They had been sitting here for half an hour and the psychiatrists had confined themselves almost exclusively to irrelevant chatter. That they were carefully exploring each other for odious orthodoxies and a plateau on which they could congenially meet, he did not know.

Now James wore a ruminating expression. He lit a long cigar, then frowned at it. Dr. Parkinson ostentatiously coughed. Dr. Grassner produced a pipe. Dr. Parkinson scraped back his chair a pace or two. The two psychiatrists stared at the fire for long moments. Then James said, "Of course, psychiatry is the irrational science of irrational behavior. Nietzsche once wrote, I believe, that if a man despises himself he still has great esteem for the despiser within himself. We psychiatrists preach that for mental health we must love ourselves, which is possible only for the stupid. Jerry was never stupid, except for the stupidity of youth. Would you say, Doctor, that Jerry despises himself?"

"Certainly. He is an intelligent man, from all I have heard. Now he has come to grips with what he despises. At least, that is my fumbling opinion. I did not know him before. When did you see him last, Doctor?"

"Call me James, please. I saw him, though not his wife, fifteen years ago. Strange." Dr. Meyer stared intently at the fire. "I just remembered. I thought him greatly matured. I was wrong. He was the same Jerry I always knew, but kept in a self-made jail. Of course, he was older. He seemed abstracted at times, but he had the young way of throwing his head back and shaking it, like a colt tossing its mane or, to use a battered metaphor, a war-horse who hears a distant drum. But he was no longer eager and voluble in speaking. It was as if he was guarding something, probably some fragile aspect of himself, which he was afraid of shattering. It was that constraint which made me believe he had matured from the wild youth he had been, all vaulting with ambition and dreams." James paused, pursing up his full lips and slightly shaking his head. He scratched the gray-red curls on the back of his thick neck. "He showed me photographs of his wife and children. Like all children, they were pudding-faced and uninteresting. I can't fancy why American parents adore them so much. But the English proletariat does that, too. It's as if they found no significance in their porridge lives but their children, and no importance. Sad, that. Middle-aged peasant juveniles worshipping immature juveniles, all one smirking family of dumpling-heads. Well. His wife seemed to be very pretty

27

in the picture, though she was half hidden by the obese bodies of her children and was clutching their shoulders tightly with her hands, like a mummy monkey. Saw just one half-face of her. No character, I thought. I did notice that she had the usual gleaming American teeth, evidence of a good dentist, or toothpaste. Sorry."

Emil Grassner laughed. "Oh, Lucy Jerald's a wonderful woman. She never has anything to say, and says it constantly. A flaccid woman, except when it comes to her children, then she has the usual American woman's syndrome of getting all emotional over her offspring. You know, the quivery voice and the gulping throat muscles. She doesn't get very emotional over Guy. Deep down, she's extraordinarily shallow, like most women. She probably has as much concern as she can muster for Guy. But she is incapable of knowing the terribleness of what he is enduring. I know it is terrible, but what is destroying him I don't know. I am hoping you will help me find out."

"Thank you—Emil. As I said, I am only Jerry's friend, not his physician. Mrs. Jerald mentioned his muteness. Pathological or psychotic?"

"Neither, I think. I believe he is perfectly capable of speaking, if he wanted to. He doesn't want to. Why? I don't know. He's crouching over something which he is controlling, because if he stops controlling it, it will shake up his life, and he's not ready for that, or not willing, or is afraid. Of course, that's only my opinion as of now. He did say one word to me, over a month ago. 'Death, death.' I asked him what he meant, and he stood up and walked away. I've mentioned this to him many times but he only looks at the floor between his knees, as if he hadn't heard me. But he hears all right. Nothing physically impaired."

Dr. Parkinson intervened. "He had a small stroke, the result of the—the accident." His dry voice lifted to shrillness. "Aphasia." The two psychiatrists looked at him, but he went on, doggedly: "He still has extreme hypertension, 240 over 110. He could have a major stroke or a coronary occlusion at any time."

James spoke to him soothingly. "And all the treatment

he is receiving here, all the sedatives, et cetera, don't bring the pressure down?"

"No."

"Then his mind and his emotions are going full speed ahead," said Dr. Grassner, nodding. "He isn't communicating with others, but, by God, he certainly is communicating with himself! And the conversation is getting more frenetic every day. The hypertension is functional, organic. No sign of atherosclerosis."

"Just what medication is he receiving?" asked James.

"Well, as he's not psychotic, I am, at present, using a conservative approach. I don't see any signs of the typical anxiety neurosis. Small doses of sodium amobarbitol; using it with caution, of course; haven't attempted any deep probing as yet; I feel it's too dangerous. Tranquilizers, in small doses. As you know, James, sometimes drugs ally themselves with the neurosis, and that's disastrous. A psychoneurosis is a hell of a thing to try to treat, for every man's neurosis is unique. Not the usual frank signs of mental disease. Again, in my opinion, Guy is as sane as you and I—and possibly saner. At least he is confronting whatever is tearing his life apart, something which men generally avoid."

"Any danger of his attempting suicide again?"

"No. He's carefully watched all the time, but unobtrusively. I think he's decided that suicide is cowardly and he'd better face up to things and make up his mind. Whatever he decides will be all for the best, though possibly devastating for others, if not for himself. In short, he's dueling, and is both fierce adversaries. Which one will win I don't know and probably never will know. He will, however."

What nonsense, thought Henry Parkinson. A simple case of a mild stroke, and continuing hypertension, but psychiatrists turn the most ordinary things into egos and superegos and conversions and phobias and libidos and the unconscious, and God knows what other drivel. What they all need is to be born again, and turn their lives over to Jesus, and clean out the toilets in their own minds.

29

They're all septic tanks. Did anyone ever see a superego or a libido or a phobia? No. And what you can't feel or smell or touch or hear or see doesn't exist, except religion, yes, and the soul. When I suggested a sodium-free diet for Guy, and bland nourishing food, and a quiet atmosphere, and the regular treatment for hypertension, Dr. Grassner grinned at me! Well, when Guy has a cerebral accident or a coronary, perhaps he'll agree with me, when it's too late.

Dr. Grassner said, "Did Guy, in his younger days, ever seem to have a latent rigidity of character?"

"No," said James. Then he lifted his hand. "Odd. I just remembered. A little incident, which never repeated itself. He was a corporal then, just before we were mustered out. It was reported that one of our men had raped a young Italian girl. Yes, really rape, not the contrived sort. And Jerry almost beat the chap to death, with his fists. Perhaps he deserved it, yes. But Jerry seemed to take it personally. No, he had no sisters, and of course he wasn't married at the time. I never saw him in such a rage before or since. And he never explained the excessive emotion, nor would he talk about it."

"Did he ever talk about his early life, James?"

"Yes, but only occasionally. His father, he said, owned a very large but poor farm outside this city. His parents had separated. His mother had a miserable rooming house for the sawmill workers in Cranston. I understand she was a bit of a Tartar, though he seemed fond of her enough. But he was very fond of his father, whom he described as a hellion. An old devil, and such, foul-mouthed and intransigent and a ne'er-do-well, and an 'old soak.' Jerry spent his summers with his father; it appeared he enjoyed that, and helped his father about the farm. What they both made, he said, just was enough to pay the taxes—"

Dr. Parkinson broke in, leaning forward stiffly in his chair. "That nine hundred acres of worthless farmland became the most valuable piece of property near Cranston! When Guy inherited it, it was said it wasn't worth a dollar an acre. He sold part of it when he inherited it, three years after he came home from the war, and then decided to develop the rest of it, with partners. I don't know why, but he got the banks here, and in Philadelphia, to lend him outrageous sums of money. I've got to admit," he admitted with reluctance, "that Guy had a keen head for business and knew the way the city was growing, which is more than can be said of the rest of us. I remember. I was almost as young as Guy at the time."

The two other men looked at him with deep interest, and he pulled his chair closer to them, almost preening. "That land now has apartments on it, and expensive houses, five first-class motels near the edge, on the way to Philadelphia, office buildings—everything. A town in itself, they say. Supermarkets, department stores—everything. And very well arranged, I must admit. Nothing cheap or sleazy. I'll say that for Guy."

He looked at them proudly. "Then he bought adjacent land, as much as he could, and built another community. But that was before the farmland development was complete, otherwise he couldn't have bought it as cheap as he did. A real fox, when it came to business. He brought the best architects in, from Pittsburgh. The first town, or village, is called Jeraldsville, the other River View. It's on the river, you know."

He had the complete concentration of the two men now, that Jew and that headshrinker from Philadelphia. "And while all that building was going on Guy went to work part time in our main bank, just as a teller, and all that money beginning to come in! Now he's president of that bank, and chairman of the other. The first one— Lucy's father was president of it, and it was on the edge of failure. Too much money lent to too many lazy farmers out in the country, and a bad investment in an office building in Cranston, among other things. Well, there had been the Depression, and we were just coming out of it, and the war had ended, and Guy is very shrewd, though where he got the business sense I don't know. His mother was just a poor hard-working boardinghouse keeper, and his father—I knew old Jerald. If the Chief of Police hadn't

31

been a good friend of his he'd have been jailed a dozen times. Drunk and disorderly, driving while intoxicated—he had a very old car which was always falling apart. We used to wonder where he found the money to buy whiskey; he was a scandal. For a long time he had a slut living with him in the broken-down farmhouse; Guy used to call her Aunt Sal. I remember that. They would all get drunk together, after Guy came home. They weren't considered a very nice family, you know? I'd hear all about it in the summer, when I was home from medical school in Pittsburgh." He hesitated. "I heard that the old Chief of Police himself, when off duty, used to riot and drink with them in the old house. Disgraceful."

For a man only in your middle years you're damned prissy, thought Dr. Grassner, amused. James was also amused. He once knew these old farmers in England, reckless, enjoying their lives mightily, sturdily unregenerate, reckless, rollicking, drunken, and in love with living and with women. Too bad grim Socialism has eradicated their sort; they gave vivid color to the landscape. It's strange that no one as yet has equated Socialism with evangelism, or Puritanism. Anything to take joy out of life and reduce all men to a dun and dreary condition of labor and hopelessness and monotony! Nothing strange or lively or unorthodox allowed, nothing sporty or vehement, no danger, no excitement, no raising hell or dancing under the stars, no laughter or authentic music, or gaiety. Everything reduced to the lowest possible level, and regimented, under commissars, though they, in England, call themselves public servants. All working for the public weal or something equally lifeless, squalid and loaded with punitive taxes against those who dare to aspire, to dream, to invent, to work, to create. In other words, to be fully men. A welfare jail is just a jail when you come down to it, except that the guardians are even more grisly than the regular jailers; and far more ruthless and full of envious hate. I think I'll emigrate, if Emma is willing, with all her Swiss francs and German marks. Clever old girl. Wish I'd taken her advice years ago. Well, I have that land in

Canada and I've done well in private practice and there is still some of the old estate left. Yes, I think I'll emigrate. Where are you now, you merry men of England?

The day was definitely dark now and the wind was becoming tumultuous among the wild trees. The fire rustled. Glasses had been refilled for the two psychiatrists, but not for Dr. Parkinson, who had nobly refused and had looked at the two other men with covert reproach. They had not noticed this gesture of righteousness and self-congratulation.

"When may I see Jerry?" asked James.

"Tomorrow. And alone, too. I'll keep out of sight," said Emil. "Do you think he will recognize you?"

"Yes. Well. I've put on some weight, I must admit, and I've lost most of my hair in the past fifteen years, but I think he will know me. Thank you."

They stood up, and Emil asked, "Where are you staying, James?"

"At the Cranston Hotel, and very comfortable, too."

"I am staying at the Old House, an ancient German establishment, and cozy and warm and homelike. Why don't you join me there? We have plenty to discuss."

James agreed to move. He was a very affable man in appearance, if one did not observe those very sentient eyes and the cleft lines about his mouth.

Dr. Parkinson said with much stiffness, "Guy was agitated this morning, one of his nurses reported. He hadn't slept during the night."

"But not too much barbitol," said Dr. Grassner. "Better let him fight things out for himself."

Dr. Parkinson was angry. They had treated him as if he were a medical student and not too intelligent at that. Now his resentment turned against Guy, and he wondered how such a lovely lady as Lucy Jerald could have married such an oaf.

3

That night James called his mistress in London and said, "Old girl, I must remain in America a little longer than I anticipated—"

Emma interrupted in her strong and lively voice, "How old is she, what does she look like, and is she after your money?"

James laughed. "I just thought of a certain lady, the wife of a very ill friend of mine. She is vague, about your age, love, and has pots of cash, and is a damned fool into the bargain. I can't imagine her—"

Emma interrupted again, "Let's not be coarse, love. We're not in bed. Are you getting her into the loony bin?"

"She is not intelligent enough to be insane, dear. It does require a certain amount of brains to go around the bend, you know. Cretins never go mad. They're too aware of reality, and too in love with themselves. The lady is a cretin. It's her husband in whom I am interested. I told you about old Jerry a long time ago and mentioned I would see him sometime while I was in America. He, poor chap, is in a very expensive loony bin, from which I propose to rescue him."

"Old Faithful," commented Emma. "Do your bit, love, and come home soon."

"Emma, I intend to emigrate. Are you infatuated enough with me to come to America, later, or Canada, or Australia or New Zealand, or perhaps Andorra, or possibly the moon?"

Emma answered with cheer. "They probably have the pure-in-hearts and the true believers—passionately avid for cash they never earned themselves—all over now. Remember that very old stanza:

"To share your wealth the liberal's willing.
     He'll tax your pennies and keep his shilling."

"Yes. Well, the vermin are everywhere. Candidly, I think the whole world is now dotty."

Emma gave an elaborate sigh. "Except you, love, except you, and perhaps myself. I'll go anywhere with you, as you know."

"I'll even make an honest woman of you, Emma."

"God forbid!" said Emma with fervor. "So far the vermin haven't taxed sin."

"They will, love, they will. You can bank on that."

James found the elderly German hotel, the Old House, exceedingly comfortable, with very little glass and no chrome or neon or vinyl, and with good fireplaces all pleasantly roaring. He and Dr. Grassner had a most euphoric breakfast in the morning, and James filled himself with thick big sausages, ham, pancakes and syrup and eggs and hot muffins and scrapple and large cups of coffee yellow with cream. He felt quite benevolent towards the world when he emerged with Emil into the cold damp air and the harsh wind. The sky was whitish and dull and Emil said, "It feels like snow. Button up."

The trees were lean black skeletons against that white sky, and the gutters were filled with oak leaves the color of blood and there was a smell of grit and dust swirling about. The aspect of the street was deserted and barren and James felt quite at home. When the two psychiatrists entered Emil's big car James said, "I like your car. Not one of those minis where a man can't stretch his legs. Are governments trying to reduce us to pygmies again?"

"Without doubt," said Emil. "In every way, James, in every way. You mentioned emigrating last night. Don't come here. Our politicians imitate England constantly, and the more punitive the taxes, the more enthusiastic they are about them. If England begins to tax bowel movements, as sure as God Washington will begin to tax them here, too. There's no refuge in the world any longer, no escape from bureaucrats."

James gloomily stared at the street and the traffic. "It's very peculiar, but it's always the minority which creates bloody revolutions and tyranny. The majority never seem

35

to revolt against the minority despots, and murderers. Look at Russia: The Russian people never voted the communists in. They just imposed themselves on the people. They're so bloodthirsty, vindictive and ruthless and greedy. I wonder why we, the majority, don't serve them up their own brand of death."

"We're too civilized, James, and too busy obeying the sound rules. We believe in law and order and justice and decency, and may the best man win in the game of living. We believe in the sanctity of life and honor and pride."

"Um," said James. "Perhaps we should develop some ruthlessness of our own, and gird up our loins and be men, as the Almighty advised Job. But somebodies have corrupted us with sweetness and light and general mildness and meekness and that abominable thing called 'tolerance.' Wasn't it Christ Himself who advised men that if they lack a sword to sell their cloak and buy one? Yes. His Apostles carried swords, too. Nothing like going armed in a dangerous world, and the Liberal/Socialist/Communist Cabal have made it extremely dangerous, indeed, for an honest and upright man."

"To keep myself from having an overly optimistic view of the world, James, I often refresh myself by reading Roman history. When the Vandals came into Rome, the noble Roman Senators, wearing a very noble expression, repaired with nobility to the Senate, and there sat nobly in their noble white robes and scarlet shoes, awaiting the Vandals. To 'communicate' with them, no doubt, and impress them with noble sentiments and dialogue. The Vandals just went around to the Senate seats and quite ignobly cut off the Senators' heads, one by one. I guess that's all they deserved anyway. Where in the hell were their own swords?"

"Probably their Catilinas had confiscated them," said James, and laughed roughly. "Sword control, you know."

Emil smiled but without merriment. "Yes. Disarm the citizens and lay them wide open to the Vandals, and their bureaucratic masters. A very old story. I think we should
36

now teach the boys in schools the arts of wa̶r̶
lessness against their miserable enemies."

Emil's square farmer's face had become less pl̶
he talked with James, and James thought there was
of Odin about him. No, not Odin—Thor, the ha̶m̶m̶er
thrower, the most virile of Emil's ancient gods. James himself was losing his earlier resemblance to a fat and massive
Toby jug, and his vital eyes had taken on a Draconian
gleam. They had not talked of Guy Jerald this morning.
They had a tacit if silent agreement that James was not to
be influenced by another's opinion, and that he was to be
regarded only as a solicitous friend of the desperate man.
But a quiet rapport had risen between the two men, an
understanding which words merely underlined.

James said, "In my father's house, in London, a very
big and ostentatiously vulgar house—to him vulgarity was
highly amusing—there was a very bad engraving of the
Paris mob storming the Tuileries during the period of the
French Revolution. The street rabble. There they were,
bloated and vehement and violent and conspicuously ram-
pageous, their faces contorted with malicious and grinning
hate and envy—oh, the sansculottes!—pouring up the
magnificent steps, brandishing clubs, swords, pistols,
scythes, and what not, lusting to loot all the beauty within
the Tuileries. But they really preferred to destroy it and
trample on it, for it represented to the rabble the majestic
loveliness and glory which ignored and scorned them, and
to which their ferocious and barbaric souls could never
aspire, or understand. Yes, yes, the murderous rabble.

"Nearby, watching with enormous contempt and disgust
and genuine hatred stood a young corporal, Napoleon.
Under the engraving was a legend '*A bas le canaille!*' Yes,
indeed, 'down with the cattle.' I was about ten years old
when I became aware of that engraving in my father's
library, and I became devoted to Napoleon from that
minute on. To this day I read everything published about
him. He not only loathed the rabble, or the 'street people'
as they are called now, but he understood their swine souls
and their mindless impetus to demolish and kill and eat

37

rink and breed and rape and sack. So—he gave them
wars, and they served him well."

"What did you think of Hitler, James?" Emil gave his
new friend a sidelong look.

"The perfect example of the rabble come to power, as
was Stalin. I once heard this century called 'the century of
the common man.' Yes, indeed. The world has lost all its
capacity for grandeur. I can't see any man anywhere,
among our politicians, who has lofty and aristocratic
spirit; a man of strength and fire and intellect and physical
force. The world badly needs heroes. Now we have Socialism or liberalism or humanitarianism or 'love' or 'compassion,' but it is all the primitive manifestation of
Neanderthal man. The lusting and rapacious beast, making
mewling sounds and slinking, conjuring up personal
enemies in natural thunderbolts.

Suddenly Emil said, "I just had the oddest thought. I
wonder if Guy had come to these conclusions himself."

James nodded abstractedly. "I was thinking of something else, too. If I were superstitious—and perhaps I am—
I would be convinced that behind it all looms the most
terrible power of personal Evil, which is very cognizant,
very wise, very puissant, and which is elaborately plotting.
It knows all the mean and viscid traits of mankind, all its
innate repulsiveness and ghastly insanities. And—it is
using them."

Emil chuckled. "You mean Satan. My parents believed
in him implicitly. I sometimes thought they believed more
in his verity than in God's."

"Well," said James. "He does seem more imminent, I
daresay."

They were now traveling swiftly through the countryside. Overnight most of the trees had lost their foliage
except for an occasional twig clutching a few brown leaves
like the scorched and shriveled pages of a once glowing
book. Black trunks, black branches, stark thin scribblings
against that white sky, appeared to be a casual etching,
done at random and upward, from a dull and sepia earth,
without direction or intent. Far beyond them rose the
38

brown tumblings of the mountains, struck here and there by the acid green of a fir or a spruce. The car raced by silent farmhouses and silos, and chimneys fluttered with rags of smoke. It appears dead, thought James, but in reality this is the busiest time of the year for nature, who is laying down seeds in the sodden ground and banking them with fallen leaves to protect them against the winter and to fertilize them. Perhaps that is also true of the autumn of our life: In the last years of our lives we are burying the seeds of the spring of our resurrections, the ripened seeds of our experiences and our knowledge.

They crossed an arched wooden bridge leaping over a narrow stream which glimmered dimly with leaden lights. Now they passed a number of brooding cows grouped near a hedge, and a dog ran after them with bustling authority and a great deal of noise. The landscape did not remind James of England in the least. Everything in America seemed designed and created on a vast scale, and he found it slightly disconcerting like the reverse of claustrophobia. The smooth road bent to the right and now the buildings of the Mountain Valleys sanitarium came into view, quite abruptly. James was surprised at the size of the sanitarium and its calm beauty, for Cranston was not a large city. Emil said, "Mountain Valleys is very well known. Patients come here from Pittsburgh and Philadelphia and even from New York. It's very beautiful, the country, in spring and summer and fall, and the sanitarium has an excellent staff, some of the best men available from other cities. In the center"—and he pointed to an impressive larger building—"is an old mansion once belonging to a coal baron; it's five stories high and remarkably handsome inside, and carefully modernized so as not to ruin the fine mahogany paneling and oak floors and molded ceilings and heavy oaken doors. They let the enormous Venetian chandeliers alone and restored some of them, and the staircases are really grand and imposing. The original oriental rugs are there, too—priceless, they tell me—and some excellent landscapes, two alleged to be by Landseer.

"The first two floors are the administration and staff

sections, the three upper stories are what we don't like to call 'maximum security,' but it is. Those tall windows are barred so tactfully that you'd think they were only casement windows. It's also the richest section, suites and such and big finely proportioned rooms. The wings on either side are only three stories, the rooms smaller and filled with modernistic furniture, all very expensive chrome and vinyl and cheery paintings and razzle-dazzle rugs in bright colors. Supposed to be mood-lifting. But comfortable for all its insistent gladsomeness. The right wing is for the ladies, the left for the gentlemen, and they are identical. There are common rooms, too, where they have dances and movies and TV and libraries, and kitchens, of course, and a large common dining room. We believe in being as coed as possible. We're really quite advanced; we know now that mentally ill people of all ages haven't lost their sexuality. You'd be surprised at the keen perking up that goes on when the sexes meet for arts and crafts and cards and games and the plays they put on themselves, under enlightened direction. A considerable number of very satisfactory marriages had their beginning here. Nothing like sex to stimulate sanity and health!"

"I've noticed that," said James, laughing, and looking with interest at the sanitarium. The buildings were all of white brick, quite vivid in the shadowy morning light, and every window was framed in glistening black shutters. The grounds were very considerable, almost parklike, with groups of evergreens and white birches and oaks and maples and elms, and many flower beds now scrupulously bedded down for the approaching winter. Surrounding it all were high and elaborately artistic iron fences and gates, the latter with lampposts. A long drive curved through the grounds to the double front doors. There were a few men about, quietly raking leaves. A man in a gray uniform appeared suddenly at the gate and scrutinized Emil and his passenger, then by some magic the gates silently opened.

"All this," said Emil, with some bitter irony, "is not to protect the community from the loonies inside, but to protect the loonies from the community. Especially from unwelcome relatives with an eye out for inheritances and hope high in their black hearts—this covers most children. I've had many a talk with sons and daughters, who earnestly asked me, with big tearful eyes, if I weren't an advocate of the 'happy death,' meaning euthanasia. 'Dad—or Mom,' they'll whimper, 'is just a vegetable now and didn't I think—' I always say no. And I, and the physicians here, do everything possible to keep Dad and Mom healthily alive, and aware, and legally protected. We have some patients with very modest incomes, and we have a quota for the poor souls who live on Social Security and nothing else. It isn't odd that their offspring aren't in the least anxious for these parents to die."

James said, "But your practice is in Philadelphia, isn't it?"

"Yes. But I have an interest in Mountain Valleys and I have a number of patients here myself. People who have about given up trying to cope with our present world, and I don't blame them. I can't always cope, either." After a moment he added, "The psychiatrist in charge here is Charles Witherspoon, who is cynical about psychiatry. He knows damned well that most patients would be cured without any so-called treatment at all—if they just had a little peace of mind. A very able man, with many credentials. Well, form your own opinion of him."

The double doors opened silently and a very pretty young lady, a receptionist, greeted them with the typical American smile, "wall-to-wall teeth," as James ungenerously called it. But she had very nice legs, he observed. Emma was noted for her own nice legs, almost as admirable as these, one of her beauties, thought James, who found Emma's ugly and gay and animated monkey countenance the most fascinating in the world of women. They entered an immense hall, the walls lined with long and enticing sofas, the walls heavy with portraits and landscapes and seascapes, many of them valuable. The floors were thick with elegant oriental rugs, and a huge and sparkling chandelier, lit on this gloomy day, hung from the ceiling of the second story.

41

"Dr. Witherspoon is waiting for you, Doctor," said the young lady, who looked hesitantly at James. But Emil merely nodded to her genially and let her lead him and James to a door at the end of the hall. James noticed that the warm air was fresh and fragrant, and not institutional. He saw tall live plants in brass buckets scattered everywhere. One was actually blooming with broad pink flowers. He touched them furtively as he passed them. Thankfully, they were not plastic. He had no objection to plastic; it was really very useful; but he did not like it in quantities, and especially did not like it when it was designed to imitate, quite cleverly, the authentic article. There were enough imitation people, he reflected, without making the whole environment fraudulent, too.

The young lady touched a discreet bell near the door, then coyly opened the door and glanced within. She must have received a signal, for she held open the door for the two visitors and stood politely aside, still smiling that fixed Cheshire smile. James found such smiles very pathetic and he wanted to pat the girl consolingly on the bottom, and say, "There, there, lovey."

The office beyond the door seemed to be a very handsome living room, with a bounding bright fire on a black marble hearth—which had a mantel above adorned with valuable objets d'art, and above which hung a Venetian mirror framed in ornate gold. A choice oriental rug in dim blue and yellow covered the wide floor, and the furniture discreetly arranged were genuine antiques. James recognized a Duncan Phyfe here and there, and a piece of Sheraton, not to mention old red leather chairs embellished with brass studs. A Florentine desk, carved discreetly, stood under still another shining chandelier, and there was a scent of chrysanthemums and fern and wood smoke happily floating about. The room was very quiet and had a feeling of repose and peace. There was not even a clatter of a typewriter to be heard here, nor a distant banging of a door, nor a voice.

A tall man of about sixty was standing behind the desk, and though he was slender and compact he gave the instant impression of being strong and immovable. He resembled a still statue made entirely of gray granite, from his severely cut hair to his immobile slab of a face, gray clothing, gray hands, gray lips, harsh nose and rudely carved cheekbones and small colorless eyes like remorseless pebbles. There was no friendly expression on his face; it had the fixity of stone and was, James thought, about as gentle.

James, the astute, knew at once that here was a man almost excessively good and kind and perceptive, a man of probity and filled with great and awesome compassion, and a profound intuition. James had met very few men like this psychiatrist, and always felt, when meeting them, that he had been given some kind of absolution. Of such were the saints made; it was a gift of God to know them. James was not surprised when, after introductions, he found the granite hand to be hard yet sensitive and shy.

Dr. Witherspoon inclined that rude head towards James and said, in a rough voice like gravel, "Will you have coffee, Doctor? Or tea, perhaps?"

"Coffee, please," said James. He smiled at the other man. "I detest tea."

Emil was relieved. Charles had instantly accepted James, as he accepted few men. Charles might be the best of men but he was no soft accepting fool. He did not suffer fools gladly, either, and he had no patience with the pretentious and the frauds and the hypocrites. His opinion of mankind, Emil knew, was not exactly benevolent, for all his greatness of soul. No one could deceive him. Emil honored him as he honored no other man.

The pretty receptionist brought in a silver tray, very polished and ancient, with delicate cups and saucers and spoons and a bright coffeepot also of silver. The three men sipped thoughtfully, and James found Dr. Witherspoon studying him with the calmness of marble.

"I understand," said Charles Witherspoon, "that you are not here in the capacity of Guy Jerald's psychiatrist, but only as his old friend. Emil told me yesterday."

James made a disarming gesture with his thick rosy
43

hand. "Only as Jerry's friend. We called him Jerry in the Army. Jerry and I were close friends. I wasn't popular, for a number of reasons, and it comes to me now that Jerry wasn't either. Our relationship with our fellow soldiers was sometimes dodgy, to say the least. I can understand why I wasn't the chap from the local pub, but I don't understand why Jerry and the others weren't matey. Strange, I never realized that until now." He looked thoughtfully into his cup and frowned. "Jerry had every trait considered to be necessary if one wants to make friends. He was very steady, considerate, would lend money, was interested in others to a certain extent, and generous and never backbiting or mean or treacherous. Malice was beyond him. He was always straightforward. I never knew him to do a contemptible thing, or show any greed."

"Perhaps that's why he didn't make friends," said Charles Witherspoon.

James glanced at him, startled. He considered. "Yes. Very probable." He paused. "It isn't pleasant to think that one has to be a thoroughgoing rascal to be loved by one's fellow men."

For the first time Charles smiled. It was a smile like a bleak light falling momentarily on granite. "But it's true, just the same. 'Night calls unto night, and deep unto deep,' to quote the Bible. So does rascality call to rascality, and we're a world of scoundrels, you know. We are uncomfortable in the presence of decency."

The heavy hoarse voice had subtly changed, and James recognized the change as incurable sadness. Charles picked up a folder on his desk, glanced within it, then put it down.

"As Emil has probably told you, and Guy's physician, too, we haven't much to go on concerning your friend. I never knew him before he came here, or was brought here. I have to rely on others, including"—and again that bleak smile—"his wife and children. It seems Guy, or Jerry, as you call him, isn't very communicative."

James thought, with dismay: If you haven't been able to communicate with him, I haven't a prayer.

"I have a tentative diagnosis," said Charles, "my own, and I admit I haven't any real grounds for it. Guy Jerald is as sane as anyone I've ever known. But he is in such a depression that he might as well be blind and deaf and locked in a black dungeon. He's shut the whole damned world out—while he makes up his mind about something. That's only my opinion, of course, and Emil agrees with me. We are giving him as little medication as possible. He doesn't need sedating, he doesn't need tranquilizing, he doesn't need mood-lifting drugs. He needs, I think, to be let alone. We are letting him alone as much as possible. We'd go along with that indefinitely, but he is showing signs of an impending physical collapse, too. Possibly willing himself to die. If this keeps on, he will die; there's no doubt of it. The point is: Do we have a right to interfere, to force him to live against his will?"

Those very small expressionless eyes focused directly on James who was again startled. "Well," he said, "we are supposed to have a reverence for life, and to extend it as long as possible. We are supposed to alleviate pain of both the body and the mind."

Charles sighed. "Jerald is in pain, all right. Terrible pain. No doubt unendurable. We can't possibly understand it. What is one man's trivial trouble is another man's tragedy. From what I've heard there're no circumstances in his present life which have precipitated this conscious, or unconscious, drive to death. Nothing wrong anywhere. Nothing unusual has happened to him, nothing disturbing. From all accounts his outward life is serene. Emil mentioned that you told him that for a number of years his letters to you were lifeless and indifferent. That is indicative of intense depression. Yes. He has no disease which threatens his life, nor has his family. On the surface he should be the happiest of men, instead of the most wretched."

He waited for some comment from James, then when James remained silent Charles went on. "Have you any ideas—James?"

"I'm sorry to say, no. None at all." Then his vivid eyes
45

came even more alive. "I just thought of something else!" He sat up quickly in his chair. "When we were in the war together, Jerry was very young, younger than myself. He had had, he told me, only a preparatory—high school—education, as you call it in America. But I saw he had a really tremendous mind. Actually, it was most unusual for a raw country lad, as he called himself. Or, rather, he called himself a hillbilly." James paused, and began to frown to himself.

"I understand he went to college under the G.I. Bill," said Charles, and now the stony eyes were deep and interested.

"Yes. So he wrote me. He studied architecture, I believe, though didn't complete the course. His mind was so enormously restless. Well. We were in a little town in Germany, and resting, so we could let the Russians have the honor of being the victors." James smiled derisively. "Those were the orders to both the Americans and the British. I was an ambulance driver, by the way. I used to race cars at home, and I suppose, in their dreamy way, the authorities considered me just the chap to drive an ambulance. Well. I always had the thought that there was something else he wanted. To study medicine. It's a little obscure to me just now, but I think I was on the right track. That's not the point I wanted to bring out just now, though.

"A friend sent me a book of poems by my favorite poet, John Donne. One of the most lucid minds of his generation. Jerry would listen to me while I read the poetry to him, and I must say that he became very alert during those sessions. There was one stanza of a certain poem which he memorized, and would quote aloud, to himself:

"Go, and catch a falling star,
    Get with child a mandrake root.
Tell me, where all past years are,
    Or who cleft the Devil's foot.

"Now, why that particular stanza so fascinated him is beyond me. He never explained. It is a very eerie piece at
46

that, and if you try to understand it precisely it escapes you. You have to know it by a supercerebral process—or something. It's more a matter of feeling than of precision and cold reason. Some would call it extrasensory perception. At least, that's my opinion."

Charles had listened closely. Then he nodded. "That's my opinion, too. There's a clue there." He stopped. The three men looked at the fire, and it was as if each were entirely alone. Then Charles sighed again, and spoke as though he were reflecting aloud.

"Contrary to the general opinion—and the opinion of psychiatrists, too—routine is not the deadening process it is ritualistically supposed to be. For the majority of us it is lifesaving, a source of unshakable security. It's what makes most lives endurable, even significant. It keeps instinctive terror under reasonable restraint, chaos ignored, the universe comfortably explained. It is the nursemaid and the maternal protection of timid little souls.

"But for the rare personality, security, comfort, the attainment of long objectives and ambitions, routine, can be deadly, actually killing. It can destroy life itself. An old doctor once told me, 'When a rut becomes deep enough it becomes your grave.' Yes. I think we have a dim clue here, though not the whole picture."

"Nobody ever saw the whole picture of anyone else," said James, "That's what makes life so dangerous, so intriguing, so poignant, and interesting. We move about like blind beasts in a forest at midnight, without a star or a moon, sensing the presence of each other, feeling terrified, running, avoiding, and sometimes, pathetically, trying to make contact with another frightened warm body. That's what bothers me about a lot of my fellow psychiatrists. Many superbly feel they understand everything about the human psyche; they carve slots for others to neatly fit in. That's arrogance of the worst kind, and the most blasphemous. We can only fumble about, hoping to touch others once in a while, or hear an answering voice. Pardon me. I am riding my favorite hobby-horse—"

Now a smile of deep sweetness appeared astonishingly

on Charles's face. "I think," he said, "you'll be very good for Guy Jerald. What do you think, Emil?"

"I'm sure of it," said Emil, standing up. "Now, it's agreed that James shall be alone with Guy, completely alone, and for as long and as frequently as possible."

4

Emil and James were almost literally wafted to the fifth floor on velvet ropes. A few men and women occupied the elevator with them, all nicely clothed in country tweeds or trim city garb. All seemed preoccupied but none appeared distressed. They murmured together in calm tones, and no one fidgeted or showed any agitation. James pondered on this. Either mental illness was comfortably accepted as almost normal among the rich, or they honestly did not give a damn for those unfortunates whom they were about to visit. Either attitude was depressing to him.

Then he noticed a woman at the rear of the elevator who did not resemble the others at all. She was unusually tall for a woman, and thin nearly to the point of emaciation. She seemed to be a woman approaching fifty, and obviously not as well-to-do as the other occupants of the elevator. She was adequately clothed against the weather in a heavy brown wool coat with large black buttons, and she wore a green tam-o'-shanter on a rather disheveled mass of fine and brilliantly copper hair, straight and hastily pinned at the temples. Her boots were sturdy and there were evidences of mud about the soles. Her gloves were brown wool; she held them in her right hand and James saw that her hands, surprisingly classical and slender, were red and rough about the knuckles, and the nails were clean but unvarnished. James was firmly convinced that he could tell the character and status of people by their clothing, and their attitude towards life, and he found himself thinking: Why, here is a typical English lady in for a few hours from the country. Not too horsy, but very much county, and an obvious dog lover. She makes the other women in this elevator look like the pretentiously genteel, the low-bred nouveau riche. A fine woman.

He stared openly and with increasing interest at the lady, who was not in the least "glamorous" or even pretty in the American sense of the term. Her face was too thin and too strongly marked with intelligent and indomitable character, though the features were delicate and sensitive. She was in profile to James, and he saw that that profile had a certain humorous pugnacity about it, accompanied by a subtle blend of irony and challenge. Here was a woman who tolerated no nonsense. She wore no cosmetics: her skin was fair but heavily layered with bright freckles. Her nose was blunt and upturned and a trifle fleshy with flaring nostrils. Her mouth was very pale but beautifully formed, and her chin small and firm. She seemed intent on some deep thought, for the coppery eyelashes, fine but thick, scarcely moved in any blinking. She was at once very plain yet fascinating, and her appearance was unusual and well bred.

She must have felt James's concentrated regard, for she suddenly turned full face to him as if he had addressed her. And so he saw her eyes, startlingly large and full and radiant with intelligence. They were the color of a certain Hungarian wine he particularly liked, Tokay, tawny and sparkling and inclined to be heady. They were most aware and perceptive, and suddenly, to James, she was beautiful in spite of her lack of artifice, in spite of her frank plainness; in spite of her extreme thinness and lack of feminine hips. He also saw, in a flash, that here was a most sensual and passionate woman, and he was stirred to a deeper admiration.

Then he heard Emil say, "Good morning."

She smiled at Emil, a faint smile both remote and polite, and she also said, "Good morning—Doctor." Her voice was unexpectedly warm and deep, if reserved.

Emil was hesitating. Then the door opened and they all trooped out. James lifted his eyebrows inquiringly, but Emil only shrugged and waited until the woman had approached the receptionist's desk, which was manned by two pretty nurses in smart uniforms. Then Emil said in a low voice, "We don't know who the hell she is, but she comes at least once a week to ask about Jerald. She's given only her name. Just calls herself a 'friend.' The girls have been trained not to give out information to unidentified people about any patient, but there's something about this woman— I usually leave a message for her, as reassuring as possible."

"Jerry's mistress, perhaps?"

Emil laughed shortly. "I don't think so. Not his type, from what I've heard and obviously too old for him. No charm; no seductiveness; nothing coquettish, nothing overtly sexual. All we know of her is that she is a Mrs. or Miss Turner."

The woman was leaning over the desk and one of the nurses was apparently giving her the message Emil had left for her yesterday. She was listening with a profound attention. She showed no emotion. Then she left the desk and was coming towards the two psychiatrists, and the elevator. She looked paler than before. She was so preoccupied that she almost collided with the two men. Emil gently caught her arm and she uttered a faint sound.

She said, "He isn't getting better, is he?"

Emil hesitated. "Miss Turner, these illnesses take time to heal. He's no worse, let us say. His condition is stationary. We hope for some improvement soon."

"That really means nothing, does it?"

James smiled. Yes, the challenge was there and the impatience of a challenger. Emil said, "It means something to me. Miss Turner, why do you refuse to let me tell Mr. Jerald you come here to find out how he is? It might help him."

She shook her head and a strand of that violently red-copper hair fell across her face and she pushed it back. "No. He has to ask for me himself. He knows where to find me. He must make up his own mind."
50

"About what, Miss Turner?" Emil spoke gently but with interest.

"About many things. Until he does he will be ill."

"Really? What makes you come to that conclusion?"

"I know. That's all I can tell you." At once those tawny eyes were dark with pain. "And I have your promise that he mustn't know I come here." It was almost a stern admonition. "It could only make him worse."

She nodded quickly and went into the elevator. Emil said, "Quite a mystery, isn't it?"

"The lady intrigues me," said James. "I know her sort well. She is a rarity in America, I'm sure. I'd wager she never told a lie in her life, not because she has principles against lying but simply because she is incapable of it. Noblesse oblige, courtesy of nature."

"She doesn't look very prosperous, James."

"One can't be sure of that. She dresses exactly like the county ladies in England, no fuss and feathers, just plain common sense and sturdiness. All utility. I'm positive she could afford fashionable clothes, if she liked. But she doesn't 'like.' What cheekbones she has, broad and almost transparent. An aristocratic face, imperious, gaunt, dauntless, intrepid—totally brave and heroic. I think there's more to this situation than meets the eye."

Emil said again, "From what I've heard, she isn't Jerald's type. I went into that thoroughly. About half the women he'd had all over the state, and in New York and points east and west, north and south, oddly resemble his wife. Just sheer vapid prettiness. The other half—well you can find them in the less expensive bordellos. Coarse, rowdy, stupid, and oozing raw sex. Miss Turner, or Mrs. Turner, if that's really her name, doesn't look like his wife or his whores. There's nothing very attractive about her, though I admit she has extraordinary eyes and a certain air."

They were walking down a broad corridor handsomely paved with thick lengths of oriental rugs in very vivid colors. Small crystal chandeliers dripped twinkling light from the high arched ceiling. The corridor was lined with carved oaken doors, solid and closed. There was nothing institutional about this corridor. Nurses passed them, but they moved in sedate silence, no bustling, no hurry. Doctors gravely consulted each other outside of those mute doors, or had retired to an occasional bay-windowed alcove filled with excellent furniture. One could not tell, from looking at the tall windows, that they were barred. They merely seemed latticed. A gentle warmth flowed down the corridor. As usual, everything's overheated in America, thought James. He felt uncomfortable in his thick tweeds.

"There are only suites on this floor," Emil said. "This is the most expensive section of Mountain Valleys. Only private nurses in attendance. Guy has three of them, all around the clock. As he never stops smoking, they are necessary. Not that there is much danger of suicide—but we take precautions. Guy is never alone. I have the impression that that infuriates him, but you can't tell."

"As long as he doesn't become passive—" James suggested.

"Well, sometimes he doesn't move for hours, but there's nothing passive about him. That lady we just encountered knows more than we do. She's come to the same conclusion about him without having seen him since he was brought here. Damn it, I wish she'd open her mouth and tell us! Looks like a schoolteacher, to me."

They were passing another alcove. Emil paused and looked within. A tall old priest with a very angry face was standing in the center of the alcove, and was moving his arms rapidly if stiffly, emphasizing what he was saying in a rude rough voice. His tone was not only enraged but disgusted. Facing him, and seated, were two silent and richly suited ladies in their thirties. One wore a sable jacket, the other a short white mink coat. Their brown heads were smoothly coiffed, as if made of polished wood, their cheeks daintily tinted, their mouths sad and deliberately meek, their gloved hands folded over each other. They greatly resembled each other and
52

James judged them to be sisters. They had nothing of the splendor of Miss—or Mrs.—Turner about them.

The strong old priest was not using any profanities, yet his voice and gestures expressed pure and raging profanity. "Psychiatric care!" he was shouting. "And you offering to pay for it for him, when he should be hanged from the highest tree! Damned if I wouldn't like to pull the trap myself!" There was a hint of Irish brogue in his roaring voice.

One of the women spoke in a dolorous voice whining with piety, "Father, Edith and I suggested it out of compassion. We don't bear any malice—"

The priest came to sudden halt in both speech and gesture. He bent forward to scrutinize the lady who had spoken and his long hard face tightened. "And why, may I ask, Gertie, why don't you?"

The other woman, Edith, spoke. "Father, that's a strange question. Gertrude and I are only trying to be truly Christian—compassionate—understanding."

The priest turned his small fierce blue eyes on her. "Now, is that so, Edith? 'Compassionate!' What a weasely word. Compassion for the man who murdered your mother? Why haven't you been compassionate about her, Edie? And your father, dying of grief behind that door there? Haven't you any blood or guts or life, you girls? Or—is there something else?" He was studying them with increased ferocity, and he looked very formidable. The two women shrank.

"I don't know what you mean, Father," said Gertrude. "Certainly we grieve for our mother; certainly we pray for our father and hope he will regain his senses. But—will revenge restore Mama or cure Dad? Will one evil cure the first?"

"It's words like that which keep our streets running with murderers and other criminals," said the priest, and he was angrier than ever. "It's words like them which make the poor po-lice blasphemous. It's people like you who've corrupted our judges with sweetness and light and got them

53

ro release fiends on us again. And where did you pick up that nonsense, that wicked, dangerous nonsense?"

A glint of absolute malice blinked in Edith's eyes. "Father Gurney speaks about it often, Father McQuire."

Again the priest seemed about to erupt into profanity. "Ah, yes," he bellowed. "Little young Christian martyr Jack Meany! Of sweet and modern and aggiornamento St. Catherine of Sienna Church! I know him well!" The brogue was thick in his words now, almost stammering with his anger. "At least your mother didn't suffer the Mass of Christian Burial from that spalpeen! It was from my church that your mother was conveyed to her grave, God rest her good soul! Not from Jack's." The old priest's face was swollen and scarlet, and he shuddered.

He then noticed the two men who were listening, James with fascination. An enraged priest was something new in his experience, except for his late mother's confessor. Emil said, "Good morning, Father McQuire. May I introduce Dr. James Meyer, from London, a colleague of mine?"

The priest's face candidly said, "What the hell are you interrupting for?" and James pressed his lips together to keep from smiling. The clergyman's engorged color did not fade when he grunted his acknowledgment of the introduction, but his big hand was clammy and tremulous and James was concerned. Hypertension there, he thought, and no wonder. The ladies, happy for this interruption, swiftly got to their feet, murmuring, and hurriedly brushed past the three men in flight. The priest followed them with his infuriated blue eyes, then he sighed.

"And how is your friend today, Father?" asked Emil.

"Bad. Very bad." The priest sighed again and the sigh was like a sob. "They'll be calling me for the Last Rites soon, I'm afraid."

"I hope not," said Emil. He turned to James and said, "Mr. Jordan's wonderful wife, Ruth, was murdered in her house a week ago, by a young thug who thought the house was empty and had entered to rob it. He saw Mrs. Jordan, and he knifed her to death." Emil paused, and all at once his face was as savage as the priest's. "He's only a child,

54

the social workers say. 'Only sixteen.' They're trying to put him into the category of 'youthful offender.' In short, just naughty delinquency. That means, if they succeed, that he'll never be tried for murder. He will be sent only to a tender correctional institution, and will be out on the streets again within a year, free again to rob and kill. 'He never had a chance,' the social workers say. To be brief about it, he had strict parents who tried to bake rotten and diseased flour into a sound loaf of bread. His brothers, though, are good boys and were never in trouble. Just this one stinking bastard who should never have been born. I don't know who to pity more, Dick Jordan or the boy's parents. Funny about heredity, isn't it? Skips a couple of generations or more, then comes on full blast in a new generation. Some murderous ancestor came out in Billy Johnson's psyche."

"Yes," said James. "The criminal is born, not made by environment. Once we knew that in Britain, too, but the sobbers are at it there just as in America in these days. If one didn't try to be very rational one would suspect an international conspiracy, designed to drive nations mad so they could be the more easily conquered and subdued."

"I do suspect a conspiracy," said Emil, in a flat tone.

"So do I," said Father McQuire, "and it was spawned in hell." He rubbed his flaming face with both his hands, a pathetic gesture of defeat. "And Ruth Jordan's daughters want to get a loving psychiatrist to treat their mother's murderer! It's daft they are—or something worse." As if he were afraid he had said something unpardonable, he flickered his hand and almost ran from the alcove.

"Why do you suppose those daughters want to do that?" asked James.

"Well," said Emil, with an ugly intonation, "their mother had the money in the family, not their father, and I understand that the daughters get two thirds of it. Christ! But I'd put nothing past any human being now. Maybe, in their weasel souls, as the good Father would put it, the daughters are unconsciously grateful to their mother's murderer."

James was not shocked. They had walked on again.

Emil stopped before a door and knocked. He said, "When you are ready to leave, the nurse will call me; I will be here for at least five hours. Let's have lunch, about one-thirty." He glanced at his watch. "It is eleven now."

The door was opened and a bright middle-aged face with the traditional nurse's cap appeared, and a happy little body came briskly into the hall. Emil said, "Dr. Meyer, this is Nurse Halstrom. She is on duty with Mr. Jerald until three, and she has been told about you. Nurse, Dr. Meyer, a friend of Mr. Jerald's."

She nodded and her pink cheeks dimpled. "Good morning, Doctor. Yes, Dr. Witherspoon has told me about you. I am to leave you and Mr. Jerald alone until you ring the desk for me." She beamed at James with curiosity, and he found himself smiling as ruddily. "How is Mr. Jerald?" he asked.

The rosiness paled a little. "Well," she said. "About the same, I think. He did have a restless night, I saw from his chart. Walked the floor for hours. He isn't given much of a sedative," and she glanced at Emil. "He smoked a great deal, and ate very little dinner. Pretty restless, I think."

"Good," said Emil. He nodded to the nurse, who moved off rapidly to the desk with the other nurses; her cheery voice echoed along the hall. Then he touched James on the arm and nodded again, this time at the door. James entered Guy Jerald's suite. It was very dusky here, he saw, the dimness of the day increased by the half-drawn rich green curtains across the two high barred windows. This was the sitting room, excellently furnished with real or reproduced antiques, wing chairs, polished tables, mirrors, two bookcases, a Queen Anne sofa, an electric fireplace in which a quite realistic group of white logs simulated wood-burning, even to the flutter of artificial flames. Fine prints hung on the pale green walls, and there were fresh flowers about. Beyond was the bathroom and bedroom. It was a quiet and comfortable suite. There was an ormolu clock on the mantelpiece and it chimed in fragile music.

James thought of the moldering old sanitariums in England all paid for by National Health, and so naturally all shabby and decaying. Yes, indeed, there was a great deal to be said in favor of private enterprise, even medical.

He looked about him cautiously, standing near the closed door. At first he did not see Guy Jerald, so dusky was the room. It had an air of emptiness, as if no one had been there for hours. However, there was a heavy odor of tobacco, and, as usual in America, it was entirely too warm here. Still, in spite of the cigarette smoke, the air was fresh as if changed regularly. Then James saw the thin figure of a man in an opened white shirt and dark trousers crouched in a distant wing chair near a window. James came farther into the room, and he was strangely uneasy.

The man's head was bent, his arms folded on his knees, his gaze fixed on the floor. James could see more clearly now. The thick black hair, interwoven with gray, had an unkempt look, half fell over the bent forehead. James could see the colorless cheek, the fixity of feature, the clenched lips, the absence of expression. He was shocked. Could this immobile creature be the Jerald—Jerry—he had known? Could it actually be the vivid and sometimes exuberant and often wild man he remembered even from fifteen years ago? The almost fleshless face seemed made of pale wood, the muscles unmoving, the throat still, as if it did not possess a sound box or even a larynx. Then James saw that the fixity was the fixity of still agony and the long and aquiline nose testified to anguish, for it was translucent.

"Jerry?" said James, and his voice was weak with pity. The man did not move. The thick black eyebrows did not lift; there was no sign of life in him anywhere. Only the cigarette smoking between two attenuated fingers gave any clue that this man lived at all. The long emaciated wrist finally moved; an ash was deposited in a cloisonné ashtray on the table beside the chair. So, thought James, he is quite aware, even if only mechanically aware. The man gave no other indication that there was a stranger with him, or that he was thinking.

James turned on a brass lamp and a warm light moved into the dimness. He stood helplessly, still gazing on this man who had apparently withdrawn into the darkness of a living death. The clock chimed again and James started. Then the man lifted his head with a slow movement, as if his skull were made of iron and it was nearly impossible to lift it or it took all his strength. He looked at James.

"Jerry?" James said again. Again he was shocked. The face that confronted him resembled the face of his old friend, but it was as if an uninspired artist had carved it, giving it the remembered features but none of its implied motility and vital glow. The dark eyes were larger in that shrunken face, yet they were inert, those once animated and lively eyes full of emotion. They were unseeing, far removed, empty. They were like the eyes of a dead bird, filmed and opaque. The once splendid bones of the face, sharp and defined and clear, appeared to have dwindled, become smaller and vague. The remembered mouth, quick to express amusement or annoyance, was only a line, pent and dry.

Unable to look away from that devastated face, that dead face, James moved to a chair facing his friend and sat down. A cool sweat came out on his forehead. He had left the door, the lamp, yet Guy's eyes fixed on the spot he had occupied. Then the head fell again, the stony chin on the chest. Once again the room was abandoned.

James lit a cigar. He was usually a voluble man, energetic of speech and forceful of language. Yet he fumbled through a cloud of words and could not grasp any of them. He had a sensation both of grief and helplessness. This was worse than he had anticipated. He rubbed his damp forehead. His wits evaded him. Then the warmth of the room irritated him, and he heard himself, to his own astonishment, speaking aloud.

"Why the hell do you people keep everything so blazing hot, like a jungle?"

The fallen head moved and lifted, slowly, slowly, and the deathly eyes looked at James, without recognition or cognizance. It was if it were responding to a harsh touch
58

only, a response out of a nightmare. James felt the poignancy of his own pain as he stared at Guy, and a kind of inexplicable fury at what had come to his friend, and he did not understand why he stammered, "It's really all there is, all there is!"

What in hell was he talking about? he thought with despair. It was as though someone else had spoken with his own tongue out of vast madness or memory. Had he been trying to say, out of that despair and fury, that there was only despair and fury in the world, after all, and nothing else?

Then, to his awe and his own trembling, he saw that for an instant those terrible dead eyes had flashed with life and a remembered wildness. A black glow had lit them, like exploding light on polished coal. James leaned towards Guy. He said, and his voice was broken. "Jerry, for God's sake—!"

He knows me, he knows me, he heard me, James suddenly thought with a shaking exultation.

Once again the eyes became dead and filmed and the head dropped. James did not move or speak. He felt the enormous retreat of the spirit of his friend, but in some way he knew that the retreat was not into nothingness this time, but into something else.

"I tell you, Jerry, there ain't anything else. This is all there is, I'm telling you, all there is! So help me God! And I'm a damned heathen, and I can say that!"

It was a hot August day in 1946 on a farm near Cranston, a large stony farm which could be coaxed to yield only by the most intensive effort and tons of fertilizer, none of which it got regularly. Even when listlessly tended, it was "played out," as neighboring farmers said derisively. The soil was mostly infertile, and barren, and many acres were sheer wasteland, full of strangling bush and snarled half-dead trees. The apple orchard produced wormy little apples which tasted like acid wood and usually fell long before any signs of ripening. The pear trees were blackly blighted and no one had removed them. Only the small acreage of bottomland could sustain a stand of corn or wheat, but because of neglect these were almost always brown with fungus, or stunted. The bare land stretched far into the distance, and beyond that distance the foothills, fiery in the August noon, were burned and eroded. Behind them the green and purple mountains lifted ancient battlements against a sky white with heat.

What timber was on the land—it had been cleared ruthlessly of good timber long ago—was second-growth and scraggly. As if in celestial malice this growth had been frequently struck by lightning, and the charred logs lay at the feet of the weak growth above them. Here it was dank, the dark earth teeming with toadstools, the air heavy and fetid.

The surrounding farms were green and fertile and blooming, full of sunshine and ardent crops, pastures thick with grass, fields bursting with life. The Jerald farm was a desert among them, somehow sinister and silent and abandoned. The neighboring farmers, husbandmen all, mourned for the land.

The farmers, however, could not make derisive remarks about the stock. The few Holstein cattle and the six Angus cows were fat and sleek and complacent, the three hundred chickens plump, and vigorous about laying large eggs, and the Poland China swine were bigger than those belonging to the neighbors, and their flesh succulent. It was suspected that the intelligent and curious guinea hens were kept solely as pets, and on a large blue pond several geese and ducks lived in total amity. There was one dog of pluralistic ancestry, who gravely did duty as a watchman and took that duty with the utmost seriousness and never pursued cars on the road or quarreled with other dogs. "The stock got better sense than ole Tom Jerald," the farmers would say with some envy. "Wonder where he gets the money to feed them, he and his drinking and his blowsy Sal."

Tom Jerald raised considerable truck, too, and it was a

constant amazement to his neighbors why his vegetables and melons were so gigantic, grown as they were on a small patch of fertile land. His strawberries, also, were prized in the market, and his raspberry bushes were scarlet with juicy berries. But his old tractor was rusted and unreliable. It amused the farmers that Tom plowed in an anachronistic way, with a plow of the sort never seen in the neighborhood since 1915. It was pulled by a hearty mule who seemed to be a pet, too, and who laughed at the neighbor horses with high glee, much to their sedate discomfiture. Tom owned an elderly car of unnamed vintage and make, which aroused all the dogs in the country, it was said, when Tom drove it into town. It not only smoked, it rattled like a bevy of cymbals, and its fenders seemed imminently about to drop on the road. But it ran, and that was all Tom cared about, and he drove it as considerately as if it had been a new Cadillac, and he kept it waxed and polished.

The small farmhouse, which had a red silo, was as battered as the car, and there was no sign of paint on it. It was now silvery with age, and its shingles curled and its doors were warped and full of slivers. But its windows were brightly polished and showed cheap white muslin curtains, made of worn sheets, and it was always buried in a teeming and colorful mass of flowers from spring to autumn. That was Sal's doing, of course, Sal who had been born on as worthless a farm as Tom's, and a member of a family of twelve children who now made their livings in town in a dubious fashion. Sal herself was known to be "no better than she should be." Hadn't she kept house for Ole Schiller, a farmer on the other side of Cranston, and hadn't his three sons openly accused her of sleeping with their father as well as cooking for him and raising the table vegetables and the chickens? Ole Schiller had left his mortgaged farm to his sons, but he had left three thousand dollars to Sal and the huge brass bed on which he and his "woman" had slept for quite a number of years. Sal was forty-three, Tom Jerald fifty-nine, his son, Guy, nearly twenty-four. Guy had gone off to the war, drafted, of course, and was now home on the farm.

Everyone felt sorry for Mary Jerald, Tom's wife, who kept a boardinghouse for workingmen who had no other home. At least she was respectable and went to church, and had left Tom years ago when she could no longer endure his "rioting" and general worthlessness, and drinking. A good son would have disowned Tom Jerald as a father and stayed with his exemplary mother. But—"what's born in the bone will come out in the flesh." It was obvious that Guy preferred his father, even from earliest childhood, though that was the only crime he had ever committed, to the neighbors' knowledge. He had worked in one of the sawmills since he had left high school, and in the winters he lived with his mother. In the summers he helped his father on the farm, and was often with Tom during the winter holidays. But he was now considered "queer," in that he had become very quiet and was sometimes morose and never seemed to smile and certainly was never "neighborly."

Tom was sitting, this hot August day of 1946, on the broken steps of the stoop in front of the farmhouse. He was a small and satyric man with a grin that was described as "fiendish," and he appeared made of faded wood and leather thongs, with never an ounce of good flesh. He had a dry browned face with blue eyes and a fair beard as scraggly as his trees and a very prominent nose and big yellow teeth. He was as quick and restless as a sparrow, which he somewhat resembled, and his head was bald and freckled and as brown as his face. If his house was filled with decrepit furniture and had no rugs except for the hooked ones Sal had made, it also harbored many books, which puzzled the few neighbors who had ever entered the house. For it was rumored Tom could not read or write. He never received a newspaper, though he had a very old radio which squawked with static when used, which was almost always.

Tom was never without a pipe or one of his homemade cigarettes which had a very strong odor, "like manure," the neighbors would say. He was now tamping his pipe with a thin and grubby index finger and was staring up at his son, who stood before him. His grin was both ironic and very wide, and not too kind.

Guy "took after" his mother, Mary Jerald, in that he was much taller than his father and lean rather than flesh-less. His uniform was neat and fitted him well, unusual for a common soldier, and his boots were polished. His shoulders were broad, his waist narrow, his hips taut and hard. He had a good face, the neighbors had to admit, and quite handsome, thin and dark and mobile, with excellent features, large black eyes, a sullen but expressive mouth and a rounded chin full of strength, with a hint of obstinacy. His mother, it was said, came of a "nice family," working-class but respectable, and her father had been a bricklayer with a commendable income. Guy had her round head and her thick black straight hair, very abundant, and neatly combed.

He stood, now, before his father, his arms folded some-what obdurately on his chest, one big hand holding a cigarette. He was smiling slightly, but the smile did not radiate as did Tom's lively grin.

"Yes, sir," said Tom. "That's all there is, son, your life, and it's the only life you'll ever have and no one can live it for you. You got to live as it's your nature to live, or, sure as God, you'll pay and pay bad all the rest of your years on this earth. And you can't whimper it was only your duty that you ruint your life and it ended up in the privy of 'responsibility.' That's one thing the angels, I heard, never accept as an excuse. You can't blame other folks, either, for the stink you make of your life. You did it all your lone self. It ain't anybody's fault but your own." His voice was naturally high and a little shrill.

"I wish you wouldn't pretend all the time that you're illiterate," said Guy, in his strong young man's amused voice.

"I sure am illiterate in not wanting what other folks want, to their death," said Tom, puffing on his pipe as he lit it. "Besides, if the people hereabouts even suspected I
63

went to a good university downstate, they'd sure think I was crazy, or worse. But, it's my life, and I'm living it as I want to live it. That's all that matters, Jerry, my lad."

"But what will you do when you get old?" asked Guy, smiling wider but with evident reluctance.

"You've never asked me that before," said Tom. "What'll I do?" He thrust out one scarecrow leg in its patched denim. "I got a leg full of shrapnel I got during the other war and I get two hundred dollars a month compensation from the V.A. Eighty percent disability." He cackled. "Probably'll get more later, and maybe a pension. And I got this farm, such as it is." He pointed with the stem of his pipe. "This farm's near Cranston. There's going to be a lot of building on bought farms around here. Suburbs. Not that I'd sell it so long's I live. A man buys land; he don't sell it. Maybe that won't be enough for you, Jerry, when you get it when I'm dead. But—you do what you want to with it. It's your life."

"You were never ambitious," said Guy, in a neutral tone. He put his cigarette to his mouth and smoked thoughtfully.

"Now, why the hell should I be?" asked Tom, with some irritation. "I got enough to live on, if I'm careful. I got a roof, some good stock and truck. Got a Sunday suit and another pair of shoes. My life ain't the life other people would like. But I like it. It suits me. No hustle, no bustle, no fretting over bank accounts and investments. No competition. It's my life. No apologies. I don't give a damn for other people and their opinions, son. Once you do you've set yourself up in a jail, with the bars made of other people's judgments, and a locked door made of other people's chatter about you. You ain't yourself anymore. You're what your neighbors, and the community, made out of your living soul. Except it ain't living any longer. It's the creation of other people. So, what's left of what you were born with? Gone, gone forever. Your unique mind is composed of the echoes of other people's thoughts, just as they were the echoes of others before them. What a life! Son, my life's not your life, and I'm glad you still

64

have a life of your own. I never hounded you to be like me or anyone else. It's your life, like I said. God help you if you don't live it as your own and no one else's."

Now the grin faded, and a strange and sober look replaced it and the light blue eyes were sharp and compassionate. "Ain't that what I've been telling you all your life? I thought you listened. Not in one ear and out the other."

"I've been doing a lot of thinking," said Guy. His father grinned again.

"A bad habit," said Tom. "When did you get snarled up in that? You wasn't like that when you left here for that damned war. It's made you solemn or something else bad. Nothing like a war to change a man around and ruin him."

"I've had experiences," said Guy, and again the somberness was on his young features and his polished black eyes took on a certain ferocity. "And, I'm older. I'm not the kid who went away. I'm a man now."

"Maybe that's good, maybe that's not so good, Jerry. You got to keep a lot of childhood in your soul. Wonder, and such, and an eagerness for the future, and adventure. Lose that, and you lose something that's vital, and you'll just become a drudge in living, even if you get to be a millionaire. Remember what Livy said, couple of thousand years ago! 'Seldom are men blessed with good fortune and good sense at the same time.' A man can get along without good fortune, but, by God, he can't get along without good sense. One's being a robot, the other's being a man in charge of his life."

He looked at his stiff leg again. "Once I kind of lost my own way. Got drafted for the other war. Had experiences, too. Saved my pay. Got a bonus. Thought I'd go back to teaching somewheres. Never told you I was a prof once, did I? It don't matter. Then it came to me: I didn't want to teach. I didn't want to go into any kind of business. I wanted to live my own life. So, here I am, living it. Aimless, useless, worth nothing, the other folks say. But to me

65

it ain't aimless or useless. It's fascinating. No worries, no sweat. And I got me a good woman this time."

Guy frowned, glanced at the open door of the farmhouse. "I couldn't live like this," he said, as if to himself.

"Good. Who's asking you to live like this? Live as you want to live, Jerry. Do what you want to do and be damned to anyone else, including me. But be sure it's what you really want and not what you think you ought to do. Say, one time you told me, before you went off to that damned stupid war, that you wanted to be a doctor. You said you'd always wanted that. So, why don't you?"

But Guy said, "We all can't live the way we want to. That's chaos. A doctor? There's no money. And I'm twenty-four and never went to college. So even if I had the money to go to medical school after college it would be at least fourteen years before I'd be ready to practice—or go into cancer research, as I'd like to do, perhaps even fifteen years. I'd be thirty-eight or -nine.

Tom held up his hand. "One thing at a time. You say there'd be chaos if everybody'd live his own life. Well, as the Bible says, most men are born to be drawers of water and hewers of wood. That's what they'd like, most people, to do useful heavy work on the land or in factories or building, or such. Why should their parents force them into academic studies, where they'd be miserable? False pride. What's wrong with labor? Chaos is created by discontented and overeducated men, and we've got millions of them now and that's going to be bad for an orderly society. Men who've been forced to work at something or learn something they despise. Is that living? No, that's real chaos, when it's in the mind or the heart of a man. Chaos.

"On the other hand, there're men whose whole aim is to go into the professions. Why don't they? Money? What's that got to do with it? They could work at any job and go to school at nights—I know dozens who did. Exhausting? Sure. But the hell with exhaustion. As the old Romans used to say, 'He is able—if he thinks he is able.' Everything has its price, sonny boy. The Spaniards say, 'Take what you want, says God. But pay for it.' I decided on a profession myself when I was young. But when I got it I saw it wasn't for me, after all. So—here I am, living as I want to live. I paid for everything in my life, not just money, and I'm glad I did. Now I'm content. No chaos in me. But, there was before. Miserable years when I tried to conform to what people thought I ought to do. I was desperate. Had a revolution come along I'd have joined it, fooling myself I was joining a Cause. Anything to run away from the mess I had made out of my life. Got a dose of common sense just in time.

"I hear about this new G.I. Bill. That'll help you to do what you want to do. To take up the slack—get yourself a job doing anything useful. It'll keep you in bread and butter and a shelter over your head, if no luxuries. A small price to pay—for being a whole man. You say I'm not ambitious. What about you, son? Being ambitious means being ready to pay the price for what you want. Aren't you man enough to pay the price—of being a man?"

Guy threw his cigarette away and his young face became recalcitrant and dark. "You talk as if I've got all the time in the world, Pa."

"So you have. What're years? Just a delusion. In the meantime, while you study and work, you are living, and when you live, time is not measured; it is an eternity, with no limits." He paused and screwed up his eyes in the sun and stared at Guy. He spoke in a quieter voice but a more insistent one. "What're you afraid of, Jerry?"

"Oh shit, Pa! I'm not afraid of anything, after that war!" He hesitated. "You forget Ma. She's fifty-four years old and works hard. How about duty, my responsibility to her as her son?" He looked down at the ground. "I've got to do something to make money—fast."

Tom chucked hoarsely. "Your ma's a pretty tough woman, kiddo. Always was, even if she's a roaring Bible-shouter. So, you got polluted after all, with all that 'duty.' When a man's manacled by duty he don't do himself or anyone else any good. He's filled with hate, and it usually is projected on the one who received all that duty. Many's the man I know who thought he should spend his life in duty to his wife and children, and parents, and he ended up wishing they were dead, or he ran away. Sometimes, in extreme cases, he murdered. It was a sickness all around. A chained man is bound to become wicked, one way or another. And who suffers at the last? Not only him, but the ones he sacrificed himself for. Think they were happy? No. Many's the man these days dying of heart attacks, or strokes or suicide, because he sacrificed himself in the name of duty. Hell.

"Back to your ma. When I left teaching a lot of muttonheads—most students now are muttonheads—I found this place, after a lot of wandering. Just what I wanted. Land—with a little good acreage. Just enough to provide for me. And, being still young, I needed a permanent woman, to help on the land and to screw. I didn't want to spend my life on a good rich farm, sweating my life out. Just enough to live on and to look on this damned mysterious world and think and read and ponder. Only that's living, when you live in your soul and your heart. Well, anyways.

"I found your ma in Cranston, working in a boarding-house. A good hefty woman, and I thought, no foolishness about her. She still isn't foolish, except when it comes to her stringent religion. Then she's an idiot. But somehow, I, being a man, a religious woman, I thought, was bound to be pure, and that's what I wanted—a pure, hard-working, sensible woman who hadn't been obliging every Tom, Dick, and Harry around. See how stupid I was in many ways? What's traffic around the genitals got to do with the intrinsic worth of a person? Later I found out that Magdalens make fine wives, when they fall in love, whereas the 'pure' women usually ended up using a whip on everybody in sight, and imposing their 'morals' on husbands and children and making their lives miserable, and talking about duty to man and God all the time. Wonder what God really thinks of such women—and some men, too— who live entirely for 'duty,' and create a hell on earth for others in their vicinity. If God is anything at all, He is a

God of joy and love and laughter and humor and youth, and not some old Party glowering over the walls of heaven with hellfire and damnation like thunderbolts in His Hand: ready to hurl them on those who love 'illicitly,' as it is called, or not doing their damned 'duty' as regulated by the parsons. Hell, son, a man who is faithful to his wife when he detests her is violating the great Law of Love, which rules the universe—if there is any law at all.

"Say, I'm wandering, maybe. You'll remember that it was Christ who refused to condemn Mary Magdalen, and prevented her death by stoning. He said, 'Her sins are forgiven her—*for she loved much.*' There ain't any sin in the world, Jerry, that can't be forgiven, if a person loves. The great sin, and maybe it's the unpardonable one, is *not* loving. A strictly virtuous and dutiful man or woman is a great sinner, in spite of Bible-shouting and going to church and living a 'good' life—because they didn't love. They sinned against God Himself, who is a God of Love."

He paused. Guy had been listening intently and now his dark face was lighted by a brief smile. He said, "I guess, then, that God must love you a lot, you being a great sinner, Pa."

Tom grinned anticly. "Well, I love Him, in my fashion. Most sinners do. Only the virtuous really hate Him in their hearts—they think He's a taskmaster, full of hate, too, for anything beautiful and joyous and delightful. And deep in everybody's heart is the sure knowledge that joy is a celebration of the God of Joy. So, the 'virtuous' deny joy because they think God is purely a God of wrath who must be appeased at any cost, though they know, by instinct, that's wrong. So, they violate their God-given instinct, which is to love wholly and completely. That's what has always led to religious cruelty and persecutions —in the name of a God of hate—who doesn't exist, anyway. The lovers of a God of hate are the most evil people in the world, in spite of their prissy faces and their talk of 'serving the Lord, and mankind.' If there's a hell, which I doubt, it's full of such folks.

"Now: I met your ma. A tall, good-looking youngish

woman who knew how to work hard and had a good figure and fine legs. I thought there must be hidden fire in her. I was wrong. There was fire, all right, a fire of duty and 'serving,' and denying life. Besides, I was getting hot. Hadn't had a woman for a long time. I'd have settled for jumps in the hay and ass-patting and love and fun and laughter. But not your ma. A 'good' pure woman. So, to have her I had to marry her. I should have been warned; she didn't even drink a glass of beer. Now, there're people who shouldn't drink, for health or other reasons, and I got no quarrel with them. But a man or woman who 'refrains' out of some damned idiot principle or other is again denying God. Remember what David the King said: 'Oil to make the countenance shine, wine to make the heart of man glad.' And he didn't mean grape juice, either. The fruit of the grape is a gift of God, if it ain't abused, as no good thing should be abused, including sex.

"Your ma didn't think she'd like to live on a farm, but she'd give it a try. She did; she tried very hard. It was no use. Maybe if she'd been happy with me she'd have made do. But she wasn't happy. I wouldn't conform to what she thought was 'right' and 'decent.' She'd accuse me of not being 'dutiful' and responsible. She tried to make me into the kind of man she thought was worthwhile: Slaving and looking grim and righteous and begetting children who'd also be grim and righteous, and living in the Name of the Lord. She tried to make me go to church. Now, I ain't got any prejudices about going to church. Maybe if more would go it would be a better world—if it was kept in proportion. But to live for church and not for day-to-day life is soul-killing and joy-killing. That wasn't the Lord's intention. 'Make a joyful noise until the Lord,' said David, and that didn't mean groaning out hymns and sitting in silent pews really hating everybody. A joyful noise. Your ma never knew about that. All her 'noises' were sober and sour. It must have made God wince. Remember: Christ did preach occasionally in the synagogues, but most of what He said was said out in the hectic world, on hills and in fields in sight of the green shining waters, and in roaring cities teeming with life."

Tom sighed. He drew heavily on his pipe. "Like a lot of young men I was more interested in what was between your ma's legs and not what was between her ears, and in her heart. So, we got married, and within a year you were born. She'd had a hard time. So no more bouncing in bed, or, even worse, she'd show no joy. I hadn't noticed that at first. So, when you was five, she lit out, with all the money I could find for her, and opened that boardinghouse, where she takes in only prudent and serious men, God help them."

A great oak tree near the farmhouse tossed its serrated leaves in the sun, and every leaf shone. A cooling breeze ran over the land, filling the air with the scent of dust and hot dry earth. The door opened and Sal stood on the threshold. "You fellers like a cold bottle of beer?"

Guy was impatient at this interruption, but then he had to smile. There were few who could not smile at Sal. She was forty-three years old and short and plump and as downy as a peach and resembled a rosy peach, slightly browned by the sun, and ripe, and full of sweet juices. She was not in the least pretty; in fact, she appeared very earthy and more than a little coarse. But her round face was gay and cheerful and she was always either smiling widely or laughing, and her spherical brown eyes, with their rowdy expression and intimation of innocent lewdness, were very endearing. She had a short thick nose and a jolly full red mouth filled with small glistening white teeth, which seemed to twinkle with mirth all the time. Her bosom was very ample and strained against her blue cotton dress, and her hips were broad and ample also. Her hands were short and broad, showing signs of constant labor. Her hair was an untidy mess of curling dark hair, always spilling about her glowing cheeks in tendrils which crackled with exuberance and vitality. There was a lust for life about her, a bountiful lust for living and for giving, and the vivacity of lush summer, fruitful and warm.

Tom turned, as he sat on the steps, and patted and

pinched her bottom. He said, "Sure, we'd like a cold beer, Sal." His thin browned face was alert with love and humor for this almost illiterate farm woman who had never read a book in her life and who was engrossed, when at leisure, with the radio, and with food. She ate as heartily as she lived, and drank happily with Tom, and was an enthusiastic bed partner who kept Tom as vital as a youth, and as potent. Whatever he wished to do she was joyful to do also; she never complained and never was petulant or sulky. Health leapt out of her like a fountain, inexhaustible. She was, as Tom had often said, truly a woman, lustful and romping and kind, buoyant and, always, alive. Her conversations with Tom might be without depth or literacy, but she had the strong wisdom of a loving woman, and a certain sprightly bawdiness. Her laugh might be too loud and raucous, but it was the laughter of spring, without sniggering, and without restraint. Malice was unknown to her; she had a humorous attitude towards the world. "Hell, Tom," she would say. "The only thing is to be happy. Anything else is an insult to the good Lord, even if you are in pain, or something, and things go wrong. You gotta trust Him."

She was truly religious, as Tom often remarked. Her love for God was as simple as an animal's, and as accepting. She was aware of evil, as she was aware of cold dark winters without life, but she waited it out and greeted the end of it with laughing thanksgiving, and without resentment, and rejoiced in each day. She never condemned anyone, not because she was charitable but because she knew nothing of condemnation, and was incapable of it.

Guy thought of what his mother often said harshly and with bitterness of Sal: "A bad bold woman with no more morals than a mink. Well, God will judge her, and she'll deserve the judgment. She was always a scandal since she was fourteen years old. She's just right for your pa, and all he deserves. A woman with her reputation, all bad. She's disgusting. But so's your pa."

Sal looked down lovingly at Tom. She pinched his

72

cheek. The air seemed to vibrate about her, an energy of being. She went into the house and brought back two nondescript glasses and two bottles of icy beer. She poured the beer with gusto, blew off the foam, and handed the glasses to the two men. She sighed ecstatically. "What a beautiful day," she said. But all days were beautiful to Sal.

For a moment Guy was envious of his father, who lived as he wished to live, unburdened by duty and righteousness, and who had Sal. Then he became conscious that she was looking at him, a little less light on her face, and her beaming eyes were darkening with what he uneasily suspected was pity. "I got black-eye peas and sauerkraut and spare ribs for dinner," she said. "And cherry pie."

"You'll make me fat, Sal," said Tom. "And everything you cook is full of fat, thank God."

"I half promised Ma I'd go back for dinner," said Guy.

"The hell with Ma," said Tom genially. "She counts crusts. Sal, call Mrs. Jerald and say Jerry ain't going back for dinner tonight. She'll save the dinner for tomorrow, and be thankful." He grinned at Sal. "And stay in the house. I'm giving this boy of mine some advice, which he don't like, it seems."

Sal rose promptly, again pinched Tom's cheek, and ran back into the house, singing some questionable song in a loud but not unmelodious voice. Tom shook his head, smiling. "I sure was lucky when I met Sal," he said. "The Chief of Police's coming tonight, with his girl friend. We'll have a party."

Guy sipped his excellent cold beer. Tom never refused to spend money on comforts. He said to Guy, "You've been back two weeks. Found any girl yet? If not, Sal will find one for you."

He became curious when he saw his son's face becoming bleak. He waited. Guy looked into his glass and said in a pent voice, "There was a girl in Germany, in Berlin. Marlene, seventeen years old. She—we let the Russians take over the city. Eisenhower's orders. Marlene—she died in the subway, with hundreds of other women, young and old, and even children, when the Russians found them. They raped the women to death; little girls and grandmothers, too."

Tom studied his son's averted face with compassion. He said, "I read something about that, on a back page in the newspapers. Just an item. The women and the children are always the real victims in a war, Jerry. I'm sorry. And wasn't there something about Operation Keelhaul, too?"

"Yes. Millions of men and women and children from East Europe, running away from the Communists. Eisenhower, at the point of bayonets, had his soldiers force them into cattle cars and sent them back, and they mostly died. They—they even tore the women and children out of the churches; they were clutching the altars and begging for mercy—some they bayoneted."

"I heard," said Tom, and now there was hatred in his shrill voice.

"But I saw," said Guy, and his lips had whitened. "There were other things, too. Our flyers bombed the little Italian coastline towns and villages, and they had only old men and women and children in them. And there was Dresden, in the closing days of the war, an open city. The women and children and nuns were out in the streets, celebrating the beginning of Lent. Our noble flyers dropped napalm on them, burning thousands to death."

"I know. I heard," said Tom. "God damn. Wars. Once it was man to man. Now the innocent are the sufferers. The world's getting worse every day, seems. I'm glad I'm not a day younger. The atom bomb. You can be damned sure when nations invent a new weapon they're going to use it, sooner or later. America's got that on her conscience, the only country to use that bomb. But she won't be the last, and you can bet on that. You know something, Jerry? This world is full of hate and murder now. I'm a student of history; in fact, I taught ancient and medieval history when I was a stupid instructor and then a professor. Full of horrors. But none so bad as what has happened recently, and what will happen in the future. Sure, there used to be pogroms in Russia. But never was there any attempt, before, to wipe out a whole people as Hitler's attempt to wipe out the Jews, the Gypsies, the Ukranians, the Poles, and others. The whole goddamn world is now a slaughterhouse. And every country is just gathering its breath to do worse.

"That's why I tell you, now, to live your own life. Live the life of others, and you'll be a victim, too. At least, if you live for yourself you'll have had a taste of what life's really about—before you die. That's all you have, your life. There's nothing else."

He waited, but Guy was silent, his face still more averted. Tom said, "Look, I have a little money. And there's the G. I. Bill. And there's always part-time work, son. If you want to study medicine, do it. It'll be rough, but what the hell. When wasn't real life tough?"

"But what about Ma? I really owe her something."

Tom sighed. "All right. I'll screw up a little money for her, even though she's thrifty and probably has more than I have." Again he waited, but Guy said nothing, and again Tom sighed. He repeated, "Your life. That's all there is. There isn't anything else." He pointed about him with his pipe. "You think this farm is a wasteland? No, it ain't. But the whole damn world is, now."

What in God's name? thought James Meyer, who had been watching his friend acutely, and had seen the terrible flashes of thought on Guy's face, and the anguish. What is he thinking about? What is he feeling now? It is something, I'll swear to that. Memory? Of what?

"Jerry?" he said, in a low tone.

That suffering head lifted itself again and it was more like a skull than ever, and wild. Then it dropped and the dull wooden mask of pain covered Guy's face and he leaned back in his chair and closed his eyes. A deep sigh, as if of mortality, came from him.

Still, there had been something. James waited. The wind hissed at the windows. The artificial fire brightened the dusky room.

I reached him, thought James. But how? Can it be done again? I can only try.

He stood up. "I'll be back soon, old mate," he said to that shut face and those shut eyes. There was no response. James left the room and summoned the nurse.

"I am joining Dr. Grassner," he said. "I'll be back, later."

Slowly and thoughtfully, he walked down the hall and called Emil.

5

"So," said James Meyer to Emil Grassner, "he did recognize me, he did hear what I said. He came alive, and with vivid suffering, after I said something that reached him, but damned if I quite know what it was. It may be it was when I mentioned 'despair and fury.' I don't know. But I hope you agree with me that we must push this thing faster and faster, before he has time to sink down into that morass in his mind again."

"I do agree with you," said Emil. "So get on with it this afternoon. I feel very relieved. We never had that response from him before."

They were sitting in the sanitarium's very well-appointed dining room for the staff, and the lunch had been excellent. It had begun to snow, the patient wet flakes falling silently and clustering together on the windows and on the sills. The sky had darkened considerably, but the wind had fallen.

"I wish I knew what it was that stirred him so," said James. "He's got to face something in his mind. I'd like to know what it is. I can only fumble."

Emil poured them both another glass of wine. "Just keep on fumbling the way you did this morning," said Emil. James frowned, trying to think, and rubbed the fringe of red-gray hair at the base of his skull. He shook his head, sighing.

"It's worse than I suspected," he said. "He has a dying look. He's got to resolve something or he will surely die. God help him."

'You will meet his children this weekend," said Emil. "Perhaps they can help you. I don't know. They couldn't help me. They aren't too bright, by the way. Simple sort of creatures, like their mother, but not quite so stupid."

Dr. Parkinson came hurriedly into the dining room, glancing around. He saw the two psychiatrists and pushed his way between tables to them. He looked at them both with hostility.

"I've just seen Guy," he said. "What has happened to him? He's very agitated, worse than ever before. He's even groaning, and wringing his hands. He needs a heavy sedative, at once."

"No!" exclaimed Emil. "Under no circumstances. He's come alive, if only a little. He's got to come alive, or he'll die."

They did not invite him to join them. He gave James a glance of pure if feeble hatred. James smiled under his nose, but Emil stared at Dr. Parkinson formidably. The latter shook his head with resignation and walked away. He went immediately to the nearest telephone and called Lucy Jerald. Her negative and colorless voice held no alarm when she asked about the condition of her husband.

"I'm afraid," said Dr. Parkinson. "Look, Lucy, it's that —that—English psychiatrist, if he's English at all. I suggest you give orders immediately that Guy is not to have visitors except the family. That—Englishman—claiming to be Guy's friend—he's doing him great harm."

"But—" There was a short silence as Lucy tried to gather her thoughts together. "Dr. Meyer isn't treating Guy. Dr. Grassner is. Why don't you ask him to do what is necessary, at my request?"

"Lucy," said Dr. Parkinson. "Dr. Grassner is a well-known psychiatrist. He's had books published. I can't give him orders. I'm just your family physician. He doesn't want me around at all—Dr. Grassner. I'm not even treating Guy at the present time. Grassner lets me stay around, because I am the family physician and a friend. That's all. You're the only one who can do anything."

"Well." There was a pause. "Dr. Meyer did come to see Guy. He didn't impress me much. He looks very poor and shabby to me. Not in the least a gentleman. But he did come to see Guy, for old times' sake, though what on earth Guy could ever see— I just don't know. The children will be here Saturday. We'll all come to the sanitarium for a consultation and see what's best to do." Her uninterest astounded the poor doctor. She added, "We're having an early snow, aren't we? Do you think we should bring Guy a heavy robe?"

Dr. Parkinson came very close to screaming an obscenity, then he hung up abruptly.

In the meantime James had returned to Guy's suite. Guy's nurse informed him that Mr. Jerald "hadn't eaten one single bite of his nice lunch, and it was chicken à la king, with sherry, too, and a delicious mushroom soup and an apple tart."

"I hope you didn't let it go to waste," said James, twinkling.

"Well, no." The nurse giggled childishly. She patted her round belly. "I was raised never to waste food. It's a sin."

She took her dismissal from the scene with pleasure and James closed the door and looked at Guy. Guy was seated again near the window in the big wing chair. He was exactly as James had left him over an hour ago, totally immobile and endless leagues away in his mind. James sat near the fire and automatically raised the legs of his trousers to the slight heat, as he always did in London. He thought. Now, he said to himself, it is I, the psychiatrist, who must try "free association," as I did this morning. But what were the magic words which could arouse that desperately ill man?

He could see the snow, falling heavier now, so that it was a thinly gleaming and trembling curtain at the window. The fire, and the snow, reminded him of the large dark and cluttered house of his father, with fires bounding on every hearth in every room, and a promise of
78

Christmas—or was it Chanukah—in the air? He chuckled to himself. He had had a lovely childhood, with his noisy and vehement father, and his Chanukah sovereigns, and his serene and smiling aristocratic mother with her Christmas trees, and lilting carols and many gifts. The best of two worlds, thought James. Perhaps we should have had a Moslem member of the family, too. He thought of his many trips to Egypt, and his visits to the mosques and the stunned faces of the worshippers. He said, aloud, "In the Egyptian language the word for death and life is the same word. No distinction. Very wise, that. Very subtle. Life and death—the two great mysteries. We should go mad if we dwelt on the mystery too long. So we invent banal phrases to explain both. If nobody died, what would the parsons do for a living? They are trained to explain the inexplicable, so they use dogma and cant which soothe but clarify nothing. The more the mystery is elucidated, the more impenetrable it becomes."

Had he heard the faint sound of movement in the room? He looked at Guy through the corner of his eyes. Guy's posture had not changed, nor his shut face and half-closed eyes. Yet James felt that something almost inaudible had stirred.

"Banality," said James, "is the real opiate of the people. But without banality, how could we endure living? Forced to gaze into the fixed face of the Eternal, we should truly perish. The Beatific Vision is not for mortal eyes—if there is such a Vision. So let us be placid and forget both life and death and live for the instant hour, in all its coziness—that is, when it is cozy. Never question. That's the real mortal sin. But—it is sin that makes man superior to the other animals. And it's sin that makes man a thinking reed, slender and vulnerable though he is. Sin, I am afraid, is the mother of wisdom. The expulsion of Adam and Eve from the Garden of Eden was their expulsion from bondage, the bondage of a sweet but meaningless dream, the bondage of nonthought. They say God is all-Prescience. So He knew that His two human creatures would commit the sin of seeking freedom even before He

79

created them. Freedom is the very breath of existence. Without the 'sin' of freedom, there would be no philosophers, no art, no science, no cities, no marketplaces, no gaiety, no joyful naughtiness, no explorations, no music, no excitements, no sudden songs in the morning, no laughter at midnight, no spicy dishes, no wine, and, of course, no wars and no books. Perhaps sin, in its deepest meanings, is truth. At any rate, it does have a bad effect on myths."

He glanced at Guy again and a thrill like electricity ran through him. For Guy's eyes had opened and he was staring before him. James could see the dilated eyes, the whites glimmering in the dimness. He was almost afraid to breathe. He sat very still, and waited.

"Don't you tell the kid that goddamn myth of old Brownlow going to heaven yesterday!" said Tom Jerald in a voice unusually irate for him. "We don't know where he is. Maybe he's as dead as a dog; maybe he's joined the second law of thermodynamics or something. You could be honest for once, Mary. You could have said, 'I don't know.' For, damn it, you don't know. Nobody does. I'm not going to have you or anybody else stuff this kid with fairy tales, just so his soul, or whatever, won't be forced to ask questions or share in the noble misery of human conjecture. Better to be wretched and desperate than to feel nothing at all, and comfort yourself with nonsense."

It was an early April day in 1928. The spring had come grudgingly. The distant foothills still showed eroded mounds of snow, and the mountains beyond flashed with whiteness. The buds of the trees were still stiff and as cold as iron, though the land was greening warily here and there, and the river, in the approaching evening, was a vein of fire in the wet dark earth. The sky had become a blue translucence, and there was a vast unseen throbbing of expectation which could be felt by both flesh and spirit. There sounded a flutter of eager black wings across one window, and suddenly a robin sang, its voice a pure and thrilling resonance in the great stillness, at once melancholy and piercingly tender. A faint smudge of rose like a scarf concealed the lowering sun, and above it a young star began to scintillate.

Tom paused, looking through the window, and he was all-listening and all-seeing, and suddenly there was reverence on that dry and Panlike face, a bemusement, the intimation of a young smile. He said, with a gesture, "That's what it's all about—out there. Life coming out of death, but not the way they tell it in pulpits. The Resurrection has a greater meaning than the clergy ever knew, a greater significance, a greater joy." He paused. "And that's what I want the kid to understand someday. I want him to know that Christ's message is out there, and not in some dark church with stained-glass windows. Christ is not a cold dead lily. He's a vital rose."

"You'll never get over being a Catholic," said Mary, Tom's wife. Tom sighed with exasperation.

"A heathen," said Mary.

Tom's fingers moved as if counting beads. "The Joyful Mysteries," he said. "All joy is a mystery. That which isn't worth knowing or understanding."

The big brick kitchen was warm from the heat of the wood stove. The wooden walls gleamed with the endless coats of shellac Mary had painted on them, and the wooden ceiling gleamed. The linoleum on the floor might have lost most of its pattern but it shone also. The stove was black with polished steel trimmings, and some of the lids were glowing. The two windows were framed in white scrim curtains with fringes. There were buckets of water from the well standing on a scrubbed counter, and a pot of soup was simmering, the warm air alive with the odor of onions and beef and tomatoes and cabbage. A cat drowsed on a windowsill; from somewhere came the lonely and echoing bark of a dog. The cattle in the old barn answered, and a duck on the still half-frozen pond added to the chorus.

Little Guy sat in the wooden armchair near the other window. He had been listening intently, and Tom knew this, though Mary always insisted that he was too young

81

to "know," too "innocent." But Tom did not believe children were stupid and vapid, and had no comprehension. He remembered the long thoughts of his own childhood, the vast and amorphous thoughts that engulfed both mind and body, and the spirit as well. In adults, thought was restricted, set in a pattern, set in a frame of iron references that could be equally absurd and imprisoning, meretricious and without validity. Shut in from knowledge in the narrow stockade of banality, of what was accepted. Tom believed there was only one Frame of Reference, and that was the Unknowable, the Concept without words. He had tried for years to impart this to Mary, and she had only looked at him with superior amusement and had only said, "I don't think you know yourself what you are talking about." To which he had replied with satire, "Who does?"

He knew Mary was afraid of everything. She was afraid of the glorious terror of love, and had only sensed it at a far distance and had never approached it. She was afraid of "what people would think," and afraid that she was not doing her "duty" at all times, afraid that she might be forced from a safe threshold into the enormous windy spaces of chaotic thought. Mary's favorite word was "comfortable." It was not "comfortable" to question where there was no answer, though, in truth, she did not fully know that there were no complete answers. Above all, it was sinful to question that which had been "proved" through the ages, and what had been written in Scripture. To accept was to be secure. Not to accept everything was to open yourself to danger and fear. She did not put these thoughts into words, for her mental vocabulary was very limited, but she felt them in her soul, and shivered. To have one's neighbors think ill of you was to be rightfully ostracized; to live as you wished to live, in defiance of what was "moral" and approved and conventional, was to be an outlaw. She believed Tom was an outlaw, and was considering, more and more, leaving him. It was bad enough when he talked "crazy," as he was doing now. But it was even worse when he "drank" and laughed and danced and sang. She shut herself out from the knowledge that he often did something unspeakable of a Saturday night. She knew, from whispered gossip, that he sometimes visited one of the few brothels in Cranston. She ignored this knowledge as much as possible, for it was a relief that he didn't "demand anything" of her any longer. If she had ever loved him she had forgotten it. It had been enough that he had "a little money from the war," and that he had a farm, if a poor one. Mary did not like the country, but land was land, and could be sold. Moreover, she was thirty years old at the time of her marriage and was weary of being a drudge in a dirty rooming house filled with raucous men who were attracted to her thin but pretty figure, her long smooth legs, the promise of fulfillment in a generous bosom, her dark but handsome face, her really beautiful black eyes and black hair. That she had a prim and forbidding expression was not at first noticed. She had never cut her hair and so it was a gleaming mass of braids wound about her small head, and seemed made of black glass. Moreover, she was clean and "tidy" and unapproachable, and this teased the earthy men in her aunt's boardinghouse. Her voice, however, had no strong intonations; she spoke in a neutral way without inflections, and her little narrow convictions were outspoken and firm and inflexible.

"Your mother," Tom would say years later to his son, "was a 'good' woman, and that was her curse, poor thing."

Mary was also without true intelligence. Things were what they seemed to be, and had no subtleties, no protean character. The evidence of her senses was her only truth. She was as certain of her restricted religion as she was of her opinions, which were all based on what she had learned in church. Wonder was alien to her, delight was incomprehensible, laughter was suspect, "too much education" was effete. Work was her true god, and she totally believed that God labored without rest, and gloomily monitored His only world. A laughing God would have seemed blasphemous to her. She knew the cant that "God is

Love," but she did not know the meaning. She loathed sex, considered it "sinful" even in the marriage bed. She agreed with St. Paul on the subject. That God had created male and female to have joy and pleasure in each other would have seemed obscene to her, if she had ever given it a thought. Never once had she felt an exhilarating response to any man, never once had she trembled in his arms and felt the eager tremors of ecstasy. A wife did her "duty," and above all she was responsible and worked every hour she was awake.

She never recovered from the hot bloodiness of birth, and the "shame" of it. A child was living proof of lasciviousness, of hectic movements in the dark. She had been a virgin, of course, when she had married Tom Jerald. She could not now remember why she had married him, though marriage was the proper state of a woman. She never forgot her first night of marriage, and tried never to remember.

"You are a Calvinist," Tom once said to her in disgust, angrily disappointed that the promise of the full breast had been a lie.

Mary did not know what Calvinism was. But it seemed to her that Tom had thrown a curse at her.

It took him at least two years to learn to tolerate her, and even, at times, to be sardonically amused by her. He taunted her for her rigorous religion, and she prayed, somewhat vindictively, for his soul. She firmly believed in hell, and that hell was Tom's ultimate destination. Now she was convinced that to live in the house of an unregenerate man doomed to damnation, was a sin, and that she must leave him if she were to escape the wrath of God. Even more, she must remove little Guy, for his father was a threat to his eventual salvation and his entry into heaven. As much as it was possible for her to love she loved her small son. She must teach him, unremittingly, that he had been born to work and to serve God and do his duty and accept whatever arduous responsibility God inflicted on him. His father, in short, was an evil influence. Guy would never know pleasure, if she could help it.

The Roaring Twenties, with their hedonism, bootlegging, wantonness, and general disregard for the accepted moralities, had come belatedly to Cranston, and somewhat costively. Even Mary could not be unaware of all this, and so she clung with passionate sternness to her religion and her convictions. Her skirts never rose above her slender ankles. Her skin had never known rouge and powder; her lips were pale and unyielding. Now, at thirty-six, she was a paragon of grimness. Tom sometimes, and with amusement, considered safe ways to "put her out of her misery."

Once he had bought her a bottle of jasmine perfume. That was three years ago, on her birthday. He was quite aware that he was being teasing, but he could hardly wait for her remarks. She had opened the bottle and had sniffed at it and then had thrown back her head in repulsion, as if, he thought, she had smelled dung. She had poured it out on the ground in black silence, but had thriftily kept the bottle for condiments. She never started a flower garden. That was a waste of time. She had come to hate the farm. The lusty odors of earth and cattle became indecent to her, too reminiscent of the marital bed.

Now it had become her "duty" to leave Tom. She had remained with him for nearly six years in the hope that she could "convert" him and save him from his heathen nature, and possibly save his soul. The hope was gone.

Years later Tom was to say to his son, "A 'good' woman can do more evil in the world than Hitler or a Stalin, or any of the other monsters of history. Those bastards could only kill bodies. But women like your mother can, and do, kill souls." He would add, "And they never know how much terror and death and agony they inflict on others, and how they deprive others of life. Stupidity is a worse crime than murder, and to

85

believe that your truth is the only truth is an insult to the God of variety and versatility."

Mary never knew that her husband was an educated man. To her, education beyond the basics was decadent, a condition which was unnecessary, time-wasting, and contemptible. When Tom used words and phrases totally alien to her she would regard him with suspicion and would believe he was "showing off." The "parlor," a dank, dark little room, was filled with his many books, which she hated and suspected. They were "worldly." She never asked where Tom had acquired them, but she resented his spending hours reading them when he could be "making the farm pay."

She now agreed with her neighbors that Tom was beyond redemption, and that he was a menace to herself and her son. She would take Guy and make him a "good man," living always in the "fear of the Lord" and doing his duty, and shunning "sin." Guy would never live as his father did, heedless, unworthy, lacking in ambition, disdainful of money, despising work, blaspheming God.

It had taken this vernal evening, this evening full of the fragrance of the carnal earth, the voluptuous earth hinting of open thighs and procreation and wild exultant jubilation, to fix her "duty." She clashed the stove lids with unusual vigor, and her pallid lips were a cruel and righteous slash in her face. Her eyes almost disappeared in her taut and bony cheeks; they were merely a vicious glint in the falling light. All her gestures and motions expressed her deep rage and disgust. Tom did not appear to notice. He was still staring through the window, and Guy, in his rocking chair, was watching him, and his infant face was bright with love and expectation. When Tom was present the very air became alive and sparkling, and full of laughter. The more outrageous his words, the more gleeful, and though Guy rarely completely understood he felt the import, and would often clap his small hands. When Tom sang shrilly, in his high voice, Guy would sing with him, to Mary's anger. "What filthy words!" she would cry.

"Now, how would you know?" Tom would ask, reasonably. "Never thought you'd ever heard them. Maybe there's more to you than I ever knew, hey?"

"In front of an innocent child, too!" Mary would say.

"No kid's innocent, thank God. And how's he going to learn about the world of men unless he knows the vulgar vernacular, too? Nothing wrong with good Anglo-Saxon words. 'Evil to him who evil thinks.' That's what your Bible says, old girl."

He would grin at Mary without kindness. How in hell had he come to marry such a stupid wench, such a completely mindless female, if you could rightly call her female?

"You'll pay for it someday!" Mary would promise him, with a rare relish.

"I started to pay the day I married you," said Tom. Such altercations were the common way of his life. Mary kept a clean house and was a sound cook, if uninspired, but she never helped with farm chores. Otherwise, he ignored her. He accepted afflictions as casually as he accepted living. Nothing much enraged him except stupidity and "virtue," and the general hypocrisy of mankind and its furious obsessions about the nature of the world, and its often stringent rectitude.

Tonight Mary glanced at her husband with suppressed fury. "I wish you'd stop your crazy talk and get some more water for me," she said. "Before you feed the stock. I can't stand their bawling."

But Tom said, as if speaking to himself, "When I married you, old girl, I thought I was marrying the good earth. I didn't know I was marrying a rock pile. If I can help it this kid here isn't going to marry until he reaches the sense of years, say forty or so."

"Get me some water," said Mary, who had heard this many times.

"He's going to have every hot little bitch he can

lay his hands on, before he gets married, so he can learn about women. As if any man ever did learn much about them!"

He smiled down at his little son and Guy had the impression of light. The kitchen was darkening rapidly, but the great stateliness of the land outside increased. Tom said, "Now, about this business of old Brownlow next door to this farm, kiddo. Your ma said he had 'gone to heaven.' Hell's more likely, for if there was ever a pernicious old bastard he was the worst. Mean, grasping, covetous, hateful, malicious, and full of that hardheartedness your ma's always talking about. His family hates him, and why shouldn't they?

"Son, we don't know where his soul is, if he had one, which is very doubtful. He never committed what folks call a 'sin' in his whole life."

"Stop talking that way to that poor child!" cried Mary. "Of course Mr. Brownlow wasn't a sinner. He was good to the church. He was saving and careful and has a fine farm, which is more than you can say of yourself, Tom. He knew his duty. Guy, Mr. Brownlow's gone straight to heaven, which he earned."

But Tom was concentrating on the child and his face was unusually earnest. He said slowly and emphatically, gesturing at the land outside: "There's heaven, sonny boy. There's all the wisdom you need to know. There's life and immortality. Nothing's dead. Every stone has its being, every morsel of earth is living. Every grain of sand is sentient—I mean, it kmows. Everything has its destiny; it moves in harmony with inscrutable laws. Only man is tumult and confusion—because there is no law in him. He is the most lawless when he believes he is law-abiding. He obeys the laws of death, and not the laws of life."

"You think that little thing knows what you're talking about?" demanded Mary, with contempt.

But Tom was looking down into his son's grave little face. "You know, don't you?" he half whispered.

Guy nodded. Tom held out his hand. "Come on," he

88

said. "We'll go to the barn and feed the cows and then the pigs. Get your sweater and your cap."

They went out, hand in hand, Tom swinging a pail. The far mountains were outlined in pure scarlet and seemed to pulse, as if some gigantic heart was beating behind them. The wind was suddenly sweet if cold in Guy's face, and the air was pungent. A pellucid light filled the arch of the sky. The earth was soft and yielding under the feet of the man and the child. There was that stillness all about them, that joyful waiting, that invisible upthrust of sentience. Guy felt his little heart rising and he was awesomely happy and did not know why. He wanted to shout, to cry, to run, to laugh. Yet something restrained him, and in restraining gave him love and set him free. He had no words for it.

Tom gazed at the mountains. He said, " 'The mountains have no kings.' Hosanna!"

They went to the well together. The ropes creaked and squealed as the water was drawn up. Guy peered over the edge of the well and looked down at the darkly shining water. He saw, reflected in it, the sky and the hills and his own face, so like his mother's, and the smiling face of his father. A bird called and Tom whistled in answer. There was the throb of wings and the bird came closer. It perched on a leafless tree and insistently queried, and again Tom replied. Guy was only a child but he thought there was something bird-like about his father and he would not have been surprised if wings had sprouted then on Tom's shoulders. He glimpsed the bird's red breast. It twisted its head and peered down inquisitively at the man and then groomed itself. It gave the impression that it was among friends and it had nothing to fear. Then it opened its beak and once again the air poignantly vibrated to the long drop of a robin's song, cascading, as it were, from the very sky itself like the fall of silvery bubbles.

"Sounds sad, doesn't it?" said Tom. "Touches your damned heart. You could make up poetry hearing it. Yet, it's only a male robin's warning to other males not to intrude on its territory. That's no poetry, though. It's a fact. Still, without poetry the world would be a muddy place, wouldn't it? Myths, I reckon, do have their place after all, if they don't deceive you into believing they are truth. Sometimes I think myths, if they aren't sniveling lies without any beauty at all, are God's works of art. If they are beautiful—well, they do have a truth of their own. Like the symbols of ancient Greece. Not the modern ones, though." He looked at the bird, who was still singing. "Go on, old fellow," he said. "You are singing war songs, and establishing your territory. I wish men could do that as sweetly."

He put down the filled pail. "Let's look at the cows," he said. "I hear that young heifer complaining about something. Females are always doing that."

"Shouldn't I take the water back to Ma first?" asked Guy.

"Now why?" said his father. "She ain't in no real hurry, and that heifer sounds like she's in trouble. Hell, I hope she isn't freshening too soon. Her first calf."

They went into the warm and musky barn. The building might be battered but the roof was tight against the weather and the floor was clean and the hayloft was still piled pungently high. The long light of the evening filled the barn, and the seven cows languidly looked at the boy and man, patiently standing in their stalls. The floor rumbled. Segregated, the young Holstein bull had decided to join the complaint of the young heifer. "Too bad about you, boy," said Tom. "It's you that caused the trouble. Want to help?"

He said to Guy, "Take the water and bring back the milk pails. If your ma tries to keep you, tell her I just sent you and told you to come here for a while. She does talk all the time about honoring your father and mother, and obeying them." He chuckled. Mary had always insisted that Guy not be present at mating and

90

birthing. She considered them lewd and revolting. "We mustn't pollute his mind," she would say of Guy.

"If we don't, God will," Tom would answer. "God arranged it this way, and I say it's blasphemous to consider His arrangements dirty, whether it's man or beast."

When Guy gathered up the milk pails and his mother grumbled, he thought of something which had troubled him over his short years. "Ma," he said, "why does Pa call me Jerry, and you call me Guy?"

His mother looked down at him, the replica of her except for her expression. Her eyes smiled a little. "I like the name Guy. Read it in a book once, a novel, which was sinful, reading novels. The hero was called Guy. It sounded refined and good, and he was a good man. Your pa never liked the name but I had it given you in baptism." She paused and her dark face became resentful. "He didn't want you baptized, and he a Catholic, at that! I thought they was always for baptism and such, though I'm a Baptist and we don't baptize until the age of reason, or something, about thirteen. He never did tell why he didn't want you baptized then. Just being contrary, that's all, and your pa's a very contrary man. Just want something, and like as not he'll say no, just to be contrary even if he wants it, too. Anyways, I took you to a Methodist church, and you was baptized Guy Somerset Jerald. Somerset's my maiden name. Your pa never called you Guy. It was always Jerry, just to be mean. Well, run along with them pails and tell your pa as soon's milking's done he must hurry back. Want to listen to the gospel songs on the radio, after supper."

Guy went back to the barn, very slowly, thinking. Ma was contrary, too, if she had had him baptized so early when it was her religion not to baptize until one was a grown man of thirteen. There was so much conversation in the house about "God," and always in a vituperative manner by his mother—and in a laughing and mocking voice by his father. He could not recall a single encounter between the two that was amiable and friendly and gay or comfortable. God seemed their major dispute. God was Peace, his mother had once told him, but Guy doubted that, if He could provoke such intense animosity between two people.

Troubled, Guy looked at the elegiac sky. More stars were becoming visible and all at once the child halted and stared up at them earnestly. Pale fire, they were remote and cold and mysterious. A profound awe came to him again, an urgent wonder, clarified and vivid. Then he went on.

Tom had hung a lantern from the wooden ceiling, though the light of the sky still filled the barn. The heifer was bellowing in evident distress. The other cows munched and the bull rumbled loudly. The barn seemed warmer; there was the strong smell here of the cows' pads and hay and urine and thick hides. Tom was standing behind the heifer, whom he had tethered. She was crying loudly with pain, and shuddering, her young body convulsed with contractions. Tom said, "Come here, boy, I want to show you something."

Guy approached the stall. The bell cow had also become restless; her bell tinkled nervously. Tom was standing at the heifer's side, out of reach of her plunging hoofs. "Here, boy," said Tom. "Careful. Circle her. Stand at her flank. Now, look."

Guy looked. He saw, in a bloody hot aperture, two very tiny hoofs, glistening, jerking a little. The smell of blood was both startling and atavistic.

"Calf's got caught somewheres in there," said Tom. "Can't get him out, just pulling. Poor girl. I think it's his head, in the pelvic bone. No time to waste or we've got a dead calf." He rolled up the blue sleeve on his right arm. He plunged his arm into the steaming aperture, level with the hoofs and legs of the calf. Guy winced. The mystery of birth was not unknown to him, for after all he lived on a farm and his father had been explicit more than once concerning sex and its functions. It was not a sly and sniggering introduction to the realities of life, though Mary, more than once, had expressed her disgust and her aversion for the whole process and had attempted to project her revulsion on her child. Guy was not revolted. Tom's explanations had been as simple as water, as casual and forthright as if discussing food or taxes. "Trouble with your ma is, she hates life. She thinks it's dirty," Tom once had said, laughing humorously. "Got to watch out for the life-haters; mostly they're very religious. They retreat to a sterile heaven where, I've heard, there's no marriage or giving in marriage, and everything's pure and bloodless and the boys and girls don't embrace or romp. That's your ma's idea of heaven, anyway. I have my own opinion."

Guy's wincing was for the young cow's pain. But he saw that his father, though probing with strength, was also very gentle. He was crooning to the cow, reassuring her, soothing her. She listened, apparently. At any rate, she was not lurching and kicking now, and only shuddering, understanding that Tom was trying to help her. She still bawled, but she tried to stand still. The light of the lantern brightened as the first dark approached. The bell cow was peering over the top of her stall. The other cows munched. The bull threatened.

"Just as I thought," said Tom. "Head's twisted in the pelvic bone. There, girl, just a minute until I turn your youngster's head. There! Loose now. It's all right." He withdrew his arm, glistening with wet blood, and took the two small hoofs in his hands and gently tugged. In a moment the little body of the newborn calf was lying on the straw of its mother's stall. Guy looked down at the miniature creature—a bull, he saw, its hide fuzzy and matted and dripping. He saw the small head, the heaving flanks, the opening innocent eyes. Why, thought the child, he's seeing the world for the first time, and I guess he's thinking about it.

The scent of blood was even stronger in the barn now, and to Guy it was exciting. It was the smell of life, flowing, vigorous life. Tom was attending to the heifer. "Don't we wash the calf?" asked Guy.

"That's for the mother to do. Just wait a minute."

The heifer, quiet now, turned in her stall and bent her head over the calf. She licked it, poked it with her nose. It continued to lie there, unmoving except for the rapid rising and falling of its rib cage. The heifer nudged it impatiently, muttering something deep in her throat. The calf stirred, and its eyes took on a peevish expression. Tom laughed. "He's a boy, and he's already pitying himself for being born and I guess I don't blame him too much. Besides, being born is an uncomfortable experience, for the kid as well as for its mother. Now, a female calf is much quicker to get on her feet, I've found. Hurrying to get into mischief; can't wait. This calf would just as soon lie there and be pampered and saying 'Pity me,' under its breath. But he's got to get going in the business of life."

The calf whimpered, but his mother pushed him more roughly with her nose. Actually sighing, the calf turned and straightened his forelegs and rested on his rear. He stared blindly about him. Now his mother poked his buttocks, and he struggled to rise on his legs with her help. Then he wobbled to her side, his mouth fumbling for her udder. Tom surveyed the scene with gratification.

"Son," he said, "that's truth, that's the real swear-to-God truth, the real verity. All the rest is humbug, thinking, conjecturing, agonizing, yearning. That's man's curse, that he thinks but doesn't accept disagreeable conclusions. He rejects what isn't pleasing to him and accepts only that which pleases him and reassures him. That's freedom of choice, sure, and I'm all for that. But why accept lies when the truth's plain to see, no matter how painful it is? I'm all for mythos, provided it doesn't interfere with reality, with freedom and what is. As Christ said, 'The truth will make you free,' but, as usual, theologians misinterpret that, too."

After the milking had been finished, Guy awkwardly attempting also, they went out with the full pails into the evening. It was dark now, and the stars throbbed and glittered in the calm zenith. Tom looked up and quoted from Milton:

"Where the bright Seraphim in burning row
Their loud uplifted angel trumpets blow."

Guy was only five years old but his heart lifted also, for he knew the import of what his father had said.

At dinner that night James Meyer said to Emil Grassner, "Again, I don't know what it was I said—I wish I knew—but Jerry came suddenly and violently alive for a few seconds. That is, he actually stood up and walked a few steps, then sat down and shivered, clenching his fists in extreme agitation. But when I asked him a question he subsided and fell into a deep apathy, an apathy, I suspected, of resistance, a refusal of what he was remembering. A fear." James paused and frowned and rubbed his bald head and stared down at the excellent sauerbraten he was neglecting. Emil watched him without speaking and detected a deep uneasiness in his friend.

James continued. "Jerry is as attached to his suffering as an unborn child is attached to the placenta. It is the only thing which keeps him alive. He draws sustenance from it. Perhaps only through painful rebirth will he enter the world."

He half laughed. "I am beginning to wonder if banality, again, doesn't makes life possible for the majority of mankind. Most people, God help them, are immobilized by their own banality, which paradoxically is their shield against a reality they cannot face. But when the rare intelligent man is immobilized by the general banality, or chooses it, he is to be condemned."

"So, our patient is to be condemned," said Emil, with a serious smile.

James hesitated. "Perhaps 'condemned' is too harsh a word. I don't know." His uneasiness increased. He shifted in his chair, looked restlessly about the small

95

snug dining room of the Old House, where the somewhat obese diners were avidly devouring the plain and plenteous food. James said, as if talking to himself, "I often conjecture if a psychiatrist doesn't sometimes catch his patient's own malaise, as if by reflection. I myself am feeling depressed. Something is bothering me, personally. I'm trying to find out what it is, but it's like trying to grasp a slippery goldfish in a bowl. It eludes me, yet it seems necessary to grasp it. For myself? For Jerry? I don't know." He drank a little beer. Again, he rubbed his head.

"Perhaps you are too emotionally involved with Guy Jerald," suggested Emil. "It's happened to me myself sometimes."

James thought about it, then slowly shook his head. "No. I wish I knew what it was. On the other hand"—and he laughed without mirth—"I'm afraid it has something to do with me, all by itself. I haven't felt this way for a long time. It's as if I, too, am being stirred up like a cold pot of porridge, with the fire under it."

"You're a very successful man," said Emil, watching him. "Your books—your practice, your fame. No wife, no children, no worries. I think you are to be envied."

"My lovely life," said James, almost inaudibly. Then he started. "What the hell am I talking about? I think I'll have some brandy. The anodyne for pain—alcohol. No wonder alcoholism is now such a tremendous problem in the Western world, the affluent world, the comfortable, easy world, where everyone has everything and nobody has anything of value. Why do we need anodynes? Alcohol? Drugs? Flights into wholesale sex? Wars? What are we running from? I often remember what a general said to Napoleon, before Waterloo— The general declared that a new campaign was 'unthinkable.' Men were weary of war, and would not have it. And Napoleon replied, 'Yes. They will. I will be rescuing them from button factories.'"

He mused. "Yes. Button factories, well lighted, well warmed, clean, comfortable, regulated, surrounded by 'benefits,' all hazards removed, all very neat and bright. Like a blasted spa, or a nursery filled with nannies with

96

soothing syrup and nursing bottles. No wonder men are losing their minds and will resort to anything to get away from all that damned monotony and safety. I don't always agree with Nietzsche, but he did say that man was created for war and woman to recreate the warrior. In a deeper and more psychological sense I interpret that to mean man was created for action, for exhilaration, for danger, for excitement, for color and change, for the seeking of new worlds to conquer, for the hunt, for battle, for the pitting of his strength against another strength, physical and mental. Stodgy comfort is the grave."

"Tell the unions that," said Emil, with a wry smile.

"Oh, I'm all for unions," said James. "The Industrial Revolution has had its bloody and despicable side. But we've gone to the other extreme. Yes. Well. I'd like to know what is bothering me myself, and it has nothing to do with Jerry, poor lad."

He added, "I am thinking, vaguely, of writing a book to be called *The Decline of Western Morale*. The title's come to me but not the context. I feel a deep boiling in myself, yet the words won't come yet. It will be like nothing I've written before. But then, all of a sudden, I'm not as I was when I came to Cranston, and that is why I am uneasy in a world I made myself."

"We all make our own world, banal though it sounds," said Emil. "I'm a great one for coining clichés, but clichés wouldn't have existed so long if there weren't a universal truth in them. Let's go and look at television. So many complaints about it—but I find it restful and interesting. They do try their best, and perhaps that is the trouble."

James said, "You know, I think God deliberately created Lucifer, knowing exactly what Lucifer would do. The Jews, the old ones, say that without evil there could be no good. It is the conflict which is the challenge, the problem, the excitement. Perfect good—how damned boring! Just as complete evil is banal."

6

James awoke the next morning to a world of total white, from the shining alabaster mountains to the undulating earth, all under a turquoise sky filled with cold radiance. He thought it far more beautiful than spring or summer; it reminded him of his mother's statue of the Blessed Mother, immaculate, clothed in blue and white, crowned with gold. For the first time in years the memory of his mother was acute and poignant to him. She had been lovely and gentle and quiet, with a face constantly simmering with kind mirth and tiny flickering dimples. His rowdy and rambunctious father had adored her and she had adored him in return, finding even his fierce moods humorous, his fierce shouts amusing. She knew him for what he was, that emphatic Austrian Jew: A completely good man, ferocious in his pursuit of justice, sentimental, roughly tender, full of ancient Yiddish and Hebrew wisdom and stories. He had a story for everything, to illustrate a momentous point, and James had suspected, even as a child, that he invented quite a number. They were often too apt. James's mother must have known, too, for her whole face would twinkle and she would say, "Yes, love, of course, love," with admiration for his ingenuity.

James looked at the snowy scene outside his window, and sighed. For a moment or two his ambiguous malaise lifted at the memory of his parents. A man who had had good parents was twice blessed, first when they were alive and second for the memory of them. The remembrance could often be accompanied by pain, as all happiness has its darker side, but it could also be a holy place, a sanctuary. That Guy Jerald's childhood had not been so delightful was quite evident, though James was not one of those psychiatrists who attributed all aberrations and mental illness and despair to "childhood traumas." Life never failed to inflict its traumas all the days of a man's life. There was no escaping them, though men themselves increased them.

His father had been killed during one of his bolder attempts to rescue some of the fellow Jews in Germany. His mother died of grief, though James never saw her in tears. Her heart literally broke, in silence. Now the poignancy of his own sorrow became fresh again and he said, "God damn it, and we've got the same thing today! Call it Fascism or Communism, it is the same mortal curse."

Was that part of his present malaise, which had nothing to do with Guy Jerald? From what had he been hiding all these years, refusing to see what was to be seen? A feeling of dull helplessness came to him. There was no longer any place to hide these days, no new continents, no fresh land, no escape, no refuge. The whole spiritual atmosphere was pervaded with millions of malignant eyes, watching, waiting. The new holocaust was coming; it was inevitable. Yetzer hara, he thought. Who would be the victims this time? The Jews again, or all freedom-loving men in general? There was a malevolent murmuring in the world, audible but to a few. "It can never happen again," people said.

"No?" said James, aloud, as he tied his tie. He was glad he had no children, that he had never married. At least he had not been guilty of begetting new victims for the men of terrror to torture and kill and oppress and silence, and enslave, to pervert and corrupt.

If I were a father, he thought, I would feel as guilty as hell now, for being a fool in believing that the world was improving and terrorism could never smear blood on a doorstep again, or that the knock in the night would never be repeated. The history of man was written in blood, and men were not more "good" than their fathers and grandfathers. Rather, they were worse. They were like tigers in the arena who had smelled torn flesh and spewing arteries.

"You seem depressed this morning, James," said Emil Grassner, as James sat bemused with the breakfast menu before him. James started, and smiled sheepishly. "I've been thinking," he said. "Nothing original, of course. It was Solomon who said, 'There is nothing new under the sun.' Nothing improves, nothing changes. What is it the French say? 'The more a thing changes, the more it is the same.' Yes."

He drank his orange juice. "I am just remembering something from before the war, when I was just a lad. There were two men in the world, of whom Mahatma Gandhi, the Archbishop of Canterbury, Winston Churchill, George Bernard Shaw, André Gide, Otto Kahn, the historian Toynbee—that great 'liberal,' and the president of some large American university whose name escapes me now—well, of the two men big in the news in those days, these eminent gentlemen said, 'I would have been with him in the beginning!' 'The world owes him a debt of gratitude.' 'Progressive!' 'Superman!' 'The one great figure in Europe.' 'Man of peace.' 'Behaves like a genius.' 'I particularly admire the diversity of his methods.' "

He sipped at his coffee. Emil waited, then said, "Who were those two paragons those eminent men so fulsomely praised?"

James gave a short laugh. "Mussolini and Hitler."

"No!" exclaimed Emil, aghast.

"Embarrassing? Yes. But it is true. I look at the newspapers very carefully these days to find what particular man, or men, the new eminent gentlemen are praising so highly. There is an old saying: 'Put not your faith in princes.' But I say, 'Beware of those who are praised by allegedly great men.' Eminence is no guarantee against imbecility—or, perhaps, treason and something even more sinister. The world rarely praises a prophet, a noble man, a true hero. In fact, the world will destroy such, if it can. Evil instinctly recognizes evil, and where is a virtuous man these days? I don't outright accuse the eminent gentlemen I've quoted as being absolutely evil; in fact, they may just have been fools, which is even worse."

Emil was shaking his head. Then he smiled. "You're depressing me, James."

James found himself, somewhat to his own astonishment, replying vehemently, "I wish to God the whole damned world was depressed! There would be some hope for its survival then!"

Emil said, "There does seem to be a lot of pessimism around these days. We put a vague name on it, we psychiatrists, and blame it on a 'too rapidly changing world,' or something else as foolish and superficial."

"Strange, I'm by nature a somewhat optimistic man." James paused. Am I? he asked himself. Or have I just been cynically complacent? He said, "But for the last few days I've become a pessimist myself, and I don't know why."

The new uneasiness, without a name, returned to him and he lost his appetite, which was usually a voracious one.

When, a little later, he saw Guy's nurse, outside the door of the suite, she looked troubled. "Mr. Jerald was so upset this morning. He ate nothing. He did go out on the covered terrace with me, and he stared and stared at the mountains. He didn't speak, of course. He just stared. Some ladies and gentlemen spoke to him but he didn't answer them; it was like he hadn't heard. Then he almost ran back to his rooms. I had a hard time keeping up with him."

So, thought James, we are progressing. The nurse hesitated. "Dr. Parkinson just left. He says to ask you to order something to quiet Mr. Jerald, or at least you were to ask Dr. Grassner."

"Let us see," said James, and entered the suite. He saw that the sitting room was empty and dim. He went into the bedroom. Guy was crouched on his bed in the sad fetal position, but his eyes were open and he was gazing at nothing, nor did his face express any emotion. James sat down near the bed. He lit a cigar and puffed at it for several long minutes. Then he said, "Jerry, I know you know me. One of these days we'll have a long talk together, as we used to do. It's been too long, perhaps for me also. The years scamper away like mice, and before you have

101

hardly glimpsed them they are gone, with the merest flicker of a tail. Do you remember—'Tell me, where all past years are, or who cleft the Devil's foot'? Then there comes the day when we say to ourselves, in our old age: 'Why, I never lived!' It's too late then, isn't it?"

The merest grimace, or the ghost of it, touched Guy's face. Then he closed his eyes, as if to sleep. But James saw the tenseness of every rigid muscle. He said, "Jerry, you were a very brave boy when I knew you during and after the war. You weren't courageous. You were something much better—a brave man. We are all afraid of something, aren't we? But the brave man is more afraid than the average, yet he overcomes his fear by faith or the power of his own will. Bravery is more than courage, for it knows the terror it faces. But courage is only hope that the terror is less than it appears, so take it on."

The closed eyes suddenly flew open, and stared, but not at James.

"What does the Bible say?" asked James. " 'Perfect love casts out fear.' Perhaps you loved, or love, someone now. I don't know. It doesn't matter who you love or how you love or when you love, for the eternal imperative is to love. Without love, you only have courage. With love, you are brave."

I'm talking at random, thought James. But I feel I am reaching him.

There was still no real response from the crouched man. James thought, his life has been like the "sunless sea" of Kubla Khan. But each of us travels through the "caverns measureless to man." How idiotic it is for any of us to pretend to know another, or to measure the caverns through which we individually wander.

Absently, he sighed, and then said, "Yes, Jerry, you have always been brave. Until recently?"

The white and stony lips moved soundlessly in that still face.

"Well, anyway, kiddo, you were a brave little bastard to take on all those brutes," Tom said to his son, now ten

102

years old. "Your ma probably shrieked at the sight of that black eye and that cut lip and that puffed chin, but then she doesn't know anything about bravery. She could drive off a raging young bull, or a strange dog, with a shout and a flutter of her apron, but that was only courage. She didn't recognize the danger, or minimized it. But you— and I'm proud of you, kiddo—you knew what you faced, but you went ahead anyway."

"Ma called it violence," said young Guy, wincing as he touched his wounded face. His whole body ached; his ribs felt broken.

"Now, did she?" asked Tom, interested.

They were sitting on the farmhouse stoop that gold and green June day in 1933. Guy could see the glittering chartreuse of distant young trees, the brown steaming earth which Tom had plowed and which was now pricked by the young corn he had planted, emerald spears rising in rows. The chickens in their flimsily contrived fenced yard were scrambling in the heated dust which rose about them in a golden cloud. The cows were black-and-white movements in the new freshening fields and the infant pigs squealed in their pens. The mule wandered around as he willed, teasing the cows and laughing at the bull, which kept charging him. The mule would prance out of the way of that charge, his high laugh echoing, and the frustrated young bull heaving sweatily and frothing at the mouth, would charge again. The orchard showed more promise than it would fulfill. The sky glowed with blue light, and the distant foothills wore cloaks of aquamarine velvet against violet mountains. The fir trees had tips of jade. Tom had planted a few rose bushes in a careless bed, and they were bursting with red and pink and white and yellow a few yards from the house. Everything was pervaded by the intense sweetness and fervid fecundity of June, and the hot sun caused the scattered poplars and sycamores and elms to blot black shadows on an ignited earth.

Today, Guy had arrived to spend the summer with his father.

"Tell me about it," said Tom.

Guy looked sheepish, then he glanced down at his fingers, which were tangled together. The knuckles were red and raw and sore. The wooden step of the stoop was warm against his buttocks. He sighed happily. He was glad to be out of the city, glad to be away from his mother and school, glad to be free. Yet, he frowned.

"There isn't much to tell," he said.

"Now, don't be modest," said Tom. "Your ma always said you were a quiet baby and kid, but I know better. There's wildness in you, Jerry, thank God. And violence, too. You'll be a fine man, that is if you don't let life subdue and geld you, and break you to the harness so that you trot along sedately with a bit in your mouth and slapping reins on your back. Go on, tell me. And why's your face getting red all of a sudden?"

"Well," mumbled Guy. "It wasn't anything, I guess. But the kids at school don't like me, never did—"

"That's good," said Tom, encouragingly. "When people don't like you that's proof you aren't what they are, for which you should give praise—to something or other. Never saw a man amount to anything whom everybody liked. The world's approval is God's disapproval. And wasn't it St. John who said, 'He that loves this world is an enemy of God'? That is, the world of men. Not the riotous earth. Well, go on."

"I don't know why they don't like me," said Guy, with obvious reluctance. "I don't bother them. I don't play with them. I hardly speak to them—"

"That's good," Tom repeated.

"Ma doesn't say that's 'good,'" Guy said, defending his mother. "She's always telling me that if you're good that's pleasing to—God. She says the world's full of good people."

"More fool she," Tom said. He pulled a long blade of green grass, and began to chew on it thoughtfully. "She's always quoting Scripture, for her own purposes, poor soul. Did she ever tell you what someone said? 'Why do you call me good? None but God is good.'"

"Is that from the Bible?"

"It sure is. A young man approached Christ and called Him 'good Master,' and Christ said that—'Why do you call me good? None but God is good.'"

"I must remember to tell Ma," said Guy, and his great black eyes filled with laughter. "Where's it from?"

"St. Luke. I've got a Bible in the house. Read it for yourself. But tell me about the fight."

Guy's face changed and again he stared down at his injured knuckles. "I—I don't suppose it was really anything. But it made me mad."

Tom studied that young profile, the aquiline and sensitive nose, the strong mouth and chin, the broad forehead, the rough black hair which fell almost to the eyebrows.

"They said something about me," Tom remarked. "That's it, isn't it?"

"How did you know?" The boy turned admiring eyes on his father, then he looked away, flushing.

"Easy, son. You and your ma live miserable blameless lives in that damn town. Your mother is known as a 'respectable' woman, ever since she left me. She works hard, pays her bills, goes to church, and does all the expected things a good woman does, the wretched dreary things. There was never the slightest touch of scandal about her. She never bedded down with another man but me. So, the fight couldn't have been about anything but myself, anyway a fight that marked you up like that. Go on, tell me."

"Well," said the boy with even more reluctance. "They didn't think much of you as a farmer—or anything else."

Tom laughed, his shrill light laughter. He pulled on his ragged fair beard. He was already half bald and the ginger freckles were bright on his skull. "I can tell you the rest of it. They know all about the parties I have here, with the rollicking lads of the town, running away from their damned pure women on a Saturday or Sunday. They know all about the moonshine I buy, and the moonshine the boys bring here. They know about our girls, fine hearty girls with fat legs in rayon stockings. The town thinks I am a disaster, and so do our pucker-lipped neighbors, who spread the gossip. They know I've spent many a night in jail, after a particularly raucous party here. I even know the names the town calls me. Womanizer, drunk, shiftless, idle, no account, a lecher, perhaps even a thief just because I help myself, once in a while, to a peach or an apple or a watermelon from my excellent neighbors' orchards and patches. I know it all; it's no news to me, kiddo. So, they told you that, didn't they?"

"Well, yes," said Guy. "And even worse. They said you once—you once—"

"Raped a neighbor's woman? Hell, son, she was more than willing, but when her husband caught us she yelled 'rape.' That's a woman for you. Is that all?"

"Just about," said Guy.

"And you lit into them. Why? It's the truth that they told you. So why?"

Guy could not say, "Because I love you, Pa. And I know what you really are." So he only mumbled, "Well, I didn't like it. There were six of them. I wanted to fight them one by one, but they all piled on me at once."

Tom nodded. "Of course. Aren't they all upright young Christians, bursting with Queensberry Rules and fairness? So all six of them jumped you."

"Yes."

The boy had turned his head aside. Tom looked at him, ruminating, and his small blue eyes squinted in the sun. "And that's all? Ain't there something else, too?"

Guy quickly glanced at his father with amazement. "How did you know?" he asked, marveling.

"Oh, I'm psychic. The names they called me came afterwards when you objected to something. What was it?" He reached out and tumbled his son's hair with a tender hand.

"Well, it was that kid Elsie Braden. We were in the schoolyard, all of us. She's just a little kid, about seven, and kind of sickly. They made her cry, and they pushed her and knocked her down and then they kicked her.
106

They kicked her in the nose, too, and made it bleed. So—"

"You were Sir Galahad who had the strength of ten because your heart is pure," said Tom. "Only, you didn't have the strength of ten. Tell me about that little kid."

But Guy's face had turned a brilliant red and he averted his eyes. "Just a kid they were picking on, all the boys."

"Why were they picking on her?"

"Don't know," Guy muttered.

"Come on, son, you know. Tell me. Is the kid poorer than most, in this damned Depression? Ragged, maybe, hungry?"

"Well, no. She has pretty good clothes, and she brings a good lunch, better than the others."

"That's enough to make them hate her," said Tom. "All right, go on."

Guy blurted, "It's her mother!"

"Her mother? Where's her dad?"

"She doesn't have any. Never did."

"I see," said Tom, after a long pause. "And how does her mother get the money for good clothes and food, in this Depression?"

But Guy was silent. Tom, watching his son's bent head and averted face, lit his pipe and contemplatively puffed on it.

Finally he said, "I'm being psychic again. The mother, poor girl, prefers to sell her body to selling her soul to Welfare. That's it, isn't it? Come on, son. You're old enough for us to talk man to man. I've told you as much as you can take in. Now, I think it's a damned rotten world when a woman is forced—I say forced—to sell herself for shelter and food for herself and her child, but even that's better than charity. It's what they call the 'oldest profession,' and I can't see any harm in it, if it's necessary to survival. We all have to live, even though it escapes me why just now. So, Elsie's mother is a whore. Whose business is that but hers? It would be different if she was one of those women who prefer to sell them-

107

selves rather than work. But what work is around here now, in these days?"

When Guy, still bright red, did not answer, Tom went on. "All in all, I think Elsie's mother is an honorable woman. Many's the whore who is a better and more decent woman than the righteous bitches who have never been hungry or homeless, and have been parasites all their lives. Our Lord had more mercy for a 'bad' woman, whom He would not condemn, than He had for any of the lady Pharisees, who prided themselves on their worthiness. Substitute virtue for lack of temptation and need, and you have it."

"Ma wouldn't agree with you," Guy said, and rubbed his smarting cheek. "When I told her what happened in the schoolyard—she said I was very wrong, in defending a bad woman's child. It was all Elsie deserved, she said."

"Oh, she would say that, Jerry. Nothing like a good woman cursing the innocent and the defenseless. So, then when you tried to help little Elsie the other kids called me names, didn't they?"

"Yes."

"So, without considering the cost, as the courageous do, you were brave instead. You knew what you were facing, and you faced it. How many licks did you get in first before they all jumped you?"

Guy began to laugh. "I made a few noses bleed, maybe one of the fellows lost his teeth, I mean, maybe a tooth, and I kicked one in the knee and he screamed like a girl. That's why Ma said I was violent."

"Oh, so you were supposed to let them go on abusing that little girl and you were supposed to turn the other cheek and kiss them when they jumped you and beat you up. Yet again, it was our Lord who said that if a man lacks a sword he should sell his cloak and buy one. Why buy a sword? For decoration? No, to use it with violence to protect yourself first of all, and then to protect the weak. People forget our Lord was a 'violent' man, as God is violent when necessary. The Bible's full of stories of rightful violence, and some, I admit, of not so

108

rightful violence. Our Lord didn't hesitate to use a whole lot of damned violence when He overturned the tables of the money changers in the Temple, and His language, at times, was often less than peaceful. Violence is the strong color of life, when it is nobly aroused."

Guy looked at his father with love, his large black eyes dilating. Then the great gaze became opaque and he glanced away. He said, half to himself, "Ma whipped me for what I did. I don't blame Ma, in a way. She has a lot of worries, the men in her house getting drunk sometimes, and sometimes forgetting to pay her. She works awful hard. She's tired a lot, though I help her after school, and she has that old lady, Mrs. Thorope, who comes in to lend her a hand couple of times a week. Sometimes I hear Ma crying in her room."

"Well," said Tom. "She's one of those who work themselves to death out of a sense of virtue. I'm sorry for your ma. She never got anything out of life, except you, kiddo. And that's her own fault. She denied life. Life was something dirty to her. So she takes her profit to the bank every week—and a dollar ain't no substitute for living."

A squat middle-aged woman with a sour face appeared at the door, a grim woman who "did" for Tom, and who came of an even less affluent small farm some ten miles away. "What you want for supper?" she demanded in a coarse husky voice. Her eyes looked at Tom with contempt.

"What you got?" he asked in reply. "Good God, woman, do we have to have a major consultation every day about what we put in our stomachs? From the looks of you seems like that's your biggest preoccupation. We don't care what we eat, so long's it's enough." He smiled very nastily at her. "And you can bring us a couple of glasses of that wine I made, unless you've drunk it all up yourself."

The woman was outraged, and her broad flat face turned crimson. "I don't hold with liquor, Mr. Jerald, even if you calls it wine, and I don't even want to touch it. It's against the law. You kin get it yourselfs. You making that sinful stuff, and the law says you can't."

"If a damn-fool law says I can't enjoy myself with a gift from God, then be damned to the law," said Tom. "Go on back to your washtubs." He stood up and stretched, and Guy thought of a deer he had once seen, dappled and thin and lithe.

The woman said, "It was grape juice the Lord made. You ain't going to give that kid any of that stuff, are you?"

Tom looked into her vindictive eyes. "Yes, I am. And if you mention it to anybody I'll be telling about that load of lumber your man took, feeling himself free to do it, because he is 'poor.' Go back to your washtubs." He pushed past the woman and went into the house. She looked down at Guy.

"Take my advice, sonny," she said. "You got a good ma. Go back to her. Don't stay with your dad." She turned and went inside.

Tom returned with two chipped glasses of his homemade and very potent wine. It tasted of both grapes and cherries and was refreshingly dry and even acrid. "The Jews," said Tom, "often bless the Lord for giving them the 'fruit of the vine.' So do I. And it ain't grape juice the priest drinks at the altar." He raised his glass. "Blessed be the Name of the Lord that He has given us this gift, to raise our hearts and brighten the dark places of our lives."

Guy eagerly took the glass Tom gave him. He smiled and his young face became wild, as Mary called it, and gay. The man and the boy toasted each other. They sipped contentedly together and looked about them on that warm waning day.

"Coming back to what we were talking about," said Tom, "there is a time and a place for violence. Justified violence against evil. Violence and bravery often go together, like Castor and Pollux. You've got to be brave in every aspect of your life, or the world will beat you and it's all you deserve."

He heard a sound and listened. "I think that's young Jennie in the pen, groaning about something. Let's go see."

They finished their wine and then went to the pigpen, which had an aroma even Tom could not say was pleasant.
110

But he had pointed out to Guy many times that swine were among the cleanest of animals and that they wallowed in the mud to rid themselves of tormenting insects. There were two pens, one for mothers and their endearing young piglets, and one for the "matrons" and the boar, who had an evil look. Jennie had six little piglets, who now stood about her anxiously as she lay on her side and groaned. She stared up at Tom with a piteous look, which was rare for her, for she was a young sow who was usually willing to challenge anyone. Tom leaned on the fence. "What's the matter, Jennie?" he asked.

Guy looked over the fence also. "She looks fat and sleek," he said. He looked closer. "But her belly's swole up. If she was human you'd give her a dose of castor oil." At this moment the poor young sow audibly, very audibly, farted.

"Now, why didn't I think of that?" asked Tom, scratching his beard. "Thinking of being a vet, Jerry?"

"No. A doctor."

"When did you get that idea?"

"Long time ago, when I was young," said Guy

Tom laughed. He patted his son on his shoulder. "Good a thing as anything. If you do get around to it, remember it's just as important to find out what castor oil the soul needs as well as the body. Well, I'll get the pig laxative for Jennie."

Later they carried out the swill from the kitchen to the trough and Tom mixed it with various other edibles. The late afternoon was increasingly still and glowing. They could hear the cow bell at a distance and to Guy it had an infinitely melancholy sound as well as musical. The mule had tired of his games with the bull and was placidly eating grass nearby the herd while the bull patrolled his womenfolk, threatening the whole world occasionally with a savage bellow. The chickens were fed. Tom scattered the corn and Guy helped him. Tom was quite silent and he showed a rare gravity, as if thinking. They returned to the stoop.

"Think I've got something to read to you, about that

111

doctor business," he said. He went into the house and returned with a shabby book, its spine held together with tape. He squatted on a step and turned the pages, humming to himself.

"These are all quotations, Jerry, and they're like old silver coins worn thin, but still valuable, as they pass through men's hands and minds. Here's Voltaire: 'Doctors are men who prescribe medicines of which they know little, to cure diseases of which they know less, in human beings of whom they know nothing.'" He chuckled. "Here's one from old Ben Franklin: 'God heals and the doctor takes the fee. He's the best physician that knows the worthlessness of most medicines.' And from that cynical Frenchman, 'The best doctor is the one you run for and can't find.'

"But here's something else, better than it all: Juvenal—'A sound mind in a sound body is a thing to be prayed for.' But the Greeks said it first; the Romans could just repeat, they being worthy men who found action easier than thinking. Now. We got these psychiatrists these days—we used to call them alienists—preaching the new gospel about the human body and the human soul. It all comes from that old Austrian, Freud, who disliked his father and was in love with his mother. He believes, to put it somewhat simply, that copulation is all. If your soul is sick, you are either fantasizing about copulation, or you want to sleep with your mother, or perhaps your sister, or even perhaps your brother or other male friend. He didn't believe in the dark night of the soul. It was all a matter of genitals. Now, I've got nothing against genitals. Most wonderful things God ever created, as you've seen right here, son, and as you'll know when you're older and have had experience with life. For the genitals are glorious life itself, especially the male genitals, and never be ashamed of what you've got. Be proud. Well. I've been wandering away from the subject of medicine.

"It's an art, they say. And it is. But an artist knows when to refrain and listen to the soul. That's being a good physician, too. Know what I mean?"

Guy had listened with fascination. He nodded, and again his young face was brilliant with love for his father. Such a peace came to him then, and he leaned his head against Tom's knee, and Tom stroked his hair. Guy had never seen his father sad. When he did look up, Tom was smiling.

"I preach too much," he said. "But there's so much I want to tell you, Jerry, and life isn't long enough for that. Knowledge is like a river, too full and wide and vast for a man to drink in a thousand thousand lifetimes. So, we have the well of words, filtered through the earth of tongues, from the river, and we can fill our cups and be satisfied—for a time." He looked at the mountains, now floating in a silvery mist like moving gauze. "Yes, there's a limitation to words and to speech, but there's no limitation to what a man thinks. There's a whole universe there to be explored, and each man has his own universe, full of fiery planets and dead suns."

They ate a somewhat greasy but filling supper, then went to milk the cows. Tom carried the milk pails into the house but Guy remained, waiting for his father to return. The sky at the zenith was palpitating with a mauve light, but over the mountains stood a lake of emerald green and the shadow on the earth was the color of lavender. The silence was more intense.

Tom looked at the west. The evening star was rising, purely grave, immaculate as light, gaining luster moment by moment. The man and boy stood side by side, content, watching. Not even a leaf rustled, but a night bird called.

Then Guy thought of his mother. She would say, of this "idleness" of father and son, "Wasting time, fooling away time, when there's work to be done!"

A dark uneasiness came to Guy. Then Tom began to sing in a clear and vibrant tenor, from *Tannhäuser*, "O Star of Eve!"

Guy listened, as the ecstatic but mournful song lifted to the sky in what the child thought of as moving reverence, and his eyes filled with painful water and yet a kind of rapture was in his heart.

113

"Get to work!" he heard his mother say.

"O Star of Eve!" sang Tom, and Guy wanted to cry and did not know the reason. There was only that worshipful voice celebrating God and His glory, and though Guy had never heard the thunderous climax of the song, he heard it in his soul.

My God, thought James, and he was much stirred. Is that actually a tear that's running down Jerry's cheek? Or is he asleep, and crying? And what is he crying about? The tear was gone, but it was as if lead had settled on James's chest; he had been moved as rarely as he had been moved before. Another man's anguish was both a noble and a sacred thing, not to be intruded upon. Not even comfort could be offered, for what, damn it all, was human comforting?

James did not see Emil Grassner that night, for Emil had returned to Philadelphia for the weekend to be with his family. James went out into the snowy night and his thoughts were inchoate and miserable, but they had nothing to tell him except pain. There was something far back in his own mind, he knew now, that he did not want to face, though what it was he did not know. He could only sense regret and sorrow and self-reproach—but about what, he could not fathom.

He could only walk restlessly through the trembling haze of falling snow, feeling frost bite at his nose and chin but not caring. It was a long while before he returned to his hotel, and he was very tired. I am getting old, he thought, hoping for his own comforting, but he knew it was something else.

He called Emma and she said with joy, "Damn it, James, it's five o'clock in the morning here in London. Where have you been? Carousing?"

"No," he said, smiling. "It would have been better for me if I had."

"How do you mean?" she demanded, and her robust voice was now anxious.

"The dark night of the soul's on me, Emma," and he laughed weakly.

There was a little silence. Then she said, "Yes. Well. Dear Jimmy, that's the Jew in you. You can't even be merry with the heritage from your mother without your father putting in his ponderous thoughts."

"My father was never ponderous," said James, and then he asked himself: Wasn't he?

He suddenly remembered one winter evening early in 1939 when his parents had stood hand in hand, forgetting him, on the street, looking up at one clear and icy moon.

Without any perceptible cause his father had said, with passionate emotion, "Hear, O Israel, the Lord our God the Lord is One!"

And his mother, in her gentle and shaking voice, said, in tender counterpoint, "Holy Mary, Mother of God, pray for us sinners now and at the hour of our death. Amen." She blessed herself and began to weep.

Yes, it was the early winter of 1939, and there was terror in the air.

James said to his beloved mistress, across three thousand miles of black and stormy water, "There's terror in the air, Emma."

"Yes, love, I know, I know," she said.

7

That night James Meyer dreamt of his parents. It was a strange and haunted dream. It was like a jigsaw puzzle, the pieces not quite meeting, other pieces out of place and at an angle. It was a chill late-summer day; the dream was pervaded by the odor of coal gas; the roofs and chimney pots outside were steaming with the moisture of a recent rain. They were in the bedroom, the parents' bedroom, and James stood on the threshold, watching. His mother had something on the bed, and she was

115

anxiously doing something to it. Luggage? Was she packing a small case?

His father stood at a window, staring out, his big hands in the pockets of his hairy tweed jacket. He was saying, "Love, I have to go, you know. I have to." His mother turned to him quickly and said, "Yes, I know you do. But that doesn't keep me from being terrified for you, my darling." His father turned from the window and literally ran to her, hugging her in his mighty arms and crying, "O God!" he said. "O God."

The wavering and disjointed pieces fell apart. James looked at them in horror. But out of a dimming of light his father said to him, "Jimmy, it's up to you, a long, long time from now." His voice was hollow and echoing, as if from a deep well into which he had fallen.

James woke up, trembling even in the cold bedroom. Was the dream a memory, or had it happened? He could not remember. He never saw his father again. Where had he died? In some concentration camp in Germany? How had he died? Who had killed him? Had he suffered? Had he been shot or had he perished in some gas chamber?

If it had not been a dream, then it was a memory? What had his father meant when he had said to a youth barely sixteen, "It's up to you, a long, long time from now." The time had been late August, a dull rainy August, of 1939. He could remember that. Or was that just part of the dream?

What have I been shutting out all these years? he asked himself.

He thought: I should never have come here. Something's happened to me here, something's upsetting me. My lovely life. He shivered in the cold of the room. He had all that a man could desire, the love of a most unusual and fascinating woman, money, fame, respect, health, success, comfort in spite of the horrific taxes, and in general, peace of mind and a contented cynicism. He had once heard, "Life is a tragedy to the man who feels, a comedy to the man who thinks." He had been a thinking

116

man. Coming down to it, he thought, I haven't felt much lately.

Once his mother had said, "This world will either break your heart or turn it to stone." It had broken his mother's heart. Was it turning his own to stone? A petrified man—perhaps I am a petrified man, he thought—does not feel. He may think, out of his stony isolation, but he does not feel. Have I lost the art of feeling?

Then he said to himself, out loud now, "Why, I'm running away from something, just as Jerry is running, God help us both!" But what it was that he was running from he did not know, just as he did not know from what Guy Jerald was running. A dim ripple ran across his mind, exciting a spiritual pain, but from what thrown rock had the ripple come?

For the first time in many years he could not eat breakfast. He drank only a cup of coffee. Emil had left his car, and his chauffeur, for his personal use, for which James was grateful. During the night there had come a warmish rain, and the blameless snow was pitted with dark melting spots and there was a stringent scent in the air. The sky tumbled with gray clouds and out of it came a bitter wind. He was taken to Mountain Valleys. Tonight he would meet the children of his friend. Lucy had invited him to dinner in that ghostly Georgian house where no one lived.

James felt very disheartened. True, in some way he had moved Guy, but how and with what words was still hidden from him.

The nurse told him, "We've had a very bad night. I hear he didn't sleep at all." The thought came to James like a shock: It's about time he stopped sleeping! And a second thought: And perhaps it's time for me, too!

Guy was sitting in the wing chair. He was neatly trimmed and shaved, and he wore a white shirt, a blue tie, and a gray flannel suit. "We took a nice little walk on the open terrace today!" said the nurse, very brightly. "Then we looked at television for a while, didn't we, Mr. Jerald?"

117

Guy did not answer. Then James noted, with dread, that Guy's right hand showed the mark of teeth. The nurse saw James's expression and sighed, and shook her head. She left the room. James sat down near the throbbing artificial fire from which came a diffused faint heat. He felt weary to the heart, and could not remember that he had ever felt this way before. He said, "You're getting to me, Jerry, blast it!" His voice was accusing, almost despairing. It's that dream I had, he thought. He looked at the bitten hand of his friend.

He spoke aloud again, hardly knowing what he was saying. "I had a dream last night, a terrible dream. About my father. Or was it a memory? I never saw him again. He—he was smuggled, in some way, into Germany; I never knew how. It was just before the war. He went to rescue some people; he had been doing that for a considerable time. But that was the last time. He was murdered."

No movement, no sound, from the stricken image in the chair.

"My father was a great man, a noble man, though he never did learn to speak English without an accent. He was a boisterous and laughing man, with thick red cheeks and bright blue eyes, like blue crystal, and curling red hair, as mine used to be. He was a powerful man, a wise one. You don't see his like anymore. He had the heart of a lion, the mind of a philosopher, the soul of a hero—and a blasphemous tongue. He made a lot of money, and often wondered how he did it. Money was nothing to him, though he regarded it as a reward, not as something to hide behind because he was afraid of life—"

Guy stirred. He lifted his head, stared intently into space as if listening, not to James, but to someone else. For an instant his face was lighted with anguish. Then the light died and his face dulled and his eyes closed.

"You've got to make money in this world," Mary Jerald was saying to her sixteen-year-old son. "People hate you if you don't have money. Not that I blame them,
118

though the Good Book says the lust for money is the root of all evil. But I did hear, once, in church, that if you was good the Lord rewarded you, and you never starved. If you did your duty and worked and worked and worked honestly and hard—you got rewarded. God takes care of His own. Duty, work, work at anything, and you won't want, Guy. Besides, people hate you and despise you if you don't have money. That don't mean a fortune, I don't think. But making money as fast as you can. Some folks think money is evil. It isn't. It's a blessing from God, if you earn it and use it wisely. Look at your father. Penniless. Hardly ever had two dollars to rub together. He said he wasn't afraid of not having money. But I tell you, Guy, not having money is a terrible thing. It shows you aren't in the Lord's favor, and you know what He said about the grasshopper."

She added, with bitterness, "Your pa's a grasshopper, and no wonder folks laugh at him and hate him. You've got to have money, Guy, you just got to have it, or the world'll eat you alive. I know."

For the first time the listening youth, who had been faintly smiling, was afraid. He looked at his own neat but shabby clothes. He looked about his mother's house.

It was a tall thin house wedged closely between its neighbors; there were hardly three feet on each side. It was built of old wood, gray and somber, and was three stories tall, with little arched windows and a splintery porch; it had a lawn about twelve feet by ten, which was ruthlessly cut, with a few spindly bushes near the basement walls. Located in a very poor neighborhood, it was clean and tidy, if dreary, and was in a section known as Old Germantown, for here lived indigent and elderly Teutons who worked endlessly in order to live; their wages were very meager and hardly kept them alive, and there was not a man on the street who was less than sixty years old. But they worked. Depression or not, these old people could always find "something to do," for they had pride. Though chronically hungry, they had not gone on "relief" in the worst of days. For weeks at a time

119

they had lived on scrapple and a tiny portion of pork, with no bread or fruit or vegetables. Yet they were hardy and proud and there was a nobility in their desperate poverty. Their clothes were neatly patched, and they went to church of a Sunday and asked the pity of none, and would have refused any offered help with outrage.

Abandoned by children who were often as desperate as themselves, they talked together sparingly in their guttural "low Dutch," and kept their windows shining, their porches swept, their lawns cut, their tiny gardens in perfect order. Mary Jerald, at forty-seven, was the youngest among them, and they highly approved of her diligence, her cleanliness, her pride, and her unremitting work. Of German stock herself, she often exchanged a curt nod with her neighbors and a few brief words. Sometimes, when she could afford it, she would take a loaf of bread she had just baked and would receive, with thanks, whatever little they gave her in return. They all had one thing in common: They distrusted and feared President Roosevelt, for he was a Democrat and they were all Republicans, and he was promising to relieve the nation of its awful plight. "Plight?" they would say among themselves with suspicion. "We've got roofs over our head, haven't we, thanks to the Gross Gott, and something on our tables." But their greatest fear was of "that Hitler, with his threats of war." They had fled, as little children, with their parents, from the rule of Bismarck, and they remembered their elders' tales of Socialism. Most were Catholic, but they were very tolerant of Mary, with her evangelism, because she was so "young," as they said, even when she tried to "convert" them.

According to the more affluent in Cranston, this area was a "slum." They never knew it, these sturdy old men and women. They scrubbed their porches and even the walks, every Saturday, and they somehow managed to have a few flowers in the garden in the summer, and their rooms, though very bare, smelled of soapsuds and fresh air. A few, like Mary, "kept roomers," men who worked in the almost empty factories and in the sawmills. Mary

120

paid one of her neighbors thirty-five dollars a month in rent, and never was she a day late. In the last few years she had added "supper" to the payments her "roomers" gave her, for a dollar a meal each, and she ate the scraps herself or gave them to the old woman who "helped out" in this eight-bedroom house, or, if there was a slice of ham or a sausage or two left intact, she would give it to her neighbors.

"A good decent frau," those about her said. "Even if she talks Bible all the time, and that boy of hers is a good boy, too." Though they knew of Tom they avoided mentioning him to mother and son. It was understood that this was a very private topic, and being private themselves, they respected Mary's privacy and independence. Some believed her to be a widow, though she never claimed this.

Tom had given her literally his last penny when she had left him, some eight hundred dollars, and with this she had bought second- or third-hand furniture from the Salvation Army shop and had refinished and mended and upholstered it herself. The rooms might be almost empty but they were clean, if depressing and uncurtained and barren. For a free supper once or twice a week one of her roomers would stoke the furnace in the morning and take out the ashes. The house was mournfully chill in the winter, but the exhausted men hardly cared. Mary served them a supper that was filling if not particularly appetizing, and the beds were tidy and the sheets changed once a week and the old blankets, if patched and mended, were warm enough.

Her roomers were, for the most part, sober and hard-working men, and if, out of their despair, they sometimes bought a cheap pint of moonshine whiskey, Mary did not particularly object so long as they drank it in their bedrooms, which often slept three men. But she insisted that the rent be paid on time, as she paid all her bills at once. There was a long thin "parlor," hardly more than a hall, and there were a few comfortable chairs in it, and one old sofa and a radio, to

121

which, if the men were not too tired at night, they listened. Few could afford a newspaper. When one appeared it was meticulously refolded after reading and passed along to the next man. When the weather was particularly grim and harsh, and after Mary had washed the dishes, they could, with her permission, retreat to the dingy kitchen, still warm from the last meal. But Mary never stayed among them. She went directly to her room, which contained only a bed, a rickety dresser, and a single kitchen chair. Guy's room was as ascetic.

For the past two summers Guy had not gone to stay with his father on the farm, though he managed the long streetcar ride and the long walk on weekends and on holidays. He was working himself, in a sawmill, ten hours a day, six days a week, for ten dollars weekly. He gave his mother seven of them.

He knew what poverty was, and had never feared it, until today. He continued to listen to his mother, but not with his usual lighthearted admonishment and and his hope for the future.

He listened with a closed hard face, and with his first fear, and his first feeling of despair. Yet there was a resolution growing in him. He said, "Ma, don't worry so much. I know all about money. We've never had it. We will, someday. I know."

Mary, cooking a large kettle of spare ribs and sauerkraut this Sunday afternoon, nodded her head shortly. "You're a good boy, Guy. You work very hard. You're not like your pa at all. Someday you'll amount to something." She looked at him where he sat near the wood stove. "You'll be working full time now, won't you?"

The acute new anxiety in Guy increased. "I did think of finishing school, Ma." He put out his hand and touched the three books which lay on the table. Each Sunday he returned the books to his father and Tom gave him a fresh selection from his library. The dim warm kitchen, this summer evening, was heavy with the smell of pork and kraut. The wooden floor had no linoleum as yet, but the wood was scrubbed sedulously at least three times a week.

"What for?" Mary demanded in a sharp voice. "Going to school's no way of making a living, Guy. Waste of time. You've got to be thinking of a full-time job now. You're sixteen years old; a man."

But Guy's face was set as stubbornly as her own. "Ma, this is my last year at high school. I've been talking to the boss at the sawmill. He thinks, if things pick up, he can give me part-time work after school. Ma, it's my senior year. When I finish it I think I can get a job in the office of the mill. I'm taking typing at school, too. An office job will pay more than working in the mill."

"How much more?"

"Two or three dollars a week more."

Mary looked at the dilapidated ceiling as if imploring angels. "Guy, you'll be wasting a whole year of work! We need the money, right now. Education isn't for our kind; work and duty is all there is for us, and thank God for that. Books! Guy, you're just an ordinary boy; nothing special, nothing very bright, though you are a good boy, I admit. But—books! Look what books did to your pa! Nothing ever came of it, him with his fancy talk and all. He got that talk out of the books. Addlepated. Do you want to be like him, with never a cent to bless yourself with?" In her exasperation she swept the books to the floor and glared down at them as if they were deadly enemies. In truth, she considered them so. "Haven't you a duty to your mother?"

She waited for his answer. Her lean dark face was shining with anger; her beautiful black eyes flashed. The coil of thick black braids on her head were ribboned with white. Her body was thinner than ever and she had lost the bosom Tom had so admired when she was younger. Her housedress was gray and mended, her "house shoes" broken, and her stockings were of coarse cotton. The hands on her narrow hips were scoured and red and rough with labor.

"Of course I have a duty to you, Ma," said Guy. He loved his mother and his compassion for her was never absent. "And I intend to fulfill it. That's why I must finish

123

school and get an office job. I'll make much more money. Just this one year—"

She put up her hand as if to fend off any further argument. "How do you know you'll get more money? In the meantime we need your wages. Work hard, work very hard, save a little if you can, and maybe someday you'll be a foreman in the mill, if you work very, very hard, and mind your manners and learn the business and keep your head down, and show respect. Never talk back to your superiors. Always be ready to do a little extra work, even if they don't pay overtime any longer. Things can't get worse than they are now. They're sure to get better, and then your wages will be better, too. Haven't you any respect for Labor?"

"Sure I have, Ma. What do you think I'm doing this summer? I'm working, as I did last summer, and as I'll do next summer, and winter, too. But I've got to finish school. My last year."

"It's all foolishness, Guy! Books aren't for you. Waste of valuable time. School! All you need to know, folks like us, is to write a neat hand and do figures, so you can watch the bills. You try to climb out of the life God ordained for you and you'll suffer for it! It's in the Bible. You've got to make money, Guy. Things are bound to get better and a good job in the mills is a start. Money. Money. If you don't have it people will despise you. And we need the money *now*. Not next year, in some fancy office you imagine, but right away. Money." She spoke the word with reverence and avid desire.

Why, she worships it! thought Guy, with mingled contempt and pity. It's not a matter of need. She's got nearly a thousand dollars in the bank now. It's money for money's sake—that is what she wants. Just money, for itself. Poor Ma. She's had a hard life, I know, but others have it harder and they don't talk of money as if it's holy and all there is in life.

He had never told his mother that his father was a man of high education and that once he had been a professor of history in an excellent university. She would not have

124

believed it, or she would point out, triumphantly, that all that education had come to nothing. It had not produced money. That Tom had deliberately forsaken a fine profession to live as he wished would have been incredible to her.

"If you've got money, you've got the world," said Mary. "And you can look people in the face—with money. You can toss your head at them. It's all there is, Guy."

He bit his tongue to keep from saying, "How about your God? Doesn't He come first? You are always saying Christ was an uneducated man, and a hard-working character. But you never knew that He had attended the school at the synagogue for many years, and that people called Him 'rabbi,' which means teacher. An uneducated and illiterate man was anathema to the Jews. No matter how poor they were, their sons received an education, as Christ received one. He knew all the laws and the prophets; He knew all history. But you always call Him 'only a poor carpenter.' He was a carpenter to earn a living, but He was always a student, and to learn and to read were the most important things in His era. Pa told me and showed me all of this. Pa wants me to have an education so I will understand the world of men and make up my mind what part I wish to play in it. Books, he says, are the paper doors opening on eternity and grandeur."

No, he could not say this to his mother, who reverenced money and thought it the one good in the world, not just for security or peace of mind, but as the most valuable of all things.

But he did say, "The more education you have, Ma, the better your position in life, and the more money you'll have."

"Nonsense! Look at the teachers and the educated men who are starving or are on relief! It's in the papers every night. Now, if they'd have had a good sound job, like yours, and like the other men in this house, they'd be able to pay their way and not be beggars. But their soft hands are just like their soft minds. Useless, in days like these and in other days, too. What did their books ever bring them? And doctors. I hear doctors are starving these days, too, or taking pay in vegetables and a little meat, when they can get it from the farmers. There's no substitute for a good sound job, Guy, with regular pay. Books! Wish they'd never been invented! It would be a happier world—and money in the bank, too."

Guy looked about the kitchen; he thought of this house. Was this to be all his life? The fear sharpened in him, and the new despair increased. In a way his mother was right. Money was the most important thing in the world. But it could not be earned to any great extent in a mill. It could be earned—how?

I've got to get it some way, somehow, the young man thought, and his determination made him clench his fists. I can't live like this all the rest of my life; I can't live like the wretched men in this house. I've seen it all myself, but never really saw it before. Money is indeed everything. It is freedom. It is the golden door to life.

He said with hard stubbornness, "Ma, I'm going to finish this last year in school. I'll work after school and all summer, and next year I'll work full time. And I'll start to think how to make a lot of money—"

Mary stared at him. "You'll not make it through books, son."

"I suppose not. But I'll get an office job, after I'm graduated. More money. There's no money in that mill. You'll never get rich just working for a living. There must be other ways. Thousands of people have found the way to become rich. I swear to God, I'm not going to be poor all the rest of my life!"

He had begun to sweat in the extremity of his emotions. Suddenly he hated poverty above all other things. He hated the poor. His father was deliberately poor. That was another matter, and his own business. But he, Guy, would find the way to be rich. One day.

That weekend he did not go to see his father. He wrote him a letter instead. "There's a lot to do about the house, Pa, and Ma needs my help. I'll see you next week, if I can." But he did not. He was afraid he might repeat this conversation to Tom. He could see Tom's cynical smile; he could see him shrug his lean shoulders. He could see the look in Tom's small and penetrating blue eyes. Tom might not understand the new desperation and resolute will of his son.

He saw his father the last weekend before school. He said, "Pa, I'm finishing this year, and I'll be graduated in June. I'm going to get an office job, for more pay."

Tom said, "An office, hey? Never saw an office that wasn't teeming with silent misery. Mean little minds, mean little grubs with ink-stained fingers. Why don't you go to college?"

"Now, Pa, with what?"

"You can work at anything during the day, and go to college at night. Somewhere, if not here. You can support yourself by any kind of work, and pay your way through school. I knew many a man who did that."

"Did *you*, Pa?"

Tom was silent a moment. Then he said, "I never told you much about my parents. My father was a very successful businessman, God help him. My mother had been a teacher, poor soul. I ache for teachers. My father sent me to college— If I'd worked my way through I might— No. I'm content as I am, far more content than my father ever was. He knew nothing but work, and it finally came to him that he had worked himself to death, and for what?"

It was the summer of 1939.

The world exploded into fire and thunder. Suddenly American factories became busy and bustling. Suddenly the Depression was over and men were working again, making munitions and other war matériel. The President announced the absolute neutrality of the United States, though shipments of munitions and food and other supplies and contraband were shipped to "the Allies." It was not a matter of neutrality, people said. The contraband was being paid for, and lavishly.

Suddenly there was renewed talk, renewed old talk, of

German "bestiality and atrocities." The great and famous flyer Charles Lindbergh helped form the America First Committee.

Guy returned to school. In the summer of 1940 he was making fifty dollars a week in the sawmill. The next winter he was making eighty.

Mary was jubilant. "See, I told you!" she cried with joy.

Guy did not say to her, "And young men, like me, are dying and fighting. And for what?"

He said to himself: This is not what I want. I want money, not this dribble.

After his father had tried to talk to him about the war, and discovered that Guy was not interested, and that a new quiet had come to him in spite of the wildness that now lived constantly in his eyes, Tom refrained from discussing the dreadful events of the day. He knew that Guy loved him more than ever, but of what he was now thinking he never told Tom. His father had his life. But he, Guy, must make his own life, and, as his father did, he must go his own way.

He had abandoned the idea of working in the mill's offices. He had discovered that the salary there was much less than his wages. By the end of 1940, during the "phony war," his wages were one hundred dollars a week.

He bought a small secondhand car, much to his mother's dismay and expostulations. He used it to visit his father.

They talked of many things, but they did not talk of the war. They did not talk of Guy's education. A sad hiatus came between them, but Guy resolutely refused to surmount it. He had his life to live and it was not his father's. He bought no books for himself. He borrowed no more from his father. His gaze was on what he called "greater things." He was saving some money.

In June 1941, Hitler invaded Russia. In December, Pearl Harbor was attacked. A few months later Guy was drafted.

"I could have claimed you were needed on the farm," Tom said. "I'm not getting younger, and it's the truth."

But Guy was filled with an unformed excitement. He was sick of the mill, sick of his endless days of work, sick of the monotony. He would see the world at least. He would see some "action." He would find a way to make money, to become rich. His mind was closed to his father's cynicism.

"If we'd just have let Hitler alone when he attacked Stalin," said Tom, "the two murderers would have finished each other off, and the war would soon be over. But no, some sinister men in America had a reason to save Stalin, and I know why. It all started with the Bolshevik Revolution. It started in 1917. The war never really ended. I remember that Wilson said my war was to 'make the world safe for democracy.' He didn't know it but he was making the world safe for Socialism—Fascistic Communism. The same thing. And this war is only to extend its power over all the world. So this damned war will go on until Fascism can't be challenged any longer, not even by our country. All I can say, kiddo, is that the world we have known has gone forever and the Age of Tyrants has begun. Let the idiots blabber of a 'free world.' I'll never know it again, in my lifetime, and you can bet, Jerry, you'll never know it either."

James sighed, as he watched the man in the wing chair. I wonder if I'll ever reach him, after all, he thought.

Then, to his amazement, Guy sat up in his chair and stared fully at him. James got to his feet and slowly went to the other man. For a long moment they looked at each other.

"Jerry?" said James, his heart fluttering with hope.

Then Guy spoke for the first time in months. "Go away, Jim," he said, in a rusted voice. "Go away, for God's sake."

James held out his hand, and he saw it was shaking. Guy shook his head. He leaned back in his chair and a gray tide flowed over his face. He relapsed once more into his self-induced stupor.

"I'll be back," said James. "You never left me when I almost died, so many years ago. I won't leave you, Jerry. You and I have things to face together. You and I."

8

Sherry? thought James, as the silver tray with its five crystal little apéritif glasses was presented to him. Abominable stuff. He was tired and beset and he did not know why. There was a black veil moving painfully at the back of his mind and he acknowledged frankly to himself that he was afraid to look behind it. So with polite irritation he declined the sherry, murmuring something about his liver.

"Oh! I thought the English——" said Lucy Jerald, with a helpless wave of her hands.

"My father," said James, "was an Austrian. We drank schnapps at home." It was not like him to be impolite, especially not to a woman. Helplessly again, Lucy glanced at her brother, Hugh Lippincott, who gave James a sardonic smile. "What the hell, Lucy," said Hugh. "Don't you have any whiskey in the house?"

"You know I do," said Lucy. "I just thought—the English—"

"Dr. Meyer just finished telling you he likes whiskey," said her brother. "And so do I."

"Schnapps," said Lucy with vagueness. "I don't think—"

"Do you ever?" muttered her brother, but only James heard. "Same thing, Lucy. Whiskey, or a reasonable facsimile thereof."

Lucy glanced at her son, William. "Billy?" she said.

"Sherry's good enough for me," replied William.

"For me, too," said his sister, Marcy.

Lucy raised her empty blue eyes to the maid. "Whiskey
130

for Dr. Meyer and Mr. Lippincott, Susie," she said. She folded her heavy hands in her lap, meekly.

"I didn't know you liked sherry, Bill," said Hugh to his nephew. "On a diet?"

"No. But I really like sherry," said William, sipping at his glass and struggling to keep from making a grimace. "Besides, Mother's cook is wonderful. No use drinking strong stuff and ruining the dinner."

They were sitting in the beautiful but cavernous living room of the Jerald house, which, though there were five people present, had a hollow feeling to James. The white walls, with their silver moldings, enclosed a room of superb proportions, long and wide, and a white marble fireplace with a marble hearth showed a fire of substantial warmth and cheer. An incomparable interior decorator, probably from Philadelphia, had been responsible, it was apparent, for the gold and blue and light jade and white silk furniture of a Louis XV design, and, thought James, if they are not authentic they are damned good reproductions. The draperies were of gold silk drawn over filmy white gauze curtains and the rug, obviously genuine, was a fine old Aubusson in shades of blue and rose and dim yellow. Everything was in the best of taste and most elegant and beautiful, then why, thought James, did it appear so cold and distant and untenanted? Why even repellent? His father's great warm and cluttered house, furnished by himself in a mixture of several heavy and ponderous periods, made James ache with nostalgia. Emma's large house in London was similar to the house James remembered from his youth. Dear Emma, so ugly, with such gorgeous legs and big breasts and monkey face sprightly as a Pan's, and with such an endearing wit and with such loud joyful laughter, and with such kindness and indecent language and innate tenderness! Emma, Emma, he thought with real hunger and yearning. You are flesh and blood, Emma, but my unfortunate hostess is composed solely of specious gilt, papier-mâché and plastic. He had not planned on talking to Emma tonight, until the vast dimness and pain in himself had subsided, but now he felt an

131

urge to return to his hotel and speak to Emma at once. Without explanations, she would understand his malaise.

The maid brought in a decanter of whiskey and a bucket of ice and large crystal glasses. "It's good whiskey, Bourbon, Guy's favorite," said Hugh seeing James's apprehensive expression. William glanced at it longingly, then resolutely drank his sherry.

Hugh Lippincott, Lucy's brother, did not inspire trust in James. He said, "No ice, if you please, Mr. Lippincott." "English," murmured Lucy. Hugh raised his eyebrows, lifted the decanter, and said, "Say when."

He began to pour. James watched. When the glass was almost half full he raised a finger. "Water in another glass, please," he said. "No ice."

Mother and son and daughter exchanged swift looks. Hugh smiled widely. "Same here," he said. He filled his glass and saluted James. He's amiable enough, thought James, and seems to be the only one of this family with any intelligence. He had hoped that Guy's son, who had once made a perspicacious remark about his father, would reveal some intelligence, too, but James was disappointed.

Hugh Lippincott was a large man, almost as large and massive as James himself, with a plump and sallow face which showed all the discretion of a banker. He was as blond as his sister, and he had a wary look for all his size, which meretriciously enough denied the very little hidden blue eyes under thick yellow brows, the grotesquely small nose like a cherry and approximately of the same color. In spite of his ease in his chair he had an alert aura, as if ready to pounce at any moment. His apparent relaxation was meretricious also, James concluded. He wore an excellently cut suit of a deep "banker's" blue, and his shoes, no doubt handmade, were as brilliant as black mirrors. He was, from his appearance, an overfed and self-indulgent man of about fifty-nine.

William Jerald, son of Guy, was a young man of twenty-six, not very tall, not even as tall as his mother, and he was frankly quite fat, with sloping shoulders under his gray suit, a vivid red tie, and dusty boots. He, too, resembled

132

Lucy in that his thinning hair was blond. But he had light brown eyes, the color of sandpaper and as abrasive, and a loose full mouth. Cunning, but not bright, thought James. I wouldn't trust him around the till. Avaricious, too, judging from his eyes, and he's been doing too much womanizing from the expression of his mouth, and there's a twitchiness under all that candid air of innocence and that American aspect of boyishness. Good God, he is close to thirty and looks as if he has been playing cricket all day! But I shouldn't carp. We've got a generation or two of him in England also. *A bas le prolétariat!* They're turning the whole bloody West into a bankrupt spa, filled with sharks.

Lucy's daughter, Marcy Blanchard, was hardly more prepossessing in James's uncharitable opinion. True, she had her father's coloring, in that her eyes and short straight hair were black, and she had his aquiline nose. She was not tall but was stocky, with a round dark face and a tight petulant expression and a thin mouth too highly colored by the wrong lipstick. She was never still a moment. She had her twin brother's twitchiness but it was more pronounced. She was constantly crossing and uncrossing her thick blunt legs with the muscular calves, and tossing her arms about so that quite frequently she upset a piece of fine Meissen ware on the table beside her. She never stopped, it seemed, from saying "Whoops!" when her flying elbow overturned the delicate little flower girl with her miniature basket of roses. She would impatiently slap it back in its upright position as if it had mortally offended her. (Lucy, finally, removed the objet d'art, to James's relief.)

Marcy wore a white silk blouse with the inevitable shirtwaist with sharp collar points, and a long black silk skirt which was always in disarray, revealing her unattractive legs. She wore but one piece of jewelry, a gold gemmed wedding ring. Lucy, in her blue dress, which concealed the offensive huge "bum," was almost dainty in comparison with her daughter. James thought, of Marcy, that she resembled one of the new hockey mistresses now

133

in the "comprehensive" schools in England, who rose, not from some aristocratic stratum, but from a mill. James had no objections to mills and the people who worked in them—good sturdy folk, or at least they once were—but he did not care for the company of their daughters. Marcy, to add to the general unappetizing picture, had a loud hoarse voice tinged with whining, whereas her brother's voice was high and thin and piercing. Hugh rumbled, which James found preferable. Yes, he admitted, he was feeling irritable tonight, and irritability was not one of his usual moods. He was also bored and resentful. As yet, no one had inquired about Guy Jerald.

"How long are you staying in America, Dr. Meyer?" asked Hugh Lippincott, as if very casually, but James became alert.

"I just don't know how long, actually," he said. "This is a sort of holiday for me, you know."

"A refill?" asked Hugh. James was surprised to discover he had already drunk his whiskey. "Thank you," he said, and held out his glass, and Hugh poured it a third full of whiskey. Again, the quick exchange between mother and children.

"Been in America before?" asked Hugh.

"Many times."

"Like it?"

James paused. "It's becoming more like England every day, or perhaps England is becoming more like America."

"Is that a compliment or an insult?" asked Hugh, and he smiled, and this time there was no wariness in the smile but a bland attractiveness.

"I'm no lover of Socialism," said James, "and it's name is, really, Fascistic Communism."

William said, "Isn't that a contradiction in terms? Fascism isn't Communism."

"Sorry, Mr. Jerald, but it is. Both Mussolini and Hitler visited Russia, before the war, long before the war, to study things at first hand, how to brainwash the people, how to subdue and oppress them, how to herd them into slave-labor camps, how to kill them more or less

134

quickly if intransigent, how to silence dissent, and how to torture exquisitely, and how to terrify the people with random arrests and the knock on the door in the night. In short, how to brutalize a nation. Poor Russia, poor Italy, poor Germany. The last two, especially. Italy and Germany had never known such evil before. Of course, there was Bismarck and his Socialism, from which tens of thousands, millions, of fine Germans fled, to the advantage of other countries. And Italians, when they could do it more easily, ran from Mussolini, also to the advantage of other nations. Most of them came to America, and I think, if ever your country throws off the present and impending tyrants, the Italians and the Germans will be the ones to lead the counterrevolution."

"Tyrants!" exclaimed Marcy, of the short, muscular, and flailing arms. "We're a free country, Dr. Meyer!"

"Are you?" he asked with bluntness. "I am afraid I must disagree. America may be a little freer than England—still—but not so much. The whole world is seething with tyrants. There is not a peaceful spot on this earth any longer. Surely you read your newspapers! If it isn't a bloody outright revolution going on, it is something more sinister, a very old plot by the self-designated elite to rule and master and oppress all the peoples. It started with Robespierre and the bankers who financed him, and the very wealthy—outside of France. But it is too long a story to go into at this time—this pleasant evening. I am sure we have something closer to us to talk about."

William blinked those sandpaper-colored eyes and gave James a superior smile. "But this conversation is interesting, a different point of view. How did you come to your conclusions that America isn't a free country any longer?"

James quietly ground his teeth. He was tired of being polite. "I read your newspapers, several of them, every week, in England—even if you do not. Your schools, grammar schools—or, as you call them, public schools— are uniformly teaching conformity, as our schools in England are teaching our young. Both countries are now bringing up a whole generation to be meek, docile, fun-

135

loving, illiterate, lazy, irresponsible, immature, overfed, infantile— Education is in poor repute. The young must be served, especially with drugs and amusements and fairy tales. But never honor, never patriotism, never manliness, never pride—and never, of course, education in the true sense of the word."

Hugh said, "I agree. You should see and hear the new applicants for jobs in our banks and our business. Men and women, in their late teens and early twenties, unable to speak a sentence in decent English, unable to write legibly, unable to follow the simplest written directions, unable to use the simplest of machines, unable to concentrate for more than a few seconds; restless and useless. Their sole preoccupation is 'fun,' money, food, coffee breaks, dancing, and sex. No wonder so many of our businessmen are dying of heart attacks—having to deal with such rabble."

"But—" said Lucy, with one of her vapid gestures.

"Really!" exclaimed Marcy. "Our schools are wonderful, our boys and girls are wonderful! So much brighter and more aware than our—your—generation, Dr. Meyer! My children go to a progressive school—the things they learn—!"

"What?" asked her uncle. Apparently he had never used that harsh tone of voice to her before, for she blinked and stared at him a moment before answering.

"Why, things relevant for today! How to get along with your peers. Life styles. Awareness!"

"The things which are relevant today are irrelevant for tomorrow," said her uncle, in that hard voice. " 'Awareness' of what? I've never seen such blank faces as I see on children these days, totally unintelligent, like rabbits. As for manliness, they wouldn't know a fist if they saw one."

"We should all like America to be a gentler country," said Marcy.

"In an eminently ungentle world?" James broke in, with exasperation. "You've got to give Russia credit for one thing: Young men and women, when they reach the age
136

of twelve, are ruthlessly examined for scholarship and literacy. If they are only average or are under-average in intelligence, they are sent to work in the fields and factories, to learn agriculture or hard labor. To learn to make themselves useful. They are taught militarism. Above all, they are taught patriotism. The Russian people would never die for Communism. But they are taught to honor, respect, and love the Motherland, and they would die for her, as we all know from the siege of Stalingrad. So, the Russians are hardy. Each young man, and often strong girls, too, are taught the art of war, and how to kill and how to survive. For what are the Russians arming and making themselves indomitable? To advance a 'more gentle' nation? What nonsense. Give the Russians respect: They have never deviated for a single moment, even in a fraudulent period of 'détente,' from informing the entire world that they intend to conquer and subdue it—and that includes your country too, Mrs. Blanchard."

"But—" said Lucy.

Marcy directed a glance of pure hatred at James. "I don't want my children to grow up in a militaristic world," she said.

"If I had children," said James, "I shouldn't want that, either. But we must face the fact that we are now confronting an envious and hostile world. You cannot go unarmed any longer, sad to say, unless you are willing to be slaves."

William gave a snicker. " 'Better dead than red.' "

James looked at him with quiet rage. "Too simplistic, as you Americans would say. Let me tell you something. Immediately when Hitler took power he had all the arms of the unfortunate German people confiscated. The reason is obvious. They could not fight back."

William interrupted. He snickered again. "Well, he did a good job on the Jews, anyway!"

It was rare for James to feel the impulse to murder. He made himself breathe less furiously. He said, "If we do not all begin to protect ourselves the Fascistic Communists will do a good job on us, too."

He thought of his father, who had died in an effort to save the helpless. He felt the corners of his eyes fill with water. Something behind the black veil in his mind shifted, moved, murmured, exhaled. The malaise in him quickened, almost choked him.

He added, "The great prophet Isaias said, 'My people are going into captivity, because they have no knowledge.' And it is as true today as it was then. Captivity. That is what our schools and our whole establishment are silently, mercilessly, and subtly preparing us for: Captivity."

He paused, looked about him. "The most terrible captivity of all—the captivity of the human mind and the human soul. Sealed into speechless conformity. Humanity deprived of humanity. To serve its masters—and they are in every capital of the world today, plotting against us. And the 'knowledge' of which Isaias spoke is kept far from us, or we refuse to learn it."

He saw that Hugh was watching him and suddenly he no longer disliked that ambiguous man, for all he was a banker. Those very small blue eyes were fixed on him with great intensity and there was no unfriendly glint in them.

He continued: "It's not just Russia, though she is more overt than the rest of us. It's the men in our great capitals, the plotters, the tyrants, the murderers. Power."

Marcy, the stocky and sinewy, gave a whimper. "I'm thinking of the children," she said.

James was freshly infuriated. "I don't quite understand that American phrase, 'the children,' Mrs. Blanchard. Whose children do you mean when you say 'the children'? Your neighbors', the children in every school in America, the children of the world—whose children?"

She glared at him again. "Why, I mean *my* children!"

James nodded. "I thought so. But there are millions of children in the world, madam, besides yours, though perhaps you never considered that. What of them, besides your own?"

She was so angered that she blurted, "I don't care about anyone else's children except mine!"

138

James nodded again. He was so tired. "I thought that was what you meant. I sometimes get a little confused over American—vernacular. When I say 'the children' I mean the children of the whole earth. I believe that is proper usage."

She did not hear the ironic insult. She was fumbling wildly in her purse, which was beside her. She dragged out something with which James was only too familiar: a package of cellophane envelopes packed with photographs. She thrust the package at James, as if it were a weapon, and said, "These are my children!"

Returning to politeness, James accepted the package and was confronted, as he was often confronted in America with dozens of photographs. They were Marcy's children, of course, a boy of about four, a girl of about three. They, too, were bland-faced and grinning, overfed, almost obese. Marcy, or her husband, was kneeling behind them in all the photographs, too, clutching their shoulders as if the children were crippled or blind or threatened. Threatened. Of course they were threatened. All the children of the world were threatened. And their parents sang sweet songs to them, overwhelmed them with toys and food and 'fun,' and lied to them constantly, at least in America and England.

William said, when James had murmured something and had returned the precious bundle to Marcy, "I wish you could talk to the kids at Harvard, Dr. Meyer." He was smiling nastily.

James raised his red-gray eyebrows. "Kids—at Harvard?" he said, as if bewildered. "I didn't know they are now letting little children, in America, into your colleges. Strange."

"Oh, you know what I mean," said William. "Kids just out of preparatory school, eighteen, nineteen." His nasty smile had lessened, but it was vicious.

"I don't call men that age 'kids,' Mr. Jerald," said James, in a deliberately insulting voice. "Or are they just 'kids' mentally?"

Hugh laughed aloud and slapped his knees. "Men

139

that age do designate themselves as 'just kids,' Doctor, and refer scornfully to 'adults.' Precocious, eh? Whoring and drinking and copulating all over the damned landscape, and they call themselves 'kids,' not the adults they are."

William turned to his uncle, and his light brown eyes blinked rapidly. He lowered his voice but it was still malevolent. "The kids know much more, these days, than their parents ever knew. That is why they are rebelling—"

James suddenly lost his control. "Rebelling? A great English writer, Malcolm Muggeridge, just recently said, 'They are not rebelling against anything. They are just degenerate.' He is correct. Degeneracy of the mind, the heart, and the soul. And who has corrupted them? Look at the schools, and in England, too. Look at the silly materialistic parents. But don't look at the churches! They have nothing pertinent to say any longer."

There was a short silence, and except for Hugh Lippincott, the silence was not amiable. Three pairs of narrowed eyes were fixed on James. Then dinner was announced. It was notable, to James, that no one as yet had mentioned Guy Jerald.

Lucy's cook was indeed superb. James's rage had kept him reasonably sober. There was a saddle of lamb, parsleyed potatoes, peas, a fine salad, hot rolls, and a good vintage of Burgundy. James was not particularly fond of lamb, but this was artfully seasoned with fresh herbs and ginger and garlic. Lucy presided with exaggerated elegance, but James, hopelessly mellowing, overlooked it. Marcy glowered blackly at her plate; William kept shifting in his chair. Hugh Lippincott was giving James furtive and amused glances. He was not accustomed to intelligent and informed conversation, and so he was grateful to James— for all I am a banker, of sorts, he thought, with more amusement.

He said to James, "Lucy has told me you are an old friend of Guy's, and a psychiatrist who has published a number of books on the subject of psychiatry. I under-

140

stand you see Guy every day. Tell me, what is your opinion of his condition?"

"The same as Dr. Grassner's, I believe. Jerry is fighting out something in himself. He must resolve it, or he will die, or go mad."

William put on a very solicitous expression and leaned towards James. "But he's mad now, isn't he?"

"No, not at all. He is absolutely sane, and that's why he is confronting something more strenuously every day— in spite of himself. When he has solved it all, he will be well. But it is a tremendous decision he must make."

William looked puzzled, glanced at his mother and sister. His voice was very pious. "Poor old Dad. Dr. Parkinson thinks he had a stroke—result of the accident, or perhaps the cause of the accident."

James said, looking fully at Guy's son, "Let us not pretend, among ourselves. He tried to kill himself, because, at that time, he didn't dare confront what he must confront, or he was fighting the confrontation."

"Sounds too psychiatric to me," said William, and his abrasive eyes were outright hostile now. "Just what do you mean—Doctor?"

"Exactly what I said. Surely it isn't too complicated for even a man in Harvard's School of Business Administration to understand? Every man when he reaches the middle years—that is, if he is intelligent—must face himself, must decide what he wants. As Dante said, 'In the middle of the journey of our life, I came to a dark wood.' Your father has entered it. He must find his way out of it, all by himself. If he had faith, perhaps, it would not be too hard, or at least less hard. He would be able to tell himself, 'God gave me my life, and I must live it as I must, or perish.' "

Marcy said, still glowering, "Well, for one, I don't understand either. What does Dad want? More money?"

"Don't be a fool, Marcy," said Hugh, and once again James looked at him with reluctant liking. "What Dr. Meyer is trying to tell us is that your father has come to the

141

decision that he must live his life, not as others want him to live, but as he must live. Clear?"

"In what way, Uncle Hugh?" asked William, now intent.

"God knows, Bill. Only your father knows." Hugh looked down at his lamb. "I've made my own decision. I came to it faster than Guy's doing. That's why I—" But he stopped, thinking of his wife. This was not the time.

"Well, why can't Dad come to his own decision, too?"

Hugh smiled, and the smile was not pleasant. "Maybe he has a higher sense of duty, or something. Who knows?" He looked quickly at his sister.

"You're mixing me all up," said William. "What's duty got to do with it?"

"What, indeed," said Hugh, and his rumbling voice was satiric. Now, here's a man of perception, thought James.

Lucy said with shrillness, "I do not believe, I will not believe, that Guy tried to kill himself! I don't care what anyone else— He has everything to live for—a wonderful family which is devoted to him, wonderful grandchildren, security, wealth, health, this lovely house, his business, his banks—"

"But, Lucy," said Hugh, "you know damn well he tried to kill himself. You accepted that from the beginning."

"But why?"

"He probably couldn't stand all that 'wonderfulness' any longer," and Hugh laughed and only James detected the bitterness. "No one knows what he wants, or what he wants to decide. Only he knows."

"And none of you psychiatrists can help him?" said William, and now his tone was avid, and so were his gleaming eyes.

"None can help himself but himself," said James. "If I sound sententious, I'm sorry. But it is the truth. All we can do for your father is to show him, if possible, that it is all up to him and nobody else."

"How can he make any decision if he's out of his mind?"

"Mr. Jerald," said James, very slowly, "again, your

father is not 'out of his mind.' He's been compromising. Just my opinion. Now he realizes the time for compromising is over."

" 'Curiouser and curiouser,' " said William, with mockery. "Dr. Parkinson told Mother today that the case is hopeless, and that Dr. Grassner"—he looked pointedly at James—"isn't doing Dad any good at all, and that he is only getting worse. Hopeless. I never did believe in psychiatry, anyway."

"I don't, either—that is, not often," said James. "The human soul is beyond the comprehension of any other soul, except fleetingly. We do get glimpses, but it is like will-o'-the-wisps in a swamp. We are never certain. We can only be supportive and do as little harm as possible, and help the sufferer to get an insight into his own misery, and what has caused it."

Marcy said, "I read in the newspaper—new drugs for mental and emotional illness. What are they?"

"Palliatives," replied James. "Mostly. To help over the rough places. But the least thing your father needs at this stage is palliatives. He needs strength. It is my opinion that he is gaining it."

"Such riddles," sighed Lucy. "What is to become of us?"

"And the business, and the banks," said William. He glanced at his uncle. "Uncle Hugh is carrying the whole load, though I'll be able to help after I am graduated. I don't think Dad will ever be able to go back—"

So, thought James, remembering the two women who consciously, or unconsciously, were grateful to their mother's murderer. He clenched his fists on his knees. He said, "For the last time, your father isn't mad. He's not insane. Insanity is a legal term, not a medical one. But I am not here to give you a lecture in psychiatry. If your father wants to return to his 'business,' he will. If he does not—" and James spread out his hands.

"But why shouldn't he want to return?" asked Marcy.

"He hasn't yet told me. Perhaps he will, perhaps he will not. That, too, is his decision."

"I don't think it's fair to me and Uncle Hugh," William began.

Now Hugh raised his voice and it was grim. "Never mind the fairness to us both, Bill. Your father is the one who needs fairness if anyone does."

William was honestly surprised. "Why, Uncle Hugh, it was you who said, only a week or so ago, that 'something must be done,' about Dad and his affairs."

Hugh turned crimson. He threw down his coffee spoon. "Perhaps I was wrong, damn it! Dr. Meyer has given me some insight, for myself, too."

James felt a sudden compassion for this man he had at first disliked. Et tu, Brute, he thought. He felt he had an ally, a new defense against these vultures. But William was obviously dismayed. He stared at his uncle. "You don't think we should apply as 'conservators'?"

"No!" Hugh almost shouted. He pushed back his chair. "Why the hell don't you let your father alone to fight his own battles and decide what he wants to do? He's not senile, though you seem to want to believe he is. I never particularly liked Guy, but now I do, God help him. You've heard Dr. Meyer. I happen to know something about him. I respect his opinion, and Grassner's, too, and not that fuddy-duddy Parkinson. He wouldn't recognize a neurosis even if it kicked him in the balls!"

"Uncle Hugh! Mother!" exclaimed Marcy, pretending shock.

Hugh uttered a worse obscenity and Lucy covered her ears and closed her eyes. "I've known Guy was neurotic for years," said Hugh. "I knew he was fighting something. But I had sense enough to keep out of it. It's his affair, and his only."

Lucy said, almost sobbing, "I've been such a good wife, such a good mother. I did my best. Everything for my home and the children— Never a thought of anything else." Her pale blond head bobbed up and down and she glanced about her imploringly. "I have nothing to reproach myself with at all. It was a few years ago— Guy began to act very strange. I should have advised a psychiatrist right

144

then, instead of waiting. He would stay away overnight—
He would never tell me where he had gone. I never
thought—"

"Perhaps there was another woman," said Hugh, obviously enjoying himself.

"Uncle Hugh!" Marcy was again in shock. "I'm sure
Dad never looked at another woman since he married
Mother!"

"More fool he," said her uncle. "And I don't believe
it for a moment. Guy's human. He's a man. And any
married man who tries to tell me that he's never 'betrayed'
his wife is either a liar or has been castrated. It isn't
normal for a man to be 'faithful,' as they call it, to his
wife, after a few years, or even earlier. The male psyche
isn't built that way. We're a polygamous sex, Marcy, and
I'm sure your Alan hasn't worn a chastity belt all the time
he's been married to you."

"Uncle Hugh! Alan never did anything in private that he
didn't do in public!"

At this Hugh and James burst into ribald laughter while
Marcy glared at them. "Women!" shouted Hugh. "Marcy,
do you understand exactly what you said? If you don't,
then you are sillier than I suspected."

Lucy whimpered, "I'm sure as I can be that Guy never
looked at another woman—"

William, who had not listened too closely to this conversation, was now very glum. "What was it Dr. Parkinson
told you, Mother? That"—he looked at James—"Dad
shouldn't have any visitors but the family? I agree."

Hugh stood up. He was extremely grim. He leaned his
fists on the table and fixed his eyes on his nephew. He
spoke slowly and in a deadly tone. "Now, I say that Dr.
Meyer must see as much of your father as he wants to,
and when he wants to. If any of you interfere—I have
ways of standing in your way, and you had better believe
it. I know what's on your minds. I say—halt it, or you'll be
sorry. Very sorry."

"He's incompetent—Dad," said William, with defiance.

"You are the incompetent one," said Hugh. "Not your

father. I'm warning you. I am a lawyer, too, remember, and don't forget it. I know all the tricks sons can work against their fathers. I know them all."

Hear, hear, thought James, with some unholy satisfaction. He stood up also, though he usually awaited the signal of the hostess. "Mrs. Jerald, may I be excused? I fear I am coming down with a chill."

James called Emma, his mistress, when he reached the Old House. She said at once, on hearing his voice, "Well, love, what is bothering you now?"

"I need you, Emma, my darling," he said. "I never needed you so much as I do tonight."

"Ah," she said in a voice of deep and tender sympathy. "You never told me that before, but you must tell me that again when you are home."

"About emigrating, Emma. Perhaps. But not to America, say, or the moon. How do you fancy me buying an island somewhere, a lovely island in the South Seas, where we will have peace together?"

There was a little silence. Then Emma said very gently, "You are in a bad way, aren't you, sweet? Do you remember what God said to Job? 'Gird up your loins and be a man.' I think that is it."

The black veil in his mind shifted strongly as in an impending gale, and James was appalled. He said, "And what the hell do you mean by that, love?"

"I don't know, quite, Jimmy, but I feel your thoughts even if I can't put them into words. 'He is wounded, but not slain. He will lay him down and bleed awhile, then rise and fight again.' With armor, this time with armor."

He was more appalled, and he sweated a little and the red-gray curls on the back of his head grew damp, and then he became frightened and closed his eyes.

"Emma, you don't know what I am talking about."

She sighed. "I love you, Jimmy."

His voice trembled as he said, "It's enough for me that

you are alive, my love. I love you, I love you, and perhaps that is all I need."

"Not quite, Jimmy. There is something else and you will probably know soon."

9

It was Sunday, a gray moist Sunday, full of low gloomy clouds and despondent wind. James felt both weary and unable to rest. His dreams had been very bad all night, but though he could not remember them they oppressed his spirit. He was driven to Mountain Valleys. Guy's family had mentioned seeing the sick man that day. James profoundly hoped it would rain and storm and they would not go out. Americans, he had noticed, did not particularly care for bad weather, and found nothing very bracing about it. Frankly, he thought, neither do I. We are all effete these days. We prefer to look at inclement weather through polished windows.

The sanitarium was already milling with visitors. But Guy's family had not yet arrived. Everyone, James noticed, looked damp and bad-tempered, as if visiting their "loved ones" was quite an imposition on their day. Some had sternly dutiful expressions. They are probably calling on their private gods to congratulate them for their forbearance, James commented to himself. I'm glad I have no relatives to "suffer" for me when the time comes. Only Emma, who will be cheering me up on my deathbed and commenting on pretty houris.

The nurse was in Guy's suite and she seemed happy to escape the dismal atmosphere and murmured something about coffee and Danish, which puzzled James. Perhaps she means crumpets, or jam and toast, he commented. He was further oppressed by seeing Guy huddled in the usual wing chair. Then Guy looked at him with full recognition, and his gaunt face, for a moment, wore a strange expression, and he turned away.

147

"Well, well," said James, taking off his deplorably old gray tweed coat and laying it down. "Bad weather, isn't it? A real English winter day in London. Do you remember London, Jerry, and all the humid girls in the rain? And their hectic cheeks? And the dreadful weekends when everything was closed up tighter than a virgin? But somehow we usually managed to find a whorehouse doing a splendid business, and some scotch, didn't we? Ah, youth. Thank God it's over."

Guy said nothing. It was as if he were alone. James sat down and rubbed his hands before the fabricated fire. He detested it, but then there were no ashes.

He said, "At least there were fires in the brothels, though not in our rooms or barracks. Fire. To me it always meant both life and death. Odd, that, isn't it? Fire is alive —and yet in a way it is dead. It's hard to put in words. Resurrection, or destruction. Creation, or annihilation."

Then Guy spoke. "Oh, my God." It was a voice of total suffering. James leaned towards him. "Yes, mate?"

Guy turned his head away and pressed his face into the back of the chair.

James watched him as long minutes passed. Once Guy's shoulders lifted in a silent sob. Then he was as quiet again, as if he slept. But James knew he was not asleep.

It was the winter of 1948. There had been a slight depression after the war but now things were exuberantly "booming," as the newspapers shouted. Guy had reached the eminence of assistant foreman in the sawmill, and there was inflation, and his wages were one hundred fifty dollars a week. He gave his mother thirty-five, which she sedulously banked, and he was living, as always, in her house. She was charging higher for board and room but her boarders were happy and euphoric, though her table had not much improved. There was sometimes a roast for Sunday, or a big platter of fried chicken, and Mary was leaner than ever and the ribbons of white in her hair were very broad, and her expression was more formidable, her nose longer and harder and more prominent, and she
148

appeared more bitterly determined as her prosperity increased. She always seemed "on the run," Guy thought, and wondered if she had always been like this. Yes, but not as fierce. She was fifty-eight and looked like a somewhat underfed hawk, and there was a kind of obduracy about her in her pursuit of—what? Security, of course, but that was not the paramount thing. Money. She was a middle-aged and hungry virgin in some dilapidated gaunt temple with no music and no footsteps but her own. Pursuit, not of ease and contentment and love—no. Guy, thinking this, would call himself uncharitable. But then, he would reflect, he was no better himself, and he was no nearer being rich for all his modestly growing bank account. A job was not enough. A small mean pension in his old age was not enough, even bolstered by Social Security. His one besetting thought—and he was no longer ashamed of it—was money also. He was twenty-seven now. The way was no clearer than before to a worthwhile future, free from hard labor and obscurity. How did one get money, not a few thousands, but millions? Education? He told himself he had no gifts, no talents. He no longer even had books. He had not read a book in three years.

The hiatus between his father and himself had grown more painful and more obstinate than ever before. Guy visited Tom two or three weekends a month, and he did not acknowledge to himself that those visits were loaded with restraint, sadness, and often long uncommunicative silences. He knew when his father looked at him intently, as if waiting, but he would never return those looks. His father had nothing to offer him but thinking, and Guy did not want to think of anything any longer but money. Once Tom had said to him, " 'The world is too much with us; late and soon, Getting and spending, we lay waste our powers.' " But Guy had thought, with inward derision: getting what? He saved his money almost as grimly as did his mother. He hoped to buy some stocks in a few years. But—how much? He did not confess to himself that he was afraid and growing more frightened every day.

He had no friends. He felt no rapport with the rowdy and meaty men with whom he worked and whose pleasures were simple if very enjoyable. Their conversation was confined to the subjects of women, automobiles, the new ones after the war, and drink and poker, their pettish wives, and, sometimes, "the kids." None had any authentic ambition. Some were proud of the tract houses they were buying, and exchanged information on crabgrass in the summer and complaints of heating bills in the winter. Some were discontented with their unions, or spoke of strikes. No one worked more than eight hours a day now, or five days a week—but the discontent was growing. Guy's contemporaries, and older men, remembered the days of the Depression and the hopelessness, and rejoiced in their "decent" present wages and their new "benefits," which meant paid hospitalization, insurance and "sick leave," and paid vacations, and pensions. They talked of the day of their retirement and how they would buy a small boat and go fishing. Their comprehension of anything else did not extend further than the sumptous moving pictures, which were another world of sleek women with jewels and finely tailored men, fast cars, great houses, and constant feverish leisure, and nights of dancing and wenching.

The new discontent was growing. It was not based any longer on fear of being out of work, fear of starving, fear of homelessness, fear of broken shoes and hunger, fear of illness and the "poorhouse." Those days, they believed, were gone and happily forgotten.

It was a different discontent now, a sullen resentful discontent, and a rising dull hatred. It was pervaded by envy and hatred for "the rich." This was not true of the older men, who thanked God nightly for the new life for the working class, the new access to a few luxuries, the new safety. But it was true of the other men, of Guy's age or younger. It was greed, a hating greed. Why should they, they asked, not have what the "rich guys" have, without any effort? Why should the "bosses" have handsomer and more expensive cars than they had? And prettier women and imposing houses? Yes, they could send their children to college now, if they wished, but that was not enough. They did not for a moment believe that riches were often a reward for superior gifts, intelligence, invention, harder work, more ambition, more determination, more planning. They harbored the idea that they were the victims of thieves.

It was contemptuously amusing to Guy that it was not the men of enormous inherited wealth who aroused their cupidity, envy, and hatred. For these they had an almost abject awe and admiration. The men whom they resented with such a dangerous resentment were men they called "no better than me, and how did he get all that money?" The middle class was their target of smoldering rage.

Tom had recently said to his son, "Why, it's clear, Jerry, what's going on. Men ain't being encouraged any longer to work hard, aspire, sacrifice, think—though what the hell most people want with a lot of money I don't know. Among the men you work with there must be some who are incipient draftsmen, engineers, inventors, craftsmen, and all that. There is free night education for them, or education at little cost. Why don't they attend good trade schools or colleges at night? The old American dream of making it on your own, and competing for the prizes of life, is gone. You should know why, Jerry. The whispering men who sneak among these discontented workers, the lethal deadly men who mutter the working class is being 'exploited' and abused and kept from their lawful 'rights.' They never tell the men that many of them are making more money than most teachers, and some foremen and truck drivers and carpenters and such have higher incomes than many a professor or newspaperman or younger banker or lawyer, even, perhaps, a doctor. The middle class. That's the target of their discontent, Jerry.

"And you know why. At least I have been telling you. Things are moving faster and faster now, and the spew comes from Washington. It is coming from all the capitals in the world. Fascistic Communism. The destruction of the middle class, which is the only protection for the workingman against the power seekers. Once the middle class is destroyed through the mindless hatred of the unthinking and the envious and the ignorant, then it is all over. It will be over, sooner or later. Then a nation of the enormously rich and powerful—and slaves, a slavery they never heard of before, or can't possibly imagine. The greatest way the middle class is now being eliminated is through vengeful taxes—though the tremendously rich pay little or no taxes. Old trust funds. Inherited guarded wealth, foreign investments, national investments. Foundations. It was planned that way a long, long time ago. And, it will succeed, unless the working class are enlightened as to their real enemies. Who is going to enlighten them?"

Guy did not see the hope on his father's face, the waiting.

Guy said, "I don't give a damn about the noble workers, for God's sake, Pa. I just want money myself. A lot of money."

"Well, then, why don't you go to night college?"

"Why? Just to become a middle-class man? That's not enough for me, Pa. I've seen the middle-class sections in cities. Nice little houses, with larger lawns and rosy wives and fat children—and mortgages and taxes and no tangible security, and endless worry. Not enough. I want to be rich. The hell of it is, I have no talent, no gifts, no genius for money."

"How do you know?"

"Oh, for Christ's sake, Pa! I'm not a kid any longer. I am going on twenty-eight. At least I'm not married, with a family, as a lot of idiot slobs are, and kept in a prison of debts. I pay a woman occasionally, and no obligations. But—I can't see the way to get what I want."

Tom sighed. "I suppose I'm lucky that I never wanted much, and there is no fever in myself for what I lack. But, your life is yours, and it isn't mine. We're getting off the track. I don't know if you fully understand what is threatening this world of men, or don't care. We can't all be crusaders. No apologies. Me—I see it all before me and I lay low, and glad I'm not a minute younger. Well. I

152

still hope you'll find your way, as you want to do, and I only hope it will give you some deep satisfaction. But—find your way, boy, find your way." He added, "I think you had a dream, once. But you've forgotten it."

"A dream," said Guy, with despairing contempt.

He had not noticed that for some months his twiglike father, his birdlike father, was becoming very thin, almost transparent, much older, more sad, and sometimes withdrawn. But his high shrill laughter was as ready as usual, and he often looked at the world about him with joy and pleasure. He had Sal, he had his land, his stock, his little farming, and above all, his books. His hair was almost gone, his beard just a scraggle, and his clever fine hands were sometimes clasped together for a long time, as if contemplative. "I'm getting old," he once said. Guy did not hear.

He went to see his father in January of 1948, on a Sunday. He did not stay very often now for the full weekends. Before he left, his mother said, "You're not going out to that farm, are you?" Her voice was accusing and rigorous. "I guess you forgot. There's a church supper tonight and you promised to go with me. A good chicken supper, a dollar apiece."

"I forgot, Ma. I didn't see Pa last Sunday, and I told him I was going today."

"It's bad weather and it's hard on the tires and the engine and the gas. Gas's expensive; takes more on those roads. Tell him you can't come. You promised your mother, Guy, and you got a duty towards her, though seems like you don't often remember it, leaving me alone on a Sunday all the time."

"I'm going," he said. For some reason he felt oppressed more than usual in this drab thin house. There was already much snow on the ground, and more had begun to fall. From the kitchen window he could see the rear of the house and the dilapidated rears of others on the next street, and the sheds with their garbage cans and the long streamers of snow twisting over them. The bleakness seeped into his very bones. The radio was inanely babbling

153

away on a kitchen counter, and from the cadence of the man's voice, sonorous and portending, Guy gathered that it was a late sermon being broadcast. At any rate, the man was castigating those guilty of "sins of omission and commission." Mary had been listening with a properly subdued air. She said, "He and that sinful woman he's got living there with him. Can't bear to think of it. You really going, and I'll have to go alone to the supper and it costs——"

Guy threw down a dollar on the table. He did not speak, usually, so roughly to his mother, but he said, "I'm going. I just feel uneasy and I don't know why." She looked at the dollar and picked it up deftly.

"And at his age, too. He ought to be ashamed."

Guy left without speaking again. His little elderly car, pre-war, was indeed showing signs of fragility outwardly but the sturdy engine ran with no trouble. He thought of his father, as the windshield wipers strove with the fast-falling snow. At least the farmhouse would be warm and Sal was adept at making the most ordinary food delicious, and there would be conversation with his father, however much conversation with him now angered his son only too frequently. Guy supposed that it was the way between the generations—lack of understanding, though he had an uncomfortable thought that his father understood him too damned well. He loved his father with a mature love, not a child's, and all at once he said to himself, "Why, damn it, Pa's the only friend I've got in the whole shitty world! But I always knew that. He's like the only real thing in my life."

The truth of it shook him and he made the car move faster. I think I'll tell him today. I haven't told him for a long time how much he means to me. I just took it for granted that he knew. And another thing, I've never heard him complain in all the time I can remember, no matter what happens.

Guy thought of Sal, and it came to him that she had not lately looked at him with her broad and bawdy smile, but had greeted him somewhat tersely for a considerable time, and that all her laughter was for his father and never for him. If Guy spoke to her lately she would reply quite shortly, and direct her conversation to Tom, and her merry eyes would well with tenderness and love, and she would listen to every intonation of his voice. Now, what the hell have I done to her? Guy asked himself, with some irritation. Perhaps she's angry that I don't stay weekends all the time any longer, but just Sunday. But, hell, I work hard, and sometimes Pa's sermons get under my skin though I can't explain exactly why. He always talked like that. Sal. Now, I like her far more than I do poor Ma. She's really alive, at the least. The car moved faster.

When Guy finally drove up to the farmhouse the day was darkening, though it was but one o'clock, and the snow was increasing. But the big kitchen window was bright with the kerosene lamp, as if greeting him. He opened the splintered door and a gush of warm air enveloped him like a welcoming friend. Sal was peeling potatoes at the "dry sink" with its pump handle—a fairly new installation—and his father was sitting near the ancient wood stove with its high warming shelf and its comforting fire. Tom was reading and smoking his old pipe. He looked up when Guy came in, stamping, and his face became as bright as the lamp.

"I was afraid you'd decide not to come today, son," he said. "Bad weather and getting worse." He held out his hand to Guy, and Guy could feel its unusual heat, and its new fragility. Sal had not looked up from the sink; she kept her head over her work.

"I didn't come last Sunday," said Guy. He looked at the woman, far more plump than a few years ago but clean and fresh in her gingham red-and-white frock and her worn sweater. "Hello, Sal," he said.

She said in her new abrupt voice, "Hello, Jerry." That was all.

So something had annoyed her and with impatience Guy wondered what it was. The constraint in the kitchen grew sharper and finally Tom noticed it. He said, "What's the matter, Sal? Don't you feel well?" His voice was anxious.

Sal drew a deep breath. "I'm well enough," she said.

155

Her own voice had become uncertain. Guy shrugged, and hung up his snowy coat on the hook on the wooden wall. He smiled at his father. Tom was gazing at him very closely, and then he smiled. "Sit down, son," he said. "Right near the stove where it's good and warm. You're getting to be quite a man, kiddo. It's always a new shock to see that you're no longer a kid."

"Well, I'm twenty-seven, for God's sake, Pa. I'm not young any longer. I'm a man."

But Tom was gazing at him with deep love, as if he wished to impress Guy's image on his eyes and mind and now the smile was faintly sad. Then observing that Guy noticed that, he laughed. "What is it Stevenson said? 'For God's sake, give me the man who has brains enough to make a fool of himself!' I hope you take time enough off to make a fool of yourself, Jerry."

"Oh, I do," said Guy, thinking gloomily: When? A bought girl occasionally, a movie once in a while when I can persuade Ma it isn't sinful, and listening to the older boarders cough at night, drearily, and that damned mill!

"There's nothing like a fine woman, Jerry, nothing like wrestling with her in bed. But I hope you don't marry too soon, not until you have some sense. I didn't have any, and I was older than you. But what are you standing there for, with that sober look on your face?"

Guy sat down and lit a cigarette and again studied Sal. Her black ringlets romped about her cheeks, but for all their rosiness the cheeks were taut, and her large red mouth was not smiling. Then she put down her knife, pulled on a very ugly old coat, took up a basket, and started for the door. "Need some eggs," she said.."Out in the chicken coop."

"I'll go for them Sal," Guy said, and stood up. She gave him a quick denying glance, shook her head, and started for the door. He snatched up his own coat and followed her, to Tom's wonderment. Guy found her running down the narrow snowy path in the direction of the shed, and she moved as if fleeing. He caught her halfway. "Sal," he
156

said. "What's wrong with you? What have I done? You hardly speak to me anymore."

She pulled her arm fiercely from his hand and looked up at him with tears in her eyes and something else—bitter reproach.

"I wouldn't give you the time of day anymore, Jerry," she said.

"Christ, what have I done?"

To his moved surprise the tears ran down her trembling cheeks.

"You haven't noticed anything, or do you just don't care?"

"About what?"

"Your dad."

A savage blow like a fist struck Guy's middle. He blinked the falling snow from his lashes. "You mean about my coming every Sunday?"

"Oh, God!" she cried. "He's sick, Jerry, he's terribly sick! And you never saw it all these months! Don't you look at anybody but yourself? Don't you think of anybody but yourself?"

"Sal, what do you mean he's 'sick'? I did notice a change in him lately, I think. But he's getting old."

"He's dying, you fool! Only a blind person couldn't see that!"

The giant fist struck again. "Dying? Who the hell told you that?"

She hit herself on her great breast with her clenched hand and the tears were now running over her shaking lips. "No one has to tell me. I know." She gulped and added in a broken voice, "I thought you saw—I thought you would help me. But you didn't see, you didn't care."

"What has he been complaining of?"

"Nothing. That's the worst. But he knows. He doesn't know I saw him vomiting blood behind the barn, a month ago, brown blood like coffee grounds. When he came in he was whistling or singing as usual. I was too scared—and he had a look, I couldn't ask him anything. I—I haven't heard him complain of anything all the time I've lived here with

157

him. He isn't the kind you can talk to about any sickness, if he has it. But couple of months ago or more he was off his food. Stopped eating meat. Looked like he was in pain afterwards. But never a word. Always had a good appetite, he's the wiry kind; now hardly eats at all. In bed—in bed he turns and groans, sometimes, and I know he isn't asleep, though he pretends to be when I ask what's the matter. When I first found out he was feeling bad, I asked him to go to a doctor, and he laughed and said, 'What for? I'm fine. Just getting old, Sal.' "

A great terror seized Guy and made him numb. Then he reached out and took Sal by the arm again and she fell against him and put her head on his shoulder and cried aloud, enormous sobs that racked her from head to foot. She clutched him. "Help him, help him!" she moaned. "I love him, even if nobody else does!"

Guy's lips were thick and icy and his heart began to pound like a stricken machine. His father—his only friend, the father he had loved so intensely since childhood. The world felt empty, forlorn, forsaken, abandoned, and the terror in him was increasing. "No," he muttered. "Not Pa." The wind tossed particles against his cheek like cold fire. A pale crystal sun had come out and intensified the sensation in Guy of desolation and wild despair, of ruin and devastation. Never before, in his lonely young life, had he felt the horror of unalleviated loneliness. The whole landscape was a white hell and he in it, alone. There was no voice, no change, no being.

He tried to speak again to the woman clutched to his body. His voice was just above a whisper. "It may only be ulcers." Sal shook her head violently.

"No, no, he is dying. I can't make him go to a doctor. Help!"

"Yes," he said. After a moment he said, "He mustn't know we've talked. I'll talk to him, Sal. Go back to the house. I want to think a minute." He had to make her go; he was too weak to move just yet. She looked up into his face, her own distorted with anguish, but there was now a
158

little hope in it. She withdrew herself, and he took the basket from her. "I'll get the eggs."

"Couple of weeks ago, I said I'd do the milking, and I thought he'd get to argufying, but he only said, 'Thank you, Sal, but just for a little while.'"

She went back to the house and Guy stood, a dark haze now moving before his eyes. He tried to draw deep breaths but his ribs felt like iron, unmoving. Clouds of vapor from his mouth puffed out, resembling the gasps of a faltering engine. There was suddenly a hard and monstrous pain in his temples. The agony in him quickened. Then he forced himself to go into the chicken shed. He never remembered gathering eggs, and then he found himself walking slowly and feebly towards the house, the basket feeling too heavy in his numb hand. He had the sensation that he had grown very tall and fragile and that his legs were mere bending sticks. He had a sudden overpowering need to urinate, and he did so, in the snow, fumbling in the cutting wind. The terror was almost more than he could bear; not even during the war, and under fire, had he felt such a crushing fear; such a wild desire to run, to hide, to look for shelter. There was no shelter. Not even when he had known about Marlene Kaufmann, that young murdered German maiden, done to death by Russian soldiers by rape in a Berlin subway, had he felt such blind rage against life, such unbearable suffering, such tormented denial.

One awful word insinuated itself into his laboring mind, but he refused to say it to himself.

The weight of the door was almost too much for him. He entered the hot kitchen and saw his father standing at the window, smiling and puffing on his pipe. He turned when he saw Guy. "I thought Sal had brought the eggs," he said.

"I sent her back, it was too cold," replied Guy. He could hear his own voice from a hollow distance. Sal took the basket from him and again her eyes were desperately imploring. He nodded. He looked at his father's back, saw his emaciated body, the fallen shoulders. But nothing could have been more tranquil than Tom's attitude.

"I like spring and summer," said Tom. "They're like a quilted spread thrown over the hills and the land, all colors mixed together, and warm. But the winter—I like it best. Look at the land and the hills and mountains, son. Like white embossed velvet, laid over everything. Austere. Noble. The sun's out. The hillocks of snow have hollows made by purple knives carving new ivory. Come and look. What a beautiful world."

"Pa," said Guy. "I've got to talk to you. Please sit down." His voice sounded as if it came from a far and echoing distance. Tom turned, surprised. He went back to his chair. There was a clarified light in the kitchen now and by it Guy could see the full ruin of his father.

Tom's fair skin was a grayish yellow, the lines deeper, the declivities sharper. There was a skull-like appearance about his smiling face. His teeth appeared larger between ashy lips. But his blue eyes were living and vital as usual, the thin beard as jaunty. Guy closed his eyes for a moment. God curse me, he thought. Why didn't I see this before? No. I was too wrapped up in my own sullen reveries and resentments and wants and demands, my own damned self-pity. I put a wide space between us. I wouldn't let him come close—because I was afraid of what he was saying. Whether I was right or wrong doesn't matter now. I wouldn't let him come close, after all those years. I gave him the face of a shitting little bastard who wants his own way and sees nothing else. I gave him the face of a child when he needed a man. He needed a son.

"What's wrong, son?" asked Tom, and for the first time Guy heard the effort his father had to make to speak.

Guy pulled his chair closer to his father's and held him with his eyes, which kept dimming in his rage. "Pa, don't kid me any longer. I—I've seen it for some time." Sal made a faint noise near the stove. "You're sick, Pa. I didn't like to speak about it before, but now I have to." There
160

was such a thickness in his throat, dry and hard. "You've got to see a doctor at once."

"Oh, hell," said Tom, with indulgence. "Nothing wrong with me but age. We all come to that, eventually." His antic face, his satyr's face, changed, became melancholy as well as amused. "What is it the Bible says? 'The days of our years are threescore and ten, and if by reason of strength they be fourscore years, yet is their strength labor and sorrow. For it is soon cut off, and we fly away.' Yes. And Panin says, 'In youth the days are short and the years are long. In old age the years are short and the days long.' Yes, son. In youth is the time to prepare for old age. I did that. I'm content."

Guy bent his head. Tom looked at him with unusual gravity. "If you want contentment later, boy, start looking for it now for your middle age and old age. When you're fifty it is almost too late—and fifty will be on you before you realize it, with all its doubts and its glooms and regrets. Then tomorrow you'll be old. What have you then but yourself, and a love to warm you, if you're very lucky? A love to warm you." He glanced at Sal, who was gazing at him with agonized love. Tom slightly shook his head, as if in regretful pain. Then once more he was smiling. "Son?" he said. "Never reject love, in your arrogance or because you want no commitment or involvement. Hell, I'm wandering in my old age. It's age, not youth, that has long thoughts, despite what the poets say. Well, if you reject love, feeling yourself of one piece and not needful, then you'll have barren years and cold."

Guy, with acute intuition, knew that his father was trying to distract him from the idea of medical attention. He lifted his head. "Pa," he said, "I am going to take you to a doctor tomorrow. If you refuse, then I'll leave now, and I'll never come back." He wanted to add: I couldn't stand it.

Father and son stared at each other in silence. Then Tom said with gentleness, "You mean that, don't you, son?"

"Yes, Pa, I do, so help me God."

161

"Tomorrow's Monday."

"The hell with tomorrow, and work. This is more important. Well, Pa?"

"I don't like doctors, son. But if you had been one—"

Guy shut his eyes for an instant. "Never mind what you feel about doctors. Well, Pa?" He stood up. "Do I take you tomorrow, or do we say goodbye?"

Tom chuckled. "Always knew there was steel in you somewhere, kiddo. Now, let's discuss this—"

"No discussion, Pa. Yes or no?" He reached for his coat.

Tom gave an exaggerated sigh and looked humorously at Sal, who was one listening ear. She was nodding fervently. "Jerry's right," she said. "And if you don't listen to him, Tommy, then I'll pack my things and I'll go, too."

Tom spread out his hands and shook his head over and over. "You want to kill me off. That's what. Doctors and their brews! Remember what Holmes said? 'I firmly believe that if the whole materia medica as now used, could be sunk in the sea, it would be all the better for mankind and all the worse for the fishes.' Correct. Can they cure old age?"

Guy felt beset. "I'm afraid, Pa, you've been substituting quotations for common sense."

"That's the way to get a reputation for being an erudite man. Saves time, and study. All professors know that."

A huge nausea hit Guy's viscera. "Pa, it's getting late. Yes or no? Now."

Tom again gave that elaborate sigh of surrender. "All right. If it makes the two of you happy."

Sal uttered a cry and ran to him and pulled his head to her big breast. He leaned against it, and Guy saw his exhaustion, saw his eyes. He turned his head again, but not before he saw his father put his arms about Sal like a child, like a child who was home. Sal was weeping. Guy felt another huge pain, a new desolation.

Tom was very lively at early dinner. He had never spoken so well and so pithily, while his dying face shone with affection for these two he loved. He kept touching

162

Sal's hand and smiling. He kept looking at Guy with profound emotion. "I'm a lucky man," he said. "A very lucky man, with you two."

Guy noticed that he ate almost nothing of the good dinner, and that, as he swallowed, he winced. And I never looked, I never saw, he said to himself. There's no forgiveness for that. It was plain to see, but I never looked. The wood stove crackled, the day darkened. No one really tasted the dinner. Death was the fourth guest.

At four o'clock Guy looked at his steel Army-issue watch and then called his mother before she left for the church supper. "Ma. I'm not going home tonight. Pa and I—I'm taking him to the doctor tomorrow."

She almost screamed, "But tomorrow's Monday! Work. You'll lose a day's pay!"

He nearly hated her. "Did you hear me, Ma? Pa's sick —I think. He needs a doctor."

"Why doesn't that sinning woman of his take him? Why you, Guy, wasting your time? Let his fancy woman take him, that bad wicked woman, everybody knows what she is—"

Guy glanced at Sal and his father. They were holding each other's hands in brimming love, and all at once Guy envied his father.

"Goodbye, Ma," he said, "I'll be home Tuesday. Perhaps." He hung up.

Later, when it was dark and the winter storm was raging and bellowing and rattling his windows, he lay in his old room on his old sagging bed, and could not sleep. Conscience tore him like tenterhooks. Tom and Sal lay in their ancient brass bed, and Guy knew that Sal held Tom in her arms. Tom groaned softly through the night and Guy sweated with anguish. I never knew, I never knew, I refused to know, rang the mournful accusation in his mind. He heard Sal murmuring like a mother. The dolorous wind was an accompaniment. In that warm brass bed there was love and consolation and vows, and it needed no speech. What have I? thought Guy.

He could not sleep. He got up, carefully shut all doors.

He turned on the radio in the still-warm kitchen, as softly as possible. The New York Symphony Orchestra announced that its next selection would be Schubert's *Unfinished Symphony*. Guy had heard it once before, in Munich, that shattered city. He had heard it later after Marlene had been so monstrously murdered. As the first muted strains began he could see Marlene's delicate little face, her pale long hair, her great blue eyes, her tinted cheeks, her frail little body, her expression of bewildered innocence, her trusting hesitant smile. An arctic moon was running between clouds outside the kitchen window, bloated and glittering, alternately causing the snow-filled landscape outside to gleam like polished marble, then obliterating it to gray ash and black shadows.

The music climbed into a crashing crescendo, and behind his closed eyes Guy could see enormous fiery-white wheels whose spokes were interwoven with flashing swords; he could see mountains falling and the land roaring up into mountains—and then the tender melody like the touch of a translucent hand. He thought of his father and he began to weep as he had never wept since he was a child.

He thought he must have fallen asleep out of his exhausting pain, for he opened his eyes. His father, in his old-fashioned nightshirt, was standing on the threshold, listening and looking at Guy, and he was not smiling now. He held out his hand and said, "Son."

Guy could scarcely get up and walk to him and take that febrile hand, so dwindled in his now. He could not speak. Tom put his other hand on his shoulder and said again, consolingly, "Son."

He took away his hand and returned to his bedroom and Guy still had not spoken. But he felt that something invincible had touched and comforted him.

The early-morning sun was clear and blinding on the snow, and the wind had gone and everything was immobilized into black and white. Sal had prepared a good breakfast. Nothing was said of the night before. Tom seemed the only one of the three who was at ease and carefree. He studied the determinedly stolid faces near him with amusement. He drank a little milk, a cup of coffee, and ate a piece of toast. "We're not going to a funeral, you know," he said. "The doctor you called so early at the Cranston Memorial Hospital this morning, Jerry, must have been pulled out of bed."

"He's waiting for us," said Guy. The food was sickening in his mouth. There were many things they had these days—for that—if it was that. He was weary and drained, for he had slept but three hours. Sal's full plump face was pale and very still; she could not take her eyes from Tom. He had always been sparrowlike, but now his small coat hung on him as from sticks. Sal wrapped a woolen scarf about his neck, firmly pulled on his farmer's cap. She had hardly spoken a word this morning. She put her arms about Tom and kissed him over and over. "Come home soon," she said. He patted her round full shoulder, touched her opulent breast. "Sure, sure," he said. "Have lunch for us. We'll be hungry, sweetheart."

Guy went out to his car and brushed the heavy snow from the windshield and studied the whole situation. He went to the barn for a shovel and cleared the wheels. He asked Sal for a blanket for his father. "Good God," said Tom, "I'm not an infant." But he pulled the rough folds about him, and tried to suppress a shiver. "Damn growing old," he said. He lit his pipe, and Guy lit a cigarette. Carefully starting, Guy rolled slowly down to the road, blasphemously praying the car would not be stalled in the drifts. But the little vehicle sturdily found its way and they were on the road, just recently plowed. Tom looked through the window, wiping the gathering mist with his mittened hand. He said, "Such a beautiful world. A thousand lifetimes isn't enough to appreciate it." He smoked with contentment, waving away the spiraling little cloud that rose from his pipe. There had been no regret, no sadness, in his high shrill voice. It had in it a note of deep tranquillity and calm. Guy's eyes were burning and sometimes he could not see to drive.

He said with irascibility, to keep from weeping again, "I thought I'd have to drag you out today. You're so damned obstinate, Pa, almost as bad as Ma."

Tom laughed. "Would you really have said 'goodbye, forever,' if I had refused?"

"Yes," said Guy.

Tom looked at him admiringly. "Damned if I don't believe you! And Sal, too." He began to sing, almost in a falsetto. " 'Woman is fickle, false altogether, light as a feather, borne on the summer wind!' Not Sal, though. She's a real old Mother Earth. A woman. A woman is a rara avis in the world now, Jerry. Oh, the whole fucking place is full of females these days, all dainty gestures and big glistening smiles and hips and padded breastplates, and brass and dancings, and pretensions and airs and graces. But they're not women; all their looks are artificial and they have artificial souls, too. Not an honest emotion in ten thousand of them. Not a throb of genuine feeling. Even their tears are fake, and probably perfumed, too. I bet their genitals never felt one joyous ecstasy. They're too careful of their curled hair to let it get mussed in a bed. But Sal. She is a woman. I hope you find a real woman like Sal, Jerry. But you'll have to look hard. Don't go off your head at the sight of a mere pretty face. You can find them in every Woolworth's. Look behind the face and the silly gestures. Look into a woman's soul, that is, if a woman has a soul."

"You're a real Turk," said Guy.

Tom laughed once more. "Remember what Nietzsche said? 'When you walk among women do not forget your whip.' Correct. Most women need the whip now. Find someone like Sal. If you can. Sal was never a beauty, thank God, and you mustn't look for that. Few real women are beauties. They are too busy taking care of what a woman should take care of to look in the mirror and paint up their eyes."

Oh, God, Pa, you don't have to make conversation just to cheer me up or something, Guy thought with the deepest pain of his life. I can hear how weak your voice is, Pa, and what an effort it is for you to laugh. And I never noticed it before yesterday. Forgive me, Pa. Guy said, "If I find the sort of woman you advise, I hope you'll dance at my wedding."

Tom was silent. Guy gave him a quick glance, and saw that his father was grave. Then Tom said in a low but emphatic voice, "You can bet on that, Jerry, you can sure bet on that."

They did not speak again until they rolled into the city, where brilliant light reflected on all windows and the roofs tumbled with snow and a fresh wind blew skeins and scarfs of whiteness into the bright air. Drifts and ridges of snow smoked with a mist like fog. Cars were all about them. "Glad that stupid hospital is near the suburbs," said Tom, and his yellowish skull-like face was drawn. "Not too far to go, not too far to get back."

The hospital was warm and bustling though it was still very early. "Dr. Smithson? Yes, I believe he is waiting for you, Mr. Jerald, in his offices." Guy prayed that the receptionist would not mention the "cancer floor," and she did not, but her eyes on Tom were compassionate. "Second floor, office 222."

Dr. John Smithson was a smiling but serious young man with a fresh face and clear discerning eyes. He shook hands with the father and son, remarked on the weather, took them into his examining rooms, and asked Tom to take off his clothes. When undressed and when Tom stood before Guy, the son experienced again that terrible pain. For he saw mortality in his father's withered and wrinkled flesh, he who had seen many of the dead in Europe. But he clenched his teeth and lips and hands and said nothing. He saw that the doctor's eyes had confirmed his terror. The physician helped Tom onto the examining table and Guy could no longer look. He went to a window and looked down blindly on the cars and the people on the street below. Once he heard his father make a cringing sound, and he forced his nails into his palms. Time passed. Dr. Smithson said to Tom, "You may get dressed now, Mr. Jerald." He drew a deep breath. "Why didn't you come to me months ago?"

"Why? I was all right until lately. It's only old age." Now Guy turned and saw the physician assisting Tom with his clothing. He saw his father's bare feet, shriveled and pathetic, the arms fleshless, the shoulder blades like pushing wood through his skin, the acute angle of his jaw, the touching beard. He said, "Doctor, X rays?"

The physician hesitated. He patted Tom gently on the shoulder. "Please go out into the waiting room, Mr. Jerald. I want to consult your son about something."

"Ah, no," said Tom. "I'm the patient, ain't I? I'm not a squealing woman or a peeing kid. I'm a man, though there don't seem much left of me, is there?" He chuckled lewdly. "What's there to know I want to know. It's my body, and nobody else's. Tell me all your soothing lies, Doctor."

"Would you like to stay in the hospital—for a while, Mr. Jerald?"

"What, and have you fellas taking away my last drop of poor old blood and cutting little pieces out of me for biopsies and shoving bedpans under me? No." His voice was still amused but his face had become a face Guy had never seen before—stern and fixed. "Look, Doctor, I know what's wrong with me. I have cancer. I knew that almost from the start."

"If you had that—idea—why didn't you come sooner?"

Tom shrugged. "I know, I know, the X rays, the barium meals, the long days and nights of pain, the degradation of slowly dying in a hospital bed. I've got cancer of the stomach, haven't I? Come on, Doctor, speak up like a man. We're all men here."

The dread word was out, like a bared sword, a murdering sword.

"You'd have taken out my stomach. Now, I'm a physical coward, Doctor. Prolonged pain isn't my pref-

168

erence. My uncle died of the thing. I had a brother who died of it, and he only twenty-five. I'm not going to say you can't sometimes cure it, but I knew from the start that you couldn't cure me."

Dr. Smithson folded his arms on his chest. "Yes, you are right, Mr. Jerald. You have a massive—tumor—in your stomach. It has already metastasized. Pancreas. Supraclavicular lymph nodes, peritoneum. I don't need X rays to tell me that. It's—gross. If you had come—"

Tom shook his head. "No. I didn't want that. Hospitals. Nurses. Opiates. Operations after operations. Bloodletting. Pitying faces. Indignities. Beds. Extension of a life that isn't a life. I often remember what Chaucer said in his 'Wife of Bath':

> "—when that is remembreth me
> Upon my youth and on my jolitee
> It tickleth me about min herte roote—
> *That I have had my world as in my time.*

"I've had my time, Doctor, and it was better than what most other people have. And I'll leave this lovely world, not as a screaming mindless lump of agony, but as a man, on my feet."

The loathsome sickness and terror in Guy had increased during this exchange. His heart was one gigantic horror and grief. He said, "Pa—"

"No, son, I'll die when I must, and like a man, with no regrets and with less suffering than the other way. When I was in my war, and could walk around with all that shrapnel in my leg, they put me to work in a hospital ward, in Old Blighty, as we called England then. I saw what endless pain can do to a man. It can reduce him to an animal, robbed of his humanity. I prefer it this way."

The physician had listened with respect and surprise, for he had not thought Tom an educated man at first. He said, "There are people—"

Tom lifted his hand, kindly. "I know. 'Who are walk-

169

ing around without a stomach.' I know. But I want to die intact. What suits one man repels another. I've loved living, more than most men have loved it. But I'll leave it with no regrets. And in peace."

"Mr. Jerald, I will be frank with you. What you have described would be quite true, and I won't lie, for you are a brave man. But you are still going to have considerable pain. All we can do for you now is to give you palliatives, derivatives of opium, and such, when it gets—unbearable."

"Will it dull my mind?"

The doctor hesitated. "Well, yes. But isn't that better than pain?"

"No. Not to me, sir, not to me. Sleeping away what's left of my life, until the final sleep. I want to be aware until the last minute; I want to be on my feet until the last, clear-minded. I know what pain is. I can stand it."

"Do you think it's fair to your family?"

"Do you think it's fair to my—family—to force them to watch me die inch by inch, instead of quick yards? Until they pray for me to die, and then feel guilty all the rest of their lives? I've tried to be a just man, in my fashion."

He was so tired that he leaned against the examining table, but when the doctor would have taken his arm he opened his eyes and smiled. Guy could not move. Tom said, "How long?"

"I don't know, sir. It could be a month, three months, six. But not longer than six."

"Let's hope it's soon."

"You are a brave man, Mr. Jerald."

Tom shook his head. "I don't know. Perhaps I'm a coward for not wanting to drag this thing on for a long time. Let the inevitable come as soon as possible."

He looked at Guy and his skeleton face almost crumpled. "Son," he said. "Let's be men. Don't make it harder for everybody. We'll tell Sal the truth, and
170

then let's not talk of it any longer. It will be easier for me, too."

Guy never remembered leaving the hospital with his father. Tom would not let him hold his arm—he remembered that. He did see the street, and it wore all the shadows of agony, all the grotesque shapes of pain and despair.

They were in the car and rolling back to the farm and there were only white dazzle and black darkness before Guy's eyes, and often the car swerved and slid. Guy felt that his voice had become frozen, petrified. A dozen times he began to speak but no sound came.

At last Tom said, "Son, give me peace."

When Guy still could not speak, Tom continued: "Socrates asked why a man should fear death. If it is only a sleep, then how sweet sleep is. If one lives after death, then that also is good."

He looked at Guy's profile, wan as death itself, the aquiline nose pinched, the mouth set in suffering, the dark face a mask of torment, the black hair as ruffled as if it had been in a high gale.

Tom said with tenderness but new strength, "There are things you should know, son. I've left Sal an insurance policy for fifteen thousand dollars. I hope she marries a man who will be kind to her, and loving, and appreciate her. But no one could fully appreciate Sal. I wonder if you could help her. I'd like that. I've left your ma all I have in the bank—two thousand dollars. And I've left you the farm, lock, stock, and barrel, and there's no mortgage on it. I paid that off years ago. And there's four hundred dollars for my funeral."

"Pa," said Guy, and the water was deep in his eyes.

"Come on, son! We all have to die, sooner or later. It's the one inevitability we'll ever know. You are still young. You have your life, and your health, and your future. What does it matter that I haven't any of that? Eventually we lose everything, through death, if not by

171

taxes. I hate to quote your ma, but she is right when she said we are only lent things in this world. They are not really ours. Except our lives, for the time we have left. Then even those are taken from us. We came out of the unknown and we'll return to it. Amen." He chuckled. "Never thought I'd end up quoting clichés."

Guy slowed down to clear his eyes and to light a cigarette. The car crawled. He did not see his father watching him with sad compassion. Tom said, "Oh, the damned paraphernalia of dying! I wish they'd invent a ray or something to touch a corpse and make it disappear instantly, without dragging out the miserable amenities. Listen to me. I don't want to be buried. I don't want the noble earth to be polluted by my wretched body. I want to be cremated, and my ashes scattered, and if you don't mind, I'd like those ashes to be scattered over my land. That is, if the accursed authorities will let you do it. Well, I hear they put the ashes in some kind of a box. You can open it yourself, some night when the moon is out, and scatter them, and no one will be the wiser. I want no grave for anyone to visit and suffer the whole thing over again. When I leave this world I want to be gone, with no trace of me anywhere."

He waited. Then Guy said, "All right, Pa."

Tom said delicately, "And, if you can arrange it, I'd like your ma not to be at the funeral, or the cremation. I don't want Sal hurt any more than she will be."

"All right, Pa," said Guy again, feeling suffocated.

"And I'd like it even better if you didn't tell her I was dying. Oh, you'll arrange everything, I'm sure. I trust you, son." He paused. "By the way, no parson. Is that understood? No public funeral, nobody but you and Sal."

"Yes."

How could the sun shine so blazingly when the only thing one loved was dying? It was a mockery, a curse. Guy was forced to stop the car on the shoulder. He folded his arms on the wheel and put his head down
172

on them. He did not cry or speak. He simply could not go on for a few minutes. Tom waited, understanding. Once he put his hand on Guy's shoulder, but that was all. Of the two he was the stronger.

Sal came running to the car the moment it stopped before the door, and when she saw Guy's face she became mute and her face lost all color and her mouth opened in a soundless sob. Tom put his arm about her. "Now, Sal, let's have no talk. It's all over. I have a month or so, and I want it to be a happy month. I want to be happy with you. Please?"

She took his hand then. "Yes, sweetheart, oh yes."

They went into the house. The wood stove was crackling, the kitchen shining with light. "I have some whiskey around here," said Tom. "A toast. To life." He kissed Sal. "But above all, to love."

A little later Guy called his mother. "Ma, Pa isn't too well just now. I'm coming home for some of my clothes. I'm going to stay here with him until he is better. . . . Now, wait a minute. I need to take care of some—things. It won't be long. . . . I'll go every day to the mill; it's near this place, almost as near as home. And I'll stop in every Friday to see you and give you thirty dollars."

"You're not a real son, Guy, deserting your mother for a father who never cared about us, and to be in the same house with that wicked woman! It's shameful, that's what it is. Haven't you any pride?" Mary's voice was an indignant shriek of outrage. "A scandal."

She did not ask about the man who had been her husband for twenty-eight years. Guy felt a surge of hatred for her, and he never loved her again.

When he arrived back in Cranston, Mary did not notice how sallow his dark face had become, how leaden his lips, how pent his expression. She assaulted him with reproaches. She followed him into his bedroom, protesting his packing. Then she cried, "Can't you say something? What's the matter with you? You ought to be ashamed."

173

"I haven't anything to say, Ma. Nothing at all. I'm —tired."

"A whole day's pay wasted! You'll be lucky to get your job back!"

"I called this morning. It's all right."

"Well." She subsided for a moment. Then she said, "I've been a decent person all my life. No one can say anything bad about me, Guy. I've done the very best I could. You know that. How can you treat me that way? And only thirty dollars a week instead of your usual thirty-five. Is that fair?"

"I won't be eating here, Ma."

"But there's your room."

He was so beset that he turned on her a frank face of hate and she saw it and stepped back a pace or two. "Rent the damned room," he said. "I may not be coming back at all. Take my things out, the rest of them, the summer suits. Everything. Put them anywhere."

"You won't be coming back? Not coming back?"

"I don't know yet. I've got to make up my mind about something."

"You've got a girl, a creature like that Sal, out there! And you know what a sinful thing that is. You're not thinking of getting married?"

"No. Please stand away from my bureau. I need some work shirts."

"Then it's some hussy, all four of you living down on that awful farm! After what I've taught you, and everything, to be God-fearing—"

He could not control himself. He shouted, "Damn your God! Damn everything!"

Mary was struck silent with horror. Then she said, "I smell whiskey on your breath—whiskey. Drunk like your father."

"True," said Guy. He closed his cheap suitcase. "I want to be like my father. I will be content if I'm ever the man he was—is."

"You can say that to your mother, who worked so hard for you, and gave you a decent home? What did he ever
174

do for you except to teach you godless ways, and to swear at your mother and curse her, and let you be in the company of an evil woman, a Jezebel?"

"I don't know, yet, what he did for me, but someday I'll find out, I hope."

He went to the outside door and she followed him, wailing, but he had no pity for her. He did not speak another word. He threw his suitcase into his car and drove off, the fenders spitting snow. Mary stood on the doorstep until the car was out of sight. Then she cried and shivered with desolation. She was a good woman. As Tom had said, that was her curse.

As if he knew that it was unbearable for Sal and Guy to hear his sleeping groans, Tom no longer groaned in the night. When Guy returned home from the mill, Tom at first made feeble protests when his son took over more and more of the farm chores. The two who loved him never remarked on the fact that he was growing weaker every day, that it was now an effort for him to speak too much, and he ate almost nothing. They knew his suffering, but he did not speak of it or betray it in any manner. Tom sat by the stove, and he did not object when Sal put a blanket over his knees. He read his books, commented on them to Guy, and listened to the radio. His remarks were as sharp as ever, his smile always ready, his quips keener. And he died a little more each day, and his eyes grew larger if dimmer. He had finally stopped smoking. He just put away his pipe and never lit it again.

Guy and Sal did not pretend that everything was normal. But they did their work as usual, sometimes commenting on the stock to each other and Tom. They did not give the air of waiting for the dread inevitable. They did not talk in subdued voices. They did not ask Tom how he felt each morning, for which he was grateful. When Sal cried it was when she went with Guy to feed the stock and gather the eggs, but her face was resolute and calm when she returned with him. Sometimes, in the dark warm barn she would throw herself into Guy's arms and he would silently hold

175

her until she wiped her eyes. But they did not talk of what was impending. They did not, in the house, assist Tom to walk when he faltered and caught the back of a chair or the edge of a table. Again, he was grateful.

They watched him die and knew that this was worse even than death. They knew now what he had spared them. He was no longer able to walk outside, but he often stood at the window looking out at the cold and silent land. One day he said, "It's February. In a month it will be spring again. I'd like to see the spring once more." Then he turned to Sal and Guy and smiled.

One late-February morning he could not get up, even with the assistance of Sal and Guy. He lay back on the plump goose-feather pillows which Sal had made and looked up at his love and his son. He tried to speak. It was too much effort and he suddenly fell asleep again. His body scarcely lifted the warm blankets. It was almost flat. He slept through the day, never stirring.

The crescent moon burned like a wire of white flame in the black sky when he awoke. He saw Guy sitting near him, his hands clasped on his knees, his head bent. Now he could speak. He said, "Son, I think this is it." His voice was only a hoarse whisper. He said, "Call Sal."

Guy returned with Sal, and they stood beside him, holding his cold hands. He looked at them and all his spirit stood in his darkening eyes. He looked until he could not see them any longer and all was a swirling mist about him.

Guy bent over him. Tom was whispering very faintly. "Holy Mary, Mother of God, pray for us sinners now and at the hour of our death—"

Only Guy heard him, and could not understand. He had never heard the words before. What did they mean?

Then Tom uttered a single gasp, and his body moved in a long shudder. His eyes stared open, his mouth gently smiled. And so he died.

It was Sal who closed those dead eyes and kissed those icy lips. Guy could only stand and gaze down at his father, unmoving, the kerosene lamp flickering on the table. There was the silence of death in the room. Guy did not know that Sal had left the room and then had returned. She was putting something in his hand. He looked dumbly and slowly down at it. It was a rosary. He recognized that, at least, for he had seen some of the men at the mill with such an article.

Sal said, "I found this the other day, when I was sorting out his nightshirts. It's a rosary. The Catholics use them, to pray with. I never saw your father use it." Her voice was still and emotionless.

"He had once been a Catholic, I think. I heard my mother say so." Guy spoke quite normally. He knew the pain would come, but as of now it was absent.

He did not know what to do with the rosary. Sal took it from him and lovingly twined it in the yellow twigs which were Tom's fingers. She bent and kissed him again. Then very simply, she said to Guy, "He isn't dead, really. He is still alive." She went down on her knees, clasped her hands, and prayed in silence. Guy left the room. The coffeepot was bubbling on the stove. The wood hissed and rustled in its iron enclosure.

Sal came into the kitchen. There were no tears now on her wounded face. She said, "Dinner's ready. He wouldn't want us to waste it. He would be glad for us to know he isn't suffering any longer."

"He isn't anywhere," said Guy, and he put his head down on the table and began to cry.

As Tom had willed, there was no funeral service. He was cremated the next morning, as he would have wished, and the only mourners were his son and Sal. Guy intended to notify his mother that night, if he could bring himself to do so. It was necessary, however. She was Tom's widow, and one of his heirs.

Tom was enclosed in a plain wooden coffin, as he had directed. There were no flowers, for he would not have wanted the living to be burned with him. There was a narrow sloping ramp down to shut iron doors, which would open to admit the dead man to its hidden fires.

The coffin began to move down the ramp. The doors silently opened. For one instant Guy did catch a glimpse of far flame. He gave a great cry. He leaned down the ramp to seize the coffin but it slid from under his fingers, faster and faster.

Fire. Fire would consume the body which had begotten him. Fire would take his father from him forever. Fire. His father had once said, "Fire creates life, and fire takes it, and it is one and the same."

When James left Guy's suite he encountered Hugh Lippincott just outside the door. He looked beyond Hugh with dismay. "Is the family with you?" he asked.

Hugh smiled broadly. "Yes, Bill's parking the car, and Lucy and Marcy have taken the kids off first to dehydrate them for an hour or two. Glad I have no children. It will make it easier— Never mind, please. Why? You look sour, Dr. Meyer."

"I've just left Jerry. He spoke once, and said, 'Oh, my God,' and came wildly out of his apathy. He is now crying, and motioned for me to leave. I'm afraid if he sees his family it might set him back. Just my uninformed opinion." His distress was eloquent. "Unless, of course, he is extremely fond of them all." He looked doubtful. "Mrs. Jerald told me Jerry's daughter was his favorite."

"Hah," said Hugh. "It's my suspicion that Jerry, as you call him, never had a deep paternal interest in his children. At least that's Lucy's opinion. She wanted her husband to be a second nursing mother to her brats, 'devoting his time,' as she called it, to the Precious Ones when they were crawlers and toddlers and brawlers. It wasn't enough that he was working at least fifteen hours a day for the holy family—how Lucy loves money and wants more and more!—but he must give the rest of his waking hours to the Children. That's the American fetish now, a driven father must not have a life of his own. It belongs to the Family. We aren't men in America any longer, Doctor. We are just money earners and then playmates, or nannies, as you call them in England."
178

James smiled. "Well, that's your damned fault, Mr. Lippincott. But the infection is now in England, too. We used to send our men-children away from Mummy when they were five years old, and our girls when they were eight. But alas, that has now changed for the vast masses of the people. Yes. Well. I don't think Jerry should see his family for a bit."

Hugh said, "It's Lucy's delusion that Marcy was her father's favorite. He would regard both his children without relish, I observed for myself, even when they were youngsters. He did set his son an example of manliness, but Lucy managed to circumvent that, too. She was always undermining Guy with her offspring. He wasn't a self-immolating father all the time. I think he did try, sporadically, to influence them, but there was Lucy, undercutting him and 'defending' them or something. Typical. So you think Guy should be protected from the fond embraces of his family today?"

"I do, indeed. I will leave you to manage that, Mr. Lippincott. He is making progress. He should not be disturbed."

"Frankly, I think they'll be relieved not to see him." Hugh's smile was wry. "I'll manage it some way, for poor Guy. Up to about five or so years ago he was quite a man, and when he could escape his family for Philadelphia or New York he never inhibited himself. It was his only relief. I often went with him. Then about five years ago he changed. I suspect some damned woman has got him in her clutches."

James thought of Miss or Mrs. Turner, of the coppery hair and delicate but womanly features and wine-warm eyes and the character that shone so strongly from her countenance. But he did not mention her to Hugh. Hugh said, "He was more or less always a gloomy cuss, except when he got out of Cranston."

"He wasn't gloomy in the Army," said James. "A wild one, at times. But then, we were young."

"Wild, eh? I can't remember him being that way, and I've known him for over twenty-five years. Always the

179

dutiful one. His mother died about ten years ago. I had the feeling he wasn't exactly devoted to her, either, but he did his duty, he confided in me once, and he said it as if it was a dirty word. I never knew or saw her, but I did hear she had been a hard-working woman in her time. Guy set her up quite luxuriously in later years, though. He was a great one for doing 'what was right,' as he called it."

"Alas," James said, and smiled. "There is quite a difference between doing one's duty, and hating it, and doing what one must, out of conviction." He thought of his father. "I never heard my father speak of 'duty.' He spoke always of heroism. That's another story, a terrible one but in a way inspiring. Well, Mr. Lippincott, I am leaving it to you to protect Jerry from his family today."

"I hear you are staying at the Old House," said Hugh. "My wife—she is visiting her own family in Philadelphia just now. Let's have a drink together, and dinner, later, if you'd like that."

"I would, indeed," James said, and was surprised to discover that he meant it and was pleased. Sunday was always a lonely day for him except when he was with Emma. He reflected that Hugh was not the exigent man—entirely—that he had at first suspected. Well, he was exigent, but he was also a man of honor, a rare thing these days.

10

The next day, at breakfast, James told Emil Grassner of Guy's sudden eruption into near violence the day before. "Good!" said Emil, smiling with approval.

"I wish I knew what it was I had said," James remarked. "It was something about fire, I think. Was he ever involved with a fire that you know of?"

"No. I don't think so. Fire. It may have been free association." He added, "I am staying in Cranston only two
180

or three days this time; my patients in Philadelphia, you know. But Charlie Witherspoon will be on hand if you need him. You may, at that, with doddering Parkinson and Guy's family. You've accomplished more in these few days than we've been able to do in months. You're good for him, James." He studied the other man. "You don't look so vibrant yourself. Something wrong?"

James tried to laugh. "As I told you before, I think I've caught Jerry's 'disease,' whatever it is. But whoever heard of a spiritual virus?"

"Oh, it's common." The two psychiatrists, this time, entered Guy's suite together. Emil noticed that Guy appeared very agitated and that he looked at the two men with a kind of fearful despair before he subsided again into his usual apathy. Emil said to him, "Fight it out, old man, fight it out. We're with you all the way."

"Let me alone," said Guy, and these were the first words, since the one, "death," which Emil had heard in the beginning, that Guy had uttered to him.

"That's exactly what we are doing," said Emil. "We are letting you alone to come to your own conclusions. That's all we can help you to do." But Guy turned away his head, and hid his ravaged face. Emil nodded at James, and left.

James at down and looked with distaste at the fraudulent fire. He said, "I've met your family, Jerry." No response from the huddled man. "I've met your brother-in-law. For a banker he is quite an honest man."

There was no response, except James saw that Guy had clenched the flaccid hand which lay on his knee. "I suppose it isn't impossible for a banker to be honest and straightforward."

"All bankers are thieves!" Mary Jerald cried to her son two weeks after Tom had died.

"But you put your own money in the bank," said Guy. He had aged; his dark face was sallow and his eyes were puffed in heavy shadows. He appeared exhausted and

181

hardly present as he sat in the kitchen of his mother's house.

"Well, I can't keep the money in the house," said Mary. "There're thieves outside here, too." She looked at her son, turning from the stove to survey him with less than affection. "I don't know what I've done to deserve all this. And you are as bad as your father, Guy, in spite of all my work and all I've taught you. You say I can't get that fifteen-thousand-dollar insurance policy your pa left that filthy hussy, but I can't see why. It's really my money; when I talked to the bank they told me I couldn't, and so did you. It's not right! And you letting her live there on my property until she finds another place, as you call it. She will, you can be sure of that. And you staying there with her, too. Shameful. I don't know, sometimes, where I'll hide my face. And all he left me was two thousand dollars! Is that right? Maybe I should see a lawyer about that insurance policy."

"I've told you, it won't do any good," said Guy.

"And I can't forgive you for not letting me know he was dead, until after the funeral. If you can call that a funeral. Heathenish. No minister, no flowers, no mourners except you and that dirty woman. Was that right?"

"Would you have gone to his cremation, Ma?"

"I wouldn't have let him be cremated! And I thought you loved him. Such love, letting your father be burned!"

"He told me it was what he wanted. Besides, it is in his will."

"Wills! Foolishness, if they're written by a sick man."

"He wasn't sick when he wrote it, two years ago. So don't get some stupid idea, Ma. I am asking you again: Would you have gone to his funeral?"

Mary glared at him. "Yes! I would have kept that woman away! I would have ordered her out, as you ought to have done!"

Guy nodded. "That was what Pa was afraid of, and that's why he didn't want you to know he was dying, or me to tell you when he was dead, until after his funeral.
182

Ma, you refuse to understand. Pa loved Sal. She loved him."

Mary's eyes became fierce with rage. "You call that love, that—that lustfulness? Cohabiting with a woman not his wife? 'Thou shalt not commit adultery.' It's one of the Ten Commandments. Adultery!"

Guy spoke out of his anger and pain. "Ma, it wasn't adultery. They loved each other. You and Pa never loved each other, and so your living together was the real adultery, the spiritual one."

"I never lived with him after you were born!" Mary's thin dark face flushed with embarrassment.

Guy nodded again. "Yes, he told me."

Mary was aghast. "He talked such lewdness to you, you, his son?"

"Ma, Pa was the most moral man I've ever known. The most decent—" His voice broke. He looked at the dreary February weather outside the window. Iron and snow. The window blurred in front of his eyes. At least his father wasn't under all that. He, Guy, had scattered his ashes as he had wished, with Sal beside him one dark night, and Sal had whispered, "God bless you, dear Tommy. I'll never forget you, never. No matter where I go, I'll think of you always, and pray for you." She had not cried. She had shed not one tear since Tom's death. Her grief was too deep for tears. She had said, while walking with Guy as he slowly scattered the ashes over Tom's own land, "He read me a poem once. I don't remember what it was, but it was something about 'he is not dead, he sleeps.' I think that way of Tommy, I really do. Sometimes I think he comes awake to see us. I often turn real fast, thinking he's right behind me, smiling that way he had."

"Lewdness!" Mary cried again. "And only that two thousand dollars, even though I never knew he had that much. We've got to sell our land, that farm. It ought to bring about eighteen hundred dollars, things getting higher as they are. We'll divide that between us."

Guy said, out of his listless sorrow, "It's my land now, Ma. Not yours, not one inch of it. Pa left it to me."

"Half is rightfully mine, Guy Jerald, and you know it! I was his wife. It's only right I get my share."

"You left him many years ago, Ma. And again, you were never really his wife. You've talked to the bank, I know, about that farm, and no doubt they told you the land was mine, it was in Pa's will."

"You're going to rob me of my share?" Mary struck the iron stove with her spoon.

"You got your rightful share—two thousand dollars. I'm not robbing you of a thing. If Pa had wanted to, seeing you had left him, he need not have left you a cent."

"You're wrong! I read about wills in the paper last week. The faithful spouse gets her rightful share of her husband's property, even if—even if she had left him because she couldn't stand the life he made her live. And he wasn't faithful to me, with that disgusting woman. Adultery!"

"You do love that word, don't you, Ma?" Guy stood up. The heavy oppression in his chest never fully lifted day or night. Only when he sat with Sal in her warm steamy kitchen, and talked of his father, did the pain lighten. She would tell him antic things Tom had said in the past, and the antic things he would do, and they would smile together, as she had planned.

"Why are you letting that wicked woman live on our farm?" demanded Mary. "It's a disgrace. People will think—will think—" She flushed again.

"I don't give a damn what people will think, Ma. Sal's got a home there as long as she wants it." He now lived permanently on the farm. He added, and with a furious desire to hurt his mother, "Sal was really Pa's wife, in every way. She and I—we helped him through his illness. You weren't there. You wouldn't have come. Sal, it was, who washed him when he had no strength left to do it himself. Sal washed him when he was dead. We comfort each other."

Mary's eyes squinted at him with malevolent black fire. "How?" she asked.

"How what?"

"How do you comfort each other, as you say?"

Guy looked at her for a long and somehow awful moment. Then he said, "I've met people with dirty evil minds before, Ma, but you are the worst. I don't need Sal. I have a pretty little chippie in a whorehouse, where I go every Saturday night. I pay her five dollars. And she's a more moral woman than you are, Ma."

Mary screeched shrilly, but Guy left her. He could hear her hard sobs and reproaches all the way out to his car. He detested himself for what he had said to his mother, but he found himself laughing for the first time since his father had died.

He had not told Mary that he had received a letter from his bank, courteously asking him to call "at his leisure, but as soon as possible, on a matter of great importance." He wondered what the bank wanted, and thought it sounded ominous. His mother would not halt at anything to get her "share." He went to the bank the next day, in the afternoon. He was now a foreman in the mill and so had a few privileges. "I bet they're up to some mischief," he told Sal, as he washed, and then changed his clothes. "Let's see: The name is Daumbler, vice-president."

"Your pa didn't owe a cent to anybody," said Sal. "What can they do to you?" But she was afraid of all authority, and she chewed her lip. He patted her shoulder. "You'll soon know, tonight, Sal."

Mr. Eric Daumbler, first vice-president of the Cranston First National Bank, received Guy courteously. He was a brisk and very sleek young man with a crew cut of sandy hair, and shrewd gray eyes, and very well dressed. Guy, in his best suit, which had been pressed by Sal, felt like an uncouth farmer. His shoes had mud about the soles. Mr. Daumbler led him into a small but very pleasant office and closed the door portentously. He sat down and surveyed Guy in a most agreeble way.

"Mr. Jerald, you recently inherited nine hundred acres of land near the city. Is that correct?"

Guy answered with caution, "Correct."

Mr. Daumbler opened a box of polished silver, and offered Guy a cigarette, which he accepted. Mr. Daumbler flicked on a silver lighter and smiled genially. His dry fair face moved into folds. Guy's caution grew.

"Mr. Jerald, we have a—client—who is prepared to offer you four thousand dollars for that land. We know it's pretty barren and the most your father ever earned on it was six hundred dollars or so a year." He paused.

"More than that," said Guy. "Enough to pay taxes, which were five hundred a year, and to feed the stock, on which my father made some money, too, and to live himself."

Mr. Daumbler nodded. "Sorry. We just took a cursory survey. Now, that land isn't really worth four thousand dollars, Mr. Jerald, but our client has made the offer and we don't know why. Very generous, isn't it, considering the original price was only nine hundred dollars?"

"You don't know why he wants my land?"

Mr. Daumbler shrugged. "Oh, we have an idea he wants it as a sort of plaything, perhaps to raise horses." The young man smiled indulgently. "You know how men with money are. Besides, it would be a sort of tax shelter."

Four thousand dollars. That was a lot of money. But something quickened in Guy. Even rich men do not throw money away on worthless land, no matter how eccentric they are. He suddenly remembered something Tom had said to him three years ago. "A man buys land, he doesn't sell it. But do what you want with it, son. The city's expanding; this land is going to be very valuable someday, for houses and such."

Guy said, "I haven't really thought of selling that property."

Mr. Daumbler's smile became fixed. "You are planning to live on it yourself, Mr. Jerald?"

"I'm already living on it."

The sandy eyebrows lifted. Why, the little bastard, thought Guy with cold amusement. He knows all about me. Something's in the wind.

Mr. Daumbler tapped his very white large teeth with the end of a pen.

"I don't think my client will go higher than four thousand dollars, Mr. Jerald. Even that is too much. But I might try to persuade him to offer you five hundred dollars more."

Guy said, "If it's worth that much to him, it's worth more to me."

Again, that elaborate shrug. "Suppose you think about it, Mr. Jerald. But we'd like to know as soon as possible."

Guy smiled. "What is the hurry?"

"He has other properties in mind. I'm really afraid we'll have to know in the next day or two."

"There's no other farm for sale in my vicinity, Mr. Daumbler."

"There is plenty of land on the other side of the city, Mr. Jerald."

Guy made himself look bored. "Then, let him buy some there."

The bland façade had not changed, but the gray eyes had become shrewd and thoughtful on Jerald. "Then your answer is a definite no?"

"I didn't say that. I said I would think about it." He could not help smiling again. "I might consider fifteen thousand," he said, and stood up. Mr. Daumbler stared up at him. Guy added, "What's his name?"

"That's impossible, Mr. Jerald. It really isn't worth—" He stopped. "I can't tell you his name. This is a confidential matter."

"Why doesn't he deal with me direct? Why all this mystery?"

"We never question our client's motives, sir. We are only the negotiating party. Our client is a valuable one. If he wants to indulge a whim we can only advise him."

"And you told him you could get my land for him for four thousand dollars. What's the bank's interest?"

Mr. Daumbler actually colored. "None, Mr. Jerald. We are only doing this for a good client."

"Now, that's damn kind of you. When did a bank ever do a favor for a client that they didn't get their cut? And banks don't encourage valuable clients to buy worthless land. Now, do they?"

"I don't think you quite understand, Mr. Jerald." Mr. Daumbler thought with dismay of Mr. William Lippincott, the president of the bank, and the owner in fact, to whose daughter, Lucy, he was engaged. Mr. Lippincott would not like this debacle in the least.

"I may not understand all the details, Mr. Daumbler," said Guy. "But do you know something? You interest me."

Mr. Daumbler became brighter. "Thank you," he said. "But please let us know very soon. Very soon. I can't promise you that our client won't withdraw his offer, if you take too long to accept."

"Then I'll cry about that later," said Guy. He went toward the door, and then there was a knock on it and it opened and a young woman stood there, her face showing a very pretty smile. She was tall and blond and she wore a white mink coat and a white mink hat to match. Guy stopped. He felt dazed and shaken.

Marlene, he thought. Yes, it surely was Marlene, grown a little older, but with the same large blue eyes, the same pale hair, the same gilt lashes and brows, the same vulnerable expression, the same delicately tinted cheeks and soft little chin, and the same pink lips. She began: "Eric, I came to see Daddy, and he's busy, so I thought I'd come in to see you—" It was not exactly Marlene's voice, but it was gentle and soft with an echo of a dead girl's voice.

Her voice faltered away, for she saw a strange tall young man before her who was staring at her with a fixed intensity, a man with a dark and aquiline face, black eyes and black hair, a man in a cheap suit and a cheap black overcoat, and hatless. He was not a handsome man, she thought vaguely, and was probably some nondescript moneyless person who was seeking a loan. But Eric did not usually interview such himself. Mr. Daumbler, rising with well-tailored agility, moved to her side. He said, "Miss Lippincott, Mr.—er—"

"Jerald," said Guy.

"Sorry," said Mr. Daumbler. "Lucy, Mr. Jerald is one of our depositors."

So you know that, too, do you? thought Guy. And you probably know I've got five thousand dollars saved in your bank, Mr.—er—

The girl extended a gloved hand. Guy took it. It was warm through the leather. It was warm as Marlene's hand had been warm, though larger. "How nice to know you," she said. She withdrew her hand and gleamed at Mr. Daumbler. "Busy, dear?"

"Not really, Lucy. Well, Mr.—Jerald—you will let us know very soon, won't you?"

Guy was still dazed. He felt sick with longing for Marlene. I never forgot her, he thought, my little love. "I will think about it," he muttered.

The cold February sun had come out and it splintered whitely against Guy's eyes, but he sat for a long time in his car thinking of the girl he had just met. He knew, from her name, that she was a daughter of the president of the bank. But—she was really Marlene, resurrected. He could feel Marlene in his arms, could feel her maiden's kisses, could see the trust in her shy eyes. He confused Lucy's blankness with that innocence and trust. He was too shaken for a time to drive away. He began to sweat with the ardent memories which came rushing in on him, the brief but poignant memories, the memories of young vows of devotion, of promise, of hope, of love.

Then he was outraged, wildly, savagely, jealous. She had called that manicured vice-president "dear." She had called him by his first name. The dampness on Guy's face became cold drops which ran down his temples. He beat his fists on the steering wheel. "Marlene," he said, aloud, and then louder, "Marlene!" His outrage choked him. He would not lose Marlene again! She belonged to him; he would have her this time.

He drove home, and when Sal saw his face she said, with fear, "What's wrong? Is there something wrong, Jerry?"

"No," he said, and he threw his coat on the hook in the kitchen. He said, abruptly, "The bank offered me four thousand five hundred dollars for this farm."

"Oh," she said, with relief. Then she sat down and looked at him thoughtfully, rubbing her rosy cheek.

"What do you mean, 'Oh'?" said Guy, with great annoyance. "Don't you think that is a lot?" He was exasperated with Sal, but knew this was ridiculous. His eyes were still filled with the face of the girl he had just met.

"Who wants to buy the farm?" asked Sal.

"The banker wouldn't tell me. What does it matter?"

But Sal said in a peculiar voice, "I wish I knew. The name, I mean. You see, there was something in today's paper. Something about a Pittsburgh builder buying property around here, farms and suburban property. To build houses on. A big important builder. I wish I could remember his name. Here, wait. I think I still have the paper near the stove."

She jumped up like a girl and began to rummage feverishly in the pile of papers which was kept to light the stove when the fire went out. "Here it is!" she cried. "And here's what it says here: 'The Chandler Development Company of Pittsburgh is considering expanding its operations on a wide scale around Cranston! Mr. Howard Chandler is responsible for the famous housing development near Pittsburgh, where the slogan is "The coffeepot never stops bubbling in Chandlertown," where homes can be bought for as little as three thousand dollars down, on an eighteen-thousand-dollar house. Mr. Chandler builds homes well within the range of what he calls the neglected majority's income, small well-built homes on curving drives, mass-produced but comfortable and solid, with garden plots and a recreation center for children and adults.' Why, there!" said Sal, with eagerness, looking up at the bemused young man near her. "I bet he wants to
190

buy your farm! It's the biggest piece of property outside Cranston!" She rushed to her feet and hugged Guy with glee.

"And he wants to buy it for four thousand dollars," said Guy, and he thought of Lucy Lippincott.

"I think," said Sal, who was no fool, "that it's worth much more than that."

"I've got to think," said Guy. "Good God, I've got to think."

But he was becoming more dazed every moment. He could hear his heart battering against his ears. The arteries throbbed in his neck. "I've got to think," he said again. He thought of Marlene and such an excitement seized him that he almost choked, and his breath held in his throat.

He said to Sal, "Does it say there that he's already bought land around here?"

Sal held the paper to the lamp she had just lit. "It just says he has bought 'considerable promising development property in this vicinity.' "

"I must think," said Guy.

Two nights later Sal had more interesting news for Guy. The farm of the Geigers, adjacent to Guy's north meadow, was owned by old Otto Geiger's widow, who was childless. She was a woman nearly eighty years old, and infirm, and farm help, in these roaring days, was almost impossible to obtain. Most men were now in the "plants," for had not Washington soothingly informed an alarmed citizenry— who were working in war factories—that they were not to be worried by the end of the war some four years ago, for there would "always be brushfire wars," especially in the Far East, "to keep everybody busy indefinitely." ("Let us all be thankful for a benign government who will invent wars for prosperity," Tom had said when Mr. Truman's office had appeasingly informed the nation that wars would continue.)

So Mrs. Geiger, left almost completely alone except for the random help of a kind neighbor—occasionally—

barely subsisted on the eggs and poultry she could raise within the limits of her strength. She had had to sell her cattle and other stock. It was Sal who weekly came to her aid with a loaf or two of fresh bread, butter, a duck or a goose, a new blanket or a fresh gingham dress or a sweater, gentle charity which was held in contempt by the other and far more solvent neighbors. ("Always trying to buy her way into God's good graces," one mean-spirited farmer said, who gave only to his evangelical church, and had made more than one overture to Sal and had had his chops soundly smacked in consequence.)

Sal had gone to see the old lady with a basket of apples, onions, bacon, butter, and some of her canned goods two days after Guy's interview with Mr. Daumbler. Mrs. Geiger was trembling with elation. "I've sold the farm!" she cried in glee to Sal, as she embraced her. "It never was much good, Sal, as you know, and it ain't but ninety acres anyways, and I've sold it for two thousand dollars —two thousand dollars!"

Sal came alert at once. It was true the farm was small but it had been quite productive in old Otto's lifetime, and the soil was rich and fertile, unlike Tom's farm. "Now, that's grand," said Sal, who did not think so. "Two thousand dollars. What are you going to do with that money?"

"Well, I got a nice niece in Cincinnati, and she's been asking me for a long time to go stay with her, even when I didn't have any money."

"The Warners bought it?" The Warners owned the next, and rich, farm.

"No, some nice man from Pittsburgh. Said he'd like a little farm for his kids on weekends and in the summer."

"Hum," said Sal. She added, "Did you take the money?"

"Yes, and I sent it to the bank and now I have two thousand five hundred dollars. God's been good to me, Sal."

Sal did not say, "You should have kept it for a while." She did not say, "I don't know about God, Mrs. Geiger, but I think you got cheated, as good people usually do, with or without God." She drank some tea which Mrs.
192

Geiger brewed for her, and her manner was absent yet quietly excited. She, too, was thinking.

"Remember the man's name who bought the farm?"

"Yes. He had a check, when I signed the papers. Mr. Prentice. Mr. John Prentice. From Pittsburgh." Sal carefully recorded the name. She got into Tom's old car, which still adequately performed if carefully coaxed, and she drove onto the dirt road, a mere two-wheel track, home to the Jerald farm. The Geiger farm was landbound, and had no other access to the macadam road that ran before Tom's farmhouse except that track. Tom had good-naturedly permitted the Geigers to use the track even when it bisected his own property, for which old Otto had never expressed any gratitude, though without the use of the track the Geiger farm would have been totally isolated.

Sal thought rapidly and concisely on the way home. She could scarcely keep herself from calling Guy at the sawmill at once. When he did arrive, five minutes late— it had begun to snow again, a cold sleety snow—she flew at him, crying, "Oh, God, Jerry, I thought I'd go out of my mind waiting for you all day, and here you are late!"

"Calm down, old girl," said Guy. "What's wrong now?"

Sal was so excited that she fell into exasperation. "You never ask, 'Any good news?' Jerry. It's always 'What's wrong now?' as if the whole world's against you and there's nothing good in it."

"Well, that's my opinion, at any rate," he said. He rarely smiled now, but he smiled at the sight of Sal's fat red cheeks and jumping dark eyes. "Don't tell me we have something good coming up—at last."

"You and Tommy all those years, and he was the best thing that ever happened to you, and maybe he'll always be the best. Well, hang up your coat and I'll tell you. I'm bursting."

"So you seem," said Guy. It was still utterly incredible to him that his father was not present in the old armchair, with his pipe and his books. He still could not believe that Tom was no longer in this world. Sometimes he was so incredulous that he would say aloud, even when alone, "Pa? Pa? Where are you, Pa?" And he would find himself listening for Tom's answer. While Sal would lay out the dinner he would wander into Tom's bedroom, more than half expecting to see his father there, or in the little dark sitting room with all the books on random shelves or on the floor. Small though the farmhouse was, it seemed enormous and empty and desolate without Tom's presence. Sal would make no comment on Guy's sorrowful wanderings, his peering into corners, his air of waiting, listening. She understood. She never let Guy see her own grief, her own loneliness, her own despondency, her own waiting, and expecting, her own longing for a voice she would never hear again. Her bright and antic joy had vanished and she was not reconciled.

"Well," said Guy, as he sat down in his father's chair and drank some of the cold beer Sal had poured for him. "What happy news do you have?"

"You know that offer you got from the bank, Jerry?"

"I've never forgotten it. I still can't figure it all out, though I've had a small idea since you showed me the paper about the Chandler Development Company. I haven't given the bank my answer. I'm waiting."

Sal stood before him, her hands clasped tightly over her round belly, her eyes sparkling, and she told him of her visit to Mrs. Geiger's farm. Guy listened; he forgot to drink his beer; the cigarette smoked away in his fingers. "Your nine hundred acres, Jerry, and right on the road! And Mr. Prentice has no way to reach the road 'cept down that dirt track that's all mud in the winter, and ruts in the summer, and belongs to you anyways. If Mr. Prentice is the company man, he knows that, too. That Geiger land ain't no good to them without yours."

"Yes. Yes," said Guy, and his heart was jumping as fast as Sal's fervid eyes. He stood up. He walked about the kitchen distractedly. He stared through the windows; he snapped his fingers. He lit another cigarette and stared at the wooden wall, where Sal's pots and pans hung. The kerosene lamp made a warm yellow splash about the old

194

kitchen; a kettle of corned beef and cabbage simmered on the stove. The late-February night had come, sulky and rebellious that the world was inclining to spring.

"But they haven't called me," he said.

"Why, sure not. They're waiting you out. Then they think you'll call them and they'll offer you less than what they did."

Guy had always known Sal was shrewd, but it always surprised him the way the sharp knife of her mind struck to the bone of any subject.

"Still, it's only three days."

"They'll get after you, Jerry, sooner or later. You'll see."

"Pretty clever fellas, having the bank talk to me, and having that John Prentice get after old Mrs. Geiger. Never showing the real hand. I can be as clever. I can wait better than Mrs. Geiger could. Now, why the hell wasn't I smart enough to buy her land myself?"

Sal laughed. "Because you didn't have a crystal ball, Jerry. And no one read your palm. Jerry, that's how some men get very rich. They never let their—well, their faces be seen if they want something. They get somebody else to do it for them, somebody—somebody—"

"Anonymous," said Guy. He was both amused and vexed. "And they thought I was a lumpen proletarian farmer. An ignorant foreman in a sawmill. I began to suspect something that day in the bank, but what it was, I hadn't the faintest idea. I just knew there was something."

Sal admired him with her eyes and her smile. "Tommy always said you were a real smart kid, Jerry, and I knew that, too. You get hunches. Tommy called them—now what did he call them?"

"A mixture of common sense, extrasensory perception, and intuition." His own elation was increasing. But when would they move? His younger wildness and impatience roared back in him, making him sweat, making his muscles jerk. He had no time to waste. The telephone rang, and both he and Sal ran for the wall where it hung, and they collided, and then Sal stepped back, breathing hard. The telephone rarely rang in this house.

It was Mary Jerald. She hardly heard Guy's voice when she screamed, in hysterical joy, "You'll never guess, son, you'll never guess!" Her voice was torn and raucous with her emotion. "The most wonderful thing ever happened to us! You'll never guess."

A cool sweat broke out on Guy's forehead. "All right, Ma, tell me. I could use something wonderful."

"The bank—I took the rents to the bank today. And, you'll never guess. One of the managers, he comes up to me and asks me to walk with him to his desk, right near the cages. Such a nice old gentleman! And he asks me real nice how I was doing, and he asked if you were living out on that awful old farm—" She had to stop, for she was breathing too violently.

Guy waited. He glanced at Sal, who was standing near his elbow, trying to listen. They exchanged glances. Sal nodded with exultant delight. "All right, Ma, go on," said Guy. "A real nice old gent, wasn't he? What else did he say?"

"You'll never believe it, Guy! He offered—he really offered—three thousand dollars for that farm, that isn't worth anything! I bet you don't believe it!"

Guy smiled darkly. "Three thousand dollars, eh? Now, I call that very kind of him."

"I do, too!" Mary breathed with a rapture she had never known in her life before. "Get down there first thing in the morning, son, and get their check."

"The bank's check?"

"Who else's?"

"What do they want the farm for, Ma?"

"Oh, Guy, who cares? They want it; don't know why. You go down there tomorrow and get the check for us, for our farm."

When Guy did not answer, she said, with his own impatience, "Oh, I suppose you're just as surprised as I was, but I tell you it is true, Guy. Get down there when the bank opens before they change their mind and get the
196

check for our farm. Three thousand dollars! Half for you, half for me."

Then Guy said, "No, Ma."

The incredulous silence that followed sounded to Guy more dramatic than a thunderbolt. He could see his mother's protruding eyes, her flaring nostrils, her gaping mouth, and the way the tendons were standing out on her neck like dark ropes. He could see her clenched knuckles, her haggard staring expression. Then she screamed, "What did you say?"

"I said no, Ma. It is my farm, not yours. I'm not selling it to the bank or to anyone else, just now. It may surprise you to know that a couple of days ago I was offered over four thousand for my farm, my farm, not yours, by the bank."

Again that disbelieving silence, that dazed silence. Then Guy heard his mother's voice again, awestruck, trembling with reverence. "Over four thousand dollars." It was as if she were quoting from Holy Writ. "Over four thousand dollars! Guy, you are right to say no to that three thousand dollars. I didn't know. So go to the bank and get their check for—over four thousand dollars! Why, what were they thinking of to ask me to sell the farm for only three thousand? I think that's outrageous."

"Ma," said Guy, and with rare malice, "you know very well that the bank knows that you don't own that farm. I do. We've been over that before. I wonder why they got after you? Did they think you could influence me?"

"I don't know what you're talking about, Guy. This is fiddle-faddle. What's yours is mine—I'm your mother."

"Is yours mine, Ma?"

"When I die, yes. Maybe, unless I leave it to the missions." He could feel her struggling with her confusion, her disbelief. She was staggered. Then she said, "You go right down to the bank tomorrow and get that check, Guy Jerald. Wait. I'll be there, too. What time do you plan on reaching the bank?"

"When they offer me one hundred thousand dollars for

197

my farm—my farm—and I probably won't take it even then, Ma. Perhaps I'll ask for more."

But his mother cried, "It's my farm! I am your father's widow! As his widow, I'm entitled to his property, first above all."

"Tell that to Pa," said Guy. "It'll probably amuse him, even now."

He hung up, smiling with pleasure, and turned to Sal. But she was regarding him gravely, and was unsmiling. "Was it necessary to talk so cruel to your mother like that, Jerry?"

Guy stopped smiling and contemplated Sal and his hard black eyes began to soften. Here was a woman who had been maligned, insulted, slandered, by his mother, spoken of with contempt and loathing and disgust, ridiculed, called a whore, assigned a special place in hell for her "sins." Yet never once had Sal uttered a condemning or taunting or scornful word of Mary Jerald, though doubtless she knew all about her. Tom had never been reticent concerning his wife, but if not reticent, neither had he been harsh or bitter for all the life she had led him for several years. Guy took Sal by the arm, and tightened his hand when she tried to draw away.

"Sal," he said, "I've just realized my mother is a thoroughly bad woman. She never, probably, broke any of the Commandments willingly or knowingly, or by what Pa called a direct consent of the will. Except for the other Commandments, such as charity and kindness and mercy. She broke them all her life. I have never heard her speak gently and lovingly of anyone or to anyone. A bad woman." He smiled and shuddered elaborately.

"You're getting to be a tough man, Jerry," she said, and she sounded frightened. "Your father was never a tough man. He was the best person I ever knew."

"She made my father's life hell, and coming down to it, she made my life hell, too, Sal."

"Not deliberately."

"Sal," he said with impatience, "the subject of my mother interests me not at all. I have thinking to do."

198

She went back to the stove. Guy walked up and down the room very rapidly, forgetting that devoted woman, and his mind exploded with firecrackers and fireworks of plans, and his exultation made his breath short and fast. He said, "So, they are desperately trying to get this land."

He forgot everything but his exultation. He would be free. And there was Lucy Lippincott—Marlene. He did not think of his satiric father, who would have said, " 'Take what you want,' says God. 'But pay for it.' It's your life, kiddo. And remember that somewhat silly poem—how does it go?

"For a cap and bells our lives we pay,
    Bubbles we buy with a whole soul's tasking:
'Tis heaven alone that is given away,
'Tis only God may be had for the asking.

"Yes." Guy, of course, did not go to the bank the next morning. His mother waited for a long time, then went away, looking old and shriveled and starving, her hands, in the cheap black cotton goods, held in a grasping position, clutching each other, as if something sacred had been snatched from them, and for which she was mortally grieving and inconsolable.

"I think it was something I said about banks," James remarked to Emil at lunch. "But I can't be sure, you know. It could have been anything."

"Well, his father-in-law owned a bank in Cranston, or at least was the president of one or two," said Emil. "Perhaps he was thinking of William Lippincott. The bank was about to fail when Guy took it over, quite a while after he married Lippincott's daughter. That is what I was told. But what could have stirred Guy about his father-in-law, who was not an intellectual giant, I heard, or much of a banker, either?"

"Well, I do seem to be a sort of catalyst," said James.

199

PART TWO

The talent for money making is unpredictable.—Anon.

11

Out of the black and scarlet chaos of his mind Guy Jerald had a rational dream for the first time in months. It was hardly a dream. It was a memory and he did not suspect he was dreaming, for he was living it again in all its original vividness.

It was April 1949, and the long snows had almost left the land and a diffused pale smudge of sun dappled the gray-white cloud cover. The bawling winds of the past week or two had lessened to a cold and nimble breeze. Guy was not a young man to enjoy the association of those whose minds and conversation were limited, and so at this period he had taken his black lunch box to sit on a step of the mill to eat it there, alone. Too, his newly restless mind was seething with thoughts and plans and wild impatience. Four weeks had passed and no one had called or written him, except his mother. Only Sal's pleading had prevented him from approaching the bank again or inquiring concerning Mr. Prentice.

As he sat there, frowning and hardly tasting the good lunch Sal had prepared for him, he was aware of the endless grind of machinery behind him, the pungent and somehow nostalgic scent of sawdust and oil, the voices of men nearby. He looked at the river, gray and quickening as if with an eagerness to reach the sea, and the broken segments of ice it carried, sweating under the sun. He could see the barge waiting for the cut wood near the wharf and, beyond the river and the brown land, the rise of the burning sepia foothills slashed here and there by new green, and beyond the foothills the dusky mountains leaning over the shoulders of the hills. He chewed and thought and frowned, always conscious of the dull throb of grief in his mind, the empty room in which his father had lived. What the hell would you have done, Pa? he asked of that jaunty wraith.

He was startled by the clarity of the reply in the echoing cavern of his brain: "What, son, would I do? Well, if it was me I wouldn't do one damned thing. If they want in, they'll come for it. If they don't, they won't. Lie low, as Sal tells you." "For how long?" Guy asked the memory of his father. "Until you outwait them, kiddo. Now, what's that you're plotting?"

Guy already knew. It was merely a matter of adjusting the pattern. He knew the taste of iron resolution in his mouth. The hell with waiting. He would make his first tentative move in a day or two. He would ask Sam Kurtz, the head foreman, to permit him to take part of his vacation beginning tomorrow. As if he had been called, the head foreman himself came out of the mill and stood on the step on which Guy sat. He said, "Spring's almost here, and that was one goddamned winter, wasn't it?"

"Yes, it was," said Guy. He looked up at Sam Kurtz, a slight tall man of middle age, who had a face which was oddly both surly and kind, and tired and absent. His once brown hair had faded to a dun color on his long lean skull, and his small brown eyes had an expression of musing pain. He was, by nature, a taciturn man, a man so deft that he often appeared uninterested in his work yet could accomplish more than any of his men by a sort of force of spirit rather than muscle or physical drive. His shoulders were thin but broad and somewhat bent, his features lugubrious in repose. He never raised his voice yet he spoke with a quiet authority which few dared challenge. There were times when he gave the impression of profound weariness, but he had never been ill a day in his life and had worked in this mill since he had been fifteen years old. His hands were scoured with work; still, they had a look of repose at all times. A deep friendship had matured between the man of twenty-seven and the older man, and there was a paternal-filial relationship between them. They respected each other. Guy knew that Sam was more than merely a simple man; he was wise in a perspicacious if somewhat unlearned way. He was never loquacious, and his remarks and observations were

203

short and to the point. Careful of speech, he was capable of a sharp and oblique humor, which could be obscene but was never cruel. He hated sloth and dowdiness of character, meanness and slyness. Guy had often thought that his father would have appreciated Sam Kurtz, who was as sound as an acorn.

Sam sat down on the step beside Guy, whose lunch box was open. Guy remembered that Sam was a widower of a number of years and that he lived alone in a comfortable old house in Cranston not far from the house of Mary Jerald, though in a somewhat better neighborhood. He was, as Mary would have said of him, "saving." He saw no reason to sell his house and buy a more modern one. His car was old, but he also saw no reason to buy a newer one as long as the present one would run. He had Teutonic thrift and hatred for mendicancy.

He once said to Guy, "No man ever got himself in trouble by keeping both his mouth and his pants shut." Which, Guy would think, neatly summed up Sam Kurtz. He was assured and seasoned and had a curious air of strength.

Guy said, noticing that Sam was furtively inspecting the lunch box with his small brown eyes, "Have a sandwich and a piece of cake, Sam. Sal always gives me too much." In silence and with a nod of thanks, Sam picked up a liverwurst sandwich and helped himself to a piece of chocolate cake. "Sal still with you?" he asked. He had never met Sal but Guy had often spoken of her. Guy nodded. They ate together and looked at the river.

"I'd like a couple of days off, beginning tomorrow, Sam."

Sam licked the chocolate from a scarred finger. He ruminated. Then he said, "Pretty busy this time of the year."

"I know. I won't be away for long. Matter of business."

Sam studied him. "Guess it's important, hey?"

"Yes. To me. If I'm ever going to amount to anything I'd better start now."

204

"Don't think you want to spend the rest of your life in a mill?"

Guy hesitated. He knew that since the death of Sam's wife the mill had been his deepest focus, for he had no children. On holidays he often came to the mill and walked about it, sniffing. Guy said, "I have other plans."

"You young guys out of the war never want to stay put these days."

"Did you, when you were my age?"

Sam looked at the river and gave his rare reluctant smile. "Well, as they had a song when I was seventeen, eighteen, I'd seen Paree, in the first war. Got ideas, too. The world was bigger'n Cranston, where I come from, and the girls a damned sight more sprightly and prettier Over There. The hell with Cranston, I said to myself. I'd work back in the mill and save all I could and then I'd get the hell out."

"But you didn't."

Sam shrugged, scraped up the remnants of cake from the box. "Know what, Guy? I found out it don't matter where you live."

"You sound like my father." Guy concealed his impatience with a smile.

"Great old guy, from what you told me. Yes, sir, it don't matter where you live, what you do. World's pretty much the same everywhere, and people, too."

I've heard that stupid aphorism too many times, Guy thought. "Still, I'd like to see more of it, and I'd like more."

Sam nodded. "Me, I'm contented with my work and what I've saved. You're different, Guy. You always was, since you was a kid. You got to live your own life."

("It's your life, kiddo," Guy could hear his father say.)

"You never wanted to be rich, Sam?"

"Now, why the hell why? My mother had an old Dutch saying, 'How much land does a man need? Six feet by three.' She was right. I like my newspapers, and my radio, playing horseshoes on Sundays, beer, poker, a couple friends, a good sleep at night, my health, my money in the bank. But you're different, Guy."

I hope so, thought Guy, and he saw the face of Marlene and there was a wilder urge in him now. But he said, "How about my taking two or three days off?"

"You'll be docked," said Sam, as if this was a very serious matter and not to be shrugged away lightly.

"That's all right. I'll save my vacation for the summer, when the farm's busy."

"Ever thought of selling it and moving to town?"

"No," said Guy. At least not yet, he said to himself.

"Well, go ahead. Take your days off. I'll get along." He studied Guy shrewdly, and his eyes had a peculiar way of seeming to see more than the obvious. "Planning to get rich?"

"If I can."

"Well, good luck. Never hurt a man to be ambitious, I reckon."

In his own turn Guy studied the older man. He saw a lonely look in the other's eyes and saw the pain for the first time. He said, "How about coming home with me to the farm tonight and eating one of Sal's good dinners? We always have beer on hand, too, and we can play a little pinochle. Or poker."

Sam usually considered everything twice before he accepted a proposal. He said, with caution, "Sure it won't be any trouble? How'll Sal take it, bringing home someone she never met?"

"It won't be trouble, and Sal is a cheerful soul and it gets lonesome for her out there alone all the time. She'll be pleased."

"Well, better call her first." The whistle blew and the two men rose and went into the mill.

When Guy called the farm Sal was happy to hear the news of a visitor. "I know you like that Sam Kurtz, and I've got a fat duck ready for the oven, and the last of the apples."

When five o'clock came Sam said, "Better take my own car. I'll follow you. No use you hauling me back to town."
206

He paused. "Got to stop for a minute or two before we go to the farm. On Griener Street. St. Anthony's Church."

"Today? It's not Sunday."

Sam gave him a strange smile. "My church's open more'n Sundays."

For some shapeless reason Guy thought of his father.

They stopped before the church. It did not look prosperous, and was built of sifting brown stone and had a squat steeple with an unusually large cross upon it. It was shabby and aged. A few people were wandering in and out in the dusk of twilight. "Come on in," said Sam. "Won't hurt you."

They went in together. Guy was surprised at the warmth, the candles, the soft lights on the walls with their Stations of the Cross, the statues, the high altar at the rear with its extraordinarily beautiful crucifix, and the flowers before the altar. There was an aromatic odor in the air, both poignant and haunting. It was incense, for there had been a funeral in the morning, and the ghostly scent lingered. Guy stood in the aisle as Sam genuflected. Sam had produced a cheap rosary and he knelt in the pew and seemed to forget Guy, who watched him with curiosity. The distant candlelight and the muted lamplight hovered over his face, and Guy saw an expression of fervid devotion and suffering on his features. Guy was both embarrassed and touched. He knew that Sam had forgotten him. He did not know whether to sit down himself or remain standing. There were a few other men and women in the pews, all kneeling and praying. At a distance stood a rack of flickering candles in red glasses. It was all very alien to Guy.

He became aware of a peace in this poor place of poor people, a pervading peace that emanated from the walls, from the very worn carpet in the aisles, from the still faces in the pews, from the statues, from the altar. He looked at the crucifix with its great carved corpus. ("Catholics!" his mother had said once. "They worship idols.") The mysterious peace welled about Guy and he felt a pang of emotion. It was ancient; it was everlasting.

There seemed to be a Presence in this place, old beyond time, young as a first crocus, a Presence celebrating joy.

Sam was standing now beside Guy. He whispered, "I'm going to light a candle." He went down the aisle and Guy did not know why he followed, but he did. He saw Sam drop a coin in a slot and then light a candle, which flared up as crimson as blood in its glass. He touched Sam on the shoulder and mouthed, "For what?"

Sam looked down into the glass. It was a long moment before he answered. Then he whispered, "For the dead."

Guy felt a moment's incredulity. What nonsense was this? He felt compassion for Sam. Of course, the candle was for the memory of his wife, dead for several years. How long did the pain of sorrow last, then? Did it never end? Sam was nudging him, and again there was that peculiar insistence in his eyes. "Light one for your father," he said.

This was absurd. But Guy found a loose coin in his old mended coat, and after he had dropped it in a slot he picked up a large kitchen wooden match from its container and lit a candle. He had done all this out of regard for Sam. He could see his father's laughing face as the candle spurted into life. He could see that face so vividly that he was startled, for it was his father's face of his own youth. He was dazed for a moment. In those antic remembered eyes there was a softness as of sadness, and conjecture. The enormous sorrow of loss and yearning opened in Guy as the candle in the glass had opened into flame. He and the flame, for a second or two, were one, and a sense of hopelessness made him physically ill, and again it came to him with disbelief that his father was actually dead, was lost forever, his voice never to be heard again.

The two men left the church, but Guy walked unseeingly. The cold twilit air struck on his face and he shivered. A streetlamp showed his face.

"Look like you seen a ghost," said Sam, as they buttoned their coats.

Guy tried to smile. "Thought I did, for a minute. Was your candle for your wife?"

208

They stood on the steps of the church. At first Guy thought Sam had not heard him, for he was silent for several long moments. Then Sam said, "No. Not for my wife. For another woman. She died two months ago. Cancer."

They walked slowly back to their cars. Sam said, "She was married. A man blinded in the war. She couldn't leave him. Not even for me. I understood." He stopped speaking. "Only woman I ever gave a damn for." He stopped again. "First war, not yours. Finest woman I ever knew. I go to her grave every Sunday."

He had spoken stolidly, almost without expression, but his pain aged him in the lamplit dark.

Guy, out of his own pain, found himself saying, "And you think she survived death?"

Sam sighed. "I know damn well she did. No priest has to tell me. I know."

Superstition, thought Guy. But, if it comforts him, what the hell. The hopelessness remained with him all the way to the farm. Queer, thought Guy, as he drove in his cocoon of silence, I never fully realized until now that Pa had gone—out into nothingness, nothing at all. That's the very worst—I seemed to have had the idea all these weeks that Pa was somewhere, not far away. Now I know, finally, that I will never see him again. The very worst. The irrevocability of death struck him with a sudden horror, and he knew, at last, that the dead can never be replaced but always there will remain in the house of the bereaved an empty room.

The little farmhouse was warm and bright and every room was illuminated by a kerosene lamp, and there were fresh white curtains at the kitchen window and a gay red-and-white-checked cloth on the table, and the few precious sterling pieces had been polished by Sal. Sal herself looked festive in her Sunday frock of black with touches of white lace; her apron was white and stiff with starch. Everything about her glowed, as it had not done for weeks; her tumbling ringlets danced about her pink cheeks and she had added lipstick, and her voluptuous bosom was well defined against the fabric of her dress and her round neck was ornamented by a small string of pearls which Tom had given her. Her dark eyes were saucy and she beamed at Sam and shook his hand and said, "Glad to meet you. It's good to have a third person in the house again. Sit down, Mr. Kurtz. Beer or whiskey?" She exuded life and exuberance and great kindness, all of which was genuine. Sam was speechless, for he had few social graces and was always embarrassed in the presence of women. But as he and Guy sat near the stove and drank their beer Sam gave Sal quick furtive glances and the tenseness of his long body began to relax. The kitchen was filled with the splendid fragrance of roasting duck and dressing and applesauce and bread, with a vague touch of Sal's eau de cologne. The big kitchen window was a frame for the stark night with its polished moon and stars.

"I milked the cows, so you don't have to do it tonight, Jerry," Sal said, giving him an affectionate look. "After all, we got company."

"Born on a farm," Sam offered. "Dad sold it. Depression."

"This isn't much of a farm," said Guy, "as I've told you before, Sam. We've got a boy from one of the farms who helps with the chores, especially in the summer, but we don't raise much, only what we need for ourselves."

"Quiet. Good," said Sam. When Sal poured him more beer he blushed like a choirboy and said, "Thank you, ma'am," in a very formal tone. He looked at her breast, which almost touched his shoulder. He stretched out his feet. "Should have changed clothes," he muttered. Guy was amused, and watching. Sal's glow seemed to pervade the kitchen with gaiety. She, too, was scrutinizing Sam Kurtz and what she perceived seemed to please her. She almost danced about the stove. "Just a plain country meal," she said, and Guy was more amused, for he detected a whiff of Tom's brandy over the duck when Sal opened the oven door. Two lonely people, thought Guy, but who the devil isn't lonely? For the first time since
210

Tom's death there was a sense of completion in the house, and no echoing. Sal turned on the radio, so that there was a lilting harmony in the kitchen.

"Maybe we'll have television next year," said Sal, critically tasting the gravy she was making. "I saw one in a store in Cranston; everybody standing at the window watching it and staring. Little bitty box. But they say they'll be bigger next year, and it'll be like the movies."

Her voice had a young note in it which had been absent for months.

"Like movies myself," Sam said, sniffing the delectable odor in the kitchen. "Go three, four times a week."

"Your wife likes the movies?" asked Sal, delicately.

"Got no wife. Died long ago. Good woman," Sam added, as if there were an acrid taste in his mouth. "Done her duty, like she always said."

"Oh," said Sal, with sympathy, and Guy was even more amused. But Sam relaxed more and more. "Children?" asked Sal.

"No. Thank God," said Sam, with a vehemence Guy had never heard before. Sal laughed. "That's why I never got married," she said. "Never wanted kids, it's a waste of time."

Guy said, "There is an ancient Chinese saying, 'The world is full of loving parents but no loving children.'" Sal gave him a sharp look. "When kids finally realize, it's too late," she remarked.

"Most never realize," said Sam. "You got no money, children don't care about you. Got money, and they wish you was dead. No percentage."

"I bet you were a good son, though," said Guy. Sam glanced at him and the pain was in his eyes again.

"I tried. My mother was left with five kids, no money, when Dad died during the Depression. Ma worked at anything she could find to do. Broke her heart she couldn't keep us in school." He gave Sal a sudden stare. "Miz Sal, minds me she looked a lot like you. Never heard a mean word from her. Died of malnutrition, the doctor said. She

211

wouldn't take relief. But us kids—we didn't starve, though Ma did."

Guy had never heard Sam so loquacious before, and his interest grew.

Sal said, "Your mother had her pride, and when it comes down to the quick, pride's what makes a man different from an animal."

Sam drank his beer and Sal replenished his glass. Their eyes met. Sam sighed, content, and Sal's smile was tender and understanding.

The dinner was magnificent. Sal produced some hard cider. Sam actually expanded and once he even laughed, a hoarse uncertain laugh. Once more the house was full and filled with warm and single-hearted pleasure. Then, without warning, Guy was both impatient and restless and a great contempt came to him for these uncomplicated creatures, these meager people of ordinary appetites, who asked nothing of life but to survive as simply as possible and with artless delights. He studied Sal and Sam and a terrible depression came to him, a longing to get up and leave and never come back. He thought of Thoreau, whom his father had often quoted, and Walden Pond, and for the first time in his life he felt a slash of contempt for his father also.

Of what use to anyone, including himself, had Tom's life been, existing in poverty and bleakness with his books, without desire, without the power of striving, without the wish to excel at anything, without the urgent competition which distinguishes the extraordinary man from a mere human beast? Day-to-day living, staring "eyeless in Gaza," content with random animal pleasures and surfeits, grateful for a stroking, grateful just for the morning, grateful for warm bread and a bed—was that a life for a man? What had Samuel Butler said? "The majority of mankind licks the platter clean and leaves nothing but a pile of offal." Perhaps they had their uses, however. They left their "offal" to fertilize the fields of men who were completely men. A turmoil of aversion took Guy as he looked at Sal and Sam, and his derision and abhorrence for them was

212

like a tornado in his mind. His depression was not a passive thing now. It was a fury. He felt choked, and he sweated.

He heard Tom's voice in his mind: " 'The contemplation of truth and beauty is the proper object for which we were created, which calls forth the most intense desire of the soul, and of which it never tires.' William Hazlitt." All very well, thought Guy. But who has time to contemplate "truth and beauty" unless he has money? Once Mary Jerald had said, with unction, " 'A rich man's wealth is his strong city. Money is the answer to all things.' The Bible."

And damned if the Bible isn't right! thought Guy. Without money you are only the yoked oxen of that Bible. You have no time to live.

He looked at Sal and Sam, who were talking together in low voices over the littered table, and enjoying their coffee. And, he thought, God forgive me, I detest them and all their insignificance. His very soul rose up in rebellion against what they represented—the mindlessness of undemanding beings, the mindless acceptance of life, the lack of stern discipline directed towards a specific goal and excellence. If a man had any reason for existing at all it was to excel, to distinguish himself from the rabble, to mark himself apart, to be singular, to rid himself of the stench of mediocrity, to be more than a pig at the trough.

I have another quotation for you, Pa, thought Guy vengefully. I, too, can quote. Robert Louis Stevenson said, "An aim in life is the only fortune worth the finding." You never had an aim, Pa. You were merely a spectator at the parade. At least you were an intelligent spectator. The others are only the dust which is kicked up. Ma is wiser than you. She had an aim, if it was only a bank account and independence. Without direction, you are only a waterspout, finally subsiding in a river which was never disturbed by you to its depths.

Guy desired, with a savage desiring, to shake off those present as one shakes off fleas who suck at life and die, sucking, and are only parasites at the great feasts, or only

213

shovelers of manure at the great games, after the games are done.

The warm kitchen became an oppressive prison to Guy, a smothering cell, bare, unfurnished. And those in it did not see the walls and did not desire to escape them, did not wish for the freedom only money can give.

Guy did not hear the silence in the room, but he started when Sam said, "What's eating you, Guy? Look like you want to fight—something."

Guy said, "I do. But it's a different fight from yours, Sam." He could not help himself, and added, "My father was never a fighter. He accepted everything and didn't give a damn. Imagine what the world would be if everybody was like that!"

Sal looked at him with concern, at the pallor under his dark skin, at the unfamiliar rage in his black eyes, at the tempest that palpably enveloped him, at the clenched fists on the table. He was staring about him like a trapped bull. Sam thoughtfully wiped his mouth with his napkin.

He said, "Maybe we'd have peace in the world if more folks were like your dad."

"We'd have no arts and no science, no literature, no aspirations."

Sam said, with a curious obliqueness, "Well, anyways. Somebody has to do the world's work. We can't all be painting pretty pictures and saying poetry. Who'd feed them, who'd wash their clothes, who'd do the farming and milk the cows, who'd empty their bedpans when they was sick and build their houses?"

Sal said, "Your pa, Jerry, had a wonderful life."

Guy looked at them. He stood up, and the mighty wrath he was feeling swelled all through his body. "I'll look at the pigs," he said, and they caught no significance in his words. He went out to the pigpen to look at the sleeping animals. Now, to him, they seemed of more value than did Sal and Sam.

The ferocious longing for money, the need for money, was such a hunger in him that he felt ravenous. Lucy Lippincott had become a symbol to him of that, as well

214

as she meant Marlene. He lifted a fist at the sky in defiance. "I'm a man," he said. "I am content with nothing."

Sal was helping Sam on with his worn coat. "Don't mind Jerry, Mr. Kurtz," she said. "He's changed." She thought. "He began to change after he came back from the war. Or maybe before. I don't know. He took his pa's death hard."

"We all change, Miz Sal," said Sam. "He's got his life. He's got to live it himself, and find out for himself." His surly if kind face smiled. "That was one grand dinner, Miz Sal, and thank you."

"Come again," she said, and her heart sang a new song.

Sam met Guy on the doorstep and thanked him, but Guy seemed far away. "That's a fine woman, that Miz Sal," said Sam, and Guy hardly heard him. "A fine woman. Not many like her, no, sir."

"Come again," Guy said, and went into the house, and Sam looked after him speculatively and shook his head. Well. Bed. Work tomorrow. He went out to his old car and he wondered at the new lightness in his mind and his body. Yes, he would come again. The candle he had lighted illuminated his desolate life and he was lonely no longer.

In his remembering dream Guy not only relived that April day and night but he was given a mysterious insight into the thoughts and actions of others. It was a sort of double vision, a double stamping of a coin. He not only was remembering but was a universal spectator, both an actor and an audience.

He had returned to the house after abruptly leaving Sam outside, and he saw that Sal was simpering like a girl to herself and singing with the radio as she washed the dishes. He tried to be casual and said, "Well, how do you like Sam Kurtz?"

"Oh, there's one grand man!" said Sal, and then colored.

"My father would be glad to hear you say that."

Sal immediately became haughty. "I don't know what you mean, Jerry."

He could not help smiling. "I forgot to tell you, Sal. I'm going away for a couple of days." His voice was affectionate as usual but Sal knew she must ask no questions; there was a certain intonation in his words. He continued: "I'll pack a bag now. I'm taking the nine o'clock train tomorrow out of Cranston." He went into his bedroom and Sal frowned anxiously. Jerry sure had changed! He was no longer the youth of a few years ago, just returned from the war. But—had he really changed? Had it been there all the time?

At breakfast the next day he said very little. His black brows had drawn close together as he thought and ate. Sal was to drive him to the station, and she was ready before he was. "Think I saw the mailman drop something in," Sal said, and opened the car window and leaned out. She brought in a letter. She glanced at it curiously and then with excitement. "Mr. John Prentice!" she exclaimed. "The man who bought the Geiger farm!" She gave it to Guy and literally panted to hear of the contents. "From Pittsburgh," she added quite unnecessarily.

Mr. Prentice, whose stationery was discreetly imposing and bore but his own name on the letterhead, had written to "My dear Mr. Jerald."

"I have recently bought a farm in your vicinity from a Mrs. Lottie Geiger, whom you may know, as her land is adjacent to yours. However, that farm is not quite enough for my private purposes and so I should like to purchase yours. I am prepared to make you an offer and should like to talk with you as soon as possible. I will be in Cranston on April 5th . . ." He concluded politely, "At your convenience. I will be waiting for your reply, which I hope will be soon."

Guy crumpled the letter in his hand. He could hardly get his breath. "This changes things a little," he muttered. Sal had read the letter over his shoulder and she was exclaiming softly, over and over, and with euphoria. "I knew it, Jerry, I knew it! Now, all you have to do—" But he
216

was getting out of the car and running back to the house. She followed him as fast as possible. He was glancing at his watch. "Only eight-thirty. I can't call him just yet; I must wait until nine at least. I wonder what the hell he does." He smoothed out the crumpled letter, but it bore only the writer's name and address and telephone number in Pittsburgh. A banker? A lawyer? A builder, land developer? The very discretion of the letterhead woke up all his suspicions. He could hardly contain himself in his own terrible excitement, and Sal was pacing with him up and down the kitchen, gasping out short and incoherent words. Everything was outlined in a subjective halo of light to Guy, and the light was objective to him, so that every object in the homely kitchen had a palpitating aura. He kept blinking his eyes against it as against the sun. He kept shaking his wrist and looking at his watch. The minute hand crawled. A lifetime passed and he and Sal paced together.

Then Guy had a thought. "Perhaps that's his home number, not his office's," and he ran to the telephone on the wall. He called the operator and said, "I have tried to call Mr. John Prentice at this number and there was no answer at his house. Could you give me his office number?" This came within a minute or two, and Guy smiled grimly to himself. There must be a reason for letting him know the house number but not the office. Guy looked at his watch again. It was nine. He called the new number and a girl's affectedly singing voice answered: "Prentice and Grace Building Company." Guy gently hung up and his harsh smile deepened. So, Mr. John Prentice had thought him a stupid laborer, a farmer, incapable of thinking and conjecturing, a bird ready for the killing. He went out to look at his car. He would have to chance the long drive to Pittsburgh in it, as the next train was not until six that evening and he had no time to waste. With care he would arrive, by car, about one. Sal had followed him out, full of eager questions, but he said, abruptly, "Wait until I get home, Sal, with something to tell you." He got

217

into the car and hurried off and Sal watched him go, fuming.

He had been in Pittsburgh only once in his life, as a child, a very young child. He could not remember the occasion too clearly or the reason for the brief visit. He only recalled it had been with both of his parents. Come to think of it, he thought, I haven't been out of Cranston for over three years; I've been stagnating, not living. He ran the car as prudently and as fast as he could. The miles poured under the wheels and his thoughts were fiercely concentrated. He kept glancing at his watch after he had reached the Turnpike, which was crowded at this time of the day. The elderly heater in the car did very little to lift the chill in the car, yet he sweated with urgent haste. He tried to recall everything he had heard of the Chandler Development Company and Mr. Howard Chandler, president. He remembered reading an article about Mr. Chandler a year or so ago, in which it was noted that his company was "the largest in the Commonwealth."

All at once he was elated, feeling a new and stronger excitement, a surge of power and jubilant satisfaction. His past life seemed to him to have become insignificant, worthless, a waste, and the earlier abhorrence he had felt for his young existence—even the war—and the contempt for all those he had known, quickened, became an actual loathing. It appeared to him that he had been deliberately frustrated, thwarted, misled, and a great rage came to him against those who had so belittled his life and who had tried to make him dwell in their own wretched house and accept their limited philosophy. Pa, he thought, you never really felt the "pale passionate land of the soul," as you had called it. All your thoughts were secondhand; all your words the words of greater men who would have scorned the manner in which you lived. Why did you try to make me as savorless as yourself? Spiritless, as accepting? He forgot that Tom had repeatedly told him "it's your life, kiddo, and it's always your choice." His resentment made his very mouth bitter and his gorge forced his heart to a hard beat. His new and desperate
218

determination not to be as his father had been, and not live as his father had lived, had become a bellicose anger. Tom was no longer the beloved father but a feckless enemy who had almost destroyed his son. He had wished to squeeze the juices of life from his son and make him as inert as himself, reading and talking his years away to nothingness, and a handful of ashes.

Twenty miles away from Pittsburgh he came to the sign he had expected: "Chandlertown, 3 miles," and he left at the next exit, turning off the Turnpike into a broad two-way road. He had stopped only for gasoline and a sandwich, and his elation made him feel both confident and powerful. He drove slowly, looking about him at the freshening fields of April. It had been raining but now a wan sun flooded the countryside. Within a few minutes he encountered, in the midst of the quiet country, two enormous pillars of brick, a suggestion of an iron gate, and a huge sign impressively proclaiming: "Chandlertown! You are now entering a modern experiment in gracious living!"

Guy entered through the gates to the right and found himself on a narrower and curving road. The ground had been turned into new lawns and young trees; redbud and maple and willow lined both sides of the road. It was a pleasant introduction to the "experiment in gracious living," if not very expensive, considering the small size of the plantings. Then the grassy areas suddenly turned into little plots and he was entering the new town itself, all the streets curving unnecessarily but with aplomb. He saw the first houses. He drove down all the many created streets, and he drove slowly, watching.

All the houses were almost exactly alike, very small on narrow and unceremonious lawns, all with a single central door, all with factory-cut windows and wooden siding and brown shingled roofs, and all, without exception, having one single lower window of broad plate glass dimly gleaming in the sun. On the second story there were three tiny windows. Not one house differed from another except for the color of the clapboards—white, green, gray, pinkish—and the color of the central door, where imagination, however raw, had been responsible for a bright red or a brilliant yellow or a glittering black. Even the meager shrubbery about each little house was the exact replica of the shrubbery surrounding all the other houses. Trees, as young as those near the gates, stood on the infinitesimal lawns, still leafless, still suggesting they had been born of one seed, duplicates of each other. All the peaked roofs of the houses rose not one millimeter above the other roofs, so that, against the uncertain sky of April, they gave a serrated impression, like rows upon rows of giant wooden teeth seeking to chew the drifting clouds. And in every "picture window" was an identical white ruffled lamp on a table, and every door had an iron knocker, a concrete step, and a white-painted suggestion of an iron railing.

To Guy, with his new and sensitive perception, it was a most dismal and soul-stifling sight, despite the curving streets, despite the central attraction of various shops and markets, despite a small moving-picture theater, two churches, and a school. The streets were very quiet and echoingly still, for the men were at work, the children in classrooms. The only activity, and that as yet desultory, was around the "Market Plaza," as it was called, and here were women old and young, with baby carriages or with grocery bags, coming and going, chattering in the windy desolation of this experiment in gracious living. To Guy, this was far more depressing than any slum in Cranston, far more lifeless, with far less zest. The very cleanliness and sterile uniformity of Chandlertown enhanced the littleness, the meaninglessness, of the faceless people who lived here and had their blank being. It was true the streets were quite broad, but this merely increased the atmosphere of desolation, of the essential torpidity of the human beings who lived in those houses, the essential uselessness. The faces of the women reflected their vacuity, their lack of unique variety, their simple stupidity, their undifferentiated minds and existences.

Guy hated them. They were part of the colorless
220

new world which was spreading all over the earth like a single drab fungus, like a grayish desert. He had seen the dreadful "Council" houses of England, built by the fervor of Socialist social planners who were hardly more intelligent than the inhabitants of the houses, and hardly more imaginative. The blight of government programs was not responsible for this horror which was Chandlertown; it had been done, Guy thought, with benevolent malice, if that was not a contradiction in terms, or by private minds as gross and little as the people imprisoned in this wilderness.

Once this had been pastureland and meadows, bright running streams, birds and animals and great trees, barns and silos and farmhouses. Now it was an overgrown toy village made of the cheapest and most synthetic of materials. Tom had said, only a year ago, "Uniformity and conformity are the new religion in this world, and soon it will be political blasphemy to challenge or denounce it, and will bring its own penalties. The most inferior minds will soon dominate our lives, for they are in the majority, and this time there will be no Renaissance, no upspurt and bursting of vital intellectual growth. The masses are going to do us in, for they are now the sacred cows of the politically ambitious, who, of course, are not uniform or conforming at all." He had added with a smiling and bitter cynicism, "It is not the bucolic mind we must fear, but the urban rabble, the fearful little people. They will devastate the countryside and destroy all that is noble and original, as they tried to destroy Versailles, and as they destroyed Rome and Greece and medieval beauty and glory. They have an inborn hatred for splendor. No matter where they will live, by government assistance and planning, they will bring with them their abysmal anonymity."

Guy continued to circle the streets, growing more despondent and coldly angry by the instant. A little more money would have made these houses distinctive; a respect for the bulldozed mighty trees would have preserved shady oases in the midst of this prim monotony. This was not a town at all; it was an extension of a factory. By the time the spindly saplings were large trees themselves, this would be a slum, however gaudy it now appeared. There was nothing worse, or more deadening than a rural slum. Eighteen thousand dollars for these potential hovels! Guy began to feel a dim pity for the inhabitants. Surely, among this mass, there were born, or were being born, a few original minds, a few souls aware of true beauty. But they would be beaten into uniformity here, unless they escaped, which, if Tom's predictions had been correct, they would have no opportunity to do. Guy began to sense, as Tom had sensed, a malignant universal conspiracy to reduce the world of men to docile slaves in an environment conducive to assent, and only to assent. Fascistic Communism. A neat zoo, and as unnatural. Guy felt he was smothering, and a new resolve came to him: He would never sell his land to become another Chandlertown.

He went to the city. It was now half past three and he found his way to the offices of Prentice & Grace Building Company, in an agreeable suburb where the houses were at least different from each other, if small and compact. The offices were of new white brick and impressive, mostly all-glass windows and steel, and only one story high, a design which Guy found depressing, including the welter of glass and metal outside. He entered a large room of brown and beige and yellow, very "modern," with a young lady seated at an ultra-modern desk inundated, it seemed, by many tropical plants. If the decor had been intended to be warm and attractive it had the opposite effect on Guy, for he believed that an office should be strictly functional and utilitarian. The young lady glanced up, and Guy was reminded of a pretty pink pig dressed in a brown suit; even her hair was pinkish. Her pale eyes scrutinized Guy swiftly, and what she saw, apparently did not please her. The little jowly face became distant, as she inquired what she could "do" for him.

"If you are looking for a job," she said, in a voice

that unpleasantly reminded him of a squeal, "we're not hiring again until the end of April."

He said, "I should like to see Mr. Prentice."

She regarded him with severe arrogance, and Guy thought of Tom's frequent quotation, "a little brief authority." ("The most presumptuous and insignificant of people are the most haughty and important," he had often said, "and you'll find this type in every bureaucracy in full force." Guy found it here now.) The girl said, "Do you have an appointment?"

"No."

The disfavor on her piglike face increased. "Then I'm afraid you will have to call for one, or write. Mr. Prentice is very busy; he sees—people—only by appointment."

Tom would have laughed at her, for the silly pretensions of the obscure had aroused both his amusement and his compassion. But there was much of Mary in her son and he felt rage and a desire to strike that swinish little face, now flushed with malicious triumph. He thrust his hands into his coat pockets to keep from hitting her. He could see, as Mary would have said, that the girl was "low class." His hand encountered the crumpled letter he had received that morning from John Prentice. He took it out; it further enraged him to see that his fingers were trembling. He smoothed the letter and asked the girl for a pencil. She lifted her head higher. "I am afraid—"

"Give me a pencil," he said, and his voice was so pent that she was startled. She pushed a pen across the desk to him, and on the reverse of the letter he wrote: "Sorry you could not see me, as I came especially to Cranston today in response to your letter. Tomorrow, I will go to see Howard Chandler, who will receive me more courteously, I'm sure. Your girl even refused to tell you that I was here." He signed his name and threw the letter at the young lady, who, for a moment or two, regarded it as if it were an obscene object. Then Guy went to the door, opened it, and walked out onto the street, slowly.

He was not at all surprised to hear running feet behind him and a squealing breathless voice calling him. He turned deliberately. The girl, coatless in the cold air, was panting after him, the pink drained from her face. "I'm sorry, sorry!" she cried. "Please come back! I'm sure Mr. Prentice will see you immediately." She caught his arm and clutched it and the pale staring eyes were full of tears and fright. "I'll lose my job," she wailed.

"Good," he said, and tried to extricate his arm. People passing stopped to gape at this curious little scene. The girl clung to him tighter. "Please, please," she implored.

It was not pity or relenting that made him turn and stride ahead of her back to the building. It was his sudden realization that he could not afford the grand gesture, much as it would satisfy him. Then he was disgusted that he had let this miserable creature see his anger; in this manner he had demeaned himself. He walked faster. He could not help opening the door vigorously and then slamming it in her panting face. But he knew, instinctively, that had he shown her forgiving kindness and had smiled at her, she would have despised him, and he never intended to be despised again as he had been in the Army, where he had encountered many such.

The girl followed him inside, smoothing her wind-torn hair. She kept muttering, "I'm sorry, sorry, I didn't know, you didn't show me the letter first—"

"Shut up and tell Mr. Prentice I am here."

He did not know for a long time afterwards that he was the subject of a discreet telephone call from a friend of John Prentice's in Cranston, a friend from the bank. "He hasn't called us, though we've been trying to wait him out. I have my suspicions the Chandler people are making him a better offer." This agitated Mr. Prentice very much, and he was just beginning a devil's tattoo on his desk when his receptionist burst into the office in a state of disarray, holding out his letter to him, and stammering, "I didn't know—he didn't say who he was, he didn't show me your letter—he didn't

224

say anything—and you don't want to be disturbed—"

Mr. Prentice took his letter, read the reverse, and swore. "Ethel, you sent him away?"

"No. No, he came back." Mr. Prentice looked at her venomously. "Send him in. And I'll talk to you later, Ethel."

Trembling and beaten, she went out.

Guy entered at once. Mr. Prentice, who was a most cautious and wary man, did not rise. He sat behind his desk imposingly, though he was a short thin man of very unimposing stature, with a crafty fleshless face and a ruddy complexion, and short dark hair, and a mouth that could smile only sourly. His brown eyes, however, were sharp and shrewd and merciless, and never smiled at all. His dark blue suit and blue tie did nothing very much to make his appearance more genial. He said at once, "Mr. Jerald?"

"Yes." Guy stood before him and the two men looked at each other and Mr. Prentice saw in those black eyes the cold implacable iron which only two men had seen before—the two Russian soldiers Guy had killed one murky quiet night in Berlin, in revenge for Marlene.

Mr. Prentice was startled. This was not the foot-shuffling ignorant farmer or mill hand he had been led to believe. But he recovered himself at once. He stood up and said, "Please sit down, Mr. Jerald."

Guy sat down in a chair which faced the desk. Here, too, was all brown and beige and yellow, and Guy found it more distasteful by the minute. He also had taken a great dislike to Mr. Prentice. He also disliked the abstract engravings on the cocoa-colored walls, again in the objectional colors. But there was an atmosphere here of prosperity.

Mr Prentice tried for an amiable smile and failed. He said, "As you know, I want to buy your farm—for my own private purposes."

"Not to build on it?"

"Why, no. Why should you think that?"

"You're in the business, aren't you?"

"I also buy land—again—for my own private purposes."

Guy smiled. Mr. Prentice studied him more closely. Guy said, "Nine hundred acres, the biggest parcel of land near Cranston? Are you going to raise racehorses, Mr. Prentice?"

The other man was so disturbed that he almost said, "Yes." He clasped his hands on his desk. A jeweled ring winked at Guy. "I don't think, Mr. Jerald, that in this transaction I need to explain what I intend to do with the land."

"That is, if you get it."

Mr. Prentice shrugged as if he were completely indifferent. Before he could speak again Guy said, "You bought the Geiger farm, and it's completely landlocked. The only way you can get to the road is by way of a dirt road my father partially built. I can close it off, and you'd have a hell of a time getting an easement to the public road."

John Prentice only respected and appreciated men as alert as himself. He began to feel a faint respect and appreciation for Guy, though he did not show it. He said, "I don't know about that."

Guy nodded. "I do. The farms which surround my land are owned by very conservative farmers, who don't like housing developments. And they would seriously object to having their own taxes raised because of any such development. My next neighbor is a brother of the mayor of Cranston." He gave Mr. Prentice a very sweet smile.

Mr. Prentice took out a gold-plated cigarette case, offered Guy a cigarette, lighted one for himself. He looked at Guy thoughtfully. Guy said, "So the Geiger land is of no use to you without mine. Let's stop dancing around, Mr. Prentice. You bought the Geiger land for almost nothing; you want to buy mine. The Geiger farm is useless to you without my acres, and you know it. What's your offer?"

Mr. Prentice's complexion became rubicund, but he
226

smiled. "As I said, I am prepared to make you a—reasonable—offer."

"Such as three or four thousand dollars, perhaps?"

"I think that's a fair offer."

"For nine hundred acres to be converted into a suburb, which will make your company millions?"

"That's ridiculous, Mr. Jerald. You know nothing about the building business."

"Yes, I do. I went to see Chandlertown this morning."

A deep brown silence fell in the office, while the two men gazed at each other like bullfighters. Then Mr. Prentice said, "What did you think of it?"

"Terrible. But—unless you meet my own terms I'll go to Mr. Chandler, in spite of the tract houses he'll probably build on my land, the instant slum."

Mr. Prentice nodded. "I agree Chandlertown is a blot on the landscape. I don't build like that, Mr. Jerald. I have the best architects, with original designs. Most of this suburb was built by us—Mr. Grace, my partner, and I. And the houses didn't cost any more than Chandler's—slum. And better built, too, and not one exact duplicate of any other. I was born in Pittsburgh and so were most of my ancestors and I have a little respect for architecture, and I hate the present tract houses now going up like tawdry weeds all over the country. They'll fall apart within ten years."

"And the poor damned bastards will have nothing except mortgages for hen houses."

Mr. Prentice did not detect any pity in Guy's voice, only derision. For some reason he felt both relieved and yet more cautious. He said, "Yes, let's get down to business. My final offer is seven thousand dollars for your land."

Guy stood up, "Goodbye, Mr. Prentice."

Mr. Prentice was alarmed at this abruptness. He looked up into Guy's eyes and saw the ruthlessness there, the amused knowledge. "Mr. Jerald! Let's not rush things. Please sit down. I'm sure we can come to some agreement. What did you have in mind?"

Guy's heart began to tremble. "I'll sell you the first third of my land near the Geiger farm—and the easement—for forty thousand dollars. A bargain."

"Forty thousand dollars!" Mr. Prentice almost stuttered.

"That's not all, Mr. Prentice. I want to get in on this deal, too. After all, there are two thirds more of my land. I want to learn the business. I don't expect to be an architect overnight. In fact, I don't want to be a licensed architect at all. I just want to know as much as possible about it. Then, if you want to buy the other two thirds, I'm a partner. Prentice, Grace & Jerald. It sounds good to me."

Mr. Prentice leaned back far into his heavily padded executive chair which was guaranteed not to squeak. It squeaked. He regarded Guy with what he hoped was total incredulity and gentle mirth. "Mr. Jerald, your—terms—are impossible. You look and talk like a bright young man, yet you make an impossible offer."

"I think the Chandler people won't find it impossible. Mr. Prentice, I don't have time to waste. Take my offer, or leave it. Consult your partner, your banks. I will be here tomorrow to hear what you have to say. Early. So, if I'm not satisfied, I may go to the Chandler people, much as I dislike them."

"But you don't know anything about this business!" Mr. Prentice had never felt so beset before, and by a mill hand!

"I can learn. You've said I'm bright. You aren't an architect yourself, Mr. Prentice, but you know a lot about architecture, as you've implied. I think I've made you a very reasonable offer. In fact, I should have asked sixty thousand dollars for that one third of my land. I'm sure the Chandler people will be glad to give me what I want."

Mr. Prentice was also sure. Again the chair squeaked. Mr. Prentice both hated and admired this bumpkin. He began to suspect that the Chandler people had already approached Guy. Guy said, "The only reason I won't consider the Chandler Development Company is because

228

I detest their tract houses. But if the worse comes to the worst—I like money, too, Mr. Prentice."

"So I gather, Mr. Jerald. I'll have to talk this over with my partner. It's a lot of money, and I don't even know, as of now, if we care to undertake the development of your land. It's still all up in the air."

Guy smiled and Mr. Prentice found that smile both knowing and disagreeable. "There's a recession on just now, Mr. Jerald, and money is tight."

"I shouldn't worry about that, Mr. Prentice. Washington will think up a war to make us prosperous again." His young voice was now bitter and harsh.

"War?" said Mr. Prentice, raising his eyebrows.

"Brushfire wars, to make war workers happy again," said Guy. "I read that in the newspapers. And only recently a State Department official remarked that 'wars are America's traditional way to pull out of depressions.' Yes, indeed. Let young men die on foreign battlefields so that the men who work in 'defense' factories can buy houses in bigger Chandlertowns."

Again the savage bitterness and harshness were in Guy's eyes and voice. "I was in the last one," he said. "My father knew what it was all about—to make the world safe for Fascistic Communism, among many other things. I saw the dead. I saw the burning cities. That war made you very rich, too, didn't it, Mr. Prentice?"

Mr. Prentice was silent. He could only look at Guy, who suddenly seemed formidable to him, a symbol of the younger generation of men who had returned home shaken and embittered, or in wooden coffins, or in wheelchairs or on stretchers.

"I didn't approve of that war myself, Mr. Jerald," he said. "I wasn't drafted, though I was only thirty-eight or -nine then, in 1941. Eight years ago. My eyes."

I wonder, thought Guy. But he only nodded. "And a heart murmur or two," added Mr. Prentice. He sighed.

"Weren't you lucky," said Guy, without sympathy.

Mr. Prentice suddenly smiled and for the first time the smile was not sour. He said, "I guess I was, at that." He

229

scrutinized Guy more closely; he no longer despised him. He began to think very rapidly, but still with caution.

"All right. I'll talk with Mr. Grace. We'll all get together tomorrow, though I can't promise you anything as of now. Where are you staying in town?"

"I haven't found a place yet."

"Let me recommend a fine motel right here in this suburb. We built it ourselves. Be our guest!"

They shook hands. Then Guy said, "We almost missed each other. The fault of that little tramp outside. I wonder how many other people she's driven off."

"I'll take care of Ethel," said Mr. Prentice, and his smile went away.

In the dream Tom appeared, as young as Guy remembered him over fifteen years ago, and he said, "I admire you, son, you dealt as a rascal with a rascal. It was even Stephen, as they used to say. But was it necessary to hurt that faceless little wretch who used her 'little brief authority' on you? What else did she have to live for? What else do little scanty people like her have to live for but their pitiable arrogance to compensate for their meaninglessness?"

12

As the dream continued it moved faster and faster, spurred by the jockey of memory.

The motel was very luxurious, at least to Guy, who had slept in but a few dismal ones with a casual girl. He was accepted with cordiality, the manager explaining that Mr. Prentice had made the reservation. The manager was proud of his establishment. He personally conducted Guy to his room, which was large and warm and well furnished, with a tiny television set and an expansive bathroom. Guy deposited his small suitcase, noting with some amused anger the manager's acute recognition of its shabbiness, and then washed his somewhat grimy face and hands and combed his hair. He then went to the dining room, sharply conscious of his old clothing and his cheap suit. He felt, more than ever before, the sordidness and the humiliation of poverty, for all the diners were well dressed. He imagined they surveyed him with scorn and repudiation. Then he remembered his offer to Mr. Prentice, and his shoulders straightened and he looked about him with a new assurance.

The meal was very good; he spent far more than he had intended, and he tipped with a careless generosity. When he opened the door to his room he heard the telephone ringing, and with elation he thought: So, they couldn't wait! He ran to the telephone and caught it up. He was surprised to hear Sal's voice.

"How did you trace me here?" he asked.

"Well, Jerry, it isn't any mystery. I did see Mr. Prentice's name and address this morning, on his letter to you. So I called him and asked him if he knew where you were, and he told me." Now her voice became excited. "I just had to tell you so you'll come home early in the morning."

"What's wrong?"

"It's just something very funny. Right after you left this morning some men came, with all kinds of instruments. And they went out on the farm and I went after them and they said Mrs. Jerald—your mother—had given them permission to be there, and had told them that the farm was really hers and she was seeing lawyers. They said they were geol—I don't remember what it was—geol, or something."

Guy moved closer to the telephone, as he sat on the edge of his bed.

"Geologists, Sal?"

"Yes, that's it. Geologists. They kept moving around, picking up pieces of clay and earth, and making notes on a pad. I asked them who sent them and they said it was 'someone.' They wouldn't give me a name."

Guy's mind clamored furiously. What in hell were

geologists doing on his land? Sal said, "I told them your mother didn't own that land, you did, and they asked for you and I said you was away for a couple days. I was going to call the police to put them off, and they said your mother had given them permission and they would tell you all about it when you came home. They're coming back tomorrow morning, early. Oh, something else funny. You know the Schwartz's farm, three miles away? They dug a well, or something, and they found oil, not a big well, but fifty barrels a day, they said. Mrs. Geiger told me this afternoon."

Oil. But his land was not in the area of the oil fields and few new wells had been discovered in the Commonwealth, and these had been hardly worth the expense of drilling. Still, there was the possibility. Unable to sit any longer, Guy got to his feet. He looked at his watch. It was nine-thirty. He could make it home in a few hours, at night. He said to Sal, "I'm coming home right now, Sal. This may be important."

"I thought it might be," said Sal, with some satisfaction. "But you must be wore out now, and then driving again for hours.

"I'll be there," said Guy.

He walked up and down the pleasant room with increasing elation. Then he called Mr. Prentice. He said at once, "I'm sorry, Mr. Prentice, but something has come up. I was just called from Cranston. There've been oil prospectors, geologists, on my land all day, and they'll be there tomorrow. So I am leaving now for home."

He could actually hear the thick silence on the telephone. He added, with some agreeable malice, "It seems oil has been discovered on some property three miles away."

Mr. Prentice's voice was both shrill and shaken. "But—but what about our meeting tomorrow?"

It gave Guy pleasure to say, "Call me in Cranston—tomorrow—or when you wish." He spoke with deliberate carelessness. He gently hung up. He found he was breathing with deep rapidity. He packed his few articles. The
232

telephone rang again. Guy smiled at it. It stopped, then began to ring again. Guy closed his suitcase and ran from the room. The night was bright with stars, and his elation made him forget his tiredness. Like many people, he believed that the roads would be almost empty at night, but the roads were roaring with the big interstate trucks and as he passed them he could feel the thunderous wind of their passage. He suddenly felt a mysterious brotherhood with the brawny men who drove these vehicles in the night, yet it was a brotherhood of the body and not of the mind. He realized, with some surprise, that he had never been one with the men who completely utilized their bodies and not their intelligences, and therefore there had always been a subtle barrier between him and them, which they had recognized at once and he had not, until tonight. That, he now knew, was the reason for the resentment his contemporaries had always felt for him, even in childhood, much to his young bewilderment, and his isolation in the Army, and his present isolation. Had his father known that all the time?

He arrived at the farm at nearly three in the morning. He saw that the kitchen was lighted, and he was not surprised to find that Sal was waiting for him and that there was a warm refreshing fragrance of coffee in the big room, and that she had placed one of her fine apple pies on the table. She was nodding in a chair near the stove, but awoke alertly at the sound of his entrance. Seeing his exhausted face, she said, "Maybe I should have waited until tomorrow—I mean, after you had breakfast."

"No, you did exactly right, Sal," he said, and in his exuberance he kissed her over and over, until she laughingly protested. He then sat down and drank coffee and ate part of the pie, while he told Sal of yesterday's events. She listened with that intense interest she had always given his father, and her approval.

"I doubt there's anything to be found in the way of profitable oil in this area," he said. "But it will give Mr. Prentice thought, and that'll give me an opportunity. Wake me early, Sal."

She was smiling. She said, "Hope you don't mind, Jerry, but Mr. Kurtz called in the afternoon and asked me to go out to dinner with him, tonight." She blushed like a young girl.

"Well, well," said Guy. "For a slow man he is moving pretty fast, isn't he? Of course I don't mind. I think we'd both better get some sleep."

But he could hardly sleep much, in spite of his weariness. In his thoughts he went over and over a coming conversation with John Prentice.

He awakened early. The April sun was sharp and piercing, as was the wind. He and the boy he had hired to do most of the farm chores went out into the wet brown fields, where, here and there, there were greening spots. At all times Guy watched the road. At eight o'clock, when he and the boy were bringing in the milk pails to the "second kitchen" for Sal to put in the separator, he saw several large polished cars driving up to the house. Muddy and damp, he went to greet the nine men and they eyed him and his clothing with cool indifference as they left their vehicles. He stared at them with a quick bright black light in his eyes and said, "You're trespassing."

An older man in his fifties regarded him with less than pleasure and said, "We have the written permission of Mrs. Thomas Jerald, who is part owner of this land."

"Mrs. Thomas Jerald is my mother, and she owns no part of this property. You don't have my permission."

The men looked at each other for a long moment, then the older man smiled agreeably and held out his hand. "Sorry. We were misinformed. I'm George Random, and these"—he indicated the watchful others—"are part of my company. Random Geological Associates." He named them and Guy merely nodded abruptly. "What are you looking for? Gold? Diamonds? Silver? Mica? Or, is it oil?"

Mr. Random apparently changed his opinion of Guy, for he said, very pleasantly, "Well, there is that—oil. A
234

small well has been drilled three miles from your land. We are prepared, if there are any indications of oil, to offer you an option."

Guy smiled, and not pleasantly. "Well, what have you found so far?"

A glaucous look came over the other's eyes. "Not too favorable. But we are still prepared to offer you an option on all your land, Mr. Jerald."

Guy leaned against a fence post and assumed a parody of a country innocent. "Well, now, is that so? An option on land you are pretty sure doesn't have oil, or only a little? Not enough to make drilling one well worthwhile?"

"We are willing to take the chance, Mr. Jerald." An ominous flush stained his bony cheekbones. "About the option. For your nine hundred acres we offer you, now, fifty thousand dollars, ten thousand paid on signing the option. What have you to lose?"

Guy studied him for several long moments. Then he said, "You wouldn't know the Chandler outfit, would you?"

Mr. Random was startled. He drew a little nearer to Guy. "Chandler?"

Guy waved his hand carelessly. "Never heard of Chandler, the builder, the land developer? He's been buying up land around here for his instant slums. I thought everybody knew him. Biggest builder in the Commonwealth." Guy was amused at the suddenly taut attitude of the other men. "Now, yesterday, I was in Pittsburgh. I've been talking to the Prentice and Grace people. They've offered me forty thousand dollars for one third of my land, with an option to buy the rest. A better offer than yours."

They stared at him in silence. Two, who had been taking instruments from their car, paused and looked at Mr. Random. "You never heard of John Prentice, either, did you?" said Guy, as no one spoke. "Well, I've been considering his offer. It's better than yours. I don't think there is oil here, and neither do you. Excuse me, gentlemen, I'm going to call Mr. Prentice now and take up his offer."

"Wait a minute," said Mr. Random. "Let's be nice and easy. Suppose I consult—somebody—and talk to you this afternoon? Come into town, at the Old House, and have lunch with me." He gave Guy a most friendly smile. "Perhaps I'll have good news for you." He looked over the quickening land, which was now steaming in the sun. The other men were quietly putting away their instruments.

"If I'd accepted your option," said Guy, "you'd have reported to me in a day or two that there was little if any indication of oil on my property. But by then you'd have the option in your pockets. And the option would be careful not to say anything about oil—just the sale of my land. For any purpose at all." He shook his head with a sad pretense of regret at human manipulating. "I think we can cut this short. Excuse me for a few minutes and I'll give you my answer." He walked away, whistling, and they followed him with their eyes and then exchanged glances with each other and shrugged.

Guy went into the house and called Mr. Prentice, who almost stuttered with eagerness when he heard Guy's voice. Guy said, "I gave you first chance, Mr. Prentice. It's now or never. I'm a fair man. One hundred thousand dollars for the whole parcel. Take it or leave it. . . . Oil? I don't know. The men are here with their instruments, all nine of them. Even if there's no oil, I want that money. That's final. But, I can always do business with the Chandler people."

Mr. Prentice said with shrillness, "What's the name of the outfit there?"

"Random Geological Associates."

Guy heard a quick sharp gasp, and understood at once. "Well?" he said.

"Let me call you back, in a few minutes—Guy," said Mr. Prentice, and his voice was almost craven with pleading. "A few minutes, yes?"

Guy returned to Mr. George Random. He saw that all the men were in a state of tense expectation. He smiled at them amiably and said, "I've just talked to Mr. Prentice. Prentice and Grace—you know? They've offered me one hundred thousand dollars for my property. I've taken it."

13

James Meyer was sitting in Guy Jerald's suite, and he had been there for nearly an hour. During that time Guy had been pacing and muttering to himself. Sometimes he paused to stare blindly, and with a kind of fury, at James.

"And that's how it started," he said at last.

"What, Jerry?" James leaned forward and spoke gently.

"My damned sweet, lovely, prosperous life," said Guy. "The dolce vita."

"Oh," said James.

But Guy flung out his hand in enraged repudiation. He left the sitting room. James waited, and when Guy did not return he went to look for him in the bedroom. Guy had flung himself face down on the bed and was sleeping, clutching the satin bedspread in his fingers as a drowning man clutches at seaweed. James saw part of his face, contorted, twisted, as he slept. James waited an hour but Guy did not awaken. James looked in on him again. To his moved surprise he saw that the anguished profile was more peaceful and the breathing slower and more regular. But it was a desperately sick man who lay there, and James knew it. He went silently from the suite and reported to Emil Grassner.

They were eating lunch together in the staff dining room, and Emil listened with profound attention. "Well," he said, "we seem to be getting somewhere. At least he is speaking; at least he let you know he knows you and remembers you." He sipped thoughtfully at his coffee. " 'La dolce vita.' The sweet life. I wonder how many countless men in their middle years come to that point—hating their lives. Perhaps that's the cause of all these coronaries, and perhaps, who knows, of cancer, too. And that reminds me. Before you came here I had consultations with Guy's wife in her house, at her invitation. I was curious about Guy's personal library. Do you know what I found? At least a score of books on cancer and cancer research, from ancient history to the present! And each of the books was stuffed with Guy's scribbled notes and questions. Most of the pages were marked. Some of the notes were extremely perceptive, almost clinical. You'd have thought a cancer specialist had written them. Questions on the psychological aspects of cancer. Did those psychological states of depression and despair follow the cancer, or did they precede it? Which was the cause? Pathological from the start, or induced by emotional distress? That's what Guy was asking.

"He'd also questioned both. How did one explain cancer in the newborn? And in very young children? Both immune from emotional illness. He had even, with amusement at himself, questioned if it was really 'karma,' you know, the reincarnation business, which is absurd, of course."

"I'm not so sure," said James.

Emil smiled broadly. "And I'm not so sure I'm not so sure. Oh, come, you don't believe that nonsense, do you?"

James said, "Well, we all have our moments of déjà vu, don't we? Yes, I know the explanation: a sudden subtle shift of the brain cells. The explanation is more weird than the possibility. And there've been times I've had vivid impressions of experiences I never experienced. Scenes I had never visited, people I've never known, emotions I've never felt, languages I've never heard. Call it half-dreams, hallucinations, whatever. I don't know. Laugh at me if you wish."

But Emil was suddenly grave. "I know what you mean. I've gone through it often myself. I was visiting friends in East Hampton last summer. I was lounging on the lawn, alone, in a long, very comfortable chair, looking at the ocean. No one else was about. I'm positive I wasn't asleep. In fact, I was thinking of a certain patient, who had, in self-defense against his family, gone into a catatonic state, though there were no evidences of overt schizophrenia, and never had been. Well. It was a very warm scented day; someone had just cut the grass, and the smell was sleepy, almost like an anesthetic. I don't remember ever being so relaxed and contented as I was then. I could hear the ocean telling stories softly to itself—" He shook his head in deep marveling.

"Then I opened my eyes. No, I hadn't been asleep. Everything was as it had been moments before, warm and sunny and quiet and peaceful. But suddenly clearer; the air was purer and fresher, and hotter. I looked at the ocean and it had turned to a blue-purple mirror, as still as crystal, and it wasn't 'speaking.' There was such a quiet, a quiet I'd never known before. Then I saw three tremendous sailing vessels, sails spread and shining with light, about two miles away. They were all gliding in single file, one after the other, like great white birds ruffling their wings. I knew at once they were on their way to the harbor. I sat up and looked at them. Four-masted vessels. Tremendous in size. Ornate, dignified—the most beautiful sight I'd ever seen. And I said to myself, 'Here they are at last.' I could even name one: the *Dove*, in the lead.

"And I knew someone was on the *Dove*—the woman I loved and whom I was going to marry. I could see her face, radiant, resplendent, young, all warm olive and rose, with a rope of hair like black braided glass. She wore an archaic costume, green velvet with gold braid. It was as if I was within arm's reach of her, and yet was two miles away. I even remember her name."

A strange pensive expression moved over his strong rustic face and his eyes were the eyes of a youth, glowing with love, and James kept very quiet, and waited. "Her name," said Emil, "was Josefa. Spanish, probably. Or Portuguese. I don't know. All I knew was that I must leave for the city at once. I didn't seem to be in East Hampton at all, but somewhere else. In fact, remembering, there was a difference—I can't explain it. Then the ships disappeared, the sound of the sea came to me, the

239

scene shifted—and I was terribly alone, and really wild with grief and wanting." He paused, and added, half inaudibly, "I've never forgotten her. Josefa. I sometimes have the feeling we shall meet again, somewhere." He smiled as if with amusement at his dreams. "Do you know what I did? I had a well-known artist paint her portrait. Don't laugh."

"I'm not laughing," said James.

"It took many sessions before he got it right. Now the portrait hangs in my bedroom at home, and it seems alive and promising, to me. I'm a widower, you know, with four adult children. They've always been curious about the subject. I never tell them, of course. Josefa doesn't resemble their mother in the least."

James said nothing. Emil gently laughed. "I've looked everywhere for her, everywhere. I did find something out. There had actually been a sailing vessel, the *Dove,* in 1793. Only it was called *La Paloma,* out of Portugal. It took me years to find out. Of course, *La Paloma* is a common name, a song— Still. I just don't know. Was it only a dream, a delusion, and was I half asleep? I have the impression I was awake, keenly awake. I can see it all, even now. And it doesn't get dimmer."

Emil looked at the silent James quizzically. "Now, what do you say to that?"

"I don't have any explanation." He paused and played with his coffee spoon. "But something like that happened to me, twenty-five years ago. I was being driven in London to my offices on a particularly miserable day, rain and soot and cold, very dreary. I looked down the street, all teeming with umbrellas shining with that peculiar mercurial rainy light only England knows, and I was depressed. It's very depressing for a psychiatrist to know that he really knows nothing, and that he's not very much help to his patients except as a father confessor, the poor souls. Then, there was a blink—that's the only way I can describe it—a blink. And I was in a carriage, on the same street but with lower buildings and little shops and
240

crowding houses right on the pavement; I knew it was a familiar street. And I had a coachman.

"A carriage passed mine, in another direction, and a lady, alone, was sitting in it, with a black-and-wine bonnet and scarlet ribbons, and she was buxom and her face was full of zest and laughter, and she was about thirty years old. She seemed to have a delight in life; I saw that even in those few moments. She wasn't a pretty woman; but she was fascinating, dressed in black velvet. She wore diamond earrings, drops. She looked into my face as we passed, and she smiled at me, the most beautiful smile, and she nodded, as if we knew each other. Her name" —and James dropped his head a little—"was Emmaline. I knew that immediately."

Emil said, "So you have a lost love, too."

"Not lost," said James. "I found her twenty years ago, at a friend's house. A widow. We recognized each other at once. Her name is Emma Godwin. It was five years ago when I mentioned having 'known' her before, and she said, 'But I knew from the start, when we met in Edward's house.' We became lovers only a week after we had met. She had been married, and had a little son and daughter, and a stockbroker husband. They were drowned, the three of them, on the Thames, when a sudden storm came up. That was twenty-two years ago. We've never married. We're afraid something will be spoiled for us if we marry. I don't know what it is. I'm a very happy man, Emil, with my Emma."

A sudden sadness came to them both, a nameless melancholy. "Perhaps," said Emil, "I'll find my Josefa somewhere, sometime, as you found your Emma. If not now, then perhaps in another life."

James involuntarily shivered. "I should not want to be reborn in the world that is almost upon us now. The Age of Tyrants. Emma and I often talk about it. Tyrants worse than Hitler and Stalin, et al. Chaos. Doomsday. The onset of a new Dark Age. You can see and smell it even now. A horror. No, if we live again I hope it'll be somewhere else, on another world."

241

He shook his whole body, as if throwing some awful portent from him. "Let's get back to Jerry. It's very interesting that you found those medical books on cancer, and Jerry's notes. I think his wife mentioned that his father had died of cancer. That often makes a survivor vindictive against disease, and fate. I've seen that happen before. Many physicians I know were impelled into their particular specialty because someone close to them had died of a particular disease. One of my friends specializes in cardiovascular disease. His wife died of it twenty years ago, and she was only thirty. He pursues his specialty as if on a vendetta. And he probably is. He's fanatical.

"As I've told you before, I always suspected Jerry wanted to become a physician. What turned him from it I don't know. But I think it is part of the picture. Cancer. The great mystery, known through all the ages. We're no nearer an understanding of the cause and the cure than were physicians in ancient Egypt."

"There may be a modern reason for that," said Emil, and his face darkened with anger. "My wife died of it. Just recently I was in a different city, where they have a renowned cancer clinic, to which patients come from all over the world. Millions pour into their research laboratories, millions. Federal grants, drives, and all that. Well, I was conducted through one of their several laboratories. Huge, glaring with light, tubes, burners, cages of mice and rats, every piece of equipment you can imagine. Never saw such concentration and bustling and milling of researchers, young and old, all in white coats and rushing as if every second was precious, and making voluminous notes on counters, and scurrying to telephones, and talking in quietly excited voices.

"I said to the scientist who was taking me about, 'Perhaps today, or tomorrow, they'll find something very important, a cure, perhaps, or the cause of the devil. That would be wonderful news for the world.' " Emil was silent a moment. "Do you know what the scientist said? He looked about the big place, with all those men and women scuttling around, and he seemed uneasy. He said,
242

'But what will happen to all these specialists and researchers and doctors, then, who are devoting their lives to this work? They'll be unnecessary, redundant. One has to think of that, you know.' Isn't that incredible?"

"In short," said James, "let's not really find a cure and a cause. There're too many people who need their jobs. Yes, incredible, but quite human. The selfishness and innate cruelty of the human primate always amazes me, no matter how often I encounter it. It really did in a lot of specialists in infectious diseases when penicillin was discovered. It wiped out many of their specialties, and no doubt they resented it, and cursed Fleming. I'm sure if they could have suppressed penicillin they would have done so, and all the other antibiotics, and all with a feeling of righteousness. I'm also sure a lot of specialists in poliomyelitis detest Salk and Sabin. I've even heard some of those lads speak contemptuously of them and call them 'those Jews'! No wonder discoverers were usually persecuted, hated and driven out and ostracized and even had their licenses lifted when they found a cure for a terrible disease. Look whose livelihoods they had destroyed."

"Our government is hand in hand with all this," said Emil. "It's always 'tests and tests' for years and years, when a scientist and/or physician comes up with some unique idea about cancer and its cure. Sometimes it's a perfectly harmless procedure even if it might not be effective. But—tests and tests and tests, and the patients die. I know of at least three substances in Europe, now being used for cancer, with some promising results here and there, but Washington insists on endless years of testing before admitting them to the United States. They learned a lesson from penicillin. It will be far worse when somewhere some obscure doctor or scientist will actually, in this country, find the cause and possibly the cure for cancer. After all, there are all those multitudes engaged in profitable research, all the pallid grim women in glasses and in white coats, and their brothers, flying about with test tubes. They'll all be out of jobs. Indeed, 'think of it.' "

"It makes one think," said James. "And when you think on it you decide the human race isn't worth saving after all, and it would be a nicer world if we were all wiped out. God, it is said, made all the innocent animals first and blessed them, and then He made man, which I think was an unpardonable error."

The next morning when James arrived at the floor of Guy's suite, he saw the red-haired lady he had encountered before with Dr. Grassner. She was speaking earnestly at the desk to the two nurses. She started when James said, "Good morning." She looked at him with her warm Tokay-colored eyes, and after a moment she smiled faintly with recognition. But her face remained grave and distressed. This time she had put a well-worn piece of anonymous fur over her brown tweed coat, and more and more James approved of her. Authentic county. She reminded him of Emma. He had a thought and he said, "Miss Turner, I am about to go to the staff room for a cup of coffee. Would you join me?"

She hesitated. Then she said, "Thank you, Dr.—?"

"Meyer." Her rather deep and resonant voice pleased his ear. They went down to the staff room, which she regarded with interest. She said, "Those poor patients. Do psychiatrists really cure them?"

"Possibly not. No one can 'cure' mental or emotional illnesses. The most we can do is to help the patient to get an insight into his problems and let him make his own decision as to what to do. I am not speaking of psychotic illnesses, which, I believe, are more or less pathological, not psychological, though many of my too enthusiastic colleagues disagree with me. They'd like to make the whole world into one mental hospital! Where, of course, they would be kings. Many of us look enviously at Russia, where the psychiatrists have enormous power—especially over dissenters. Nineteen eighty-four isn't far off, Miss Turner. As we say in England, 'Who will guard the city when madmen are the guards?' And most of us psychiatrists are definitely mad, you know, otherwise we'd not be

244

so fascinated by madness. A mutual disease makes brothers of us all."

She listened with total absorption, her beautiful eyes widening. An intrepid woman, James thought, a noble woman, for all she is no beauty and is not young. A waitress came to the table and James said, "Miss Turner?"

"Mrs. Beth Turner," she said. "I really should like some muffins and marmalade and coffee. I had a sketchy breakfast and I've discovered I'm hungry."

When the waitress had left, James said, "You are Mrs. Turner? Is your husband also a friend of Mr. Jerald's?"

She smiled at his attempt at subtlety. "No, I'm a widow. My husband was killed in Korea. A childless widow, and I am glad I am childless. I've been a teacher, you know. Now I'm retired."

He raised his eyebrows and she added, with gentle amusement, "I have a very small farm, really not quite a farm, about ten miles from Cranston, and I receive a widow's pension because of Keith, and I inherited some money from my father, and my wants are not extravagant, and I saved money all the twenty unfortunate years I taught."

Her eyes were lilting with her secret mirth and James felt embarrassed. He said, "I am not actually prying, but I am Jerry's old friend, not his physician. Anything you can offer concerning Jerry—I call him Jerry—might be of help to me. Have you known him long?"

A slight change came over her clean freckled face and she looked down at her plate. "Almost five years. We met in a disagreement. He needed my land, or at least a small part of it, for an easement on property he had brought ten miles from here, for a new development. So, our—acquaintanceship—began with a quarrel. His men had been harassing me for months, and then he came himself, to argue with me. But I knew of him. He never built the monstrosities other developers built—so, after a long discussion we came to an agreement." Her pale and beautifully formed mouth had an almost unseen quiver. "Then we became friends." She tucked a strand of her

245

shining red hair behind her ear and sadness trembled on her strong but sensitive face.

More than friends, thought James, who was liking and admiring her more and more. He cleared his throat and poured her another cup of coffee from the silver pot. He said, "It was about that time that his letters to me changed. Again, anything you can tell me about him, and your own observations, will be of enormous help." But, as he expected, she became reticent and a faint color touched her broad cheekbones.

She said, "He had problems. Not financial ones, I believe. He became restless. We had many long talks together, intimate talks. It has been my—impression— that he wasn't really contented with what he had achieved, and he was becoming—agitated." She began to eat and her eyes had a distant look, but one full of pain. "I remember my father," she said, as if speaking to herself. "He had a small but prosperous factory, and then, after a period of reflection he sold it. He went out West and bought a medium-sized ranch, and was very happy. My mother wouldn't join him. She was very upset, and I was going to school and stayed with her. Just before he died—he was forty-eight—he sold the ranch. He knew he was dying. He left the money to me."

She is telling me something, thought James, intensely interested.

"My father," she continued, "was in a turmoil until he made up his mind what to do. But he came to a quick decision, finally. He did what he always had wanted to do—and he was happy. My mother's relatives thought he was 'selfish,' but a man has to save his own life, the only life he will ever have. If there is an Unpardonable Sin, it is destroying your life in the name of 'duty'—or something else."

Yes, she is definitely telling me something, thought James, elated. She isn't a woman who is loquacious, and "communicative," as the Americans say. She goes at things, intimate things, in an elusive fashion, which is purely good taste.

246

"It's my opinion," said Beth Turner, "that some men use the excuse of 'duty' to hide the real trouble—a fear of disturbing a comfortable fixed pattern and a fixed routine. If they are troubled over their lives. It isn't always duty at all. It is—a form of cowardice. A fear of the unknown, a fear of adventure, and, in many cases, a fear of life itself. Life doesn't form patterns and routines; life isn't concerned with the prison-like walls men build about themselves. Life can be untidy, of course, but it is full of excitement—celebration. If one has the courage. What lost glories would the world have, in adventure and discoveries and music and pioneering and invention and new civilizations—if all men were careful and prudent!"

So, thought James. She was gazing at him ardently, and her eyes were eloquent, though there was a moistness as of grief in them. "I was never afraid," she said, again as if to herself, and she shook her head. "I never stifled myself with prudence. I always did what I wanted to do. If others pressed me to follow a pattern they thought best for me—mostly best for themselves!—I refused to be confined. I've taken many chances; some were disastrous but they were always interesting and exciting, even the worst. I've never been bored in my life, though I came close to it when teaching school." She laughed, and the sound was warm and endearing. "I didn't really retire. I was fired, and thank God for it."

James laughed with her. Yes, he thought, she is telling me something. What had Jerry said, with such loathing? "La dolce vita." He said, cautiously, "Some men do get themselves trapped, don't they?"

"Trapped? Yes. But they set the trap themselves. Then they lack the courage to unset it and get free. Sometimes the trap is money, sometimes it is what they call 'Honor,' and 'responsibility to others.' They are lying, of course. They're just afraid to get free from the trap. They call themselves 'conservative.' That's another lie. And—so they die in their trap and never have really lived."

She sighed, and picked up her gloves. "I'm sorry I can't tell you much about Guy. He's a very complex character, but then, most people are. I only know he—changed. He is deciding something about his life. I do know that. I wish I could help you more."

But you have, my dear lovely lady, James thought. You have told me a great deal in your elliptical way. He said, "You come in very often to ask about Jerry. Wouldn't it be easier to telephone?"

Again a crest of color ran over her face. She said, "I often come into Cranston— I like to hear about Guy. Telephones get in the way. And I—" She paused, then once more she looked at James with that ardent vulnerability. "Sometimes I hope—well, that he wants to see me, has asked for me, and I want to be there when it happens."

Lucky devil, thought James, that he has a woman like this to love him, and love him she does. She said, "How is Guy now?"

"I think," said James, "he is beginning to make a decision."

She leaned towards him. "Yes?"

"A great decision," said James. "Perhaps a dangerous one, for him."

She gazed at him, all her urgency in her eyes. "And?"

"I think he will start to—live."

Her eyes swelled with tears. She dropped her head. James touched her hand. She murmured, "Thank you, thank you, Dr. Meyer." She rose and he rose with her. He said, "My father was a very brave man. He died— violently. But he lived all the days of his life, and so his life, even in death, wasn't wasted."

He did not know why he said with impulsiveness, "Like Jerry, I have to come to a decision myself, but what that is isn't clear to me as yet. Perhaps I'm just afraid to face it."

She studied him with all her concentration. "You'll decide," she said. "And, it won't be 'prudently.' At least, I hope it won't."

14

It snowed again during the night, small hard flakes as sharp as ice, with a wind that tossed them into blizzards in the air and blizzards on the ground. James was familiar with such in Switzerland, where such a storm was hailed by skiers, of which he was one. The whole air palpitated with curtains of snow, so that everything was hazy and unreal, dreamlike and very cold. "I like this weather," said James to Emil at breakfast. "Curiously exciting, promising as spring doesn't promise. My first memory is of seeing such snow in Edinburgh; I must have been about eighteen months old. Yes, I definitely prefer it."

"I don't," said Emil, "but then I'm actually effete, like most Americans. All we need is wheels, not legs. Well, it does promise Christmas. Why are you smiling?"

"I'm remembering a discussion between my father and mother." Looking ruefully at the plate of ham and eggs he was devouring, and thinking of his weight, he became reckless and helped himself to another portion. "It was nearly Christmas. My father had just finished lighting his last candle for the Feast of the Lights. He had an enormous candelabra and the candles made a fine display. He stood over them with his hat on and prayed and Mama prayed with him, as I did. It was most solemn and inspiring. Then he helped Mama to decorate the Christmas tree in honor of the birth of the Messias. Dada then said, 'He may have been the only begotten Son of God, but He was on earth for millennia before His birth as a Man, walking unseen among men except for a few. And He carried bandages with Him, and every hour or so He would apply another bandage on the wounds inflicted on Him by mankind.' Somehow, I find that very touching."

But Emil did not smile. He said, "Of course."

"It was just one of Dada's Jewish stories," said James. "I don't know why, but it impressed me very much. I used to look at strangers on the street, asking myself, 'Is that He?' Beggars and so on, derelicts, the abandoned and the hopeless, the suffering, the lonely, the forgotten, the people with painful faces, the crippled, the forlorn, the old, the life-torn. Of course, I was just a child. But it seemed to me that every time I asked the question of myself I got an affirmative answer. Children have such imaginations."

"And sometimes what they imagine is true," said Emil. They went out into the storm to go to Mountain Valleys. They discussed Guy Jerald. James said, "I've convinced Mr. Lippincott to keep the family away from your patient, Emil, as long as possible, so he can continue to improve. He isn't improving physically but his mind is definitely focusing more and more on his problems." James then told Emil of his encounter with Beth Turner. "By speaking of her father she was really speaking of Jerry; I knew that. But she is too much of a lady to chatter of her deepest feeling, and it is most evident that she is in love with your patient."

"She doesn't look in the least like the women he prefers, who all look somewhat like his wife."

"I have the impression, lately, that his wife and all his other women are only surrogates for some other woman, though he never mentions her, if she ever existed at all." But something dim stirred in his mind, some far memory.

"She couldn't have been very important to him, if he married Lucy Lippincott," said Emil. On arriving in Guy's suite they found him standing at one of the barred windows, watching the snow. They spoke to him; he did not turn, nor did he answer. But they felt a sort of vibration about him, almost tangible. Emil left, and James and Guy were alone. James went to the other window and looked out at the snowy earth. "It looks like a wedding cake, doesn't it?" he asked.

Guy turned quickly, looked at him with his feverish eyes, then fell into his wing chair and turned aside his head. James said, "All it needs is candles, and ribbons, and a bride."

* * *

"My bride," thought Guy on a snowy December day. He had been married to Lucy Lippincott for three months. They were occupying a suite in the Old House while negotiations were being completed for the possession of Lucy's birthplace, and its renovation. She was already pregnant with her first child, and was none too pleased, nor was Guy. He knew, by now, that she was no Marlene, nor would she ever be. A man does not substitute another human being for a memory. He did not blame himself for his error; he blamed Lucy. He was now fully acquainted with her limited mind, her vacuous thoughts, her pretensions, her narrow range of responses, her inability to understand anything imaginative and tenuous, anything oblique or sensitive. Poetry was beyond her comprehension, though she had attended a very smart school for girls. An allusion would bring only a wide empty gaze, sometimes puzzled, sometimes blank. She knew only the immediate, and only that immediate which pertained to herself. In those three months she had exhibited no temper, no fire, no indignation, no profound emotion. A few times she had been petulant and dissatisfied, and, once or twice, she had been sullen when crossed. Her conversation consisted of eulogies to her father and brother, discussions of clothes, the past honeymoon and whom they had met in New York, and complaints of interior decorators. Of Guy and his desires and hopes she did not speak, though he had talked for hours about them.

She had no interest in him as a man, as a husband, as a lover. Why, in God's name, then, had she married him? He was to wonder that the rest of his life. Had her father persuaded her, when, in less than two years, Guy was a rich man, a partner of Prentice and Grace? He only knew that for some obscure reason she had decided not to marry Eric Daumbler. But the reasons she had married him, her own reasons, were still vague and uncertain. That her family approved had been evident. William Lippincott's main bank had lent Guy over half a million dollars, and with alacrity. Half had already

251

been repaid, and half of Jeraldstown had been built, sound if small houses and eagerly purchased even before completion. An apartment building, not shoddy but sturdy, was under way. Oil, of course, had not been found on the land and Guy now knew that the geologists who had visited him had had other matters in mind, matters concerned with Howard Chandler. In fact, no oil rig had ever appeared anywhere else in the farming community, and the one oil well had become dry in less that three months.

One thing only moved Lucy almost passionately, and that was money. Then her pretty tinted face would display quite a degree of vivacity, her blue eyes would shine, her mouth would become wet with greed and would glisten. Yet, she had never known the poverty of a Mary Jerald. Guy had begun to learn that greed was not felt solely by the poor and that the rich could be avaricious indeed, beyond the avarice of a beggar. The poor desired money for security; the rich desired it for status and luxury, though many, he had found, were penurious. They delighted in spending the money of others or enjoying its fat comforts when proffered by others, even if they counted every penny twice before spending it themselves. The more money a man had, the greater the honor given him, whether he was a scoundrel, a liar, a hypocrite, or a gouger, and carefully pared cheese, as his mother had called it. The average middle-class man made far more display of what he had than did the very rich, and the workingman was not far behind in his extravagances.

If Guy feared and despised the poor he had known, he was now fearing and despising the very rich even more. He had met a considerable number of them in New York and Philadelphia. His own desire for money was not the same as his original desire. He wanted to be far richer than those he had already met, so he could despise them the more. He feared yet wanted their power. He had defended himself against the poor. Now he must have more and more money to defend himself against the rich, and to detest them fiercely. Money brought independence from fools, and fools were not confined to the poverty-stricken. Gilded stupidity, in fact, was more disgusting than beggarly stupidity. There was no excuse for it.

He had finally sold his land to Prentice and Grace with the proviso that he become a partner. Then he had borrowed money, to his elders' amazement, from both a Philadelphia bank and William Lippincott's bank. For some reason, very uncertain, they had lent the partnership money and were, in a manner of speaking, themselves part of the partnership. At first Mr. Prentice had been distraught with anxiety and trepidation at the sum, but Guy had taken on a newly dauntless air which, though it hinted of danger, yet had exciting implications. Mr. Grace, an elderly man, had at first "dithered" and had issued warnings. His firm was prosperous, he would say to his partners, but not in the same category as Chandler, yet now, in this incredibly short time, they were surpassing, or at least equaling, the Chandler Development Company. That is, of course, with borrowed money. "But Chandler borrows even more money," said Guy, with impatience. "You can't get anywhere by being too conservative and not taking chances. And everyone who can lay his hands on a small down payment is buying a house. We'll give the poor bastards something for their money, which is more than Chandler can say. No Chandlertowns for us."

He was sitting, this snow-filled December Sunday, in the sitting room of his suite in the Old House, waiting until it was time to go to visit his father-in-law, whom he did not respect. Hugh Lippincott and his Philadelphia wife, Louise, would be there also. Louise was as silly as Lucy, but in a different way. She was an athletic, bouncy little woman of even more pretensions than Lucy, and she was assertive and slyly shallow, yet with a cunning mind. She never failed to bring her family into any conversation, and to display an overt contempt for Cranston and her husband. Yet, unlike Lucy, she had remembered her lessons and could surprise even Hugh with an occasional touch of wit or perceptiveness. Lucy would stare at her, unaware of not too subtle insults, merely blinking her vacant blue eyes in puzzlement, and being very proud of her sister-in-law's lineage. Moreover, Louise had inherited considerable money from her grandmother, which made Lucy even more respectful. That Hugh heartily disliked his wife, who was childless, was never evident to his sister, though it was to Guy.

Lucy was sitting near the window staring out at the snow, her pretty mouth discontented. She seldom read a book; she read only fashion magazines and magazines full of "hints" in decorating. Occasionally she did read a romantic novel, some trivial thing concerning virginal heroines and what she described as True Love, though true love was as incomprehensible to her as almost everything else. Guy was sitting at a table, studying blueprints of the apartment house, and of another he was contemplating. He rubbed his eyes and glanced at his bride and wondered again why he had married her. Of course, she did resemble Marlene, but he now saw it was only a superficial resemblance. In mind and spirit there was no comparison. That he had not loved Lucy at all, but only a dream and a memory, did not excite his remorse. He blamed Lucy for his inane marriage. He had persuaded himself that she had deceived him.

It was darkening outside though it was hardly past three o'clock. A lamp outlined Lucy's fair head with a shifting nimbus as she moved. A magazine lay open on her black velvet knees. She kept rubbing her wedding gift from Guy, a necklace of rubies, more than he could reasonably afford at the time. The movement of her fingers was sensuous, which could not be said of her body in bed. In bed she was as lifeless as a stuffed doll and as passionless. The delicate fire of a Marlene was missing; it would never be there. She knew all the gestures of affection from observation, but if she felt any real affection for her husband it was not evident. She accepted him as she accepted everything else in her life, an extension of herself, a convenience; she had done the expected
254

thing, at Daddy's suggestion, which she had not resented or protested. What true marriage was, the deepest meeting of spirit and mind and body, the deepest commitment and love, never occurred to her. She never quarreled with Guy, though she had a way of dimly carping if dissatisfied, with more than a hint of a whine in her voice, which was echoless and, Guy would think, practically bodiless. Yet she was healthy enough and could play tennis and golf quite expertly.

Guy was already unfaithful to her. If he did seek her body it was in an absentminded way, as one reaches for bread when hungry. He also did it because of a sense of "duty," and what was "owed" his wife, though he suspected that Lucy would prefer him not to be dutiful in that fashion. Still, she was his wife and therefore his property, and he had a responsibility for her. When he felt most indifferent towards her he reminded himself of his obligations. Too, he was not unaware of her beauty, which could occasionally excite him, and of her position in Cranston, and even in Philadelphia. Sometimes he was even proud of her.

"I wish," said Lucy, plaintively, "that it would stop snowing. I do hate winter."

Guy thought of his father's house, in which there had been no luxuries, and he felt a thrust of nostalgia for a moment. This was the most luxurious suite in the Old House, but to Guy it was alien and tenantless. Even its pleasant appointments had no meaning for him. It was not his home.

"I can't wait for the house to be ready," Lucy continued. She was not aware that Guy had not as yet answered her. She never noticed if anyone did not reply to her remarks. What she cared about only were her own dim thoughts and dimmer words. "I do wish they'd hurry. And I'm not sure about that rose-colored paper for my bedroom. I think I'd rather have lavender."

His mother had worn lavender at his wedding, a color not becoming to her, but it was her first real silk dress. She had been almost abject in the company

255

at the wedding and had effaced herself as much as possible. She had acquired a wild way of staring lately, as if she did not believe in all this good fortune and expected to see it whisked away like a dream. But she would not, as yet, give up her rooming house and her boarders.

She had hardly spoken at the wedding to anyone, so impressed had she become, and so timorous. She would glance at her son, marveling, and no longer resentful. Still, she thought that Lucy "could have done better." She had not liked the Episcopal church in which the wedding had taken place; it had had an unpleasantly subduing effect on her, and Mary Jerald did not like feeling subdued. At all times, she wished to feel in command of a situation, a trait Guy had inherited from her. She thought that she looked handsome in her new gown and hat and this did help her among all those strangers who were evidently so rich and important and so polite and proper. She could not understand why Guy seemed at ease with them all and looked handsome himself. She felt both uncertainty and pride. Guy perceived all this with his growing bitter amusement and almost felt affection for his mother.

My father, he thought now, did not dance, after all, at my wedding. Nor did Sal, who had not been invited, nor did Sam Kurtz, who was now Sal's husband, and also had not been invited. Guy was determined that no part of his past should intrude on his present and his future. It never occurred to him that he owed any "duty" to the woman who had loved his father so faithfully and so long, though he had given a two-thousand-dollar check to her as a wedding gift. He had never gone to their house, which was near his mother's. Sal and Sam had understood. They sent him a card on his birthday and at Christmas, but never telephoned him or wrote to him.

Lucy was continuing her meandering monologue about their house. Guy returned to his blueprints. Then all at once he was seized by a savage despair, a turbulence of mind which was nameless but almost overwhelmingly powerful. It resembled, slightly, the despair he had felt after his father's death, an incredulity, a denial. But of what he was incredulous and what he was denying he did not know. He threw aside his pencil. He stood up and began to walk up and down the warm, lamp-lighted room. Lucy watched him without surprise or curiosity. To her, he was only her husband, who was pacing the room, and she did not wonder why. It was probably only "business," anyway. That he had any thoughts aside from her and any aspirations, she was not capable of conjecturing.

She believed she loved him, not as she loved her father and brother, but she was sure she loved him. Why else had she married him? He was really very good-looking, if not distinguished, really. She was used to the abruptness and moods of men and never questioned them. That men had emotions and abysses and terrors in themselves, aside from her own expectations of them, would have inspired her perplexed disbelief. Others were as unreal to her as the characters in a play, and in company she played her expected gracious part without once wondering what thoughts roamed the dark alleys of their minds and what were their motives and emotions, what their desires and hopes and hatreds and longings. All her nebulous thoughts and her own gestures were mimicries of the world she knew, automatic reactions of a conventional pattern, mannered and unquestioning.

In the meantime Guy was beset by a clamoring but unseen chorus of despair and fury. His pacing became faster. His head beat like a drum; he was sweating. His dark skin shriveled in a suffering he could not understand. Nor could he give a name to it. It was both within him and without him. It had no form, no outline. It was just there like a storm, inchoate and murderous, battering both his mind and his body. It might be mysterious and unknowable, but it was certainly there, weakening his muscles, making him tremble.

It had some aspects of the rage and agony he had experienced when he had learned of Marlene's death.

Something, he thought in his terrible confusion, has died. He stopped his pacing and stood very still, breathing heavily, in the middle of the room. Something has died.

The thought terrified him. In an effort to escape he looked at Lucy. All at once he hated her. He projected all his torment on her.

My bride, he thought. And hated her.

"My bride," he said aloud in the darkening room of his Mountain Valleys suite. He stood up and began to walk, faster and faster, and James watched him. He saw the tortured aspect of Guy's face with alarm. He stood up, not speaking, wanting to touch that agonized man and afraid to do so.

Then suddenly Guy turned to him, though James knew he did not really see his friend. "I hated her then," he said in his hoarse quick voice. "I didn't know why, and I didn't care. You see, something had died." He put his hand to his head. "And I didn't want to know, then, what it was."

He was gasping. "But I know now. It was something in myself. I shouldn't have blamed her. She was only a symbol of the murder." He looked at his hands as if expecting to see blood on them. "But I couldn't have done anything else then, could I? A man gets driven—"

"Yes," said James. "He drives himself. No one else holds the reins."

But Guy said, "It wasn't her fault that she wasn't Marlene, though I tried to think it was, and blamed her. It was what I had killed in myself, rejecting what I had always wanted. It's only a ghost—but it's there."

"Yes," said James, "we are always there."

The blank dark face was still turned to him, and James knew that Guy was seeing something appalling in himself. Then he fell into his chair and he was gone again into the awful chaos of his mind.

Later, James told Emil of that episode. He was somewhat disheartened. "It's still dicey," he said. "He'll die soon, or go mad—or come out of it. It was dreadful while it lasted. He can't endure much more of it."

"Do you have any idea who Marlene is, or was?"

"I have a vague feeling I ought to know. I think there was some girl in Europe, just after the war. He never told me. But one night in Berlin he came back to our temporary barracks, and there was blood on his clothes. He never explained, and I didn't ask. Those were fearful times, Emil."

"Do you think it's possible he killed that girl?"

James pondered. Then he shook his head. "No, I don't think so. She was never his 'bride.' When he spoke of a bride his voice was full of hate. I think he meant his wife. And he said, 'I shouldn't have blamed her.' Yes, it's all dicey, still." Then he brightened. "He said he shouldn't have blamed her. I see a significance in that. When a sick man stops blaming someone else for his torment he has made a great stride in the right direction. He has gained some insight into himself."

"Blaming himself is a sort of absolution," said Emil. "The next step, of course, is removing himself from the place or person he has hated. That is only just, to the other, to himself."

Alone, in his room, Guy had a sudden clear thought, devastating in its ruthlessness. He started upright in his chair, and panted.

He said, aloud, "I killed what I really needed all my life, not what I told myself I wanted. I killed it because I had no bravery, and because I was afraid of it. I had told myself I had a 'duty.' It wasn't just that. I was a coward. I knew that when I tried to kill myself. I've been trying to kill it again. I am still a coward. That's why I should die. It is too late."

Then he said, "Beth. Beth."

15

When James reached the Old House he found a message from Hugh Lippincott, inviting him to dinner that night at seven-thirty. James was tired and disheartened. The depression was not caused by Guy Jerald but by something in himself. Accustomed to the psychiatrist's way of diagnosing his own malaise—a somewhat doubtful practice in many instances, and confusing—James probed at his own subconscious and could produce nothing but the memory of his father, and the strange admonition. He could actually see his father's intense blue eyes and the restless reproach in them. He was glad that he had this invitation, which would divert him at least. He told himself, with some conscious virtue, that he might discover something new about Guy. He also felt very lonely. He was not one of those psychiatrists who find their most engrossing diversion in discussing cases with other psychiatrists who were, he admitted, as much in the dark as himself when confronting the mysterious labyrinths of the human psyche. So he was glad that he would not have to have dinner with Emil that night.

He had noticed that most Americans took it for granted that everyone had a motorcar at his disposal. A man without a car was almost in the position of having been castrated, or, at least, was a paralyzed cripple. So he had the manager of the hotel call a taxi for him and refused to notice the man's upraised brows. He had to wait nearly twenty minutes for a taxi to come for him. He gave the driver the address and he did notice that the man surveyed his old tweeds with both disfavor and suspicion. "That'll cost you about five dollars," the driver said, and waited for distressed sounds. But James nodded and climbed into the cold interior. He was certain, by the set of the driver's shoulders and the bulging of his neck, that the latter suspected that there would be no tip. Also, he had pointed his ears at the English accent. They rode in dark silence through the clogged streets where the streetlamps made stark holes of yellow light on the snow. The houses became progressively more lavish with an odd jumble of big ranch residences mixed with bastard Tudor and Georgian and something amorphous which had been explained to James as "split-levels." He thought them freakishly designed and of no particular character and certainly not too inviting with their lighted windows at unexpected placements, like a badly built mass of blocks raised by a clumsy child.

No doubt they are functional, if ugly, thought James, trying for charity. But, like the ranch houses—out of place in this climate—they offered no privacy or retreat for any beset soul. However, James had learned, privacy was not cherished by Americans. Parents and children were always tumbled together like puppies in a heap, and squirming. Houses were "open," so that children could race easily from one spot to another, bellowing, always in evidence with no escaping them. Where did the master of the house retire to on an evening, for a quiet drink alone with his newspaper, after the hubbub of the day? James had also discovered that American men had been coerced, by their wives, into believing that the father of the family should be a "pal," to his offspring, listening attentively to their gasping chatter and their shrieks in the evening, and never having an instant alone to recoup his stamina and his strength. How tiring, how sapping, how proletarian and plebeian! The "hut" syndrome, as James had called it, seemed to have taken over the unfortunate country. It could also be called the aborigine syndrome, where the whole family clamored about in a cave, in a welter of "togetherness." How dreary. How exhausting, how cheap. If a man sought peace and privacy and contemplation for himself, he was labeled, according to American psychiatrists, as "antisocial."

James smiled in the cold taxi. I'm very antisocial, he thought, with satisfaction. I am an adult, a civilized man, a lover of seclusion, and possibly a gentleman. I build my

261

hedges high. Solitude is a lovely thing, a well of replenishment, a time for a man to examine his life. He thought of Guy, with an earnest pity. Had he been beset, as so many male Americans had been beset, with no time to organize his private life and reflect on his soul and cultivate his own garden? It was very possible. No wonder that most American men were neurotic, the poor sods, with women and children always besieging them. No wonder marriage had little attraction for young men now; no wonder so many of them were homosexuals. They had to escape somehow, from the omnipresence of their women, their shrill demands, their inexhaustible and meaningless jabbering, their endless complaints and petulance. They never let their men alone if they could help it. King Solomon, in his Proverbs, had had many wise remarks about women and their carping and their everlasting proximity. There was much to be said for the denounced St. Paul, who had had very little admiration for women.

James remembered that Hugh Lippincott had remarked on Guy's apparent indifference to his family. Then, thought James, there's hope for him. James also remembered that most American men referred to their houses as "homes," a vulgarism if there ever was one, and no doubt inspired by ubiquitous Mum. If American men were more and more acquiring interesting mistresses, then good luck to them! A man had to save his own life. He had to run, lest he expire in heart attacks and dangerous neuroses. The whole demoralized country had become a nursery for children or a spa teeming with women. But England's getting just as bad under deadly Socialism, thought James. Vulgarity at its worst. The aristocratic spirit had departed from the West. I must remember that! James said to himself. When the patrician imperative left a civilization it descended into mobs, with women transcendent. Then came the end. Boorishness, James reflected, thy name is Woman. (Except for Emma, who is a real womanly creature, and not an aggressive and howling banshee.) In America, there was always a cry

262

very good paintings of horses, all in stride and all very active, and all, he concluded, gelded. It was strange that a large house like this, with no bustling about it and no loud voices, could seem, indeed, noisy. Perhaps it was the large standing lamps with white shades like whiskey barrels, the white velvet "groups" of assorted small sofas and settees, all decorated with tubes of chrome, the white leather chairs alike twinkling, the thick white draperies, the occasional scarlet cushion, the white marble fireplace with, alas, another artificial fire, the white painted tables, which gave the atmosphere an effect as of vociferousness. James literally felt his eardrums ache and his eyes dazzle, though not pleasantly. The room was really gigantic, as were the windows, yet every aspect seemed shouting and imminent.

And everything was fastidious to the point of vulgarity. Even the portable bar, over which Hugh was now presiding, was white.

"A sweet manhattan for me, Hugh," said Louise Lippincott, commandingly.

"Isn't it always?" her husband returned, in a disagreeable voice. Louise shrugged, then turned her blazing smile on James. He almost recoiled. She was entirely too fervid for a woman her age and James felt some compassion. He discovered that she never stopped talking and she was always crossing and uncrossing her legs restlessly, as if in from every surface in the room and engulfed the dismayed James. He caught a faint suggestion of Mozart, but was not certain. All the instruments were fused together. Why did Americans hate peace so much, and quietude? Louise said brightly, "Those are selections from *St. Paul, Superstar!*" (She spoke in exclamation points.)

"I thought it was Mozart," said James, accepting a big glass of whiskey from his host. Hugh laughed. "It's a plagiarism of every selection of music you ever heard," he said. "Or it seems that way to me."

Louise was listening, rapt. She jerked her head at her husband and said, "Oh, Hugh. You are tone-deaf, really." She flung her body forward at the hips and concentrated all her energy on listening. James grew more depressed. He found energetic women exhausting; they made him nervous. Hyperthyroidism? Her eyes were bulging and staring enough and her skin as dry as brown paper. She was one of those women who believed she was intellectual. Over the clamor she began to talk to James of her family in Philadelphia. He caught a word here and there but blessedly the music drowned out most of her conversation. She was asking him a question. He cupped his ear and looked at her inquiringly. "I think that's enough," Hugh said, and abruptly turned off the blaring. Louise gave him a look at once hateful and despising.

"You never cared for music," she said.

"Is that music?" ___ ___ him, and

England, once Empress of the world, now reduced, in her people, to a soft blob of state-fed helplessness! The land remained, but the people—? The malaise in his mind quickened and again he saw the eyes of his father. Land of Shakespeare—land of Council houses! Land of the elegant Stuarts—land of billboards shouting, "Drinka pinta milka day!" Land of the grand Tudor Queen Elizabeth I—land of featureless Queen Elizabeth II, with her fixed smile and gloved waving hand! What had King Lear said: "Dear land, I do salute thee!" James's eyes moistened and he wept inwardly at the death of glory. But glory was dying all over the Western world, and beyond its borders the masculine Vandals of the steppes were eyeing it as a ripe if decaying feast. The West had become feminized. But Aristotle had foreseen this in every civilization which did not preserve its male authority and strength. The martial simplicity and power of the West had degenerated into a meretricious "love" for everybody, however unworthy, and had disarmed itself of the imperative to survive. More than arms was the spirit of a noble people. But where was nobility, now, in any Western nation? There remained only a a soft whimpering, a desire to be overfed and "tolerant," a desire to be cozy.

What had George Savile, Marquis of Halifax, said? "To the question, what shall we do to be saved in this World? There is no answer but this, Look to your Moat." But all the "moats" in the West were filled with stinking and dropping black water through which fetid weeds were growing. Beyond the Urals a forest of steel was rising— Perhaps we deserve no more than the knout, after all, thought James with bitterness.

But was it not the infirmity of will in the so-called leaders which had brought the West to her flabby knees? And had it, indeed, not been "planned that way"?

All this time those sentient blue eyes of James had been fixed courteously on Louise, and James discovered, to his mortification, that Hugh was regarding him with wry amusement. The big blond man sat negligently on the sofa, not too near his chattering wife, and

267

James had the startling thought that perhaps his host had followed his every thought. I have, he said to himself, too mobile a face.

Louise's father had been a congressman. She was conversing emphatically on the joys of Washington. Quaint? Surely she had not said that that white terror of a nearly Communized city was "quaint"? But she had! James was incredulous.

He fell into a gloomy pondering. Louise said with sharpness to her husband, "Hugh, really! You're neglecting me and our guest. Please. Another manhattan, and another drink for Dr. Meyer. His glass is empty." Hugh rose slowly, and Louise looked at him with flared-nostril umbrage as if he were an intransigent dog. She almost snapped her fingers to make him hurry. Hugh performed at the bar. James thought: She needs a clout. She sighed and looked at James with her extensive gleaming smile.

"Hugh is always daydreaming, which is bad for a banker, isn't it? Lately he seems to move in a cloud as if he's thinking." She laughed raucously. "Now, that's really funny—Hugh thinking! I don't think he ever had a serious thought in his life. Just money." Her tone became scornful and she glanced at Hugh with a malevolent glint in her eye. "Hugh! Don't get any ice slivers in my drink, for God's sake! Do try to make it right, for once."

James remembered Hugh at Guy's dinner table, a grim and forceful man. He was neither in his own house. Why? James had seen too many American husbands like this, silent, almost docile, before their arrogant wives, who were always ridiculing them or ordering them about. And usually the wives were insolent fools like this one, maliciously demeaning their men. They seemed to enjoy it.

Louise took her glass from her husband without thanking him or even looking at him. For an instant he stared at her, and James, with some discomfort, saw pure hatred in the other's eyes. Hugh then gave James his glass and winked at him and James thought the wink was forlorn, almost apologetic.

"Money!" said Louise, disdainfully. "That's all men

think about. They don't care for the real world, the world of the suffering downtrodden, the victims of unjust treatment in this country, the oppression, the alienated, the hungry, the unfortunate workingman—"

So, thought James, she's one of Those. What had an American writer called them? Yes—the "radical chic," who knew no more of the world than a newborn piglet, who lived in fantasies of workshops, sweatshops, and assorted social ills which had passed away over half a century ago. Many of them still thought in the dolorous clichés of the Depression thirties, thankfully far in the past. There was no use in arguing with them. They assuaged their own mean guilty consciences with loud declamations in defense of and in behalf of a legendary "Poor." But never would they set themselves to alleviating the condition of the aged, the truly deprived, the deaf and the blind and the lonely slowly dying of despair in obscure places. These, evidently, were not the "Poor." They prattled of civil rights, and treated their employees with harsh contempt and injustice, but then those employees were not the Noble Poor, not the mythical truck driver and factory worker and carpenter and plumber who earned, they alleged to believe, a "handful of dollars a week." James could not help himself. He said, "Mrs. Lippincott, I had an occasion to talk to a truck driver one day recently. He averages at least thirty thousand dollars a year."

She gave him a pitying smile. "You mean his employer nets that, not the poor driver himself."

"I do mean the driver. He works for a national firm. A big pleasant man who told me of his house and his wife and children. One of his sons is in an excellent university."

She shook her head archly at him. "Oh, dear. Someone was pulling your leg, I am afraid, Doctor. Conditions in this country are appalling. But they are better in England, aren't they, under Socialism?"

"They are very bad in England, madam. All the drive and tenacity and determination of the British have been driven out of them, and deliberately, too. There is no

269

incentive for the superior to work; they are impotent. Our doctors are leaving the country. We haven't built new hospitals in England for many years. British medicine is demoralized; British force has been killed; British originality has been extinguished. The inferior are transcendent, subsisting fatly on the punitive taxes of the superior."

But she was regarding him with a sidelong superb smile. "Oh, now, not really! I have British friends; they write me regularly."

James ignored that. "And your own country, madam, is fast falling into the Socialist-Communist slime, too, and will soon be smothering as England has been smothered. You call yourselves a democracy. Perhaps once you were, but that is true no longer. Socialism and democracy are a contradiction in terms, mutually exclusive. Socialism is a very old and primitive form of government, and it has always failed, for it is alien to human nature, and unnatural. The end result, of course, when society falls into chaos, is Fascistic Communism. And sometimes"—and now James was so upset that a savage note crept into his voice—"it is all a people deserve—the knout and the torture, the concentration camps, the forced-labor camps, the rope and the rifle, the slavery, the prisons, the barbed wire. You will get them!"

He was so tired of these people. England had them, too, those parvenus who had somehow managed to acquire illicit money or had contrived to keep it from the murderous tax gatherer. He thought of the ruling clique in Russia who lived luxuriously on the toil of their hopeless masses, and their British Socialist government counterparts, who lived as delightfully on their own countrymen. Barbarism!

"You sound like a Hitler," said Louise, with her wide mocking smile.

"Who was financed by your own bankers, and by the British bankers, too, even during the war."

"Oh, come now, Doctor!"

James went on relentlessly, as if he had not heard her.

"Just as the bankers financed Stalin, the same men who were financing Hitler."

She was aghast and incredulous. Both rows of her enormous plate-like teeth were revealed as her chin dropped. "But what would be the purpose?"

"To destroy freedom in the whole world, so that the 'elite' can rule, as they call themselves." It was no use. She was one of Those who, lacking information, believe themselves to be informed. The room had become one glare of whiteness to James and he felt a faint nausea. He looked at his host, who was listening with an inscrutable expression and frowning into his glass.

"Hugh!" shouted his wife. "Did you hear what Dr. Meyer just said about bankers?"

"I did. And it's true," said her husband. "Not little bankers like ours, of course, but the international ones who in the full meaning of the word have no race and no country."

She stared at him, all projected eyes and teeth. The rest of her face was blank and sagging and disbelieving. A maid appeared at the edge of the "conversation pit" and announced dinner. Still staring and blinking, Louise rose and the men rose with her.

The large dining room was not in the least restful. Again, there was a blaze from a modern chandelier, the beige turf of the living room was in evidence once more. The furniture had a suspiciously plastic coating, and was the color of lightly bilious feces, James thought with exasperation. Here light glared off white walls and stung the eyes. The oval table did have an authentic lace cloth and napkins and the smooth blameless crystal, if without character, at least sparkled. But there was no authoritarian weight to the silver, which was slippery in the hand. The china, of good quality, was absolutely white, with not even a suggestion of a border.

A pallid soup of undetermined flavor was served in a bowl of ice, which had a white frilled piece of paper under it. The cold rolls also were embowered in paper, and each square piece of butter nestled in those stiff frills,

271

and the lamb chops coyly displayed frilly pantalettes. The baked potatoes, to James's disappointment, had dollops of sour cream spreading miserably over the contents, and the peas were obviously out of a tin and quite cool. But the salad was luxuriant, masses of rabbity green and yellow raw vegetables and croutons overwhelmingly drenched in some dressing which James was positive was made of raw eggs, lemon juice, and mineral oil. He desperately planned on an early departure so he could return to the Old House and scrounge some proper food. He noticed that nothing here was hot, only lukewarm.

The wine was not good, if red, and it was acrid. The coffee, cool also, was served in demitasse cups, and he was invited to partake of a sugar substitute. There was no cream. The dessert, as he feared it would be, was a monster bowl of fruit, and the cheese had no élan. The house was very warm but James began to feel uncomfortably cold and he feared that he was coming down with a chill.

And Louise never stopped talking. Hugh did not listen; James politely attempted to, but the cataract of words confused him, and their loudness distracted him. If the damned woman would just say something intelligent I could focus on it, he thought. He wondered how his host could be so portly on this food and how Louise maintained the mighty massiveness of her thighs. Certainly it was not on fare like this. He suspected them of gorging secretly at noon and between meals. He became conscious of Hugh watching him with eyes suggesting hilarity, and he was embarrassed.

What was the infernal woman chattering about now? Evelyn, Marie, Tracy, Meg, Wendy, Sally, Alice, Susie, Barbara— She was speaking as if James were well acquainted with these invisible females. He had lost the thread somewhere. She spoke with confidence that he was deeply involved with them, as she was. Who in hell were they? He glanced helplessly at Hugh, who was silently laughing behind his napkin. Then as the flow of words inundated him he came to the solution: Louise was talking endlessly about her nieces. He was quite familiar with this phenomenon: Wealthy childless women invariably had large clots of nieces, all devoted and all "adoring and adorable." It seemed that all of these, in Louise's case, also had big collections of children. Husbands? They were not mentioned, except in brief passing. It appeared they were invariably of the highest society and had redundant riches.

Then, if as by magic, the dreary plastic bundle was thrust at James. Sometime, he mused, when he was semi-conscious, Louise had left the table to procure the horror. Colored photographs tumbled about him in sheafs, all of young women in overstuffed shorts and trousers and the ubiquitous men's shirts, all with gross teeth and little eyes squinting in blasting sun and all clutching children (hard to tell the sex) in very brown hands. The children were disgracefully fat and wore greedy or petulant expressions, full of dissatisfaction. But one photograph was a little attractive, a tall young man, lean and athletic, with pronounced strong Apollonian features and short fair hair and large sinewy hands. James said, "A nephew?"

Louise looked at him with acute disfavor. "My niece, Barbara. She plays in tennis tournaments." James studied the totally flat chest, the narrow hips, the brown ligamented neck, and he had an unkind thought: A transsexual, if I ever saw one. "Oh," he said. Hugh gave a strangled cough and Louise turned a truly nasty face on him. "You never did like Barbara," she said accusingly.

"I prefer the female sex," he answered.

Well, thought James, we do have a lot of women in England like these, too, God have mercy on us. What had gone wrong with their female hormones? Did the decline of masculinity in men cause it to develop in women? Was it a sort of unconscious protest against that decline?

Mrs. Lippincott had remarked something concerning Guy Jerald, and James pulled himself out of his lethargy and listened. She was staring at him impatiently and was asking him a question—apparently again. "Lucy tells me Dr. Parkinson said Guy's condition was pretty hopeless

273

and she had better prepare herself that he would have to be permanently institutionalized."

"No. Not at all," said James. "Dr. Grassner and I are much encouraged by his general improvement, at least mentally and emotionally. He has said a number of things to me. His physical improvement will follow his emotional recovery."

"Oh, what on earth!" Louise flung up her hands and eyes and her ponytail hissed swish-swish on her narrow shoulders. "If there ever was a man so fortunate I don't remember! Of course, a lot of men get a little funny around his age—" and she glanced malevolently at her husband with a meaning smirk. "They go looking for tramps, though. Nobody should be surprised. Of course, it's a bad blow to a faithful wife, and sometimes divorce is the best thing for her."

Self-disciplined and well bred though he was, James could not refrain from saying, "I deeply agree with you, Mrs. Lippincott. It is best for everybody, and I must admit, it can be the kindest thing for a woman to do for her husband."

"What!" she exclaimed, and her eyes were ferocious and the greenish tint in them sharpened. "After a woman has given the best years of her life to a man?"

Hugh broke in. "How about a man's best years given to a woman, Louise? How long does he have to stay in penal servitude?" His heavy face had taken on an alarming flush. Hypertension, poor devil, thought James. He murmured something intended to be soothing, but Hugh and his wife were locked together in some unseen combat inspired by a mutual aversion and hatred, and they had forgotten him.

Then Louise said softly, slyly, "Well, Hugh darling, you'll never get a divorce from me."

What atrocious manners and conversation before a stranger, thought James.

Then Hugh was laughing, as if he had heard James's inward remark. He said. "I'm glad to hear your prognosis —James. I wish all good luck to poor old Guy. I met him

274

when he came into the bank with his first big check, after he had concluded a very good deal with Prentice and Grace, housing developers in Pittsburgh. He swaggered— no, he stalked—into the bank, and naturally, as he wanted to deposit such a large sum, he was turned over to me. I was second vice-president then. There he was, in a shabby old coat and a cheap suit and no hat, bigger than life, and with fighting eyes which dared anybody, and he told me. Prentice and Grace had wanted to buy his whole really enormous amount of land, but he had held out for a partnership. So they finally settled for a junior partnership, and, under Guy, they've become the biggest developers in the whole Commonwealth, even bigger than Howard Chandler. Old Grace was more than a little conservative, and thought Guy a disaster—"

"Which he is," said Louise. Her husband ignored her.

"He took a course in architecture," said Hugh. "And worked during the day with his new partners. They gave him a little development to handle, and handle it he did, spectacularly. 'Quality is our guide,' it says in their advertisements, and so it is. A buyer gets his money's worth in a good house, architecturally sound and distinctive, and sometimes he gets a little more. No tract houses are built by Prentice, Grace and Jerald, though old Grace is dead now. Just old John Prentice and his son, and Guy, run the business. They've won awards and such for their houses. A thirty-year-old house built by them is in first-class condition still. No shortcuts, no cutting corners. And they won't build cheap houses, anywhere. Many of what they build are true mansions, up in the hills. No one has ever failed to float a mortgage on one of their houses. The banks trust Guy."

"Ha," said Louise. Hugh still ignored her.

"Then he married Lucy, my sister." Hugh's face changed subtly.

"Poor Lucy," said Louise. "What a mess she made out of her life, marrying that oaf. Ignorant, uneducated, rude, bad-mannered, uncouth—"

Her husband looked at her. "A man," he said.

"No family," chanted Louise, as if she had not heard him. "No background. A nobody. Poor Lucy."

Hugh smiled. "A man. The kind this country needs. We're short of such men. Entrepreneurs. Men willing to take great chances. Men with a will and a determination to succeed, and the devil with 'security.' I thought he was taking too much of a gamble, a lot of the time. But he knew what he was doing, and what looked like imminent ruin and bankruptcy turned into rousing success. I heard he used to give old Grace heart attacks, but Grace died a multimillionaire and had reams of praising obituaries in the newspapers. It was all due to Guy. No, I never liked him. I thought he was—uncouth—too, but there was a splendid mind behind that ruthlessness and drive. He seemed reckless, but he never was. We became wary friends, but I didn't really start to like him as a person until about five years ago." He paused and gave a short laugh which was not really amusement. "I think I was envious of him, actually. He had what I lacked. No infirmity of will. He had force."

Louise raised her voice. The ponytail swished. "I can tell you something about your cheap brother-in-law, Hugh Lippincott. I saw him in Philadelphia a year ago, in a hotel restaurant, with a perfectly awful-looking woman with dyed red hair and the ugliest clothes! An almost old woman. At least she appeared that way. A farm wife, or something. She wore a woolen knitted cap or hat on her head! And knitted gloves! And her clothes! Guy didn't see me. He was talking to that woman as if there wasn't another woman in the world. Really."

She saw that both men were giving her rapt attention, and she preened.

"That creature was just his kind. A nothing, a nobody. No makeup. I saw her hands. Raw and red, like a washerwoman's. They had their heads together. She looked as if she didn't have a cent in the whole world." Louise laughed her raucous laugh. "I thought he was trying to get a new domestic for Lucy, but Lucy wouldn't have such an ugly thing in her house. Lucy, I admit, has some style. Now,

276

you wouldn't believe this, but it's true! Guy took both her hands and held them and he seemed to be begging her for something. And"—she paused portentously and her malice was a bright glee on her face—"I know what it was. I followed them. They went upstairs in the elevator together! My God! Yes, just his kind. And I'm telling you the God's truth. They went upstairs together to some bedroom."

She gleamed at them both dramatically. "I never told Lucy. It would break her heart, poor thing."

"I don't believe it," said Hugh, in the flat hard voice he used to his wife. "That doesn't sound like the kind of woman he goes for. They all look like Lucy, and the younger, the better."

Louise sat up alertly. "And how do you know that?"

Hugh grinned at her. "Oh, we often go to Philadelphia together! And New York and Boston and other places. You know that, Louise." He assumed a tone of mock gravity. "He never keeps a woman more than a week or so. He's looking for some ideal, or something, and the sort of woman you describe certainly isn't what he likes."

"I asked you how do you know that?"

"I've seen him—around," and Hugh grinned at her cruelly. Again they were locked in some deadly if unseen combat. "No, Louise," said Hugh after a moment or so. "You must have been mistaken about the man."

"I wasn't! I was only six feet away. He never saw me, he was so engrossed with that awful creature. Engrossed! You'd have thought she was Cleopatra or something. I almost laughed out loud. It was the funniest sight. It was around that time that he began to show signs of his mental illness. You remember."

Hugh sat and thought. He said, "He started to change five years ago. I think I was the only one who knew it, though Lucy began to complain that he had lost all interest in his family. He seemed to be losing interest in his business, too, and in the banks." He rubbed his chin. "Well, James, what do you make of it?"

James was thinking of Beth Turner. So they had had a

rendezvous, that wonderful fine woman and the beset man. Yet—what had made him ill? What, with such a woman, had made him turn his face away from all that he had worked for since he had been a young man? La dolce vita? A mistress like Beth Turner could make any man's life noble and fulfilled, and help him to endure it.

Then he remembered what she had said to him, that Guy knew where she was and if he wanted to see her he knew how to reach her and send for her. So far he had not. Why? It was very confusing. That she loved him had been poignantly evident, and if she loved a man he must inevitably have loved her in return. Yet, Guy had not asked for her.

They went back to the abominable conversation pit for an afterdinner drink. Louise was still chattering with hating glee of Guy Jerald. "Just imagine a man in his position committing adultery with a hideous creature like that! Where on earth did he pick her up?"

"I never trust your judgment about another woman, dear," said Hugh. "She must have been beautiful."

Yes, thought James, beautiful.

"She was positively dreadful! An old bag. Her hair was a mess and such an awful dyed color!" Again the ponytail swished and swished.

James was hesitating on the brink of the pit. He looked apologetically at his watch. "May I be excused?" he said. "I think I am coming down with a chill. This weather, you know."

"It's hardly ten," said Louise, "I did want to talk to you, Doctor, about poor Lucy and her poor children, with such a husband and father."

Hugh stood up. "I'll drive you back," he said. He seemed relieved, and James suspected he was glad to leave his wife for a while. James thanked his hostess ceremoniously. He had not got used to the white glare of the house, and his eyes hurt and he was inexplicably depressed. Louise gave him her dry hand and smirked coquettishly, but her eyes despised him.

When Hugh and James drove off in the warm car Hugh

was silent for a considerable time. Then he said, "I'll either divorce that bitch or murder her." His voice was pent, and he had blurted out the words as if he had lost control of himself.

James murmured, "Well, murder is a bit extreme, isn't it? And the murderer often suffers some degree of heart failure afterwards. Very wearing."

Hugh laughed his first spontaneous laugh of the evening. "How English," he said. "You even kill with flair, don't you? And, no doubt, politely."

James smiled. "It doesn't do to be vulgar, does it? And murder can be pleasing, if handled nicely. Our lieutenant, in the war, actually apologized to a German when he bayoneted him and said, 'I wish you were a bloody Russian instead.' Now, that is being civilized."

Hugh said, "Are you really very tired? I thought we'd go—somewhere—and get something decent to eat. You've got to admit that dinner was filthy, but that's what Louise likes. It's also cheap."

"Come to think of it," said James, with cheer, "I *am* a bit famished. I'm accustomed to eating later. What have you in mind?"

"You'll see," said Hugh, and he sounded like a youth, and drove faster through the quiet snowy streets. "A friend of mine. A superb cook." The car rolled on through wide and pleasant streets of older houses, all solid and gracious. Hugh pointed out a number. "Guy is responsible for some of these. You'll notice there are no ranch houses here or split-levels. All genuine Tudor or Georgian, with a touch, here and there, of Mount Vernon. Nothing ostentatious, though."

He added, "My house wasn't my idea. But it was what Louise wanted, and she bought it herself."

He stopped his car before a house very similar to Guy Jerald's, Georgian and quietly impressive, of brick and stone, set a distance back on wide snowy lawns filled with trees. Many sedate windows were bright with lamplight and one or two had the warm crimson shadow of a fire upon them. Hugh actually leapt from the car and ran

279

around and opened the door for James. He looked buoyant and a little excited.

"Whom are we visiting?" asked James.

"My friend, Mrs. Kleinhorst, my dear friend."

"But, is she expecting us?"

"No, but she is always ready for guests."

They went up the long cleared path to the double oaken door, and Hugh rang the bell with a flourish. James could see his face, flushed and happy, and he thought to himself: So. The door opened and a tall slender lady appeared, dressed in a long black dress, her pale hair heaped gracefully on her small head. When she saw Hugh she exclaimed delightedly, "Oh, come in, darling! I'm so glad to see you!" Then she saw James, and stepped back.

"A friend," said Hugh. "I've told you about him, Marian. Dr. Meyer, a friend of old Guy's."

They entered the snug warm hall with its shaded lights and quiet and good pictures on the paneled walls. A sense of peace and relief came to James. His hostess was holding out a long soft hand to him and smiling, and he took that hand and thought: A lady. Like Beth Turner, the woman also had strong firm features, not symmetrical but attractive. Her complexion was pale, as were her eyes and brows, and when she smiled she became intriguing, beautiful and serene. She took her guests' coats and hats and put them into a closet, then led them into a living room lit by firelight and soft lamplight; a foreign room. Hugh suddenly put his arm about her and kissed her long and passionately, and her white hands reached to his shoulders. It was simply done and James thought it charming, even touching.

The room was deceptively reserved and it was filled with excellent antiques and there was a wall of books on each side of the rustling log fire. "We're hungry, Marian," said Hugh, like a schoolboy. "Feed us."

"I've got only cold ham and cold turkey," said Mrs. Kleinhorst, in a warm and gentle voice. "It's Sue's night off. I was about to have dinner myself, alone. But I'm so glad you came—Hugh."

All her movements were graceful and quiet. She brought the men drinks and sat down with a hearty cocktail for herself. She smiled at James, but her eyes kept straying to Hugh and for the first time he saw what was really meant when it was said, "Her heart stood in her eyes." She was not reticent about her emotions, nor, most obviously, her love for this man. Her every glance was candid and open. A clock chimed somewhere, peaceful and unhurried. The fire sparkled. A little white dog came into the room and jumped up immediately on Hugh's lap. There was the faintest suggestion of a Chopin nocturne moving through the wood-scented air.

The chill in James's bones began to thaw. He relaxed in his deep chair and put his feet on a footstool. Mrs. Kleinhorst surveyed him kindly and said, with interest, "Hugh has told me so much about you, Dr. Meyer. How is Guy Jerald?"

"Coming along very encouragingly," replied James. "Not fast enough to please his doctors, of course, but I have every hope for an eventual—revival."

Intelligence and delicacy shone on the woman's face and in those very pale eyes, almost silvery. She said, "I don't know Guy very well, nor his wife. Just socially. But I thought him a remarkable man. Very unusual."

There was the dimmest hint of a Teutonic accent in her sweet voice, yet her English was impeccable. She was looking at Hugh again. Hugh was stroking the little dog but he was regarding his hostess with frank love and tenderness. James was interested. This was a different man from the man in the glaring white ranch house. It was a man of gentleness and composure. He said to James, "I've known Marian since she came with her parents as refugees from Hitler."

Then why the devil didn't you marry her in the first place? thought James. Hugh said, "She had to leave her husband, in Germany. He was a colonel in the Wehrmacht. He was forty years old. She was only seventeen."

"Helmut was a good man," said Marian Kleinhorst. "At great risk he smuggled us out of Germany. He was

281

also a friend of Herr Schacht's so we were able to bring with us a great deal of our money." She looked fully at James and smiled sadly. "My father was very rich. He inherited much, much money from his father and grandfather. They were jewelers. My father was a rabbi."

Is she challenging me? thought James, with his own sadness. He said, "My father was an Austrian Jew, Mrs. Kleinhorst. He was killed, somewhere in Germany, after many excursions into Germany to save his co-religionists."

Her silvery eyes glistened with tears, and she smiled tremulously. "I see," she said. She breathed deeply. "My husband was executed after the trials in Nuremberg. He was not an evil man. He was only a soldier, and he did what he felt was his sworn duty, as a soldier. We loved each other very much."

"We set a very bad precedent at Nuremberg," said James. "What if the Western world loses in an inevitable war with the Fascistic Communist countries? Will we see our officers and generals, our armies, our rulers perhaps, executed as war criminals?"

Marian nodded, but she said, "Still, many of those executed were guilty of the most barbaric crimes."

"True. But that is so of all wars. And barbarians are not the exclusive property of any country."

Again she nodded. "My father always said that the West and the East would, one day, be engaged in the most deadly war the world has even seen. That was even before the last war."

Deftly and quickly she moved a small round table before the fire, left the room, and returned with a white cloth and napkins and silver. While the men drank another drink she laid out the services and James saw some exquisite Austrian plates of dark blue and gold and white. He found himself very hungry, and very relaxed. He stretched out his feet to the fire. He yawned with pleasure. Hugh was humming with the almost inaudible music. He appeared years younger than he had over an hour ago. One could sleep here in peace, thought James, forgetful of the terrible world outside these doors.

282

Marian left the room again. Hugh said in a low voice, "She won't marry me."

James raised his eyebrows with inquiry. Hugh said, "It's the damned banks. Everything I have is tied up in them. They've been my whole life, since I was a kid. Marian said I would come to hate her if I lost—everything. Besides, she says, she is too old for me. I need a young wife, she says, for children."

James said, with an unusual lack of reticence, "I have a dear mistress in London. She refuses to marry me, saying that marriage is often the death of love. I disagree—well, sometimes. But why would you lose 'everything' if you left your wife?"

"My dear father," replied Hugh, "never really trusted me. He adored Lucy. She was his main heir. And Louise and her family are all part of the banks, and Guy is a director." Hugh gave a bitter snort of laughter. " I mentioned divorcing Louise once, to Guy, and he came down on me like a wall of stones that had been exploded. I had a 'duty' to Louise, he said. I had a 'responsibility,' he said. That was five years or more ago. A grim bastard."

Something moved in James's mind. He remembered his conversation with Beth Turner, and some of Guy's incoherent exclamations.

"I'm not exactly a poor man," Hugh continued. "I have enough to live on, very comfortably, for the rest of my life, barring disastrous inflation. And there are other banks in Cranston, and I've had discreet offers from banks in Philadelphia. But Marian won't marry me. I think she is afraid— More than anything else. She is afraid of losing me if she marries me."

"She has a point there," James admitted. "Still, my parents literally adored each other. However, there was one thing: They were first to each other. I sometimes had the thought as a child that I was a non sequitur in their lives, a cherished incident, but only an incident. That didn't make me love them the less; I thought it quite proper, and still do. Children are visitors, but only visitors. They must be treated as beloved visitors, and friends, with

283

always the understanding that they were, from birth, poised for leaving." He added, "Be content as things are. You and I—we have more than most men."

Marian came back with a large tray filled with silver dishes and a big silver pot of delectable coffee. When she left the room for a moment Hugh said, "But, I can't stay with my wife. I hate her. Yes, I hate her. It isn't healthy for me, or even for her. We detest each other. I may not divorce her, but as sure as God I am going to leave her, and soon."

When Marian returned Hugh reached out his hand to her, took hers, and kissed it, and she bent to kiss the top of his head. James thought, as he always thought, that love between a man and a woman was the one thing that made our appalling world endurable, and that without it it was a hell and a madhouse. Such love was blessed, with or without marriage, and was the only verity.

The greatest insult to God was living a loveless life.

16

"I missed you last night," said Emil Grassner to James.

"Mr. Lippincott invited me to dinner, and I thought it would be a change," said James. "But you did get my message?"

"Yes." Emil smiled at him curiously. "Did you enjoy meeting Mrs. Lippincott?"

"It was an experience," said James with wryness. "An experience I am getting accustomed to. In America. I'm sorry."

"I can't stand the lady, either," said Emil, and they laughed a little. "*C'est formidable.* But many women are, these days. My late wife was nothing like that. She was, above anything else, a woman."

"Rare, even in England now, Emil. I think the whole bloody world is going to hell. I wonder if our ancestors thought that, too."

"Probably. Every generation has its Armageddon, but this time it's for real. I'm sorry I have children and grandchildren. By the way, late last night Dr. Parkinson called me. They telephoned him from Mountain Valleys. Guy, it seems, was very 'agitated.' Shouting, crying, cursing. 'Out of control.' "

"That's good," said James, but with some doubt. "What happened then?"

"I told them to give him a strong sedative, stronger than usual. Later I called. Guy had settled down to sleep, but moaned all night. It's very kind of you, James, to give him so much of your time."

James thoughtfully stirred his breakfast coffee. "In a way, he's giving me a lot of his time, too, without his knowing it. I'm not the man who came here. I, too, am confused, as I told you before. In looking over my life I feel it was wasted. I've got to come to terms with the thing that is bothering me in my own mind—just as Jerry has to come to terms with his own problem. At least I'm not afraid. I think."

"But he is?"

"Yes, of course. He's almost berserk with fear. I don't call that weakness. Better to have fear and confront and act with it than to lie to yourself that you aren't afraid at all, even in the midst of the mess you've deliberately made of your life. Even worse is to reconcile yourself to the mess and tell yourself you couldn't have done anything else."

They went to Mountain Valleys together, as usual. The report was that Mr. Jerald was still sleeping after an exhausting night. Emil nodded, and continued on with his other patients while James entered Guy's suite. Guy was in bed, and James sat alone in the sitting room before the artificial fire, and read a new magazine. The nurse came and went to look at her patient, to sigh and to shake her head. James finally went to the bedroom door and looked himself. The gray skull-like face on the pillow alarmed him. The sick man had a deathly look, worse than before. As James gazed at him with pity, Guy awoke

285

and saw his visitor. He said in that rough voice of his, "Are you still here, Jimmy? Why the hell don't you go away and let me alone?" He swung his thin legs out of the bed, then sat there, his head in his hands. "I don't know what you're doing to me, Jimmy, but it isn't good."

"It's always hard to look at yourself, Jerry."

Guy uttered an obscenity. The nurse came to the door with a tray and said brightly, "Well, we had a nice sleep, didn't we? Ready for breakfast, Mr. Jerald?"

He gave her a suggestion as to what she could do with the breakfast, and it was filthy, indeed. The nurse merely smiled and put the tray on the table. "Juice, creamed eggs and ham and nice hot toast, and coffee."

James retreated to the sitting room and went to the window. The sun was shining with a dazzling luster on the snow. A few short icicles were hanging before the window, as pure as crystal, and dripping. The grounds spread away in immaculate undulations and the distant mountains leaned in a strong metallic blue against a paler sky. Scintillating though it all was, James felt a familiar depression, and a longing for home and Emma. He clasped his hands behind his back and shook his head. He went back to the magazine and the fire, and his loneliness made him feel slightly sick. He heard, behind the closed bedroom door, Guy's incoherent shouts and protests and curses. At least, thought James, he's out of his lethargy. He sounds enraged, and when a man is angry like this he is angry with himself. I hope so, anyway. But total anger against one's own person can end in suicide. James highly disapproved of suicide, for it suggested not only self-pitying despair but cowardice.

The nurse appeared with the tray; the breakfast had been hardly touched, except for the coffee. "Mr. Jerald is shaved and bathed, and he is dressing," she informed James. "He'll soon be with you. He's not in a very good mood this morning."

"So I heard," replied James. "I'd like to be alone with him when he comes out, if you please."

The nurse nodded and left, and James, out of his own

malaise, paced up and down the room, rubbing the red-gray curls at the base of his head—a big paunchy man who looked, more than ever, like a Toby jug though without the amiable smile. He was weary. He had not slept well himself. He had had a troubled dream about his father. He could not remember the dream very well; he only recalled that his father had been sitting before him and had been gazing at him in a questioning silence, his fiery blue eyes waiting. James had the impression that they had just concluded a most disturbing conversation. The echoes were still in his mind, but what they had said was not only unclear to him but not remembered. He just knew, however, that his father had been reproaching him and that he had understood the reproaches. He sighed.

The bedroom door opened and Guy came into the room, gaunt and ghastly, though neatly dressed as usual. He took no notice of James. He merely went to the window, stared out, muttered something, then threw himself into his chair and stared at his hands, unseeing, turning them over and over on his knee.

James said, "I had dinner with your brother-in-law last night, and his wife."

No answer. "I also met his—friend. Mrs. Kleinhorst."

Guy turned his hands over and over, not pausing, not heeding.

"A lovely lady," said James. "He's fortunante indeed to have such a friend. Every man is."

Then Guy spoke with loud contempt. "He hasn't any sense of responsibility. If he had he'd have been content with a casual woman, not an—involvement."

James was suddenly heartened. "Responsibility? Hasn't Mr. Lippincott also a duty to himself, a responsibility, if you will?"

Guy said nothing, but he suddenly looked up at James, and James was appalled to see distracted hatred in his black eyes. "That's easy to say, Jimmy. Hugh hasn't children to think of. He draws a good salary from the banks, and is a director of my business. He can afford to—"

"What?" asked James. But Guy did not answer. He moved restlessly in his chair. Finally he said, "Of course, his woman has money of her own, a lot of it. I've known about him and her for a long time."

"And, you don't approve?"

"Hell, Jimmy, it's not my affair. Louise is a pig of a woman, and she deserves what she is getting. But, that's not the point. Hugh has also a responsibility to the banks, and my business, and a scandal could do him no good, nor me, either. He hasn't any discretion."

"A man can die of 'discretion,'" said James. "And prudence is often just another name for fear, selfish fear."

Guy shouted, and half rose from his chair. "You don't know the full implication, damn you, Jimmy! A whole lifetime of work and struggle—you don't know! You don't throw it all over for—"

"For what?"

"Yes, for what?"

"A man has to live his own life, sometime," said James, mildly. "He can't, forever, be chained in manacles he forged for himself, and put on himself."

The hatred, and something else, brightened in Guy's eyes. "Go away, Jimmy. You're just making matters worse." He dropped his head. "I made myself face it—once. And it damned near killed me. I wish they had let me die."

James sat down near his friend. "Life can be very beautiful, and peaceful, and fulfilling, if we let it, Jerry. It's a lovely world in many of its aspects, though man is busy despoiling it as fast as he can. But a lovely world still. I remember a summer in Devon, when I was a young lad. Warm trees, quiet green hills on which lambs and sheep wandered, a sweet wind, fragrant. And bees, clouds of bees, going on their innocent way. I've seen many other summers, but not one lovelier than that. I met the first girl I ever loved, there. When I think of her I remember the bees and the wind and the hills."

The only sound was the thrumming of bees in the hot July sun, though there was a soft almost inaudible murmur in the air, as if some giant was gently sleeping in the midday heat. The long narrow path was bordered by wild-flowers, among them Queen Anne's lace as delicate as if made of spider's webs, and long white daisies with their yellow hearts turned up to the fervid sky. On Guy's left swept a long drift of great oaks and maples, running down to the distant road, and on his right there lay the fields of corn, their green tassels just faintly coloring with gold as they glistened in the light. The land appeared to bask, to rest, to be at sunny peace. But the man who walked in this lovely dazzle was not at peace and the scene filled him with a peculiar sense of loneliness and frustration and a longing to which he could put no name and only emotion, as if he had lost something precious, never to be found again.

He saw, ahead of him, a small compact white house of painted wood with a red roof and brick chimneys. It was very neat, and very quiet. Then from somewhere erupted a white-and-tan collie, all teeth and tongue, barking wildly, tail waving like a ruffled feather. The animal bounced on its hind legs, threatening, though the golden eyes were laughing. Guy made a fist and bent and presented it to the dog, who sniffed at it, then ran ahead, looking over his shoulder, obviously leading the way, still barking. "You're not a watchdog; you're a farce," said Guy, and the dog laughed delightedly. As if in answer there was a petulant cackling of fowl, a grunt of a hog, the "pitty-quirk" of guinea hens, and a woman's voice calling, "Joe, Joe?" The dog barked in reply and rushed up the path, prancing.

The warm complacency of the earth was stirred by a sudden random breeze, hot and aromatic, and the trees turned glittering pale backs in the radiant air. Guy glanced at the sky with quick remembrance. Yes, in the south there were a few darkening clouds with brilliant silver

289

tops, promising rain, and one of them was stabbed by a mercurial slash of lightning. For some reason this made him feel less wretched and languid. He came up to the house and saw its small polished windows, its looped white curtains, its red door with the copper lion's head on it, as bright as fire. He stopped a moment as if with relief, and with definite pleasure. Then, at a little distance to the right of the house, he saw a woman kneeling in a huge flower bed all rose and pink and yellow and white. She was weeding. As Guy appeared, accompanied by the dog, who appeared to present him for inspection, she sat back on her heels and pushed aside a fine untidy welter of red hair with the back of a brown hand and regarded him without fear and only with curiosity. "Yes?" she said. Her voice was calm, soft yet full. Then she said, "Oh. It's Mr. Jerald, isn't it?"

"Yes."

"I've seen your photograph in the papers," she said, and stood up. She was tall, perhaps too slender, but her breast was voluptuous under the blue shirt. She rubbed her hands on a pair of very soiled blue denim trousers. She looked very sweaty and very dirty and very composed. There was mud on her cheek and on her chin. She was not in the least pretty and certainly had no beauty except for that luxuriant breast, and she was not young, possibly my own age, or a little younger, thought Guy. Forty-eight or so. But she had an intrepid air, and she stood tall and straight like a young man, and pinned her hair, which was very damp along her temples and forehead. She smiled at Guy frankly, showing small white teeth; her mouth was rosy from exertion and beautifully formed, with a fearless but also vulnerable expression. He saw her very white skin, the wide translucent cheekbones on which there was a broad wash of ginger freckles, her pugnacious nose, and the eyes, open and candid, the color of tawny wine, and the ruddy lashes and brows.

"I think I know why you came," she said. "It's about part of my land isn't it, for the easement? No." She smiled again as if amused. "It's no use, Mr. Jerald."

"Well, let's talk about it, Miss Turner."

"I've talked with your men. And it's definitely no, no. So why talk about it?" She paused. "It's Mrs. Turner, by the way, not Miss."

He was surprised. He had been led to believe she was an old maid, a former schoolteacher. So she had a husband, had she? "Is there a Mr. Turner?" he asked. He rested his foot on a small fallen log on which there was a package of cigarettes and some matches. She reached for them and lit a cigarette. Her face had changed. "No, there isn't a Mr. Turner. Not anymore. He was killed in Korea." She offered him a cigarette and he took one and she lit it, casually.

"I'm sorry to hear that," he said. He looked about him. "Any children?"

"No, thank God," she answered, with such a fervor that he reluctantly laughed. She laughed also, her arms folded across her breast, the cigarette smoke rising and fluttering in the gathering breeze. "Children are one reason teachers often didn't marry," she continued. They smoked together in a little silence. The dog lay down, panting, in the shade of an enormous maple and regarded the two with affection.

Mrs. Turner, though quite at ease, was studying her visitor. She decided that he was darkly handsome, in spite of that lowering face, and very masculine, a trait one did not see often in these days among men. Yet there was no male relaxation about him, only a pent aggression and, she saw acutely, a weariness. His summer suit of light gray gabardine was obviously expensive. She glanced at his hands and felt a pleasure she had not known for a long time, for they were implicit with strength and surety: and implied hard work. To her alarm and quick confusion, she wanted to touch those hands. She stood in the sun and there was suddenly a tension between them which astonished Guy, for he had forgotten the strange but powerful attraction which could come between a man and a woman. She was not at all the kind of woman who usually drew him and pleased him, yet he was drawn and pleased. He

291

felt the intense current flow between him and Beth Turner, savoring it and wondering about it.

He said, "You have about fifteen acres, don't you? Not quite a farm."

"It's farm enough for me," she said, still standing. He sat down on the log. "Two cows, four sows and one boar, one hundred chickens and those silly guinea hens. They're always so curious. They're asking each other who you are."

The wide sunny peace lay all about them. Again they smoked in silence. "It's all I want, all I need," said Beth Turner. "I have a little money of my own, too. I travel occasionally. I have my house. What else could a woman want?"

"You talk as my father used to talk," said Guy. "He had nine hundred acres of land, and a house of sorts, and never had a cent to his name."

There was something in his voice that alerted her and made her feel an odd compassion. She studied him closer. "He sounds like an interesting man," she said.

Guy looked at the burning tip of his cigarette and so did not see the gentle pity in her eyes. He said, "Oh, he was, all right. He was content with what he had. He had a little stock, his broken old house. And—his woman."

"A Pennsylvania Thoreau," she commented.

"An anachronism," he said, and his voice hardened.

"Too bad there aren't more of him around," she replied.

"An old hippie," Guy said. "What kind of a world would we have if most people were like him?"

"And me," she laughed. "Oh, don't apologize. Everybody to his own life. I just ask that the damned government won't hound me too much, and let me alone. My life is mine—yours is yours. There's no quarrel."

("It's your life, kiddo," Tom had said.)

"He didn't have any ambition," said Guy.

"I don't either, Mr. Jerald. All I want is to be let alone to live my life as I want to live it."

"My father had a lot of books."

"So do I."

292

Guy smiled. "My father would have loved you, Mrs. Turner."

"And I'd have loved him, I'm sure. I bet he had a low opinion of government, too, as any intelligent man would have."

"He did, indeed. If any bureaucrat had come to 'advise' him, he'd have kicked the damned fool off his land, or probably have shot him."

"Good," said Beth. "I feel that way often. When I was a teacher the bureaucrats on the local school board yammered at me all the time, in the name of the sacred children, whom they were trying to straitjacket into conformity. It's an old story of tyranny, isn't it? When I refused to 'cooperate' and sing the joys of Socialism to my children, I was fired as being 'incompetent.' But my kids learned to read and write and no nonsense. I refused to teach social studies, too. I taught my kids history, not a pack of social-consciousness lies and hypocrisies. Yes, I'd like to have known your father."

"But wouldn't you like to have more money?"

She showed open surprise. "What for? As I said, I have all I need now. I'm not interested in clothes and hairdressers and jewelry or clubs."

Guy thought of his wife. "Don't you do any volunteer work?"

"Why, no. Why can't we let people alone, to live their own lives? To live as I do is rugged at times. But at least it isn't wasted time."

"My wife," he said, "is on hospital committees, and does a lot of work raising funds."

"Poor thing," said Beth. "Yes, I've read about her in the papers, too."

"She would call you selfish."

Beth shrugged. "Because I mind my own business? What a horrible world it's becoming. Everybody sniffing in everybody else's pots. Scratching each other for social fleas, like the so-called lesser primates. Everybody doing 'good,' when the best thing you can do for others is not doing 'good' for them, but attending to your own garden."

293

Guy was becoming more and more at ease. "I often think of what Mark Twain said: Are we going to continue imposing our alleged superior ways of living on 'those who dwell in darkness, or are we going to give the poor things a rest?' "

He added, abruptly, and without a formed reason, "I was very poor at one time."

"So was I," said Beth. "But what does that matter?"

"The degradation and humiliation of poverty," he said, as if quoting.

"Who says it is degrading and humiliating? I never felt that way. I don't feel that way now, and God knows, I have very little, but that little is the whole world to me. Degradation, humiliation: They are artificial concepts. They are taught falsehoods."

The sun was suddenly dimmed as a cloud passed before it, and there was a far rumor of thunder. Beth studied the sky critically. "It's going to rain. I hope so. We need it."

He stood up. "Now, Mrs. Turner. All we want is about forty feet of your land, where all those trees are, for an easement to the main road, for the children to reach their school buses faster. As you know, I already own that tract of land—fifty acres—adjoining yours—for my new development. We'll have two roads to the main road, but we need yours, as I said, so the youngsters won't have to walk so far from the development to the school buses."

"They'd have to walk four hundred yards!" said Beth, with scorn. "Imagine that. Four hundred great big long yards! Too bad for them. Why can't they walk, as I did—and probably you did? Why should things be made so easy for the frail creatures?" She pointed to the great oaks and maples on her land. "And kill those trees—for the holy children? No, indeed. What's the matter with their damned legs?"

"I bet you weren't popular with mothers," said Guy, and he chuckled. "But seriously, Mrs. Turner—"

"No, I'll sell you ten feet of my land, as I told your men, but that won't be wide enough for their mothers' station wagons, if the weather is bad and the Loved Ones
294

might get rain or snow on them. My God, what a people we've become! And you won't be able to buy part of the adjoining land beside mine. My friends who live on that farm there are already upset about your development and the crowding it will make, and the ruin of the land with your houses and condominiums. They aren't rich people; just hard-working, self-respecting. They know taxes will be raised on their land for new sewers and so on, and because the alleged 'value' of their land will be increased. I've already talked to them. They won't sell—if I won't sell. I'm not one of those ecology fiends, but my trees are not going to be killed."

"I could get an easement—"

"With two new roads from the development to the main road? No chance, sir, no chance. Your land isn't land-locked. There are already two dirt roads on your property, and you plan two more. That's enough. Four roads leading to the main one, for a rather small development. You don't need another, you don't need an easement. Have you talked to my neighbors?"

"Yes. They're as stubborn as you." He smiled at her. He could smell the scent of her flesh, warm, clean, fragrant with earth. He studied her again, her tall body, her full breast, her long legs, slender in their trousers, her little backside. Again the tension ran between them, quicker now, more imminent.

It was growing darker; the breeze freshened to a wind; lightning flashed. Guy stood up. "I want you to think about it," he said.

"I've done a lot of thinking, and the answer is no, no, no." There was a spatter of rain. "Let's go in my house. I'll make you some coffee, and I have a pitcher of lemonade, too, and I baked a cake this morning."

He wanted to leave—yet he did not want to leave. He told himself that he had met as obstinate people before, and had always persuaded them. She picked up her cigarettes and matches and, as she bent, the neck of her shirt divided and he saw part of her smooth white breast, unconfined. He followed her into the house. "Excuse me for a minute or two," she said. "I'm pretty filthy and besides I don't wear pants in the house. It's indecent, for a woman." She whistled for the dog and he rushed in and she closed the door after him. "You old fool, Joe," she said. "We've got company. Amuse the gentleman for a few minutes. Show him your tricks." She went away quickly, whistling something indeterminate. It was a happy sound, gay, and he thought, a little ribald, and more than a trifle brave.

Guy looked about him. It was a big light room with pale green walls, and very orderly. The chairs and deep sofa were upholstered in flower-printed chintz, the rug was dark green and inexpensive, the tables round and covered with tablecloths exactly the color and design as the other furniture. There were simple glass lamps here with white shades, and there was an enormous fireplace filled with logs, with a carpet of ashes under them, and old steel tools against the wall. One wall held nothing but books, and they gave a quiet sentence to the room. Here was repose and no frivolity, few ornaments and those of brass, and it was all color and serenity. Guy moved to the books and examined them; many were very old, and bound in leather. Some were in French, some in German. They were classics, even the modern ones. Guy could see Beth Turner here, in the winter, with the fire rumbling in the chimney and the sparks leaping, with a book in her hands. The dog watched him, his tail gently moving, as if he understood.

He picked up a book at random.

He had seen a copy of this book in his father's house, all heavily bracketed, as this was, about particularly pungent quotations. (Where were his father's books now?) Apparently Mrs. Turner had the same philosophy of life as had Tom Jerald, and Guy smiled wryly at some of the more emphatic remarks in the margins. Montaigne: He had been an especial favorite of Tom's: "With the tenderness of a mother Nature has provided that our necessary actions should be pleasant. She invites us to use them not only by reason but also by appetite, and it is ingratitude

296

to break her laws. When I see Caesar and Alexander in the thick of their mighty business, enjoy to the full all the bodily pleasures—which are as necessary and proper as they are natural—I do not hold that they have demeaned their souls. No, they have exalted them by subjecting their high powers to the ordinary uses of life."

Guy thought: When have I really enjoyed "the ordinary uses of life," or, in fact, when did I last enjoy myself, if ever? When I was a youth? Perhaps—a few times, but always with that stringency my mother taught me, always with that mean sense of guilt, always with the degrading semi-thought that I was wasting time, or money.

He was shocked at his own thoughts, his own conscious bitterness. He felt he had betrayed—what? The Protestant ethic of endless work without joy, just for the sake of work? He turned a page and saw another bracketed quotation, this time by "Anon.": "Sex is not only the vital life force which rules the world, but it is also responsible for the greater part of all worthwhile art, music, drama, and literature. Yet it is considered vile, ignoble, or ridiculous. How silly."

I never found it joyous or inspirational, Guy said to himself. My father did. My encounters with women were only to satisfy an animal imperative, like thirst or hunger or sleep. It was done without gaiety or happiness or laughter or tenderness or love, and always, again, with that base guilt which I acquired at dear Mama's knee. Yet the old boys in the Old Testament, as my father pointed out to me, loved lustily and with delight and celebration, whether with concubines or their numerous wives. My father used to quote Haskin: "Do not dwell on your sins. David killed Uriah the Hittite for the sake of stealing his wife, had King Solomon by her, and everything went well."

Again he had a mean thought: Was Beth Turner happily available to any man, did she have a present lover? Was she promiscuous? He became ashamed and angry with himself. Of what importance was it to him? Was it his affair? She was a mature woman who lived her own life. Why, then, this sudden vexed inner contraction of his

297

concerning a woman he had not known two hours ago? With more energy than was needed, he pushed the book back into its place and gloomily lit a cigarette. The storm was becoming stronger; the room was darkening very swiftly, so that all the colors blended together in a dim twilight.

He stared at the many books grimly. He thought of the books in his own library. Yes, sometimes he read them, but he really retreated to the library to avoid Lucy and her friends and relatives, as he had earlier retreated to avoid his noisy and exigent children. Perhaps I should start to read again, he thought, to enjoy reading as I once did, to laugh with the authors and to think with them. Not just as an escape but as an exercise in living.

He heard the growling of thunder, the slash of rain at the windows, the drumlike roar of the wind in the chimney. He saw the lightning, scarlet and dangerous. Then a lamp was suddenly lighted and he turned to see Beth Turner in the room. She had discarded her gardening clothes and was dressed in a thin white frock and her plain face gleamed with cleanliness. The red hair had been combed and wound into a tidy knot on the top of her head; the freckles were very prominent on her wide cheekbones. She said, "I'm only afraid of one thing, lightning. I've seen what it could do to trees and animals in the open."

He heard himself saying, and with what he thought was banality, "I thought nothing could ever frighten you."

She smiled, and again she had that fugitive beauty he had seen before in her garden. "How could you know, Mr. Jerald? Coming down to it, I'm really afraid of a number of things, mostly people. That's why I'm so happy here, when I don't see anyone for days except for the postman, sometimes, and the boy who helps me on the farm with the milking and other chores."

He misunderstood her. He said, "Perhaps you have reason to be afraid of people, living isolated here alone, with all this crime."

She shook her head and advanced into the room,

298

though once she slightly cringed at a particularly vivid flash of lightning. "I'm not afraid of crime. I'm well armed, and I'd shoot to kill any intruder. I do mean that. Human life is sacred when people make it so, and it isn't sacred for the criminal. What I meant by being afraid of people is that I'm afraid of their malice, cruelty, viciousness, and, above all, by their monkey curiosity, their meanness, their greed, their willingness to betray a friend if it means some advantage for them, some nasty gratification. That's why I stay far away from others. The only thing I demand of them is that they mind their own business, and let me alone to attend to mine."

She stood near him, faintly smiling, her head cocked quizzically, and he thought again that she was too thin, too tall, for his taste, a little too angular, except for that plentiful breast. He found himself staring at it. The white cotton frock was cheap and without style. Yet she gave it a sort of flair, perhaps of innocence, perhaps of nonchalance. He looked at her eyes. She was still smiling, yet those eyes were grave and thoughtful.

"What would you like, Mr. Jerald? Coffee? Lemonade? Milk? Or, I have some whiskey, Bourbon."

He glanced automatically at his watch, and she laughed and he felt embarrassed and annoyed. "If you're in a hurry," she said, "please don't let me keep you from walking back to the road in this downpour. I know you must be very busy." The last word had a faintly amused irony in it, and he decided that she was a woman easy to dislike.

"I do have an appointment at six," he said, and he heard the stiffness in his own voice.

"I could drive you to the road to your car. Down the path."

He hesitated, then made himself smile. "We haven't settled about the easement."

"Oh, but we have. The answer is still: only ten feet."

He sat down very deliberately in a chair and regarded her closely. "I think I'd like that Bourbon, Mrs. Turner."

"Good," she said. "Ice and water?"

"Just water, thanks." He saw her leave the room. She really had no backside, or very little, and her waist was slender and long and she moved quickly, like a young girl, her legs very slender yet graceful. Not to his taste at all. He asked only one thing of a woman, that she be complaisant and simply female, and not disturbing or distracting. Beth Turner disturbed him, and he felt irascible towards her. A door opened somewhere and he could smell something very delicious being cooked in the kitchen, something, he was surprised to know, that was not ordinary but tinged with wine and brandy and herbs. Women, solitary, did not cook so for themselves alone. Was she expecting a lover? Shut up, he said to himself.

Beth returned with two plain glasses half filled with whiskey, and two more glasses filled with water. She gave him a glass mechanically; she seemed abstracted and suddenly withdrawn. "Cheers," she said, and sat down at a distance. "That damned storm," she added. "It'll be over soon, though, like all summer storms."

The storm, to Guy, seemed too enthusiastic in its persistence and violence, and the windows were quite dark. He said, "You're cooking a very sophisticated dinner. I can smell it."

"I'm very fond of good food, Mr. Jerald, and cooking is one of my hobbies. It's only one of my own hams, with wine and cognac and some herbs I grow myself, and raisins and cloves. And yams basted in maple syrup." She hesitated; he knew she was thinking of inviting him to dinner, and he wondered why. But he was pleased. Then apparently she decided against it. She leaned back in her wing chair. They sipped their drinks together in a silence he suddenly found warm and comforting. So—she was not expecting a lover at all. He did not know why he should be relieved. They listened to the storm; it made the lamp-lighted room a refuge, a safe place, protected and calm in the midst of turmoil. When had he felt this about his own house? His house was beautifully furnished and very elegant, and it was usually full of guests and relatives. Yet—it was empty, as this solitary house was not empty.

300

Here, strangely, there was an immanence, as of friends, as of laughter and joy, as his father's house had been. He had forgotten. There was no peace in his house, in spite of the large rooms. Because there is no peace in me, he said to himself, and was shaken. It was not that Lucy was demanding, except when it came to her children and money. It was that—she was not really present, Lucy, because she had no presence, no absolute verity, no passion.

Again, he found himself studying Beth. Here was a very passionate woman, in the full sense of the word, a woman who enjoyed all her senses, an intelligent woman with no pretenses, no illusions, no artifices, no postures. She also had the assurance of deep wisdom, of acceptance, of understanding, of innate merriment, and, too, of gravity.

"Have you many relatives, Mrs. Turner?"

"No. No one. A cousin or two, in Wisconsin—I don't know just where. My mother died when I was in my twenties—cancer." Now those tawny eyes darkened with pain.

"Cancer," he said. "My father died of it. He was a brave man; he wouldn't accept operations or opiates for his pain. He wanted to die on his feet, as he said, and he almost literally did that. He didn't go to bed, except at night, and on the day he died." He added, again with an impulsiveness now alien to him, "You'd have liked my father."

"Yes," she said, gently. "I know I would have. I feel I already know him. You—loved him very much, didn't you?"

"Yes. Well. We had our differences. We understood each other completely, until I was in my twenties. Finally, I didn't understand him, or I resisted him. But he understood me." His face became taut. What the hell am I jabbering about to this strange peculiar woman? he asked of himself. I'm not like this, not any longer. The house was suddenly shaken by an enormous bang of thunder and the lamps flickered. But here it was—secure?

"My father," Beth said, "decided to live his own life
301

—and he went away and left us. It wasn't his fault. My mother didn't want to join him, and I was very young and I stayed with her. My father made a lot of money—in the way he wanted to make it. Sort of inadvertently." She laughed, and he was entranced by her laughter, for it was free, with no giggling undertone to it. He still disliked her, was somewhat repelled by her, he told himself. And yet—?

"My mother had been a schoolteacher, poor thing," she said. "And so I thought I should be one, too. I don't regret it. I learned a lot about people then. Unfortunately all true, all depressing. I never lived on the proverbial pink cloud. I saw people clear, I saw them straight. A refill, Mr. Jerald?"

He was surprised to find that he had drunk his drink. He held out his glass to her. The kitchen door opened and shut as she went out and again he smelled the aroma of the dinner and was, for the first time in many years, hungry. He relaxed in his chair and listened to the storm, which was not abating at all. He had a sudden desire to close his eyes and perhaps sleep a moment or two. The tenseness of his body was leaving him; he felt every muscle become sweetly limp and loose. He was startled when he found the refilled glass in his hands. "I must have slept," he said, self-accusing and embarrassed.

"You must be very tired," she said, with sympathy. "It must be very hard, these days, to be a businessman, with all the taxes and aggravation—and frustration."

"Yes," he admitted. He looked furtively at his watch. It was six o'clock, and he did not care. He said, "But isn't teaching school an isolated and restricted life?"

"No longer, what with the school boards, and the mommies clamoring about their offspring, and engrossed with their offspring, all intransigent and interfering. The hot lunches for their children were more important to them than what went into their minds. Then they demanded that teachers 'love' their dear kiddies, and 'understand' their emotions; though what that has to do with pure learning and education I don't know. Then the school child psychologists! Mad, every one of them. Absolutely mad. They know nothing about human nature, nothing but theory, which is both ethereal and ridiculous. The rose garden syndrome, I used to call it. Education is no longer a preparation for life. It's a preparation for unreal expectations. When young people go out into the actual world they discover that the world doesn't really 'love' them, and that the world won't pamper and pet them and worry about their 'nutrients.' That's why we have so many angry and thwarted and belligerent young men and women now. They were outraged when they discovered they have to get down to the mundane necessity of working for a living. But, pardon me. I'm riding my favorite hobbyhorse. And I'm writing a book about it."

Guy found himself laughing. "It won't sell, Mrs. Turner."

She smiled at him gleefully. "Perhaps not. But it's relieving my feelings. It's about time we adults protested. *'J'accuse.'* "

Again she refilled his glass. Now he caught the fragrance of baking bread. "My father was a teacher," he said. "He taught history. He gave it up. To live his own life, as he often remarked. On a big farm, which he hardly cultivated except for a few acres. He left the rest of it to raccoons, foxes, birds, rabbits, skunks, and such. It was a wild place." He thought for a moment. "I really think my father was wild, too."

"So am I."

The alcohol was making a golden haze before his eyes and in himself. He felt such peace—

"Tell me," said Beth Turner. "How did you get into the development business?"

He saw that she was genuinely interested, and not merely pretending.

"I wanted to make a lot of money—fast."

"Why?"

(What a stupid question!) He said, "It's our only protection against the world, isn't it?"

She shrugged. "I don't have a great deal of money, and
303

I never felt I needed protection against anything. My protection was in myself. When I was young I thought I could help 'improve' the world. My mother told me that was my duty, poor thing. Then I learned that when you interfere with the world you only mess it up and, often, add to its misery. The only one you can really improve is yourself. If we all did that, instead of poking our fingers into others' lives, we'd have a better world. A social reformer is a very dangerous man."

The storm showed no signs of abating at all, and the darkness increased except for the plunging swords of the lightning. A brass clock on the mantel chimed. Seven o'clock. Guy settled deeper into his chair. He did not fully see the compassion in Beth's eyes, the shy tenderness. He only remembered it, later.

It came to him, with a lazy surprise, that this was the first intelligent conversation he had ever had with a woman—even if some of her remarks were "stupid." He was not sure he was pleased. He did not like women, though he needed them occasionally. He was certain that he did not like Beth Turner. She seemed to see too much. He was startled at this thought.

"Do you have many friends?" he asked.

"Friends? No, not really, except my animals, and my books. Perhaps I don't have the gift for friendship. I don't want anyone to get too close to me. If they do, they become inquisitive and kindly—interfering. I never get bored." She paused, and then her face became eloquent and she looked away from him. "I'm a great Bible student. 'I will lift up my eyes to the everlasting hills, from whence comes my strength. My strength comes from the Lord—' I think God is the only friend I ever had." Her voice sounded far away, yet resonant and certain.

"Oh, you're religious?" He thought of his mother with distaste.

"No, not at all, in the general meaning of the term. I am just—sure. Orthodoxies obscure the Face of God. I not only see His grandeur in the world about me. I not only observe His law and order in the universe. I see His

—wildness, too. And that's not a contradiction in terms, either. The wilderness in the human soul is really the only splendor, an echo of God. Some might call it freedom."

Then he saw the tears in her eyes, and for the first time in his recent life he was moved. Only the strong can weep, he thought, and was amazed at himself.

She said, "But what did you really want to do with your life, Mr. Jerald?"

He was jolted, and angered. He wanted to reply brusquely to this impudence, and then he saw her expression, waiting, poignant. He said, "I wanted to be a physician, a research scientist—in cancer. But, it wasn't possible."

"Why wasn't it?" She appeared surprised.

"Money, for one thing," he answered with abruptness.

She was genuinely taken aback. "Money shouldn't have been a problem. It never is, really. A doctor I knew worked for his own living since he was nine years old. He put himself through college, then through medical school."

He thought of his father with furious impatience. "You don't know what you're talking about!" he said, with hard rudeness. "My father didn't, either."

What an unhappy man, thought Beth, but she did not say this until much later. He stood up as if he could not bear this interrogation any longer, an interrogation which struck at his very inner core.

"I must go," he said. "It's half past seven."

She stood up also. "The storm is still very bad, and getting worse." she said. "Why don't stay for dinner?"

"Dinner?"

"In about half an hour. Or, are you pressed for time?"

Pressed. He was always pressed, for time, for money, for—? For what? He half turned away from her. "My wife is expecting me." He did not know that he had thrown "my wife" at her as a man might throw a stone at a Magdalen. "My wife." His look was challenging, rejecting.

"Now, about that easement, Mrs. Turner."

She sighed, a deep and profound sigh. "Mr. Jerald, I will do this for you, seeing it's the only thing which seems to matter to you. I will sell you enough land, six feet short of my trees, for your damned road. And I will ask my neighbors to sell you the rest. But only on condition that you—you—erect a chain-link fence on my side, to keep out—people. I don't want children racing over my land and frightening my animals and intruding on my privacy. And I think my neighbors will demand that, too."

He found himself smiling. "All right. Then it's settled."

They faced each other. Then, very slowly and gently, she put her hands on his shoulders and as slowly and gently kissed his lips. Her mouth was soft and sweet and fragrant. He tried to recoil from her, then reluctantly, as if without his will, he put his arms about her and felt a tremendous loosening in himself, a kind of distant joy he had never experienced before. Her body was giving in his arms, spontaneous, abandoned, trusting. Her breast lay on his. "I love you," she said.

He stayed for dinner. He stayed the night. Once, in the cool darkness near morning, he murmured drowsily, "I love you, too," and thought he meant it.

"I never forgot it, I never will," Guy said aloud in the dusk. "I never forgot that dinner, the breakfast next day. The surety, the warmth, the kindness, the generosity, the passion. I thought I had loved Marlene. But that was a boy's dream. This was reality. It was the only reality I had ever known, except for my father."

James waited. He saw the anguish on Guy's face, and he knew that Guy did not see him, nor was he fully aware of him. He was looking back in despair.

He is thinking of that fine woman, thought James. Did he ever completely give himself to her? Had he kept a distance out of fear? Fear of what? Fear of life? Fear was a murderer of men's souls. Had he mistrusted her, as he
306

mistrusted himself? Mistrust, too, rises out of fear, fear of one's own honest emotions.

James waited, again. But Guy had closed his exhausted eyes. He had fallen asleep. He looked as if he were crying in himself; his eyelids quivered and jerked. He muttered something, then subsided.

James knew there was no reason for him to remain here any longer, today. The battle still raged in Guy; it was becoming more intense, and closer. He would have to engage in it, or die. There was no other answer. Sighing, James left the suite and his depression was deeper than ever.

That night he called Emma Godwin, his mistress. "Love, would you come to America and stay here for a bit with me?"

She said nothing for a moment or two, then spoke sadly, "Jimmy, I don't think so. You're fighting something out in yourself, aren't you, dear? I don't think I can help you fight it. You must do it yourself, all alone. That's what it always comes down to, Jimmy: We must fight our war ourselves. Lonely, terrible, yes. I know you'll win, love, I know you will. And the victory will be all yours, and no one else's. That's the only victory worth fighting for."

17

He did not come again. But then, Beth would think with grief, he had not promised to return, or even to call or write her. He had promised nothing, she remembered. Had he really said, "I love you," in that early morning, or had he meant another woman, possibly even his wife? Since her husband, Keith, had died in Korea she had had a few lovers, for she was an ardent woman who loved men instinctively. So she was not inexperienced in the ways of men; the word "love" came to them easily and was said merely to please the women of the hour or to seduce them, and, in most cases, meant nothing. It was, in a way, a courtesy, a handshaking, a "thank you." Beth seriously and often wondered if a man was truly capable of loving a woman, as a woman loved a man. She doubted it. But when a woman said, "I love you," she most often meant it. God help us, thought Beth.

She remembered their one night together, sometimes with joy but now mostly with mingled sadness and a sense of humiliation. Had he considered her a promiscuous woman, a woman of superficial emotion, or casualness? True, she had made the overt approach, for she had begun to love him five minutes after they had met. Did he believe she did that with other men also? Possibly. She had delighted in his big body, the touch of his hands and mouth. He had been rough and tender in his lovemaking, and she had given him what she had never given a man before, not even Keith Turner: A wholehearted abandon, a joyousness, a total surrender, a blissful completeness. He had slept in her arms, his head on her breast, and even in his sleep he had kissed her flesh. She would remember that vividly and with longing. But why did he not come to her again?

There were times when she felt rage against him for her mortification, and his implied rejection and indifference. She remembered how she had prepared breakfast for him in the morning, and his unwilling smiles. She had caught him watching her, then he had looked away. A somber man, almost a gloomy man, a man who had moments of abstraction as if he had forgotten her, and who had answered her curtly when she had spoken to him. It came to her that he did not like women, as the laughing Keith had liked them. Even when he smiled his black eyes did not smile. After breakfast he had sat for a while at the kitchen table, smoking, covertly watching her, and she could not guess of what he was thinking, as she could with other men. He was a secret man, an enigmatic one, a wary and unconfiding man, and, and she had perceived, an unhappy one. Any attempt to probe his thoughts had been met with a taciturn brusqueness—as if she were too inquisitive. He had not known, it was apparent, that a woman wished to know as much as possible about the man she loved, not out of curiosity, but out of a desire to understand him better. Good God, she once thought, did he know that, and so had withdrawn? If so, why? I am no beauty, she said to herself, and I am not young, and he wanted no entanglements, not even at interludes. What was his wife like, his children? He had avoided the subject, when she, very subtly, had tried to discover. His wife, Beth recalled, had been, and was, very pretty, with a vague prettiness that was almost faceless. At least, damn it, she would think, other men find me interesting, but obviously he does not. And her humiliation increased.

July drifted into gold August, and he did not come. But she saw men on his land, with bulldozers, and could hear their distant and echoing voices. She had heard that he liked to oversee his operations for himself, but she did not see him among his workers. But she saw the death of trees, and was angry. She did not consider human life to be absolutely sacred; trees were often more valuable than any human being, for they were both innocent and beautiful and asked for nothing but sun and rain and air. She began to despise herself for her waiting. But she could not help taking out her binoculars—which she used to watch birds—and directing them at the distant men. She had been fond of her lovers, but had not loved them. Now, to her dismay, she rediscovered pain, a sick yearning, a forlornness of spirit, and pangs which were both emotional and physical. She had not loved Keith this way, with a ripe and mature passion, and with an aching that at times became intolerable. To her own self-loathing she once found herself thinking of calling him at his offices. But to this shame she would not descend, though sometimes her hand hovered, as if by its own will, on the telephone in her small warm kitchen.

Why had he gone to bed with her, as with a paid woman? A momentary hunger, a curiosity? She knew he was not a man of pretendings. There had been one or two instances when he had held her tightly to him, not with lust, but as if clinging to her, as if he had known her for a

309

long time and loved her. Then he would restlessly turn away, repudiating her.

Once, a year ago, in a shop in Cranston she had heard someone remark that he was a womanizer. She had heard other things but could not remember them now. That he was feared and admired, she did know; there was nothing else. She wanted news of him, for her love, instead of decreasing, was daily growing stronger. On a few occasions she would mention, to an acquaintance, that she had sold a small piece of land to him for an easement. But the only replies had been shrugs or a remark that he did build good houses and apartments and condominiums. She began to see that very few, if any, were interested in him as a man. Why was this? Gradually she became aware that he was an aloof man, a stranger, that he inspired no responses of an intimate kind, that he showed no interest at all in his fellow creatures, nor they in him.

Why, we are two of a kind! she thought, with astonishment, and her love became stronger. Helplessly, out of her pain, she began to resent him, and she fed her pain with her humiliation. She began to dream of him almost nightly, and would awaken to find her hands reaching for him in her empty bed, her damned lonely bed. She had not cried since Keith had been killed; she would now find herself crying in her sleep. "Oh, damn him, damn him!" she would say aloud, and her pain would sharpen and she would feel as one feels when a part of his body had been amputated. She was both bitterly amused at herself and enraged with herself when she started to hate his wife, to whom he returned every night and who had his name and kept his house.

August became September, and trees were fading and the fields were high with corn and the mountains became a deeper purple against an autumn sky. He'll never come again, Beth would mourn, and she knew she had lost all her pride, and had nothing left but her unceasing longing and suffering. She began to hate herself for her precipitousness. Men did not like aggressive women. They never understood that most often this aggressiveness came from
310

love, for a desire to hold and be held by a beloved man. She had sometimes overheard men discussing women with derision and laughter and with ribald ugly words, as if women were merely a pleasant lewd commodity and not of their own species at all, not of human fears and passions and pain. She had often been in Europe, where, with the exception of the English, men loved women and with admiration and honest desire. This was not true of American men. American women were too open in their love, and had no reticence. They were candid and sincere, and had few if any arts. American men were, at heart, romantics. They held chastity, in women, of the utmost importance. They made no excuses for a woman driven by love and her own extremity. Such women inspired, not their response, but their dislike and avoidance, except for short and hurried occasions when it was for their own convenience and random desires. She recalled a Victorian joke: A man said distastefully to his enthusiastic bride, "Ladies don't move!" American men didn't like women who "moved," in any way, except when with a highly paid whore. The last Puritans, thought Beth, and she reread *The Scarlet Letter*, by Hawthorne.

She spent her time, which was heavy on her now, canning wild huckleberries and peaches and plums and vegetables from her own garden. Her small clean kitchen, once so comforting and attractive with its brick floor and copper pots and pans, would grow warm with heat, as her storage shelves became loaded with jars. She could no longer find solace in her books, or in her collection of classical records. Everything pained her, especially beauty and peace. Everything was pervaded with the silent anguish of love and desolation. Once, while gathering the last roses, she found herself crying, the tears running down her face. She brushed them away with her arm and cursed aloud. The collie licked her face, looking at her anxiously. "Oh, Joe," she said, with half laughter and half despair, "it's hell to be a woman."

The first frost came and the trees wore scarlet and gold and bronze, and the annuals in the garden died, turned

311

black, withered. Beth raked and bedded down her gardens. Chestnuts dropped from trees and squirrels were busy. There was an accelerating hum in the air as nature prepared the land for sleep and the following resurrection of life. Beth could see the beginnings of houses across the fields, as the men hurried against the winter. Their voices came louder to her on the brisk air. The sky, each day, was a more intense blue. The breezes were keener. Beth found some consolation in the fire she lighted at night, but she could not give her full attention to her books and the music.

She was sitting, one twilight, before the fire, listening to a nocturne of Debussy's, when she heard a knock at her door. Then the door opened and Guy was standing on the threshold, his dark face in shadow. She had seen him so often in her fantasies that she thought him, at first, another fantasy. She could not believe it. She stood up slowly, and looked at him. He entered the room but did not approach her. He merely stood in the center of the room, his coat unbuttoned, and she felt his resistance, his sullenness, his open resentment at being here.

Beth could feel the hard pounding of her heart. She wanted to speak but could not. The collie was happily sniffing at his knees and he absently bent and rubbed the dog's ears. And he did not look directly at Beth.

"I remembered," he said, "that you told me that your birthday was around this time." Beth found herself trembling; she wanted to run to him, weeping, holding out her arms. But she could not move. Her face had become pale and stark in the half-light; one cheek was red from the fire. He was fumbling in the pocket of his coat, and then he produced a small box, like a schoolboy, embarrassed and shy. He put the box on the table and said, "I brought you something."

She still could not speak. She went to the table and picked up the box, her heart roaring in her ears. She opened the box. There was a pretty yellow-gold bracelet in it, set with a row of winking diamonds.

"Well?" he said, challengingly. "Don't you like it?

312

Women always like jewelry." He spoke with a certain crude defiance.

Oh, God, thought Beth. Why can't I speak to him? Why do I have to stand like this, just staring at the bracelet? Then she could speak. "Please sit down," she said. "Of course—I like it. But why—"

But he did not sit down. She said, and her voice was quite husky, "It wasn't necessary, you know. But thank you."

She placed the box on the table and gently closed it. "But—I'd like you to give it to me some other time. Later."

Then he said in a loud cold voice, "There won't be another time."

He means, she thought with despair and shattering shame, that he's paying me off, as he'd pay off a prostitute.

"Then, I can't take it," she said, and shook her head.

He looked at the box. He abruptly sat down, still in his heavy coat. "Why can't you take it?"

"You wouldn't understand." She stood away from him.

"Perhaps not," he replied. He rubbed the top of the box with his hand. Then he put it back in his pocket. He moved as if to rise and she wanted to cry out, "Don't go! I'll die if you go! Don't leave me!" The terribleness of her agony made her feel numb and desperately sick.

He sat back in the chair and now he looked at her. He had not removed his heavy coat. It was a rocking chair and he rocked idly, still staring at her. His face was closed and harsh. He considered her with that brute force of his which she had never forgotten.

To her horror she found herself saying, "Why won't there be another time?"

Now he looked aside. He said nothing. Then she felt a deep anger, almost a scorn.

"You've surely committed—what do you call it?—adultery before, haven't you?"

"Yes. Of course. Every married man does that, and thinks nothing of it."

"Then, what is the difference now?" She hated herself as well as hated him.

" 'You wouldn't understand,' " he quoted, and actually almost smiled. He moved again, preparing to go. She held out her hand to him.

"Try me," she said.

He shook his head. "That time—it was different."

She did not know why something in her seemed to open like wings. She approached him nearer. "In what way?"

But he did not answer. He looked at his watch, his damned watch! "Why the hell did you men invent time?" she exclaimed. "And watches?"

Now he laughed, that short laugh, that very reluctant laugh, as if laughter was alien to him. "We have to have excuses," he said.

"For avoiding something? Or for fear of something?"

He was gazing at her again, and he was actually smiling. "Perhaps that's it," he said. They looked at each other, long and deeply. Then Beth said, "Why don't you take off that coat? You must be very warm in it."

"I have to go," he replied. He stood up, and just when she was beginning to despair again he took off his coat and threw it into a distant chair.

Beth said, "I'm roasting a chicken," and wanted to cry and laugh. There was such joy in her.

"My wife's having a small dinner party tonight."

"With chestnut dressing," Beth said. "And I've made an apple pie, with my own apples."

He looked at his coat. "And I have some chicken soup, too," Beth said.

"This is a hell of a dialogue," he said. Then suddenly they were both laughing, and Beth ran into his arms and he held her tightly and kissed the top of her head. Then he reached for the box, opened it, and pushed the bracelet on her wrist. He took her hand and kissed the palm, and she closed her eyes with rapture.

The house was not empty any longer. It was filled with joy and warmth.

As before, he stayed for dinner, and he stayed the night.

314

Before he could fall asleep Beth said, holding him to her with the extremity of her love and happiness, "Why was it—different—this time, as you said?"

He did not answer for so long that she thought he had fallen asleep. Then, with his lips against her throat he said, "Because I love you, Beth." Again he was silent, while she repeated what he had said over and over, marveling, thanking God, believing him.

"Why did you stay away for so long, Guy?"

He turned his head aside as if with his own pain.

"I didn't want to love you, Beth. The other women— they meant nothing to me. I didn't even think of them when I left them. I didn't feel I was really betraying my wife, with them."

"And you think loving is betrayal?"

He was silent. "Oh, my darling," she said. "The real betrayal is not loving."

"You talk too much," he said, and kissed her again, and took her again, and she thought she would die of her ecstasy and fulfillment.

18

November 1977

Emil Grassner had gone to Philadelphia to see his other patients and his family, and the weekend was at hand and James Meyer had never been so lonely in all his life before, not even when his parents had died. His father had told him of an ancient Yiddish proverb, that a man should never go to live in a town where there was no physician. He might have added, thought James, and where he has no friends. Cranston was too small to be a great metropolis, and certainly too large to be called a town. James had discovered that the "cultural activities" here were almost entirely in the hands of women, who formed cliques and rivaled each other and undermined each other. They had an orchestra they called "The Cranston Philharmonic," which James had recently not enjoyed. He thought of the old joke, "They played Brahms, and Brahms lost." After a very mediocre couple of hours the hall became a place for dancing, with no one under the age of fifty. There was one "legitimate" theater (Wonder what an illegitimate one would be like? James asked himself), where fifth-rate ballets sometimes came and stock companies, and, on demand, a play or a moving picture allegedly for "adults only." (This was very popular.) There were also three restaurants which were not at all bad, and about fifteen which were very bad indeed, and a number of moving-picture houses.

But the majority of the elite belonged to three country clubs or entertained in their houses, where the cliques really became lively, and throats were cut with gusto. Cranston was a manufacturing city, heavy industry and sawmills, in which anonymous hordes worked. It also had some flourishing slums, and two libraries and one museum full of Indian artifacts. There were also three "youth centers," where acned youth gathered to snigger, fight, and dance to their barbaric music, and, when the occasion was right, to copulate.

Cranston was a very dull city, and on Sundays it was extremely dead, with not a bar open for the thirsty traveler, and only a few restaurants. But Cranston had many churches—and a number of brothels where hilarity reigned on Sundays and liquor was in plentiful supply.

James had a chill, and so today, Sunday, he had not gone to Mountain Valleys for fear of infecting Guy Jerald, who daily seemed to lose some more of his dwindling vitality. Hugh Lippincott had promised James that in some way he would contrive to keep Guy's family at bay, and had invited James to a Sunday dinner at his house. "Thank you, but I do have a chill," said James, shuddering. "I suppose you mean a cold?" said Hugh. "Well, drink your head off and it will disappear." Hugh paused. "I don't like my house, either," he said, and laughed, and replaced the telephone receiver.

316

James had stayed in bed most of the day, listening to the competing pealing of church bells, and reading the Cranston *Herald,* which was as dull as the city. He was appallingly bored. The hotel appeared not to be tenanted, for he heard no voice or movement outside his door. It's as bad as any English provincial town, he thought. Doggedly, at seven o'clock at night, the church bells were at it again. James got out of bed, thought languidly of room service, took several long draughts of good Bourbon, decided to dress and go downstairs for dinner. It was a beastly early hour to dine, but the dining room closed promptly at half past seven on Sundays. He took one or two more long draughts, armed himself with a number of handkerchiefs, and went down the old elevator to the dining room. There were three elderly couples there, evidently "natives," for they looked at him curiously. By the time a heavy Teutonic soup was served him he was pleasantly befuddled and his nose was becoming ventilated to some extent. He saw the very quiet snowy street outside and the lonely streetlamps. The snow looked bright and inviting. He decided to take a walk after dinner. "Nothing like fresh air," as Emma would say mockingly. "If it doesn't kill you it will cure you."

He went upstairs for his overcoat and hat and gloves, descended again, and went outside, followed by the astonished glances of the desk clerk, who knew James did not possess a car. The air was colder than James had expected, and the wind was keener and very nimble. Cars were parked along the curbs but no one was walking on the shoveled pavement, no one but himself. Was crime rampant here, too, in this bleak small city? James considered the only safe cities he knew of: Lisbon, Madrid, Buenos Aires, West Berlin, and Valparaíso, Chile, and Tel Aviv and Jerusalem—all, he reflected, with a very determined police force, paramilitary. He included Cairo in his reflections, and Cape Town and other cities in South Africa, where authorities harbored no nonsense about disadvantaged youth, and the police were not expected to be psychiatric social workers, or "understanding." Reluctantly,

James had long ago come to the conclusion that the vast majority of mankind understood only force and respected nothing but power. It was a nasty commentary on human nature—but there it was. Weak nations invariably collapsed, even while screaming "love" and "gentleness" and "peace." They were prey for the strong. James sighed, thinking of his native country and, as he did so, he felt the return of his malaise. Civilization. There was no such thing.

He looked through the windows of a few scattered shops; the goods on display did not appear very inviting. He turned down a quiet narrow street, where all sound was abated and not a car moved. Here the wind was not so strong and he walked more briskly. He stopped to blow his nose.

He felt a sharp object being pushed into his side. He could feel the sharpness through his thick clothing. He stood very still. He had not had commando training for nothing. He felt very cold, cold with rage and disgust. He sensed a large shadowy shape almost behind him, and a hoarse voice said, "Gimme your money, mister, and you won't get hurt." The voice was young and brutal.

"Yes," said James. He reached for his wallet and the weapon bored deeper into his side and he knew it for a long knife. "I'll get it," said the voice, and a bare hand flickered towards his pocket. It was then that all his commando training returned to him. He pretended to shrink; he made a whining sound as the hand captured his leather purse, then he swung around, caught the knife-holding hand in his own, hurled it upwards and outwards, twisted it savagely, brought his other hand about, palm straight as a board, and slashed edgewise at the neck suddenly exposed to him.

His assailant was a very young man. He made a gulping noise, flailed his arms, and again James slashed at him. The knife dropped to the cleared walk with a ringing sound. In an instant James possessed it. The youth was staggering wildly, and this time James lunged at him with fingers extended and hard as iron, and

318

he aimed directly at the solar plexus. He felt the soft pulp of an overfed body, and the youth fell into a snowbank. James, holding the knife, was on him at once. The face below his was gray-white and contorted and very still. James kicked the young man furiously in the side, feeling the wild joy of hatred and loathing.

He said, "I'm going to mark you up a little, you bugger." The youth attempted, terrified now, to wriggle away in the snow. He had caught his breath. He began to scream, covering his face with his hands and writhing like an injured worm. He had a slack full face, an infant's face, though he was probably eighteen or so.

"Yes," said James the next day to Emil Grassner, "I think I would have disfigured him, or perhaps"—he smiled—"gelded him. That would have been the best of all. But the police came."

Two young policemen came tumbling from an unmarked car and James, who was slightly out of breath, said, "Take him away and throw him into the dustbin. He had a knife. Here it is. He tried to rob me."

The younger of the policemen looked at James uncertainly, and with respect. James was obviously a stout, middle-aged man, and the criminal was young. One drew a notebook out of his pocket while his companion looked down at the whimpering thief and clearly yearned to kick him soundly. The policeman with the notebook took James's name and his address. They caught his English accent. He said, settling his hat on his head, "I see you gentlemen are armed. Good. Our police in England are not. Unfortunately. The police should be permitted to kill on provocation. What are you going to do with this bastard?"

"Mister," said one of the policemen, "you shouldn't be out walking alone at night."

"I'm not decrepit yet," said James, blowing his nose heartily. "And I was once a soldier. It's a fine thing that a man can't take a stroll of a pleasant evening without some frigging young sod attacking him. Take him away, please, or I'll give him a bit more."

They saw James's face and believed him. They dragged the thief to his feet. They saluted James, threw the thief into their car, and drove off with considerable noise. Nice lads, thought James. A little confused, but sound. I wonder what will happen to that wretch. Some sweetheart of a judge will probably fall on his neck, weeping and kissing him, and sympathizing with him. What a state this world has fallen into, to be sure.

It was all the fault of the brotherly-lovers, the pure-in-hearts. The dreamers, who believed, with Rousseau, that man was instinctively noble and good but was corrupted by his environment—or something. But who created "environment"? Man himself, as he created all evil. Now James was vexed. He had been informed that he should appear at the police station tomorrow morning. He had been urged to go with the police then and there, but he pleaded illness—which did not deceive them—and gave them his card. "Yes," he had said, when they stared at it, "I am really Sir James Meyer, as well as a doctor, but only a baronet, not a baron." This had confused them even more. He had wanted to pat them in a fatherly way on their shoulders. He was sorry for the police in America and England. A thankless job.

But James felt quite invigorated as he returned to his hotel, and his chill seemed to have evaporated. He was almost cheerful. He congratulated himself. He might be in his fifties but, by George, he still had the stuff to fight off an armed hooligan. He took a very hot bath, drank more of the Bourbon, and went to bed, more pleased with events than he had been for a long time. In the morning his cold had completely disappeared.

However, at breakfast the next day, Emil was not amused. "You might have been killed," he said. "In these days thugs often kill first, then rob afterwards." They went to the police station together, where James was received with a flattering awe, which he suspected came more from his ability to protect himself than from his title. He almost preened and assured the sergeant that it was "nothing, nothing at all, really." He learned
320

that his assailant had been arrested a number of times and had "a record."

"I'm sure the judge will kiss his arse again and take him home to dinner," said James, and the sergeant smiled grimly. "We need vigilantes," said James. "And, by God, we'll probably have to come to that eventually."

He and Emil went to Mountain Valleys. "You seem elated," said Emil.

"Oh, I am, in a way. But I'm not in form, I discovered last night. I must practice again. I think every young man should be taught commando tactics."

"The mothers of America wouldn't agree with that," Emil laughed.

James suggested what the mothers could do and Emil said, "Tut, tut."

James said, "They have what they call Death Squads in Rio de Janeiro, composed of off-duty policemen who are disgusted with light sentences meted out to habitual criminals, and murderers and such. Once assured that the criminal is guilty, they go out and kill him, neatly, silently, then drift away. We should have such squads in America and England."

"Think of the screams of the social workers and others who receive large salaries for 'caring,' " said Emil, "and having 'compassion.' "

James laughed. "I believe Prince Philip said just recently that we are wasting compassion on the wrong people, and I thoroughly agree with him. And that reminds me, I have been reading a very interesting book by one of your American writers in which it is explained that when the Industrial Revolution came men abandoned their traditional role of agriculturists and became businessmen and entrepreneurs and such, which removed them from their women a great deal of the time. So the ladies felt they were bereft of importance in an urban environment and so sought importance somewhere else—in motherhood. They made motherhood sacred, and then exalted their children to fortify the new role. And that's part of the terrible trouble today. In an agricultural society

321

children and women are important only when they deserve importance—as valuable contributors to labor, on the land, not as mere ornaments in bed or takers-up-of-space in the schoolroom, where the poor devils don't want to be anyway."

When they arrived at Mountain Valleys they were greeted by the day nurse, who was distressed. "Mr. Jerald spent a very bad night and he seems to have relapsed again. Mr. Lippincott did try to keep the children and Mrs. Jerald from seeing Mr. Jerald, but Mrs. Jerald got in, and she came out crying, and Mr. Jerald—well, Dr. Grassner, you can see for yourself."

"Oh, damn," said Emil. "I'll go by myself for a minute or two, James."

James waited. Then he saw Beth Turner at the nurses' desk and went to her. She looked at him and attempted to smile but her anxiety was manifest. They shook hands, and Beth said, "Dr. Meyer, one of the nurses told me Guy has had a very bad night, and isn't doing well."

He took her arm and drew her away to near the elevators. He said, "Well, we can expect these setbacks occasionally. They aren't a cause for worry. Not really."

She scrutinized his face. Her own was very pale and drawn and her tawny eyes were dim with moisture. He went on: "As you probably know, Mrs. Turner, Jerry has been talking to me and to Dr. Grassner lately, and seemed quite rational. This is a great step forward, and we're encouraged."

She still scrutinized him. Then she said in a low voice, "Does he ever ask—for me—mention me?"

"No. Not yet. I'm sorry. I thought of speaking of you, but decided against it."

She nodded. "That was very wise, I think." But her eyes were sad and heavy, and her mouth was forlorn. He saw that in a moment she would be unable to control herself and would burst out crying, so he said with haste, "Mrs. Turner, would you be kind enough to a stranger in the city to have dinner with him tonight?"

She again tried to smile. She thought for a moment,

then said, "Better still, why don't you drive out with me later to my house and have dinner with me? I am supposed to be a good cook."

I know, thought James, with pity. She wants a masculine presence in her house, one who knows old Jerry and will talk of him. A masculine presence to fill up the emptiness where once he was. Perhaps she could overcome her reticence long enough to give me some information, too. He said, "That is most kind of you, Mrs. Turner. I have an excellent cook at home, and I miss him. I also miss my friend's cook in London." Again, she was trying to smile, and he patted her arm. "Say, after lunch, if you are remaining in town."

"I am buying some supplies for my farm in Cranston. Could you be ready to leave at four?" There was an eager note in her fine voice, and a pleading in her face. "I have my car here, Doctor, and it is only a short drive of ten miles, and I will bring you back to your hotel after dinner. You're staying at the Old House? Suppose I pick you up there at four?"

"Capital," he said, and she really smiled at the old-fashioned word.

She watched him go to Guy's suite. Emil came out and the two joined in an earnest conversation. She wished she could overhear them. But what a nice man he is, she thought, what a kind man, and that is rare. Her last glance, as she entered the elevator was of that large burly back and the fringe of red-gray curls at his nape. In some way she felt comforted, and supported by a superior strength.

Emil said, "Well, it isn't so good. He's lapsed back into his lethargy. Why that damned woman insisted on seeing him, after I talked to her and advised against it, I don't know. I did mention his wife to him but he only stirred in his chair as if to get up and go away."

"In a manner of speaking, I'm sorry for her, too," said James. "After all, she was his wife for over twenty-seven years. Yes. We do get ourselves into difficulties when we get married, don't we?"

He went into the suite alone. Guy was back in his wing chair, unmoving, staring starkly at the opposite wall. He did not look at James, who sat down near the fraudulent fire. Guy's face was more skull-like than ever, taut with jutting bones, and he looks, thought James, like death. I've seen dead men look better.

James let some time pass. Guy did not move. He hardly blinked. James began to talk casually. "I had quite an experience last night," and he went on to tell of his encounter with the thief and his knife.

"A fattish well-fed bastard," he said, finally, wondering if Guy had heard him. "And fairly well dressed, too. None of those storybook rags, and starvation."

He might have been talking to a picture on the wall. Guy merely sat and stared emptily. James went on:

"There was a convention of neurologists and psychiatrists in London six months ago, from all over Britain and the Continent. It was near a college, or some other damned place of alleged education. The youngest of us must have been about forty, the oldest seventy-five— distinguished men in their field, and quite notable all over the world. I was walking beside a physician from Bonn, who has written many learned books, published everywhere. A gentleman about seventy.

"Well, then. Students from that infernal 'comprehensive' school were 'protesting' something or other, with placards, unkempt brutes. They happened to see us, and several of them surged towards us, shouting, 'Go home, old people, and die!' "

James gave a snort of bitter amusement. "The reputable Herr Doktor from Bonn stopped to look at them, and he said, *'Kinder,* you are already dead.' "

Did old Jerry stir then or make a sound? James was not sure. He continued:

"The young monsters were suddenly very quiet, glaring at us, then they shrieked, in wild affirmative rage, that they were indeed dead, though they did not consciously know it, even if their souls knew it. Dead, irrevocably dead. I am beginning to believe that the soullessness of
324

modern youth, the emptiness, is due to the nihilism of their elders, the abandonment of authority by parents and government, the lack of a moral focus, the loss of the imperative to be whole. A permissive society such as we have in England, and you in America, is anarchy, for it has no restraints, no commitments to ethics and purposes, none to the Absolute, none to order, none to rational thought.

"There were newspapermen in attendance who had heard the exchange, and all reported the incident fairly except one, a yellow rag full of sensationalism and moral turpitude and lewdness. The good Herr Doktor was reported to have 'insulted our children.' It sang the infernal song of 'the children, the children,' as if nothing valuable existed in the world except uncouth offspring of spiritually immoral parents. The children—"

Guy suddenly sat up, and turned his face to James, and it was profoundly ugly and full of rage. James leaned forward. He waited. For a long moment or two that face confronted him, black with memory, looking inward.

"The children, the children!" Lucy cried over the telephone to her husband, who was in New York. "You never cared about your children! You were a dreadful father! And now this—"

It was eight years ago.

Guy said, with pent patience, "You haven't told me what is wrong."

His wife was sobbing. The shrill gulping sounds tore at his ear. He said, "Did Bill hit someone with that fucking racing sports car you insisted on buying for him? You know he's a reckless driver; he's been in enough trouble with his driving over the past two years."

"Don't you dare use such language to me, Guy Jerald! I never heard such words in all my life! No, it wasn't the car. William is home for the Easter holidays; you know that, but you insisted on going to New York, and yesterday was Good Friday and you weren't here! Your business always came first, never your family. Never your family!" She wailed over and over.

"God damn it, Lucy! What's wrong?"

She moaned, "And he's only eighteen, only a child! A child! How could they do this to him? It was that disgusting girl, on Thursday. You knew William was coming home Wednesday night for the holidays, but you *insisted* on going to New York. If you'd been a decent father, a real father to your children, this would never have happened! It's all your fault."

Guy wished she were present in the room with him. He had never struck Lucy, now he wanted to hit her savagely, not once but many times. He began to sweat with his rage and frustration. "What girl? What the hell is all this about? Stop that damned moaning and try to tell me, if it's possible for a fool like you to talk sensibly for once."

He had shocked her. He had never called her a fool before, though he had implied it many times. Her gulpings came slower, softer. Then she almost shrieked, "It was that girl! Thursday night. On the street at nine o'clock! Her mother, a very nasty woman, is a waitress, and she claims her daughter is only eleven, well, less than eleven, not quite eleven, and her daughter, she claims, was coming home from a friend's house, where they were doing their homework!"

A cold chill ran over Guy. He clutched the receiver. Lucy was sobbing incoherently. "Go on, damn you, go on!" he yelled at her. He had shocked her again. She was dithering now.

"William, the poor child, saw her on the street at nine o'clock. You know how friendly—how good he is. It was raining hard, and that woman, that girl, was walking, and he saw she had no umbrella and he called to her, you know, from the car I bought him, and offered her a ride home. He was so sorry for the wretch. She told him she lived a long way—in one of those awful ratty poor sections, and he said he'd drive her home—"

"Go on!" he shouted, when she stopped. The sweat was

326

very cold on his face, and his heart was beating in his throat in great thumps.

She began to make sounds like a whimpering kitten, and Guy, who was trembling now, hated her as he had never hated her before. "The police—they took him—to jail— your son, your child, the poor child—they didn't let him go until this morning, until I got our lawyer and my brother— They had to put up bail— Oh, the disgrace, the poor child, how he suffered through all that! He'll never be the same again. If you'd been here it wouldn't have happened—he'd have stayed home with us both instead of going to see Kenneth Fields that night. But you weren't here, where you should have been—"

The receiver was very wet in Guy's hand. In a slow and terrible voice he said, "What did Bill do to that girl?"

"That woman, you mean!" she screamed. "A full-grown woman, and her mother claiming she isn't yet eleven, not for three months! The mother's worse than she is! A waitress in a low-class restaurant, you know, on Westfield Street, where all those dirty bars are. What is a *mother* doing working at night when she should be home with her daughter?"

Guy said, "Lucy, I swear to God I'll kill him when I get home if you don't stop jabbering. I want to know all about it."

"You'll kill— You are as bad as that evil woman, the mother, threatening your poor boy! Yes, she threatened your very own son, to kill him. My child. Oh, my God!" moaned Lucy, who had never taken that name in vain before, not even during difficult childbirth. "William's so kind, so gentle, so good. He took that young woman to a perfectly awful section, all miserable little apartments, crumbling away, to her home. A filthy place, he said, tiny little rooms and practically no heat. He was afraid for that wicked girl, so he went into the apartment with her—" Her sobs were now out of control.

"And raped the kid," said Guy, in a very quiet voice. "Is that it? He raped the little girl."

327

The sobs went on and on, interspersed with moans, long drawn out. "Lucy—"

"That's what she claims! Hugh and our lawyer tried to get you all day yesterday, and even left a message for you to call home—home, where you never are! And you never called!"

Guy heard himself saying in a dull lifeless voice, "I was out on Long Island—some property. I stayed in East Hampton overnight. I just got back to the hotel. I picked up messages, and haven't had time to look at them yet." He felt so nauseated that he wanted to vomit. He heard Lucy's groaning voice very dimly.

"—five thousand dollars bail. The judge, he wanted more. But Hugh knows him well— I had to be sedated all this time— When your child needed his father, he wasn't here, where he belongs. And that woman, the mother, came to the judge with a birth certificate, a false one, I'm sure, saying her daughter wasn't yet eleven, and making an awful noise, Hugh said. Crying and stamping and threatening—"

"Where is the little girl now?" asked Guy, dreading the answer.

There was a long pause. His knees were shaking so badly that he had to fumble for a chair and fall into it.

Then Lucy whimpered, "She's in the hospital. They said she was—badly—hurt. Her mother—she claims the girl wasn't—isn't—" Her voice dwindled.

"You mean the child hadn't reached puberty yet?"

"Oh, how awful to have to talk this way, Guy! Yes, that's what she said. And the girl—the woman—is a great big thing, a hussy. Hugh's kept it partly out of the newspapers. The mother's threatening—"

"Where's Bill now?"

Another long pause. "I called the doctor for him. After all, it's after midnight, isn't it? The doctor, Dr. Parkinson, you know, gave him some pills. He had to have them! Two nights in jail—your son, Guy Jerald, and it's all your fault. You were a very bad neglectful father. You never
328

loved your children the way a father should. Bill's sleeping, poor lamb. I—"

"How was he picked up? Lucy! I've got to know."

"I didn't know where he was all that Thursday night! I thought he'd stayed with Kenneth! So I wasn't worried. And then yesterday—"

"How did they pick him up? Who knew him?" A faint hope came to Guy.

"Oh, that appalling woman, the mother, came home to her messy little flat, just as poor William was leaving, and she says she heard her daughter screaming in the bedroom, and she ran after William, all down three flights of stairs, and he got into his car, and she got the license number."

"And—she called the police."

Still another long empty pause. Then Lucy said, "Yes. The police caught him just as he was coming into our house, and took him away. They—they said—" She wailed until his numb ear rang.

"What did they say, Lucy?"

"I don't care what the police and Hugh and the mother and Jack Whitney, your lawyer, says. William—and I believe him—says the police hit him—police brutality, you know, you read about it all the time—and it was his own blood on his clothes. On his—shorts."

"Christ," said Guy. He felt spent and weak, dazed and dizzy. A little virgin, raped by his huge stout son, his overgrown son, his son who was a man not a child. With all the whores available, the free and available high school and college girls with their Pill—his son had to attack a little virgin. Only six months ago Guy informed his son of a very secluded and high-priced brothel in Cranston, and had given him money to go there, and an introduction. Even at seventeen William was experienced, as he had frankly informed his father, and knew of "Houses" near his expensive preparatory school in Philadelphia and had patronized them. His introduction to sin in Cranston had taken place last summer. He told Guy later, with sniggerings, that this one was the "best."

I should have hit him, thought Guy, Lucy's voice a far

clamor in his ear. But—I sent him there myself, with a fistful of money. Why didn't he go there Thursday night?

He said, "Shut up a minute, Lucy. I have appointments Monday but I'll go home tomorrow. On the twelve o'clock plane. Have Hugh pick me up."

He could no longer endure his wife's voice and her moans. He abruptly replaced the receiver. He began to walk up and down the room, Lucy's last words pounding in his ear: "The children—the children—the children—"

The children. Guy thought of the twins, his son and his daughter, Marcy.

He had never wanted children. He had been honest enough with himself before his children were born to admit that many men and many women—perhaps more than sentimental society will acknowledge—are not of the stuff of parents, and have no longing to see themselves perpetuated. They have other aims, other desires, other plans. They were neither "selfish" and "unloving" or "unnatural." They were simply differently constituted. So they refrained from begetting and conceiving, understanding that it was unfair to bring unwanted children into the world. They did not condemn those who desired offspring and had them. What was normal for some was not normal for others. Scientists had proved that paternal and maternal affections were not instinctive. They were learned, they were imitated. Every zoologist knew that.

After her first dismay, Lucy was enthusiastic about producing children. (Her dismay was the result of knowing that at this time, shortly after her honeymoon, the social season in Cranston and Philadelphia had just begun, and she was old-fashioned enough to believe that a pregnant woman should not "be seen in public.") When the twins had been born Guy had told his wife he wanted no more children. She had more than hinted that she wanted four children, "at least." But this time Guy prevented that culmination.

Lucy was a "good" mother. She admitted that, coyly, herself. From the very first she had accused Guy of not being a "good" father. What she really meant was that

330

a "good" father abandoned his own life, his own ambitions, his own very existence as a man, to "nurture" his children, to spend every free moment with them, with no individuality for himself. He willingly became "Daddy." He was no longer John Jones, with a soul and a mind to be "nurtured," too. He was Daddy, a surrogate Mom, constantly appeasing a temperamental wife who was constantly hysterical about her children, and uttered never-ending demands on her husband.

Guy remembered how his mother had tried to subjugate and dominate her husband, and he remembered Tom's amusedly contemptuous resistance. Guy also remembered his mother's attempts to guide his own life into her narrow circle. He was determined that his own household would not be like that. But from the beginning Lucy, even before the birth of her children, seemed fiercely fixed on turning her husband into a sedulous servant for them.

So Guy, who might have become a reasonably concerned father—but not a devoted one—resented his children from their birth. They had not been presented to him; they had been forced upon him by their mother. He fell back on the curse of his life: Duty. Responsibility. He avoided his children as much as possible, though he met all Lucy's requests for money for them. (She was careful not to spend much of her own.) He did not find his children any delight. Marcy, from her birth, was stubborn and unyielding and entirely too active, and she certainly was not lovable or endearing. Her loud voice was always upraised in complaints, in her very cradle, though she was excessively healthy. William was more sly. He "chunnered," as James would have called it, from the moment he was born, that is, he whined, half under his breath. He soon discovered that his mother doted on him, even more than she doted on Marcy, and he could manipulate her before he could even walk or talk. They were unruly from the start. Nursemaids could not endure them and their intransigence, which was their mother's fault. She would not permit the slightest correction. She bought every "baby book" extant, and would quote them volubly to the bored and angered Guy.

When Guy would arrive home, exhausted, longing for a little peace, Lucy would firmly take his arm and make him visit the "nursery." He was incessantly bored. Lucy would force him into a chair and perch her children on his knee, while she used endless batches of film to catch the "beautiful picture." The children, sensing his ennui and silent rebellion, would climb all over him, and, with malicious glee, would tweak his nose and pull his ears, laughing up into their mother's maudlin face. Then, at night, he must visit them in their "adorable little beds for a good-night kiss." He found this very distasteful, for, above all things, he was a man. Dinner conversation with Lucy was centered only on "the children." If there were guests, the women would exchange photographs of their own offspring and go into ecstasies, while the men half slumbered in their chairs. The children's bowel movements were more important, to the women, than their husbands' own needs and wants. Cattle, Guy would think, but cattle, coming down to it, were more sensible. All animals were sensible; when the young were nearly grown the parents threw their progeny out of the nest to fend for themselves, after a severe training in survival.

Guy recalled the children who had been his contemporaries. Girls and boys, in the earliest grades, hurried home to do chores, or to work on their fathers' farms. They were valuable members of society as soon as they could toddle. Tom had put his son to work, at the age of three, mounding up potato hills, and Guy had enjoyed it, knowing he was earning his own importance. There was no juvenile delinquency then, or if infrequently discovered, it earned the most painful and remembered punishment. There was no idleness. There were books and study and work, and self-respect. The children received all their "physical education" in toil, and were proud of their accomplishments. They were obedient to authority and respectful. An obese child was a rarity, even among the rich. Recreation was strictly supervised.

332

Children had no "difficulties" in school. The teacher had full rule over them, and her hand was hard. They learned. High school was a privilege; college must be earned one way or another.

But modern children, their debased mothers declared, were "delicate blossoms." The children—no fools they—took advantage of this situation and became loud, very often criminal, and endlessly demanding. Above all, they became sullen and discontented. Fathers had been forced to abdicate their authority by their women, or abdicated in hopeless despair, or, worse, became assistants in "nurturing."

They fled when they could bear no more. They fled into the arms of women who were childless, or who never mentioned children. They slept in those arms, for a brief peace. It was these women who saved, literally, the lives and sanity of the harried men, and gave them laughter and surcease.

After a few years Guy made up his mind that he was not a servant to his children. He was their father. Lucy would either acknowledge his position as head of the household or he would, in more ways than one, abandon his children. But Lucy did not acknowledge his rightful place. So he lost all interest in Marcy and William, except to provide lavishly for them. He knew his "duty."

When Marcy showed evidence of being a "tomboy" Lucy did not rebuke her, except for the times she assaulted her little brother with her flying muscular arms. William affected a sly love for his mother, and would fill his sister's bed with tacks and various loathsome objects, once even his own feces. The nursemaids were constantly in an uproar; when they attempted discipline they were immediately discharged by Lucy, who claimed they did not "love the children." (Lucy found the children of other women inferior and repellent, and competed with other mothers with exaggerated tales of the intelligence, beauty, and cleverness of her own.) Mentally, Marcy was a dullard; she was purely physical. William was a little more intelligent, but not much; his wits were always engaged in

333

finding advantages and rewards for himself. Both children, with justification, soon found their mother stupid. As for their father—they avoided him as much as possible, for, on occasion, he would slap vigorously and with dark anger, and shout curses. They soon set one parent against the other, knowing there was no love between them.

But—Guy was dutiful. He found it easier to accede to Lucy's requests for more and more for her children than to refuse them. Frequently he would tell himself that he should take some interest in his son, at least, but William skillfully subverted that. He would lavishly agree with everything Guy said, then do as he wished, knowing his mother would uphold him against his father. She was very vigilant. If Guy spoke shortly to his children she would sweep them into her arms and cry noisily with them "Daddy doesn't understand. Only Mommy does. Mommy loves her little ones." The implication was that Daddy did not. The children might not have been overly endowed with brains, but they were wily enough—an animal wiliness—to act in their own immediate interests.

Hating to return to his family, Guy took to random faceless women. So long as his affections were not engaged he did not feel he was betraying Lucy. But he did need a little peace. After talking with men all day he needed the soft and laughing voice of a woman to restore his vitality. He dreaded his house, which seemed to possess a peculiar echoing emptiness, for all the presence of his wife and children, a nursemaid, a cook and a housekeeper and a maid. As she grew into girlhood Marcy became surly and querulous, reminding him of his mother. There was nothing of Tom in William, or of Guy, but he did have his mother's fairness for all his brown watchful eyes. He was greedy, and Lucy bought him chocolates and *meringues glacées* and other dainties; in consequence, when he was only fourteen, he acquired a noticeable paunch which never left him. The children loved no one; they despised their mother, hated their father, and tormented each other and the domestics.

They went to a private school, very expensive, in Cranston. The teachers reported to Lucy that Marcy "tried," but was no scholar. She was more interested in wrestling with the boys and playing rough games with them. A teacher hinted she was very "manly." William was "mischievous," the poor teachers would imply tactfully, though he did fairly well in his classes. But he was not competitive, did not care for athletics, and had no friends. (Neither had his sister.) They were arrogant with those other children they considered less rich than themselves, and subservient to those whose parents had more money. In short, they were unpleasant young people. William did acquire a small amount of attractiveness as he grew into adolescence, but Marcy was frankly ugly, with her stiff short black hair, her narrow black eyes, her very large nose and petulant mouth, her brawny body.

Lucy was never aware that her children lacked charm. She believed them to be exquisite. When she thought of Guy denying her more children she would become sullen. She carped only in a low pathetic voice, and Guy grew to detest the sound of it.

He became more and more lonely. Was this all that would ever be in his life: the acquisition of money, which was now his sole interest, his family, his sardonic brother-in-law, Hugh Lippincott, the latter's detestable wife, and the equally acquisitive men he met in his business? He had no friends. He was isolated as he had never been isolated in his life. If he found himself taking more than a casual interest in a woman he made sure he would never see her again. He had his "duty" to Lucy, with whom he had long ago ceased to have sexual relations. He could no longer read, for despite the emptiness of the house it had a strange and unheard vibration of turmoil. He had Duty as his barren companion.

Marcy plodded through her school. William was expelled twice, and barely managed to graduate. Then he went on to the preparatory school in Philadelphia, which caused Lucy to weep copiously. He was expelled once. He was now eighteen years old. He had no ambitions

335

except to enjoy himself, which he did thoroughly at his father's expense.

As Guy, tonight, paced his hotel room, he thought of all these things, and he felt, for the first time, a wish to die and have done with his life—his sterile life. He no longer had to fear poverty, as his mother feared it, but the imperative to make money did not leave him. In some mysterious fashion he now equated money with Duty. He had no friends, no intimates. If he thought of this at all it was with the conviction that they were unimportant. Yet, he was beset. He thought of Marian Kleinhorst, Hugh's lovely mistress, and his resentment of the liaison. So long as Hugh was married to Louise he had a "duty" not to get "involved" permanently with another woman. A faceless woman, from time to time, was permissible. To love outside of marriage—no matter how loveless his, Guy's, life, was—was in some manner indecent. A quick memory of his father and Sal came to him, and he put it aside. His father never did have a sense of duty and responsibility. A reckless, useless life.

He paced up and down for nearly two hours. He drank a little, and then some more. He smoked endlessly. He found himself hating his son for getting him, the father, into such a terrible predicament. But his agile mind was already at work, looking for an escape. He tried to tell himself that there was some way out of this horror. Money could buy all things. The sweet smell of money. No one could resist it. It was a corruption beyond all other corruptions.

He lay down and slept for a few hours. When he awoke he was sluggish and sick and his body felt seventy-five years old. He could shave and dress only by the actual force of his will. He ate no breakfast. He was glad when it was time to leave for the airport. It was a damp dank day, still chill from winter for all it was Easter Sunday, and the towers of the city swirled with a wet mist and the wind was moist and heavy. The streets dully glistened as if it had recently rained. Crowds were entering churches, wrapped up closely against the chill. He thought

336

of the wild daffodils on his father's farm, the wild crocuses, purple and gold, and the new calves and the fire on the old hearth. But he put the thought aside. This was no time for sentimentality. Nostalgia was a liar.

The sun was out in Cranston, a bitter blob of pale light. The airport was full of holiday people, all talking and laughing loudly. Hugh Lippincott met Guy, and his sarcastic face was grave. Guy felt sicker than ever. Hugh took his arm without speaking and led him outside to his car. Once inside and the car rolling towards home, Guy said, "Well, tell me."

"It's one goddamned fucking mess," said Hugh, who felt a mean thrill of satisfaction that his disliked brother-in-law—his ruthless brother-in-law—was confronting an enormously difficult and dirty situation. He glanced sideways at Guy's profile, grim and pent, and at the streaks of gray at his temples and forehead. Thank God I have no children, thought Hugh, who believed in no God.

"Bill's out on bail, but Lucy said she had told you that."

Guy lit a cigarette. "What about the little whore?"

Even Hugh was shocked at this expression and for some reason he felt anger and disgust. "Whore?" he said. "She's only ten years old, for Christ's sake. Ten years old!"

"Lucy implied her mother was a prostitute."

"Lucy is not only a damned fool but she is a damned liar, if she said that. Mrs. Clancy is a decent hardworking waitress, a widow, a young widow, who is supporting herself and her child on a miserable wage and meager tips. A self-respecting young woman. She's almost out of her mind now. And the little girl, Julie, is in the hospital." Hugh paused. "The surgeons say she'll never have any children, which I'm convinced is a damned good stroke of fortune. Children!"

"Surgeons?" Guy felt a prostrating chill.

"Yes. The girl is so young, and apparently she struggled. She was terribly torn. I repeat, terribly torn. Your son—Bill—seems to have beaten her into submission. The child had to have blood transfusions, too. I've been to the hospital. I've seen the kid. If she were a child of mine

337

I'd kill your son with my bare fists. She's only semiconscious. The mother is frantic. She won't leave the kid. They've put her under sedation, too. I got a private room for them."

Guy said, "Now, that's a fine admission of guilt, from a lawyer."

Hugh had often thought, with relish, of fighting Guy to a battered pulp. He thought of it again. "Can't you understand, Jerald, that if the kid dies your son will be charged with murder? Yes, it's that bad."

"You mean the girl might die?"

"Yes."

"Jesus Christ." Guy tried to breathe in the warm moisture of the heated car. He was fighting savagely in himself. He thought of the banks, of his business. He thought, with hatred, of his son, no longer because of the crime he had committed but what publicity would do to his father's affairs. He said, "The newspapers?"

"Oh," said Hugh, detesting him, and in a heavy jocular voice, "I used quite a lot of money to keep it off the front page. Quite a lot. Remind yourself to repay me. I told the reporters that it might be a 'mistake.' One of the boys got a little obstreperous, so I had to lean on him, as the police call it. And—I've talked to my friend the Chief of Police. It'll all be kept as quiet as possible unless the child dies. If so, then all hell will break loose and your son will spend many a year in prison," where he properly belongs, thought Hugh.

"Thanks," said Guy, in an expressionless empty tone.

Hugh shrugged. "It's the least I could do for my sister's son, or rather my sister, or rather the business." His voice was even heavier with somber irony. "And as your son is my nephew, this is no fiesta for me, either. My nephew."

"What can we do?" asked Guy. "Christ, there must be something we can do!"

"If he were my son I'd let him take the consequences. Perhaps. What can we do? The mother, Mrs. Clancy, is very poor. We can offer her a lot of money, which will take care of her and the child the rest of their lives, if well in-
338

vested. A lot of money. For her silence, for her not pressing charges. For leaving the city with that damned poor suffering kid. And more money—well, it can be hushed up. I'm a lawyer, you know. We can use more money."

He sighed. "We can say it was all a mistake. That your son took the kid home, and then when he was leaving some thug came in and raped little Julie. Bill returned, and fought the thug, who ran away, just as the mother came in. A lot of money. What good will it do Mrs. Clancy if your son is sent up for, say, twenty years? She's had a hard life. She, too, knows what money is. It's a chance, but a slim chance. That is, if the child does not die."

"Have you tried coaching the mother?"

"Not yet. There's no use until the kid is out of danger."

"In the meantime, you've practically admitted Bill's guilt by getting that private room for the—the girl."

"Oh, that's taken care of! I said it was just a charitable gesture, out of pity, and because your son, falsely accused, is so concerned for the poor little thing. I had one doctor and a nurse practically weeping on my shoulder."

Guy put his hands over his face. "God, I'm sick."

"So is everyone else," said Hugh, without pity. "Louise is practically tearing her hair out. She's thinking of her nieces, as always."

"Well, thanks," said Guy. He thought he was choking. He loosened his tie. "Where's Bill now?"

"I thought it would be better if he wasn't on hand when you got home. So, he's staying with that friend of his, Kenneth Fields. Oh, I've got all kinds of character witnesses, including Lucy's dear pastor! There was never a kinder, more gentle, more considerate young boy—than your son. It's a good thing we hold a lot of the witnesses' paper, isn't it?"

"Thanks," said Guy again.

"Would you like to talk to Mrs. Clancy yourself?"

"God, no." Guy thought of his wife. "How is Lucy taking it? Screeching?"

"I talked to her this morning. She's on tranquilizers.
339

I told her the less she says to you, the better for everybody. Oh, everything's just ginger peachy now!"

"Spare me the details," said Guy, who felt so weak and faint that he thought he was dying, and hoped so.

Little Julie Clancy did not die. But she would be internally maimed for life. It was all settled within two weeks, when the child left the hospital. It had cost a lot of money.

On the day Mrs. Clancy and her daughter left Cranston, which was four weeks later, Guy called for his son at the Fields house and took him out to a quiet meadow, lonely, wet, and empty. There he beat William until the youth was unable to cry any longer and until he could not stand. It was done without conversation, without recriminations. Then Guy half carried, half walked his bloodied son to his car and took him home. Lucy fainted when she saw William's condition, but Guy would not let her call Dr. Parkinson. He said, when she regained consciousness, "We'll never talk of this again, any of us. Do you understand?"

She could only stare at his dreadful face and shudder. She had never feared her husband before, but she feared him now. She was convinced he was mad.

James waited in the suite, watching the awful memories running like dark water over Guy's face. It went on for a long time. Then Guy put his elbows on his knees and dropped his head into his palms.

"I should have let him take the consequences," he said, in a distant voice. "I shouldn't have interferred. But— there was everything on which I had based my life, staked my life. Everything. Still, I should have let him—"

"What?" said James, gently.

"My father would have called it a point of honor," said Guy. "A point of honor. But you can't cash honor at the bank."

"There's the bank of justice," said James with compassion, and he was all at sea. What was Guy rambling about, what memories were afflicting him?
340

"There isn't any justice," said Guy. "There's only money."

"My own father didn't think so," said James. "He gave it all up—for a point of honor, as you say."

Guy made a sound of desperate derision, dropped his hands, and said, "Go away, Jim. You make everything come back to me, and I don't think I can stand it any longer. You make me feel—like shit."

"When a man feels that, he has confronted himself and passed judgment. On himself. And that's the best he can ever do in his life."

But Guy turned his face away into the chair and would speak no more.

19

It was snowing when Beth Turner arrived at the Old House to take James with her. She had a little Volkswagen, cramped but warm, and almost new, equipped with what she told James were snow tires. He had been a little dubious about its lightness in the snow, but the small vehicle spurted forward like an animated toy, its wheels spurning the snow and the sheets of ice. Ground blizzards, like dust devils, twirled from the pavement, spun by the wind which was steadily rising. Beth drove expertly; James could see her strong contained profile in the whitish dusk of the day; it possessed dignity and firmness, yet the mouth was large and tender. He thought he had never seen so fine a woman, for all her plainness, and he began to wonder again about her and Guy Jerald. She asked him questions concerning England, which she loved, and they chattered together like old friends, but never with an intimate word. James saw that Beth had complete control over her speech and her emotions, an uncommon thing in a woman.

Her green knitted hood slid back and showed the rubicund glow of her hair. He saw that her hair was long and so fine and sleek that it kept slipping from its pins, and when she glanced at him he saw the aliveness and sparkle of her eyes, sometimes amused, sometimes thoughtful, sometimes absent. Now she was glancing through the steamy windows of the car with some anxiety, for the snowstorm had definitely turned into a blizzard, dry and roaring with the wind. But the little car chugged on, cheerful and determined. Beth talked of her days as a teacher, and would laugh with elaborate shudders. She talked of her parents; she talked of her farm and the animals she loved. But she did not talk of Guy. This was not due to forgetfulness, he knew. She was a woman who would never betray anyone, nor confide their secrets.

The distant mountains, for some time, had been shaking behind their trembling veils of snow. Now they had disappeared entirely. Beth turned on the headlights of the car; they shone dazzlingly on the snowflakes, which danced and whirled so that sight was cut off after a few feet. "It looks very bad, doesn't it?" asked James, to which Beth said, "Oh, this is nothing. I've seen and driven in much worse than this. Pure ice, like blue steel."

"It looks like Switzerland," he said. He found himself telling her anecdotes about his winter holidays in the Swiss mountains. He had rarely been so voluble; he had discovered she was an easy woman to talk to, attentive, genuinely interested, subtle. He found that he had been mentioning Emma Godwin, and was surprised at himself. Beth said, "You must love her very much."

This embarrassed James. He said, "We care for each other very deeply. We have known each other for a long time, over twenty years. Not only had Emma lost her husband and two little children in that water tragedy, but her whole life had been tragic. Her mother had become mentally incompetent shortly after Emma's birth, and was confined to nursing homes and institutions for the rest of her life, which lasted seventeen years. It drove Emma's father into bankruptcy, all that expense, you know; he was a barrister in the City, and doing very well until this misfortune came to him. He had hoped for a
342

splendid future for Emma, his only child, but the burden was finally too much for him. Emma had to leave school and work in a London shop, a boutique. Her father's health failed; all the savings and investments were gone; she had, for three years before his death, supported him as well as herself. She wanted a shop of her own, but there was no money. How she and her father survived is beyond me, but when he died of sheer misery, after prolonged medical care, Emma did not owe a penny. Her father had three pounds left."

He sighed. Beth nodded gravely. "Then," James continued, "Emma developed tuberculosis. She almost died. But worse than that, to Emma, was that she could not pay the bills, hospital ones, you know. She fought for her life. Emma is a very brave woman. When she was released from the hospital, with admonitions that she was to eat 'good, nourishing food,' she had nothing but her mother's betrothal and wedding rings. She had hoped never to be forced to sell them. But this was necessity. She went back to work in the shops. Then she was stricken with arthritis. It became so very bad that she could hardly walk, and her hands were crippled. It was then that Emma decided she must have recourse to God, for a female cousin had just died and left Emma with a little second cousin, a girl, to support." James smiled sadly.

"She didn't apply for any—Welfare?" asked Beth.

James was aghast. "Good God, no! Not my Emma! She would have starved first! She is a lady of immense pride. It was her pride, she said, that kept her alive. For some mysterious reason, after she took the child in—she had two wretched rooms, a bed-sitter, in a very unsavory part of London—the arthritis suddenly left her and has never returned. Her doctor was quite baffled. Well." James paused. "Those were bad times. Emma was so skillful a saleswoman, and so knowledgeable about clothes, that she was never in any danger of being sacked. In fact, the boutique flourished under her management. Still, there was little money, but Emma fought on. The child she had sheltered was, however, none too healthy. She was a wan small thing, but never complaining, and so even Emma did not guess, or know, for a long time——"

He paused again. "There was a lady who had taken a fancy to Emma; the shop carried only expensive clothing. She relied on Emma's taste. On several occasions she brought her husband with her, a stockbroker with large connections in the City. He was an excellent man, in his early forties. Emma was scarcely thirty. He invited Emma to have lunch with him several times, and she gladly accepted. It meant a saving. They were much attracted to each other. In short, she became his mistress, after some time, partly because she admired him very much and partly because her young second cousin had developed leukemia—and there was no money. The gentleman was very generous about this; for the first time in her life Emma accepted money which she had not earned, and it was not for herself. Too, there was affection."

He hesitated. "The child died, of course, but at least she had the best of care for eighteen months, with warmth and comfort and nurses and private hospitals. In the meantime, the gentleman's wife had become aware of the liaison, and there was a divorce. The wife was generous; she was rich in her own right, and so there was no question of punitive settlements. Two days after the divorce, which was not punitive, either, Emma and her friend were married."

There was a long silence in the car. At last Beth said, in a shy voice, "Is she very beautiful?"

"Emma? Not at all. She is almost ugly, but a very fascinating woman. After the first, you don't notice that she is no beauty; her personality, her soul if you will, is so beautiful, so gay, so brilliant and quick, so kind, so aware."

James smiled to himself. Even so intelligent a woman as Beth Turner was sensitive about appearances, and knew herself to be no beauty, either. Ah, women, poor women, sad women, who know their first appeal to a man must be physical, and the more pleasing, the better. He added, "Lord Godwin was a very perceptive man; he saw what Emma was, and that is why he took to her at the very first meeting. Incidentally, when Emma married her lover

344

she repaid all the old bills she had incurred. She told me they had been like an incubus on her for years."

"Are you two to be married?" asked Beth, still in that shy voice.

"Married? Frankly, we never discussed that seriously. I think Emma is afraid of marriage, of responsibility. She is afraid of—death. Not for herself, but for me. She suffered so much when her husband died, and her children. She has the illusion that if I died she would not suffer that way, nor would I suffer in the event of her death, if we were not married. She is very wrong, of course."

"Of course," said Beth, gently, and in the dim light of the dashboard James could see that her face was remembering and her lips were mournful. Now she rubbed at the windshield with her mittened hand, for the glass kept growing steamy, and several times she had to open the window to look out. "We're almost home," she said. On the last occasion when she had opened the window a great white whirlwind of snow had blown into the car, and the sound of the wind was an increasing roar. Huge blobs of snow stuck to the windshield, and the wipers would scarcely push them aside when more stuck. James could see nothing but these; the countryside was dark, with only an occasional distant light winking mistily. James was warm enough but the last blast from the opened window had assured him that it was monstrously cold outside. He said, "I miss Emma very much. I had not intended to be away so long. But I do owe old Jerry for my life. And we were close friends in the Army. In a way, we had no one else there. We were the ones outside the Pale."

Beth gave him a quick glance but made no comment. "We turn in here," she said, and James found himself clutching his small seat with both hands, for the car was rocking and swaying over a very bumpy and unseen narrow road, which he guessed was unpaved. Beth said, "Guy's men laid a wide road, on my easement, for his development nearby. I don't use it. I don't even look at it! Usually it's full of station wagons, which I call mommy

345

wagons, to the ladies' annoyance. We aren't friends. I've put up No Trespassing signs all over the boundaries of my little farm. This also annoys the professional mothers; they thought my farm should be open for the kiddies to race over freely and annoy my animals. I had to have a few obsessed fathers arrested for the trespassing. The fathers, too, thought a farm was public property. They wanted to hunt on it. Now I am the 'old witch,' and well hated, but at least I have privacy." She laughed, and it was a delightful laugh. "A mother can forgive almost anything but someone who doesn't 'love the children.'"

"It's the same in England now," said James, with regret. "Since the proletariat of the cities became dominant—I call them the street rabble—discipline, self-respect, order, a regard for privacy, for the sanctity of the individual, have been abandoned. All is now a welter of love. And hate, of course. We have a race problem, too. I often think of Moses' admonition, that God had ordained the races and the nations to be apart, to have their own identity and wholeness which must not be imposed upon, or blurred into another. The blurring leads to confusion, resentment, and finally to implacable hatred. While all mankind is one brotherhood—I suppose—one must have respect for the apartness of his brother, and his brother's need to be let alone. All this jumbling together, this assault on the dignity of others, will lead to disaster, I am afraid, and not far long from now."

The car came to a halt. "Here we are," said Beth. But James could see nothing but a few scattered lights in a wall of snow. "I leave some lights on when I know it will be dark before I get back." James opened the door and stepped into deep blowing snow, which engulfed his boots and stung his face. It was, indeed, very cold. He shivered, pulled down his hat and buttoned his coat to the throat. He plodded after Beth and marveled at the lithe quickness of her walk ahead of him, while he plunged and slipped. Now he saw the vague white outline of a small house almost upon him, and then Beth had opened the door and a path of warm lamplight struck out into the howling
346

darkness; there was a wind of such force that it took the breath.

Once inside, Beth relieved him of his hat and coat; his hands were quite numb, as was his nose, yet the walk had not been far. Beth knelt before the fireplace, set newspaper and kindling alight, and the big dry logs took fire immediately. James looked about the quiet and pleasant room with appreciation; he looked at the wall of books and the old rocking chair near the hearth. A bowl on a table, a fine Chinese bowl, held autumn fruit, and there were plants everywhere in pots, lush and fragrant. Some were blooming. It was all so welcoming, so peaceful, so inviting, so comfortable, he thought. So here old Jerry had come for sanctuary, for solace, and I don't blame him. James's acute eye saw that several pieces of furniture were authentic antiques, polished to a golden and brown blaze in the awakened fire.

Beth had taken off her own hat and rough coat, and James saw that her frock was a deep yellow wool, plain and inexpensive, but beautiful on that tall and slender body. The wind had made her transparent skin rosy; her eyes were very bright, her tumbling hair disheveled. All at once, as Guy had seen, she was beautiful, with the rare beauty of complete womanhood, and its mystery also. He saw her high rounded breast under the wool, her white strong throat. She did not resemble Emma Godwin in the least, but to James there was a strange resemblance between the two women, for they were indeed women.

"I have only a bean-and-ham casserole, and a salad, and Boston brown bread and an apple pie," Beth said, but without apology. "And some vegetable soup, which I made yesterday. But it is my own ham. I smoke them myself."

"It sounds like a feast," said James, ruefully thinking of his weight. He discovered he was hungry. He sat down automatically in the rocking chair and held out his hands to the hot fire. An honest fire, he thought, with a deep bed of old ashes. He saw there was a tall black and ancient clock in a distant corner. He was surprised to see it was quarter past six; the clock chimed, a sonorous and leisurely chime. Westminster. The window ledges outside were heaped with snow. The wind pounded the glass with a steady drumming note, and the snow hissed audibly. But here was security and calm.

"I have only Bourbon," said Beth. "It's Guy's favorite drink."

"And mine also," said James, smiling at her with appreciation. "A taste I acquired. No ice, please. And a glass of water, with no ice, either."

"That's the way Guy likes it," she said, and there was a note of joy in her resonant voice, a note, he observed, almost of gratitude.

She returned from the kitchen with a silver tray which held glasses, a pitcher of water, and a bottle of whiskey. There was also a dish of a variety of nuts. "Do help yourself," she said, and he did so. She poured whiskey for herself. She sat down quite near to him, and he saw serenity coming back into her face, and he knew, again, that he was surrogate for another man. Lamplight and firelight mingled with each other. The rumbling of the fire kept the wind at bay, in the chimney, where it spoke with turmoil.

"My house is really very small," said Beth. "This room, a very tiny dining room, one bedroom, and a bathroom. But it is quite enough for me. I am so lucky to have found it, after I was forcibly retired from the school-room. My farm is very small, too, hardly a farm, less than sixteen acres, but it keeps me in vegetables and fruit and meat and poultry and eggs. It was so very —pleasant—until Guy built his development, and very quiet. Now I hear voices almost every day, and the sounds of cars. That's why I really prefer winter, now. The voices aren't so—imminent, and I can pretend no one lives near me. In the summer my trees hide the development, too, for which I am also lucky. Do you think I am a very naughty misanthrope?" she asked suddenly, and with laughter in her eyes.

"No," said James, with warm affection. "I don't think

man was intended to be cheek by jowl with his neighbor. That doesn't lead to what the 'liberals' call understanding. It leads to—again—hatred and resentment. A man must have his wholeness, apart from others, a free air in which to live. I live in London, of course, where I have my practice, but on weekends we go to Emma's house in Kent, a lovely large old house, and we spend our holidays there, and most of the summer. It's quite a large estate, and no neighbors interfere with one, and call only when invited. England is so small—Little England now, alas—and so crowded that only a respect for the privacy of others keeps us from cutting one another's throats. It's called 'English reserve.' It's really English pride, an acknowledgment that a neighbor deserves consideration."

"You love your country, don't you, James?" asked Beth.

He was a little taken aback at her American use of his Christian name. Then he said, sighing, "Yes. At least I love what she once was, the balance wheel of the world. Pax Britannica." Now his large rotund face colored with suppressed anger. "It was one of your Presidents who destroyed the Empire, the great Empire which maintained law and order among the nations, to a great extent, for many decades. Your American 'liberals' were lovingly overjoyed at the destruction of that mighty force for peace among the various warring countries. They said they 'loved' England, but it was an evil depraved love. They caroled about 'a happy little country.' A happy little country, no longer the mighty Empire! A happy little country teeming with the risen street rabble! For that, America cannot be forgiven." He added, with intense bitterness, 'A happy little country whose requiem is sung by the shrill voice of Fascistic Communism!"

The little house shook as the gale swooped into a thunderous passage over the land. The fire on the hearth blew outwards with gusts of smoke, showering sparks. Triumphantly, the wind screamed in the chimney. Without any anxiety or apparent concern, Beth moved the fire screen more firmly into position, after turning over the glowing

349

logs. She inspected the hearth rug, absently stamped out minute embers. Uneasily, James listened to the powerful noise all about them. But above it all the clock spoke: It was seven. James said, "That is a fine old clock."

Beth looked at it and she smiled a little. "Yes. Isn't it? Guy gave it to me two years ago." Her eyes took and kept distance. The lamps flickered. She became alert, and went into the kitchen, returning with two hurricane lamps, which she placed on tables. She brought two more in. "Sometimes during storms like this the lines go down, and the lights go out. It happens in the summer, too. But it's inconvenient to have them down in the winter. My furnace stops working. But we have plenty of wood here and in the shed."

James was thinking of England, no longer Great Britain. Little England. With a surge almost of passion his malaise returned. He floundered in it while Beth refilled his glass. What was it that eluded him? Or was he eluding it? He was so absorbed in his thoughts that when he heard a gigantic crash he looked about him dazedly. "I think," said Beth, with some alarm, "that my old oak tree just blew down." She ran to a window, trying to see through the almost solid wall of snow, but it was useless. Now cold fingers crept into the warm room from cracks about the window frames. James drew closer to the fire. "I loved that tree. It was an old friend. What will shade my begonias and fuchsias now?" She turned from the window, smiling. "They're only frail little things, pink; I always think of them as being helpless. But they can survive better than the tall flamboyant flowers. Well, they'll miss our friend, who will light the fire for me next winter. Trees and other innocent things have intrinsic value, don't they?"

"And people don't, Beth?"

She hesitated, sat down, looked into her glass. "Not many, James. You see, I speak from experience. Malice is an exclusively human thing, though other primates do show a little of it, too. Does malice inevitably accompany
350

intelligence? Perhaps. But it does take brains, doesn't it, to be evil?"

James laughed. "I've heard it said that Satan was the most profoundly intellectual of all the powers and majesties, next to God Himself. Perhaps that's why God loved him more than all His other sons. And still does, probably. At least, Satan is entertaining, malicious though he is. And I confess, I find entirely good people very boring and without imagination."

The electric lamps flickered, then went out. "Damn," said Beth, without rancor. She lit the hurricane lamps and the light was soft and mingled pleasantly with the firelight. James felt very cozy, very much at home. "We won't be able to hear the news," said Beth, with no regret. "I'm so tired of hearing about wars and revolutionaries and terrorists and plots and counterplots, and threats. I once asked my mother if the world was always like this, and she said no."

"The closer we 'draw together' as a world, the more we'll hate each other," said James, in a dreamy and philosophical tone. "The brotherly-lovers don't like to be reminded of that. So they vociferously demand more and more 'togetherness.' Well, we'll have 'togetherness' fairly soon now. In one big universal cemetery." He stopped smiling. "No wars, you know, are ideological in their essence, despite the protests of idealists. As always, and forever, they are struggles for raw power, territory, expansion. The only effective challenge to wars is a stronger martial challenge. War is based on human nature, which is immutable. Peace is only an accommodation during which nations catch their breath, rebuild, and prepare for the next conflict. The Greeks, always rational, understood this and called war an art. The real art is to do as little as possible to the next conquered territory. Such as the neutron bomb."

The intensity of the storm was growing. The gale shrieked in the chimney. The fire grew brighter. James listened with a certain placidity. Now that the electric power was off the air became colder in the room, but the fire seemed to increase its warmth. Never had James been so comfortable in America. How could old Jerry have pulled himself away from this to his chill empty house, his chill empty wife, his chill empty existence? James discovered that Beth had left the room. He must have been drowsing. He heard the pleasant clatter of china and silver in the small dining room off the end of this room. The aroma of food challenged his appetite. He sipped at the glass he held.

"Dinner," said Beth, and James pulled himself heavily to his feet and followed his hostess. The round dining-room table was small but set with stiff white linen; a pot of red geraniums glowed in the center, thankfully not plastic. The silver was highly polished and glinted in the peaceful lamplight. The white napkins were huge and hemstitched, the china white with a narrow blue-and-silver border. The soup was heavy and rich with meat juices and vegetables and barley, with a hint of dill and garlic and basil. Ambrosia, thought James. The casserole of ham and beans was moist with some delectable sauce, the warm brown bread exquisite, the homemade butter sweet and soft, the salad delightfully crisp and flavored with only olive oil and tart vinegar and salt and pepper. The apple tart, thought James, rivaled any of Emma's chef's. "It's a good thing I have a gas stove," said Beth, pleased by James's obvious enjoyment and his compliments. Her plain yet beautiful face shone in the lamplight like a girl's, and again James knew he was surrogate for Guy Jerald. She brought in the coffee and thick yellow cream and sugar, and provided hearty big cups, and brandy. James chose the brandy. He leaned back in his chair, surfeited, not remembering the casual yet happy conversation which had accompanied the meal. It was the sort of laughing conversation he always had with Emma at the table. He studied Beth with fond admiration. If he hadn't his Emma, he thought, he could love this woman. In fact, in a way, he reflected, he did love her.

The clock chimed. James was startled to discover it

352

was ten o'clock. He examined his watch for verification. Where had the time gone?

"I hate watches, men's watches," said Beth. "They're so interfering. They remind people of duty and responsibility and distasteful work and routine and other dreary things, created by civilization. And—wives." Her voice dropped, became neutral. "And children. They never speak of freedom, of course." She stopped a minute. "Guy often said his father's favorite book was about Gauguin. It's mine, too. A man who broke free, at last, from his dull wife and his dull children, his dull life, and obeyed his imperative—and so saved his life and possibly his soul."

So, thought James, looking with compassion at her averted face.

"And, in consequence, gave something of limitless value to the world," Beth murmured. Then she laughed and looked at James and her eyes were bright with moisture. "Guy often said I talked as his father did. I wish I'd known his father."

James opened a new topic with delicacy. "I've met Jerry's family, as I told you," he said. "Did he ever speak much about them to you?"

"Not too much. He's a very taciturn man, you know. But sometimes, he talked. Not too directly. When he spoke with considerable appreciation of his wife I knew he was —disliking—her more than usual." She drank a little of her brandied coffee. Her cheeks flushed. There had been good wine at the dinner, and all this, and the warm intimacy of the house and the meal, had overcome a great deal of her reserve. "I don't think she and Guy had much rapport. I often wondered why he married her, but I never really knew. Sometimes he'd mention a girl he had known, Marlene, who had died; this was after he'd spoken of his wife."

"Ah," said James, encouragingly.

"I always thought," said Beth, as if to herself, "that his wife was a replacement for that girl, Marlene. But he never said so. He is, by nature, a suspicious man. Or maybe living made him suspicious. I had the feeling that he confided more in me than he ever confided in others, except his father, perhaps. His attitude towards his father seemed to me ambivalent, and sometimes I felt that he had that attitude towards me, also. A mixture of—"

"Love and hate," said James, as she halted.

Beth shook her head slowly, but not in denial. "I think we both goaded him, though it wasn't our intention. I think he goaded himself, really."

"We all do, and even if that's a cliché it's also true, Beth."

"I suppose we're our own hell, and I'm sure that's a cliché, James."

"What would we do without clichés!" said James, and they both laughed. He approached the next topic with caution. "Did he speak much of his children, individually?"

"Not too much. I bought this house some years ago. Before that, I lived in the city, in a miserable apartment with another teacher. I do remember some gossip about his son, from neighbors. The son had been arrested. I think it had something to do with a girl— Guy never spoke of it. As for his daughter—he did once say that she resembled his mother, who died about ten years ago. I don't think he was exactly devoted to his mother. He wasn't a man to talk much of his family. He did tell me how he acquired his money, though. He preferred to talk impersonally."

James nodded. "He had become cautious, which is another word for being afraid. But, what did you talk of, over those years?"

Beth looked at him with smiling surprise. "Why, mostly of his father! I just remembered. And books, and places we had seen. And people. Dozens of things. He hinted to me, several times, that he had wanted to be a doctor, really. A cancer specialist, or a researcher in cancer. But he said there had been no money. I disputed that, and he would get angry. He would accuse me of 'not understanding.' "

354

"What he meant, Beth, was that you understood too much."

"I like to think that. But, I don't know. We've been —friends—for over four years, and I know very little more about him now than I did in the beginning. Except that he trusts me; why he does that, I don't know, either. Still—" She did not continue. After a few moments she added, "He liked to hear me talk of myself. He really did. I could make him laugh and smile, occasionally. Sometimes he would actually tell me something of his own childhood and boyhood. He never spoke of his years in the war, though. He never, I'm afraid, spoke of you."

James thought the time for bluntness had come. "You know that he tried to kill himself, don't you?"

She clasped her hands together tightly and turned away her face. "Yes. I know. I often think I was to blame. I told him not to come back unless he had resolved—something—in himself. I could see, over the past years, that his life was becoming intolerable to him. I'm not sure of the reason. I couldn't stand seeing him suffer more and more acutely. Things—came to a crisis. He had to —choose. Not between me and his family, of course." She looked at James candidly. "He had already nearly chosen me. But I represented something to him— Dear God, I don't know, I don't know! It was something that included me, and I knew it. Once he told me I had made him 'come alive.' It didn't seem to please him, though. He almost threw the words at me. One time he stayed away for four months. Four terrible months. I thought he had finally chosen. He'd chosen his past life, accepted it, and it didn't include me. I almost died of grief, literally. Then he came back. I never mentioned his absence. He seemed both relieved at this and angry about it, too. I knew he had to be let alone. Perhaps I was wrong. I should have prodded him."

"No," said James. "Men always look for excuses to blame women, if something goes wrong. Or, they've chosen wrongly themselves. People should choose for themselves. The best psychiatrist"—and James laughed

355

—"is one who gives no advice at all. After those four months—when was that?"

"Five months before he tried to kill himself. I knew he hadn't resolved anything at all. He had just delayed confronting it. He looked physically ill, too. But I told him, finally, that he must leave me and not come back until he had decided what he must decide. Then, he could ask for me, or come for me." She stared at James with eyes bright with anguish. "Do you think I was wrong? Should I have just let it drift on, with him slowly dying inside?"

James considered. Then he said, "No, you were right. After all, you owed something to yourself, too. None of us can know another, and we know ourselves only dimly. But to that which we know of ourselves we owe our full fidelity, imperfect though it is. It was your right, your duty, to think of yourself first of all. Only in that way could you think of Jerry, and understand him. Self-abnegation is not really to be admired, Beth. It means abnegation of others, too, and so is unpardonable. You had the best of rights to consider yourself, and I'm glad you did."

"Even if it precipitated his attempt at suicide?"

"Even that. But I think he had been considering that a long time, anyway. Now he's confronting what must be confronted."

"Will it include me?" She leaned towards him passionately.

"I don't know, Beth, I don't know. I must tell you that honestly."

She fell back in her chair and closed her eyes in exhaustion. James studied her. A valorous woman. She would lay herself down and bleed awhile, then rise and fight again. Yes. Even if old Jerry never called for her or saw her again, she would survive. She would go on. Unlike his poor mother, who had had nothing in the world except her husband. But Beth had thousands of things. She had, indeed, "laid up a treasure" for herself, and her world was without boundaries. Sorrow might cause her to falter for a time, perhaps a long time. Then she would go on. She would survive this as she has survived many things, as Emma had survived her own tragedies, too. They were brave women. They had their multitude of scars, but these had never crippled them. They were not optimists, with silly "hope" for tomorrow. They had fortitude, and feared nothing, not even death. They would endure, without hope, but not in a gray twilight of despair.

Was he worthy of Emma? Was Jerry worthy of Beth? James doubted this sincerely. Such women were rare glories, and no man deserved them. Even worse, men did not recognize the majesty of these women. They did not know valor when they saw it. They preferred the vacuous women who had never known tragedy; such women had no aura of terrors confronted and surmounted. Men preferred cozinesses, which, in the end, were not cozy at all, but only windy nothingness. They then wondered what had happened to their lives, what had leveled the walls they thought they had built, what had blown out the fraudulent fires which had never existed, what had ruined the vanished city they thought they had inhabited.

The clock chimed. Eleven o'clock. James became aware that the storm was not subsiding at all. The little dining room was becoming noticeably cool. Beth said, "Let's go sit by the fire and have some Bénédictine, or Drambuie. Whichever you prefer." She paused. "I'm sorry I can't tell you more about Guy. I've told you all I know and a lot I've conjectured."

You've told me far more than you know, dear lady, thought James, and he went back to the fire with her, and to small crystal glasses of cordials. At least, James reflected, I understand Emma and how magnificent she is. But old Jerry apparently knows nothing of this fine woman. Or does he? Had she precipitated him from a death-in-life to the possibility of full life? Had it shaken him so profoundly that he had attempted to die?

If so, then he had been a coward, and had pretended to himself that duty was preferable to life. James was so moved by Beth that he felt an angry contempt for old

357

Jerry, who was afraid to live, apparently, and preferred the tenebrous hell he had made for himself to the savage freedom outside.

The air was full of a constant roaring like freight trains passing overhead. James came to himself, with uneasiness. "Is it still snowing?" he asked.

"I'll see," said Beth. The windows were white with snow. She went to the door and pulled at it. It would not open. She rubbed the glass. James got up. He was aghast to see huge drifts piled up everywhere, knife-edged drifts caught in the fluttering lamplight, drifts that smoked. "Oh, my God," said Beth. "I'm afraid we're snowbound. My car must be buried. And there won't be any cabs out tonight, so I can't call one for you. The roads are probably blocked, too." She looked at him, appalled.

James pulled at the door himself. It finally gave, and a mound of snow gushed into the room and the wind screamed inside the room also and nearly put out the lamps. James hastily closed the door. "Well," he said. He shivered.

"I'm afraid you'll have to stay here tonight," said Beth. "We're on the main road, though. It'll be open in the morning. Is there someone you must call?" She was no longer appalled.

"I suppose I should call Emil Grassner. If he doesn't see me in the morning he'll wonder what has become of me." He thought of the recent episode of the thug.

"I hope the telephone lines aren't down, too," said Beth. She ran to the kitchen, then called out with relief. "Still up. But you'd better call now."

So James called Emil Grassner, who said, "For God's sake! I've been worried about you and wondered where you were. Where are you?"

"Marooned out in the country," said James, without regret. "Visiting a lady."

"Ah," Emil said, and chuckled. "Have a nice warm bed. How far out in the country?"

"About ten miles. And you're wrong—"

"I doubt it," said Emil. "Nothing like a good storm."

"The plows will be out in the morning," said Beth, as they returned to the fire and fresh glasses of cordials. "I think I can make you comfortable for the night." They sat and drank and listened to the storm and felt the fire enfold them. They sat in a long and contented silence. At last the gale was diminishing.

Beth left the room as the clock struck midnight and appeared on the threshold with an armful of fresh linen. "You're a big man, James," she said. "And the sofa isn't long enough for you. So, you'll have my bed; I'll change the sheets right now, and I'll sleep on the sofa."

He smiled at her gently. She suddenly bent her head down on the linen she held and began to cry, long, deep racking sobs. He did not speak or go to her. Now she was crying, "Oh, just lie down with me in the bed and hold my hand until I sleep! Just stay with me, just hold my hand! So I can sleep!"

"It's been a long time since you've had a long sleep, Beth."

"Yes. A long time." She lifted her head. Her face was very white and wet. "I can't stand it," she said, quietly and simply.

"Yes, you can, Beth. You'll stand even this, if it's necessary."

He went into the little neat bathroom. He saw she had laid out articles for him, shaving soap, a razor, heavy towels, a comb and brush, and a pair of silk pajamas and a man's dark blue woolen robe. He knew that these must be Guy's articles, and he considered them, musingly. Again, he was surrogate for an absent man, who should be here now, and not in Mountain Valleys tormenting himself to death.

He blew out the lamp in the bathroom, and went into the bedroom in Guy's clothing, which was somewhat too tight for him. Beth had undressed. She was putting on a sturdy and sensible pale cream flannel gown; her long red hair drifted over her white shoulders. The lamplight flickered here also. James sat down on the edge of the big bed with its brass head and foot, its warm red

359

blankets, its quilts. The room was quite cold and getting colder by the instant. Firelight drifted in through the open door. The wind still battered the windows. Beth lay down on her pillow and smiled at him and the smile was that of a shy girl. Then she blew out the lamp and there was only firelight and the night and the waning storm. James lay down, and gratefully pulled the blankets over himself.

He felt Beth groping for his hand, and he held her hand tightly and consolingly. She clutched his hand with a desperate strength, and said nothing. He could feel her trembling with repressed sobs. The wind died away at last. Beth relaxed, sighed deeply and quiveringly, like a child rescued from a dark and lonely wood and from the terrible howling of wolves. She fell asleep, her hand still holding James's. He could catch the warm woman scent of her flesh, the fresh fragrance of her hair; she, in her sleep, nestled closer to him so that her cheek lay against his shoulder. He realized now, in the profound silence, how lonely he was himself, how lonely for Emma as Beth was lonely for Guy Jerald. Loneliness. The awful predicament of mankind, which is ended only in death, or briefly, in the bed of another stranger. We delude ourselves that we can ever be truly at peace, or for long, or even completely known, or loved for ourselves. We live in illusions, thought James, which is just as well. Reality might kill us.

He could not sleep. His own pain was increasing, his own awareness of mounting malaise, which still had no name. He was surprised when a brilliant bloated moon looked through the window, between the thick red draperies. So the storm had passed. He turned his head and looked at the sleeping woman beside him. The moonlight poured on her. She was starkly carved of silver and marble. Her full breasts mounded the sensible nightgown. Her hair had turned silvery also, in the sharp light. She was murmuring something. Her eyelashes quivered. She smiled. She drew James's hand between her breasts and murmured again, a sound of love and contentment. Oh, damn
360

Jerry! thought James, looking at her in compassion. The fool, to throw away all this—and for what?

He felt, to his alarm, something stirring in his loins. He wanted to shift away from Beth, in embarrassment, but she clung tightly to his hand, pressing it deeper between her breasts. He felt heat in his flesh. She opened her eyes just before the moon went behind new clouds and the wind rose again. She knew him, then, this surrogate for the man she loved. She had smiled at him, not with coquettishness or pretended shame, but with acceptance.

It seemed very natural, and right, to him then to do what he now ardently desired to do. Beth, too, was surrogate for another. In the mutual primal embrace they found comfort and tenderness as well as intense pleasure. They lay together for a long time and experienced no betrayal, but only joy.

20

James woke to a blaze of light on his face, and he sat up, blinking, confused, for a moment or two, as to where he was. Then he saw that he was in Beth's small warm bedroom, with its red blankets and red thick draperies and that it was high morning. He smiled, content. He had had the finest sleep since he had come to America, and he was full of gratitude and affection. He got out of bed. Apparently the electricity was on again, for he felt a comforting warmth on his ankles from a register. He looked through the window and saw a world of iridescence, white iridescence glittering with small rainbows as the sun splintered on high knifed drifts, some of which reached the windowsill. At a little distance there was a long drift of trees, filled with snow, and the sky was a brilliant pale blue and the far mountains shone like blue polished metal against it. It was a beautiful world, after all, a lovely world. He went into the bathroom, took a long pleasant bath, and dried himself on thick white towels. Beth might live simply but she knew when to be luxurious. He smelled coffee and grilling bacon. Yes, all was well with the world. Perhaps.

A fire was burning brightly on the hearth. James went into the little dining room, which was freshly laid with china and silver. He heard Beth in the kitchen, and in a minute or so she came in bearing a platter of bacon and eggs and glasses of orange juice. She looked at him with the sweetest smile he had ever seen on her face, and eyes that were frank and open. "Good morning, James," she said and bent to kiss his cheek. But he kissed her lips, slowly and gently. She was dressed in a crisp blue-and-white-checked frock, and her red hair was smooth and sleek and wound about her head. She looked like a girl.

She told him that the boy who helped with the farm chores had arrived in his jeep with chains on the tires. "The roads have been only partially cleared," she said. "Joel will drive you into town. My car is almost completely buried."

"I think," said James, hesitating whether he should eat two or three eggs and then deciding on the latter, "that I'd like to stay here." He saw her face change, and then she smiled again, but this time with cheerful despair. She made no comment. They ate in companionable silence. Finally James said, "I am more optimistic this morning." She poured his coffee. He sighed with satisfaction as he ate a newly baked muffin, and spread strawberry jam on it.

She said, "I never asked Guy to give up his wife and family for me, James. Never. I only told him that he must make up his mind—for his own sake, his own life's sake—how he wanted to spend the rest of his life. Whatever he wanted—he would always have me as long as he wished. But I couldn't go on seeing him until he had made up his mind, alone, with no interference at all, the way he wanted to go. If he wanted, above anything else, to keep his family and his marriage, I would still be here. If he wanted—to leave that part of his life—I would be with him still. It was his choice. It was just that I

362

couldn't stand it any longer, seeing him suffer the way he was suffering, and slowly dying of his indecision."

"Like the donkey who starved to death trying to make up his mind which of two bundles of hay he would eat," said James. "Forgive me. I'm not being facetious. It's a very apt story. And not a new one. You can't help him; he must do it himself and live with the choice."

Beth sighed. "It's not easy for him. Yes, I know I can't help him. I could only, in mercy, leave it all up to him to come to a decision. It wasn't easy for me, either, you know."

James nodded and touched her hand with sympathy. It was nine o'clock. The farm boy came in, stamping his boots free of snow, a large rosy boy with a shy smile. "Plow's not here yet," he said, after he had been introduced to James, whom he regarded with open curiosity. "But the jeep'll get through, Miz Turner. I hope."

It took two long rough hours to reach the city and the Old House, a very cold two hours. The city was floundering in drifts in the blinding glare of light, and parked automobiles looked like smooth mounds under the snow. There would probably be no visit to Mountain Valleys that day. James was not surprised to hear that Emil Grassner was still in the hotel. He joined him there at lunch.

Emil winked at him. "You look as if you had just fallen out of a warm bed," he said. "Very smug, very pleased. You work fast, don't you?"

"It's not what you think," said James.

"It never is," Emil said, and laughed and winked again.

"I was with Mrs. Turner," said James. "She had asked me to go to her house for dinner—and to talk about Jerry. Then the storm blew up and I couldn't leave last night. So, I stayed."

Emil lifted his eyebrows. His heavy farmer's face was surprised. "I should have known you British never do anything impromptu, with a stranger," he said. "Did the lady have anything new to say about our patient?"

"Not really." James became thoughtful. "She only

verified what we had already guessed. Now, there is a splendid woman. She is more than a lady; she is a woman, and a better accolade than that I do not know. She reminds me of my friend, Lady Emma Godwin. In London. They don't physically resemble each other in the least, but in spirit, shall we say, they are truly sisters. I think I can say, now, that our conjecture was right. He always wanted to be a physician or preferably do research on cancer. He can still do what he wants, in spite of his age. And that's the decision he must make: To continue to live his life as it is at this time or do what he genuinely wants to do. Mrs. Turner really doesn't enter—much—in that decision. But I do think that before he met her he was resigned to his present life, or was more or less adjusted to it, though he evidently hated it. She was only the precipitant. I think."

"I have heard, from his brother-in-law, that he was a very unhappy man even before he met Mrs. Turner," said Emil. "Then, for a while after that, he appeared happier than Mr. Lippincott had ever seen him, more at ease; so Mr. Lippincott told me. But then he suddenly changed again, slightly over a year ago, and seemed deeply distracted, even distraught, again to quote Mr. Lippincott. Yes. Apparently Mrs. Turner was the innocent precipitant. He had been ambling along for years, more or less miserably, then he suddenly came—"

" 'To a dark wood,' " said James.

"And went down into the Inferno. Where all of us go, sooner or later. Too bad we never have a Virgil to lead us back, or seldom do."

"I think Mrs. Turner is Jerry's Virgil," said James.

A waitress came in with a slip of paper for James. "It seems I had a call from London last night. About ten; three o'clock in the morning in England. Emma never called me before; I always called her. I hope there is nothing wrong," said James, with alarm. He went to his room and waited with rising dread for Emma to be called and to answer. His heart began to pound too loudly in his chest. But when Emma answered her voice was round and merry as always.

"Well, where were you, you dog?" she demanded.

He sat on his bed, sighing with relief. "I was out, ducks, visiting."

"A lady, no doubt. Well, good for you. Was she kind to you?"

He entered into the game with spirit, so relieved he was. "Very. The lady I wrote you about, old Jerry's lady. We discussed him—thoroughly."

Emma laughed. "Was that all you discussed?"

"Absolutely all."

"Now then, I'm disappointed in you, Jimmy. Have you lost your touch?"

"You'll have to tell me, when I go home." He added, "There was a fierce storm here, what they call a blizzard, and we were snowbound and I had to stay the night."

"Aha," said Emma.

James said, "You gave me a fright, love, calling at three o'clock British time. You never did that before."

There was a slight pause, then Emma said, "You've been away so long, or it seems that way, and I was missing you dreadfully and I had the thought of calling you. I couldn't sleep. I tried a very tedious book and then took a pill, and it did no good. I even had the thought of flying over to America and joining you for a time. I've only seen New York, you know, and San Francisco, and Chicago. Never Pennsylvania, which I hear is a charming state."

"A commonwealth," said James. "Well, why don't you fly over and we'll be together for the little time I am remaining? We're doing quite well with Jerry, but it may be a week or two more." The thought of seeing Emma soon made him feel like a boy, brimming with first love.

Her voice became suddenly serious. "I will let you know, Jimmy, tonight. I really think I will join you."

He felt joyous. "We'll stay awhile together. There are many places I want to see myself. No sense in rushing back, if you are with me."

"But your practice."

"Hodgkins is taking care of that for me, you know. Time for a holiday, I think. England must be gloomy now. We can go to Florida and lie in the sun, and then off to the islands in the Caribbean. What fun. You must bring your dark glasses. The sun is very strong here now, even though it is winter and deep in snow."

There was another pause. Then Emma said, "I'll have my new spectacles in a day or two. Then I'll go to you, Jimmy. Jimmy? I love you."

His love for her made him always conscious of any nuances in her voice. He became alert. "Emma? Is there something wrong?"

"Now, what on earth can be wrong, except that I am lonely and I've lost my char and have to go through the tiresome business of replacing her, and my cook, Simon, is pouting because he's afraid he'll have to tuck in and help with the housework until I get a new char. He's so damned temperamental, as you know."

But James said, "What did old Harrington say about your eyes and the headaches you've been having recently?"

"My eyes? Oh, yes. It's just old age coming along, Jimmy. We can't escape it, alas." Had her voice really become fainter, dimmer? James shifted on the bed.

"Emma. I feel there is something wrong. You must tell me!"

"Oh, Jimmy, you and your delicate 'feelings.' You're worse than an old woman, worse than some old pussy in a village. By the way, that damned cat you gave me last summer bit me yesterday. I—"

"Emma?"

"Yes, love?"

He found himself sweating. "You must tell me, Emma, or I'll be on the next plane and the hell with old Jerry."

"You don't mean that, Jimmy. And again, there's nothing wrong. I'll call you tonight." Her voice was again full. "I think I know what bothered me. Yesterday was the anniversary of the night we met, remember? Twenty years of happiness, Jimmy. Twenty joyful years. We must

366

always remember that. It's far more than most people have, poor things. We must never forget."

Now she was laughing. "I bought you a really stupid present in remembrance, Jimmy. I hope you'll enjoy it. Yes, a few weeks in the sun would do us both good. Don't be off with another lady tonight, love, until you've heard from me."

"I love you, Emma." His voice had thickened, and there was a cold darkness in him.

"So you've said before, Jimmy love, and I believe you."

"Will you marry me, Emma?"

Still another pause. Then Emma said, "I may do that, Jimmy, I really may. Perhaps." Again her voice had changed. "Oh, Jimmy! I can't wait to see you! I really can't!"

Was that a sound of shaking despair in her voice? Oh, God, make it my imagination, thought James.

"On the other hand," said Emma, "I'm not in favor of marriage, as you know. We'll see. And wait for my call tonight, my darling."

There was loud static on the line. "Emma? Are you there, Emma?"

But there was no answer. He replaced the receiver slowly. He felt sick and weak. He tried to shake himself together. Anything that touched Emma, no matter how trivial, touched him. But it must be his imagination. Emma had called him on an impulse, remembering the "anniversary." She had been lonely for him, in spite of her many devoted friends. There was nothing wrong, nothing at all. But the fear remained. He thought of the warm sun in Florida, in the Caribbean, and Emma beside him. He thought of her almost-promise to marry him. It would be their honeymoon. The telephone rang.

"James?" said Emil. "I hear the Interstate road passing by Mountain Valleys is open now. We can go there after all."

"You seem upset, James," said Emil, as they drove out of the city. "Anything wrong?"

"Do you believe in premonitions?"

"Yes. I have them regularly. And they're always wrong. Why?"

James told him of Emma's call. His hearty face was shadowed and somehow thinner. Then Emil said, "I shouldn't worry, if I were you, James. Women get whims."

"Not Emma. She never has whims."

"So, she called you, being lonely."

"It was her voice. Something—different, something not quite right."

"Well, she hadn't slept much, she told you. That happens."

"I tell you, Emma isn't like other women. She doesn't do anything recklessly."

"Well, I shouldn't worry. She'll be calling you tonight, and will probably fly over to be with you."

"It was her saying that we'd had twenty happy years—"

"The anniversary, she said. Your Emma may be different than other women, as you say, but all women are sentimental about anniversaries."

"Emma is the least sentimental of women. A pure realist."

Emil slapped his knee. "Get married here in Cranston. I'll be your best man."

"She never considered marriage to me before."

"She probably knows we're a puritanical country and openly frown on illicit love, though we engage in it all the time. We're a lusty country."

But James said, "If anything—happened—to Emma, I couldn't live."

There was a strong, almost passionate, movement in him as if someone had spoken to him in a stern admonishing voice, demanding something of him, and once again the malaise took him.

Twenty joyful years. But memories are no good, no good at all, in days of sorrow, in spite of what the sentimental say. They only enhance anguish, those memories.

"Cheer up," said Emil. "I've got a premonition of my own now, and this time it's coming true. Everything is
368

all right." He glanced at James quickly, and saw the pain on the large full profile, the beginnings of terror. He thought of his dead wife. So he must have looked himself, when he knew that she was dying. He patted James's knee again. "It's going to be all right," and hoped to God it was a fact. He had become quite fond of Dr. James Meyer.

James was not in a mood to be very patient today. After all, he thought, psychiatrists are only human, too, though sometimes I doubt that. His encounter with Beth Turner of last night, and his tender compassion for her, and his new anxiety, made him irascible. He felt no urgent friendliness for Guy Jerald as he sat near the stricken man. He saw that the draperies had been drawn to shut out the white fire of the sun on the snow, and he got up and pulled the cloths aside, exclaiming, "For God's sake, man, you may live in a tomb of your own but don't try to shut everyone else in with you!"

Guy looked at him dully, then winced as the light struck his own face. He put up his hand as if to hide. "Why don't you go home, Jimmy? You're not doing me any good, if that was your intention, and I'm not doing you any good, either. You look like hell."

"Thank you. And you look worse. Well, at least you're talking, even if you don't make any sense at all. And you are beginning to notice others besides yourself."

"Why don't you let me alone, Jimmy? It's my life, you know."

"Such as it is, and it isn't much." But James found himself smiling, and with the smile some of his malaise lifted. Guy turned his head aside, to hide from both the sun and the eyes of his friend. James settled in his chair. He began to feel concern for his friend again. So he went on with the conversation.

"Every man comes to a point in his life when he must jump, or not jump. Jump to save his life, or jump to destroy it. You've reached that point, Jerry. No one can help you make that decision." He stopped, for Guy had uttered a cry, harsh and somewhat terrible, and he was

369

staring in the distance again as if seeing something appalling, or remembering it.

"He had two choices, jump or not jump," said Tom Jerald to his son, fourteen years old, on a hot and dusty day in July. "We all have. And it's usually irrevocable. But it's better than sitting on a ledge, suffering the inevitable over and over again, before it happens."

But that was later. They were on their way, just now, in Tom's ancient car to a distant farm notable for its fine Rhode Island Reds, for Tom's young chickens had died of what he called "the roop," and needed to be replaced. The car kicked up small whirlwinds of hot yellow dust, and it clanked. The road was a secondary one and wound in its narrow way about farms, farmhouses and silos, meadows and hedges and small streams of water. The silos shone scarlet in the sun, and the sky was pale with heat and the far mountains were purple shadows against it. Cattle lay sluggishly under the shade of trees, munching on their cuds. Noisy dogs chased the car, exerting their authority. Here and there old barns had the hex sign upon them, which made Tom chuckle. "As good a superstition as any other," he said. "And who knows? Maybe there's something to it after all. Magic."

They had been discussing Mary, Guy's mother, and her increasing obsession with money, which she did not think contradicted her religion. This had led to another discussion about the Ten Commandments. "Don't you believe Moses really did bring the tablets down from the mountain?" asked Guy.

"Of course I don't! Maybe something or other inspired them, but they're pure man-made, son. You'll notice they are all directed at the male sex. 'Thou shalt not covet thy neighbor's wife,' or his maidservant, et cetera. Nothing warning the ladies not to covet their neighbors' husbands. Guess the good Lord knew better than to try to restrain women. Nobody can. Maybe that's a good thing, too. It's men who invented all the taboos and the moral laws, which they hoped, poor bastards, would keep the girls in

370

check. They never did. Fortunately. What would the world be without female sins? Damned dull and mean and colorless. They make things lively for both God and man. The Bible says God made man in His image, and from the dust of the earth, but it don't say He did that with women. The girls ain't in God's image, but they didn't come from the dust of the earth, either. They come, it says, from Adam's rib. Nice symbolism. No wonder Adam's had an ache in his ass ever since woman was created." Tom chuckled again. "God bless the girls, anyway."

His satyr's face shone with sweat and good humor. He had not as yet acquired Sal, but the nice, stupid, red-cheeked farm girl in his house was a comfort. She was also strong and amiable, and that was all Tom desired of her, in bed or out of it. Once a sheriff's deputy had come to the derelict farm and had sternly asked Molly if she was "cohabiting" with Tom Jerald. The girl had looked at him earnestly and had said, "No, sir, I ain't got no bad habits!" That had satisfied the sheriff's deputy and had made Tom roar with laughter, to Molly's bewilderment. He repeated Molly's reply to Guy now, and they both laughed, though Guy had become somewhat uneasy lately over his father's happy liaisons. "Thou shalt not commit adultery," his mother often said, in reference to her husband. As if Guy had spoken loud, quoting Mary, Tom said, "Now, if the boys hadn't made sex sinful outside of marriage, where would be the fun? You've got to feel guilty to really enjoy yourself in bed. If you didn't, you'd just be one with the other beasts, a casual mating, without God's alleged disapproval. It's knowing you've broken a taboo that gives zest to it, and romance, too, by God! And all the other beautiful things. Never heard of a Puritan composing a symphony or an opera or painting a lovely picture or carving a noble statue. Love—and sex—are behind it all, and sometimes only sex, if it's good enough. Marriage, they say, is often the death of love and the death of real sex, too, and when they die something heroic passes from a man's life. I've seen all the great galleries of the world,
371

filled with the works of men, and rarely if ever did they use their wives as models."

The road was almost empty except for themselves or an occasional clanking farm truck. The sun grew hotter, the dust thicker. Then, to Tom's surprise, other cars appeared going in their direction, overtaking them, and filled with the bobbing heads of children and women with baskets on their knees. As they passed Tom's car a sound of excited twittering came from them, twitters filled with anticipation. "Looks like a picnic's in progress," said Tom. More and more cars appeared, some pouring out of narrow side roads, and now the road they were on became suddenly hilly and Tom had to put his car into groaning second gear in going up and down. He and Guy began to cough in the haze of blazing yellow dust. An open truck pounded past them, and this also contained, besides farmers, masses of women and children, their faces fixed in excitement and strained ahead.

"Looks like a hanging going on somewhere," said Tom. "They've got that damned ghoulish look on their silly faces. You never see a mob going anywheres to do any good."

"They've got baskets of food with them," said Guy.

"Reminds me of the ladies knitting around the guillotine, and eating, during the French Revolution," said his father. "Nothing like the sight of murder to stimulate the appetite. The ladies are real bloodthirsty creatures, always were."

His straggly red beard was becoming dusty. He pulled his straw hat down closer to his eyes. Now he was becoming curious. The hills were steeper as they went on. No car seemed to be going in the other direction. Then the traffic slowed down until it came to a standstill, the road teeming with trucks and old cars. Tom leaned out of his car's window and spoke to a man in another. "What's the matter?" he asked. "Wreck somewheres?"

"Naw," said the farmer, impatiently sounding his horn. "Just heard, on the radio, that a feller's up there on that
372

there cliff, mile down this road, gettin' ready to jump. Po-leece are out, too."

"Good God," said Tom. His antic face had become quite grave. "What the hell would a man want to do that for? See? What I told you? Ghouls, hoping the poor bastard will jump to his death, and taking their kids along, and their food, to watch the fun." He uttered a sick obscenity and stared ahead with a grimness Guy had never seen on his father's face before. Tom began to look for a turnoff, but he was surrounded by cars and had to move on when traffic started again. The twitterings and shouts and laughter from the other cars and trucks sounded, to Guy, as if devils were in eager spirits, hoping for a holocaust.

"People," said Tom. The word was an expletive. "It's studying people that's made me an atheist." It was as if he had uttered a desperate curse out of some old grief, and Guy felt a dim pain like an echo.

They came on the abrupt cliff down the road, jutting up like a monument against the hot sky, emerging from a lower hill. A long narrow blade of stone plunged out from the cliff and on it Guy could see the high figure of a man on that blade. He was standing absolutely still, and looking down. There was a large grassy area about the cliff and this was choked with cars, gleaming dully under a coating of dust. People were running everywhere, dragging children, trying to get as close to the cliff as possible. The police were helpless, though they shouted and gestured and warned that if the man jumped he might kill "someone." The noise was a primal jungle noise, feral, predatory, hungry, as it rose from hundreds of hoarse throats. For the first time Guy saw raw hatred on his father's face, and a lust to kill. "Why can't they let him alone to make up his mind?" Tom muttered. "But no. They want him to jump and die, so they can crowd around him thirstily, drinking his blood. God damn 'em."

It was a carnival of horror, leaping, jumping, grinning, and howling children, and running and laughing and shouting men and women. Some of the women had already spread coarse cloths on the grass and were evacuating fried chicken, milk, potato salad, beans, cakes, and sundry other victuals from the baskets. The sun poured down on it all, and Guy thought of hell. He saw that a tall ladder had been placed against the face of the cliff, and that several policemen stood on it, gesticulating, speaking. But their voices were drowned out by the riotous clamor below them; that slavering, ravenous clamor.

Above them, closer now—for Tom's car had been forced on—stood that silent figure of a man, still as stone itself, and faceless. Guy saw that he was handsomely dressed, and that he was apparently young, for his body seemed at ease in its stillness. His hands were in his coat pockets. He was now looking at the sky, as if he were all alone and there were no human yelping animals below him. There was something at once tragically lonely about him, and brave. And helpless.

"Might as well get out," said Tom. "Maybe there's something—"

Father and son got out of the car and forced their way between sitting and devouring groups and standing men and women and children. Never had it seemed so hot to Guy, so eerie, so unreal. Then Tom said, "Don't go on, Jerry. I'll go alone."

Guy, who was taller than the average, saw his father's sparrowy figure moving quickly and lithely through the mobs, his antic face intent. He ignored those about him, and there was something about his movements, something authoritative, which made grumblers let him through. Now a long shout was rising up into the dust-thick heated air. "Jump, jump, jump!" It was a chant of glee and hope. The police made threatening gestures down at the mob and were booed, as if the beasts were angered that the policemen were trying to rob them of a colorful spectacle. They milled sweatily.

"Jump, jump, jump!" shrieked the women, yelped the children, shouted the men. Guy wanted to turn and leave, but the press was all about him. Some dogs had gathered, barking. The din was becoming tremendous. And the man
374

on the protruding blade of stone seemed unaware of anything but his own contemplation of the sky. He was wrapped in his own awful silence, and the sky was silent also, serene and uncaring and aloof.

Then Guy, amazed, saw that the police were descending the ladder and that his father was climbing it, as quick and as sure as a monkey. The din lessened somewhat, and hundreds of faces gaped upwards, watching the assent of that meager figure. The top of the ladder ended six feet to the right of the man on the blade of stone, and Tom stood there, evidently talking. At length the man turned his head to him, listening. The crowd became ominously silent, and alert. Then a man near Guy said, his face black and contorted with anger, "What's the old man trying to do? Why don't he let him jump, instead of talking?"

"Yes, yes!" cried his neighbors, wrathfully.

It wouldn't do any good to hit a few of them, Guy thought. He heard the timbre of his father's voice, but not the words. Then the man was speaking to Tom, and Tom was listening. "Get back," the police implored the watchers, and were ignored, but a couple of men made enraged gestures of dismissal, their blue shirt sleeves uprolled, their overalls stained. The women's voices rose in shrill protest at the police. They were not going to be robbed of the death.

The conversation between the young man and Tom continued, as if they were alone. Tom nodded occasionally. The young man lit a cigarette and the thin blue smoke coiled upwards in the shining air. Once or twice he made a slight gesture when speaking. Guy saw his father rub his face with the back of his hand.

"Get the old tramp down!" shouted a man, and assenting shouts answered him. "Is he goin' to stop him from jumping?" a woman's infantile voice demanded. Children were beginning to feel frustrated. A few began to whine and cry. Guy could smell the sickening odor of the food all about him. Some people were standing, chewing chicken legs, and avidly waiting. A little dog ran between his legs. Two little boys shoved him. Guy glanced at their dusty faces, and hated them, and there was something in his expression that affrighted them, for they ran blubbering to their mothers, who stared at him savagely, muttering. They had eyes like tigers. Guy saw the glimmer of their bared teeth. The stench of sweat became keener, sharper, as if it came from felines preparing to charge.

Then Tom lifted his hand as if in salute, or farewell, and slowly descended the ladder. The crowd laughed its delight, and jeered at Tom as he pushed his way through them. He came to Guy, and his face, wrinkled with dry laughter lines, was somber. He said, "Son, let's get out of here."

The man on the blade of stone waved to Tom, and Tom waved back. He took Guy's arm and somehow they were free of the crowd and they got in their car.

A great and terrible roar sounded from the mob. Guy looked back. Silhouetted against the sky was the falling and tumbling body of the young man. Guy closed his eyes. He heard shrieks of terror and pain. "I hope to God," Tom said, "that he hit a few of them. And killed them." Guy hoped so also. He had heard a nauseating thump, but he did not look back. The crowds were milling forward, pushing each other, struggling with each other, panting, cursing, screaming, even fighting to get closer to the scene of death.

They went on towards their destination, silent. Tom sighed over and over. For the first and last time in his life Guy saw tears on his father's face. He waited for Tom to speak, but he did not speak for many long minutes. Then he said, "He had two choices, jump or not jump. We all have—"

He finally told Guy the tragic tale of the young man who had leapt to his death. But Tom did not feel it was tragic; he felt it was only sad. The young man was from Pittsburgh, and of a rich and well-known family. He was socially prominent, married, and with two small children. Nothing had ever been denied him in all his life; he was a member of his father's famous law firm.

"He told me," said Tom, "that he had been everywhere in the world, traveling with his parents since he had been a child. An only child. Everything had been planned for him; life was lovely and easy. There it was: Lovely. The lovely life. Fine home, fine wife, fine children. Everything he wanted—it was given. Love, adoration, health, fortune: He had it all."

But he had nothing, Tom added. He had never had to struggle, to compete, to work. He had never been frustrated. But that was not the worst of it. He had traveled all over the world many times. But he had not seen a single thing in it. It was as if he had been blind. He had seen no glory, no splendor, no heroism, no majesty, no beauty, no light. It was as if he had been blind.

"He was bored to death, satiated," said Tom. "There was nothing he desired, for everything had been given him before he could even ask for it. He was bored. He saw no reason to live any longer in a world that was empty for him. So he was desperate. He just wanted to —sleep. To be rid of the boredom. To be rid of the lovely life, which was meaningless to him, and only two-dimensioned. The tragedy is not that he killed himself, but that he never saw what is all around us to be seen—the grandeur that is God."

Guy looked at his weeping father, who had declared he was an atheist only two hours ago.

Tom said, as if speaking to himself: "There is a poem—don't remember it all—

"The angels keep their ancient places;
    Turn but a stone, and start a wing!
'Tis ye, 'tis your estranged faces,
    That miss the many-splendored thing."

Tom halted the car. He was crying openly. "Damn it," he said, "I'm not crying for someone who just died. I'm crying for somebody who never lived."

"And neither did I," said Guy, aloud, in the blazing

light that poured through the windows of the suite. "I didn't have the courage."

James had been thinking of Emma. He was thinking of all the years of his love. He would hear from her tonight. Now he was startled to an awareness of where he was, and what he had heard. He said, almost roughly, "It's not too late, old Jerry, to have courage." (What in God's name were they talking about?) He looked at Guy and saw his tormented face. "Not too late," he repeated.

But Guy had turned away, and eventually, seeing it was no use, James left the suite.

"At least," said Emil, later, "he admitted he had no courage. Not the courage to make a clean-cut choice. But he will, James, he will—he will have courage. And, I hope, before it is too late."

21

James left word at the reception desk of the Old House that he was to be called to the telephone at any time, at any hour, and then he had dinner with Emil Grassner. Emil saw that his friend was distraught, preoccupied. Women, thought Emil, they make a hell of our lives but we'd rather have the hell with them than heaven without them. He saw James furtively glancing at his watch at frequent intervals. He said, "Calm down. Everything's going to be all right."

"Mr. Macawber," said James, sourly. At nine o'clock he excused himself and went to the desk, but was told that there had been no call for him as yet. He went upstairs, fuming, and sat down to wait. At half past nine, unable to wait any longer, he called Emma himself. Her personal maid answered, and reported that the ladyship was resting; she had a slight chill. Did Sir James particularly want to speak with her? Sir James did, emphatically. After a short interval Emma answered; her voice sounded dim and then she said, merrily, "You impatient rogue. I was going to call
378

you in a few minutes. Today—let me see—it's Sunday. No, still Saturday, where you are. Would it inconvenience you, Jimmy, love, if I arrived on Friday?"

He had a rush of elation. "Friday! I'll meet you in New York, ducks. Let me know your flight number and the time of your arrival."

"I'll let you know. Jimmy? Don't call me. I intend to visit Amanda in Torquay for a day or two. She isn't at all well, you know, with her liver."

"I'll call you there."

She hesitated. "Better not, love. You know old Amanda and telephones. She dithers at the sound of the bell. But I will call you myself. You do sound upset, Jimmy, and there's nothing to be upset about. Oh, Jimmy, we'll have such a fine time together, sightseeing and all."

Her voice trembled and all James's alarm leapt up in him like the sound of clamoring bells. He cried, "Emma, there's something wrong!"

Now her voice sharpened. "Don't be an ass, Jimmy. What on earth could be wrong, except that we've been separated for so long? Ages. But we'll make up for it, I promise you. I sound tired? Well, I do have a bit of a chill. The weather has been foul in London, fog and all that, and my throat has never been too sturdy. I'm resorting to the old standby, lemon and honey and tea, and the devil with your antibiotics. I have a new char, by the way, a real sloven, but that is all you can get now in England."

"And in America, too. Emma? You will surely be here Friday?"

Now her round voice became full of laughter. "I swear it. Jimmy, love? I love you with all my heart, I love you."

He could hardly speak for his emotion. "I love you, Emma. And we'll be married, here in America. We've put it off too long."

She laughed. "Living in sin is far more interesting, Jimmy. What is illegal is exciting; what is legal is boring. And I swore from the start that I would never bore you. Never."

James sat down after the telephone call. He felt shaken, but did not know why. He was not one to laugh too much at supranormal things; he had had some experience with the dark occult world, which no rationalizings could explain. He only knew that he felt undone and that there was a trembling in him. Emma. He could see her clearly now, as if she stood in the room with him. A tallish middle-aged woman, firm and solid of flesh, yet graceful —what was known as a fine figure of a woman. She had broad shoulders and a slender waist and full buttocks, and she was always deploring her weight. But her lusty appetite prevented her from becoming lissome. She had magnificent legs and delicate ankles and white slim hands, and she had immense style, charm and gusto, and a most endearing smile, and a splendid mind. If her face did indeed resemble an intelligent monkey's, low of brow, small and wide of nose, long-lipped and broad of mouth, it was a most fascinating and changeful face, the large dark eyes brilliant and gay, the little white teeth flashing in almost constant mirth. Her curling hair was thick and the color of ripe chestnuts, and only slightly touched with gray. James, thinking of her and seeing her clearly, actually held out his hand to the empty chair opposite him, and he said, aloud, "Emma, my love, my dearest love."

He went downstairs and engaged a large suite for himself and Emma, and a room for Emma's maid, Susan. The elderly clerk already knew him as Sir James, and was quite overwhelmed at the thought of "Lady Emma Godwin honoring us." He added, inquisitively, "Your sister, Sir James?"

James said, trying not to smile, "No. No connection at all. Just a friend, a very dear friend." In America, he thought, it was quite easy to feel wicked. At the present time, in Cranston, there was a campaign going on against young ladies of the evening and their customers, something which James found not only deplorable but unreasonable. It was Lilith, the first female companion of Adam, who had established the "oldest profession," and no doubt she had been a jolly wench. In comparison, Eve must have been most infernally dull, and it was to be hoped that Adam, in desperation, had availed himself of the happy company of the women of Nod.

He went down to the lobby, where several games of chess were in progress. Emil was waiting for him. James informed him of the almost imminent arrival of Emma, and Emil looked at him with pleasure and interest. "You look like a high school kid on his first date, James," he said. "I feel that way," James admitted. "I must arrange something for Emma, a dinner, or some such festivity. But Cranston is not exactly festive, is it?"

"But you'll be leaving soon, won't you, after you've shaken old Guy back into the world?"

"Yes." James thought of Beth Turner. The two women would get along beautifully together, they so much resembled each other in strong fortitude and generous serenity and common sense. James said, "I am beginning to wonder if old Jerry is good enough for Mrs. Turner."

James went alone to Mountain Valleys the next day, Sunday, for Emil had left for Philadelphia and his family and his other patients. James had a severe shock on arriving. He found Hugh Lippincott, Hugh's wife, and Guy's wife together near the reception desk. Hugh saluted him, gave him a wry smile, and lifted his blond eyebrows helplessly. The women greeted him with very evident coolness. Lucy's vacant face had actually taken on an expression of distaste at the sight of him, and Louise Lippincott's smile was malicious.

"We've just heard, Dr. Meyer, that Guy spent a very restless night and was very noisy and profane," said Louise.

"Good," said James. "That's better than his old lethargy. I have great hopes for him."

"We don't," said Louise, shrugging. "Really. It's too bad for all the family."

Lucy spoke in her high fluting voice: "I just don't know—"

"I do," said James. "I'm a psychiatrist, you know, after all."

Louise flared her huge teeth at him. "It's not that we aren't grateful, Doctor, for all the time you've been spending with poor Guy. Such devotion. But aren't you neglecting your patients in England?"

"Sometimes," said James, "it's most salubrious—for patients—when a doctor detaches himself from them for a while. They can then get their breath. Besides, I cleared up my most pressing cases before I came to America."

Lucy sighed. "Dr. Parkinson has been preparing us for the worst—"

"Such as?"

"He is recommending permanent institutionalization for Guy," said Louise.

"And is Dr. Grassner?"

"No, of course not," said Hugh.

" 'Of course not,' " Louise mocked. "The fees of psychiatrists are enormous."

"Some quiet pretty place in the country, perhaps—" said Lucy.

James lost patience. "Like a graveyard—perhaps?"

The women stared at him, and Hugh chuckled. Both Louise and Lucy were almost smothered in sables; they regarded James with affront. James, feeling anger, continued: "I think Guy is partly suffering from enormous boredom. Boredom, you know, is a killer in itself. More men have died from ennui than actual disease, or it has precipitated disease. Man was not made for peace and quiet and the sweet tranquil life—not for long, anyway. He was made for rude combat, for strife, for competition, for color and variety and adventure, for crude ferocity. He is, essentially, the great beast, but an intelligent beast and an active one."

"And for war, too?" said Louise, with an arch look.

James nodded. "And for war. As I've said before, no government ever gave a war and nobody came. Of course, there are substitutes for war, and we'd better find them before the last holocaust arrives with banners and bombs and burning cities. The nature of man can be restrained only so long—"

382

During this conversation they had removed themselves a distance from the reception desk, where the nurses were too curious. Louise suddenly exclaimed, with exuberant glee, "Well, look who just got off the elevator!"

They all turned. Beth Turner, her face absent, was approaching the desk. She did not see them, for people were moving back and forth around them, on their Sunday visits. Louise said, "There's that awful woman I told you about, Hugh." Still grinning, she clapped her hand over her mouth and her malevolent eyes danced above her glove. "Guy's—er—acquaintance."

"Who? What?" asked Lucy, staring at Beth, who was making her usual inquiries concerning Guy at the desk.

What a bloody contretemps, thought James, most uncomfortable. He saw that Hugh was staring at Beth, and his expression indicated that he found her less than entrancing. "You must be mistaken," said Hugh. "Old Guy wouldn't look at—"

"What is it?" asked Lucy. "Is it someone from one of Guy's offices?"

"Hardly," said Louise, and James had a passionate desire to slap her. "She's a friend of Guy's."

Lucy was vaguely incredulous. "A friend? I never met her. Some poor woman—from her clothes? He has so many charities, you know. At least, he sends checks, through me. Should I speak to her? What is she doing here?"

"I think," said Louise, "that she's asking about Guy."

"Why on earth should she?" asked Lucy, faintly.

At that moment Beth turned from the desk and saw James, and her plain face became beautiful with her smile. She came to him at once, holding out her hand. The others stared, as James took that hand; he was getting very ruddy in the face. Beth said, "How nice to see you, James. Have you seen Guy today?"

"Not yet, Beth." He felt completely helpless and he saw that Hugh was laughing silently, and he cursed him inwardly. "But almost immediately." He hesitated. How in hell was he to manage this? He saw that the others were

383

waiting, Louise with surprised and happy spitefulness, Hugh with anticipation, and Lucy with her empty stare. He did the best he could. "Mrs. Turner, Mrs. Lippincott, Mrs. Jerald, Mr. Lippincott."

Only Hugh held out his hand; the women merely nodded. Beth's pale transparent cheeks had flushed. She said, "I know Mr. Jerald. He bought some land from me. I heard he was ill, and decided to stop in to ask about him."

The two women, Lucy with her pretty tinted face and untenanted eyes, and Beth with her ardent lips and dignity, confronted each other. The wife and the mistress. The one who had almost killed, the one who would save, by the grace of God.

Lucy, the always formal, said, "It's very nice of you, I'm sure, Mrs. Turner." Her eyes strayed over Beth's country clothing, the rough tweed coat, the knitted green cap, the sensible shoes, and the green knitted gloves and simple purse. Her expression became haughty and disdainful. "Do you work for my husband, Mrs. Turner?"

"No," said Beth. Her color was fading. Now her eyes deepened with amusement. "We are just friends."

"I can't imagine Guy having friends I don't know," said Lucy. "He hasn't many friends, and I know what few he has. They are my friends also."

Louise, with a large look of innocence, said, "I think I saw you once, Mrs. Turner, with Mr. Jerald, in a restaurant in Philadelphia."

"Did you?" said Beth. She frowned slightly. "Are you certain? I rarely go to Philadelphia. I haven't been there for a long time."

"Oh, I'm sure it was you. And Guy." Louise almost hugged herself in her enjoyment.

Hugh said, "Do you live in town, Mrs. Turner?"

She turned to him with a thoughtful look, and he suddenly decided she was a most attractive woman and that she had a most sensual mouth. "No, I live ten miles out in the country. I sold Mr. Jerald a piece of my property— some time ago. We had quite a discussion about it, at the time."

384

"Oh, really?" said Louise. "Was that what you were discussing so deeply in Philadelphia?"

Lucy was looking confused. But Beth was regarding Louise with cold understanding and patrician contempt, as for an inferior, an impudent and vicious inferior. Under that steady regard Louise's glaring grin faded somewhat, and she licked her teeth, but her malign stare did not waver.

Beth turned to James without answering the other woman, and again they shook hands. Now he saw alarm in her eyes, and he understood. She was afraid that Guy's relatives would mention her to him, and he must not know that she had been here. Then to his most enormous relief Hugh said, "We've just been visiting your—friend—Mrs. Turner. He had a bad night, they tell me, and he wasn't exactly pleasant when we saw him. But he recognized us, all right. I don't think we were welcome."

"I'm sorry," said Beth. She put on her gloves. She glanced at James, and he saw her tremendous relief also, but also her anxiety. He nodded almost imperceptibly. She nodded distantly to the others and walked towards the elevators. They watched her go. Lucy said, "I can't imagine—such a dowdy woman—of course, he bought the land—"

"I noticed something," said Louise. "She had a beautiful gold bracelet on her wrist, yellow gold, with lots of diamonds, a whole band of them. Very expensive." She gave James her malevolent look as if she suspected a conspiracy.

"Then she isn't poor," said Lucy, in a tone of such relief that Hugh laughed. Hugh saw that James was giving him a slight signal, and the two men moved off together. James spoke almost inaudibly. "He mustn't know she was here, Hugh."

"I see," said Hugh. "Well, well. And that Puritan hounding me about not divorcing Louise, and talking to me about my damned 'duty'! On looking her over, she's quite a woman, and he's got unexpected taste. I suppose he gave her that bracelet."

James smiled. "How is it possible for me to know?"

Hugh cocked his head at him. "How come she called you James? Are you two old friends?"

"We've met."

"Here, I assume. Well, well. What do you know about old Guy!" He seemed delighted.

"Manage it, some way, but keep your wife from telling Jerry about Beth. As for Mrs. Jerald, I'm sure nothing remains in her skull."

"I'll manage it, even if I have to jam Louise's big teeth down her throat," said Hugh, kindly. "By the way, Marian Kleinhorst was asking for you last week. How about having dinner with us tonight?"

James accepted gratefully. Another Sunday night in Cranston, alone, did not lure him. He went down the hall to Guy's suite, thinking of Hugh and liking him. He found Guy, not in his chair near the windows, but standing in the center of the room. It was evident that he had been pacing up and down, for he had paused in mid-step when he saw James.

He looked at James with rage. He shouted, "Why did you let them come in here?"

James spoke with mildness. "Who?"

"My—wife! Lippincott! And that damned Louise!"

"Oh. Well, they're your relatives, aren't they?"

Guy uttered a very foul obscenity, and James was pleased. He felt quite heartened. "If you don't want to see them anymore, you have only to tell Dr. Grassner, you know."

"I will." Guy's voice was vengeful. He lit a cigarette; his fingers were trembling, and very attenuated. James sat down and lit his cigar. Good God, he thought, and it was so short a time ago that he was sunken in his deadly apathy! I couldn't be happier. Yes, things were brightening. On Friday, Emma would be here. If Jerry continues this improvement she and I will soon be able to leave this benighted town.

"Why don't you go home, Jimmy?" Guy's voice was strident.

386

"I will, on the very day when you tell me you've made up your mind about something, and are ready to leave here."

"What is it to you, Jim, if I live or die?"

James appeared to reflect. Then he said, with amused frankness, "Damned if I know, Jerry."

Was the other man actually smiling a little, or was that just a grimace? James said, "You know, Jerry, I never forgot you. Time and the river, you know. But I remembered."

But Guy had suddenly stopped smoking. He was staring before him, dazed, again oblivious to his surroundings. He sat down in his chair, the cigarette dangling from his lip. His taut face had become distant and full of terror.

"Life's time and the river," Tom said to his son, who was fifteen years old. "It's not a new thought. But, say, you're on a boat. It's full of your friends, and the ones you love. You're going down a long river, which came from where you don't know, and is running to where you don't know, either. And you're on that boat, in the same fix. You don't know when you got on the boat, you don't know when you'll get off. So you listen to the band playing and watch the people dancing or eating, and laughing, and you see others in corners crying, or just sitting there, looking at nothing. You try not to notice these poor souls. You're enjoying yourself with your friends, and who wants to look at gloom?

"Then you hear someone cry out, begging, hopeless, and you see some of your friends falling overboard into the water. You run to the rail. But you know you can't help them. No one can—in that river. You watch their heads bob in the water; you see their hands held up to you. You can't do a thing. And the boat just goes on and the band still plays. And one by one your friends, the ones you love, fall overboard, and are lost. And you shiver, and wonder when it will be your time, knowing that when it comes the boat will keep on its way, and the people will laugh and dance and eat and sleep and shit
387

and screw, and cry and sit alone, and they won't even know you've gone. That's life, son, that's time and the river. The sooner you know it, the sooner you'll be reconciled."

"Reconciled to what, Pa?"

"To living while you can, without looking back for one minute. Enjoy what you can, and be grateful, and don't think of the dinner last night or what the dinner will be tomorrow. Today. That's all that counts."

"But you've got to plan for tomorrow, too," said the young Guy. "You just can't leave things to happen by themselves."

"I've got no quarrel, Jerry, with planning for tomorrow. But it had better be only tentative. You never know what is waiting for you—tomorrow."

Guy was silent. Tom looked at him, half smiling. "There are men who pass up today, for tomorrow. They give up their whole lives—for tomorrow. They deny themselves joy and pleasure and laughter—so they can have joy and pleasure and laughter—tomorrow. Didn't Our Lord say we're not supposed to take heed for tomorrow? The time comes when those who lived for tomorrow find they've lost their whole lives—and tomorrow is here and they have nothing. 'Remember thy Creator in the days of thy youth, before the evil days come when thou shalt say I have no joy in them.' There, see, I can quote Scripture, too. Remembering your Creator helps you to have joy today—and today is all you have, son. Oh, I'm for planning, too. But share it up! Live today, with some prudence, if you're prudent, for tomorrow—it usually comes—but don't pass up what comes this very minute. See what I mean?"

Guy was not certain. So Tom went on. "Look, in the spring I plow and plant my crops, hoping for the harvest in the fall. But I don't forget to look at the sun while I'm plowing for tomorrow's harvest, and I drink the beer of the last crop at night, the one that was harvested yesterday. For, when you come down to it, tomorrow, today, and yesterday are all one and the same thing. Dividing it up in your mind, like so many do, is the biggest falsehood a man ever told himself. It's a lie that deprives you of joy and life."

They were sitting on the grassy bank of the river this warm July day, fishing. The grass was full of minute daisies with golden hearts, among which the grasshoppers were frolicking, their green bodies a-glisten in the sparkling sun that danced through the leaves of the trees along the bank. Birds shrilled sweetly to each other and flew down on the grass to devour a worm, then darted up into the trees again. Guy could see them jumping from limb to limb, busy with life. The narrow but hasty river flowed before them, scintillating with light on its small crests, and green as the grass itself. It wound around other banks behind and other banks still ahead. A heron stood in the shallows, preening its blue feathers. Dragonflies stitched the bright air, their radiant wings like whirling jewels. Frogs croaked under cool leaves. A few rabbits hopped down to the brim of the water to drink, their white cottontails quivering. Some jagged rocks, here and there, jutted up, wet and mossy, from where the river was shallower. They made minute rapids, white and frothing, in the rushing waters.

When Tom stopped speaking Guy could hear all the sounds of the day and the voice of the river, and he was full of contentment. He had caught a trout, which now lay in the fishing basket. Tom smoked peacefully, the smoke of his pipe rising straight up in the windless quiet. He looked about him, and nodded happily. "It's not just catching fish that's the satisfaction," he said. "It's fishing, all by itself." Guy felt a little drowsy. They had brought a lunch with them, and cool beer. "My father," said Tom, "never went fishing. He didn't have the time." He laughed shortly, but there was no real merriment in his laugh. "He just had time to make money. For tomorrow. And tomorrow never came for him. Look at all the fishing he missed."

He glanced up, then swore. Guy looked also. A youth, in a canoe, was coming downriver, very fast, his paddle wet and flashing in the mingled shade and sunlight. "Of all the damned fools," said Tom. "Thinks he's an Indian, maybe. And heading straight for those rocks." He stood up and shouted and waved a warning, and Guy also stood up, alarmed. Then it suddenly became clear to them that the youth was desperate, and struggling to keep the canoe from overturning, and that he was an amateur. Sometimes his paddles merely skimmed the water and the canoe rocked wildly. "Turn!" shouted Tom. "Rocks!" The youth sent them a look, and now they could see his face was contorted with terror. The canoe spun, rocked, swayed. "Rocks! Move out!" Tom yelled, pointing.

But the youth, who seemed about sixteen, panicked. He had seen the rocks. Instead of guiding the furious canoe towards the farther bank he struck the water with his paddles the wrong way, and the canoe raced to destruction. It hit the rocks with a cracking and splintering sound, dipped deeply, threw the youth into the water, then flowed on, a wreckage. The paddles swirled after it.

The youth disappeared for a moment or two, then his head bobbed up, and he was floundering in the water. He was hurled towards the rocks. He slammed into the nearest, and caught it in his arms, his head barely out of the river. He turned his ghastly gaping face towards the two on the bank.

"Rest a minute!" shouted Tom, going down to the brim. "Then swim over here."

The boy cried back, feebly, "I can't swim! Help me!"

"Christ," said Tom. The boy's forehead was now dripping with blood from a wound and the blood contrasted vividly with the whiteness of his terrified face. Then Tom was pulling off his shoes. "Pa," said Guy, with his own fright. "Nobody can swim there!"

"Somebody's got to," said his father. He paused for an instant and gave Guy a strange look. He was tearing off his trousers. The boy was shrieking in mindless fear. He clung to the rock, and sometimes the small rapids flowed over him, bursting into glittering foam in the sun.

Guy caught his father's arm. "Pa, even I can't swim there!"

"So we let him die?"

"I'll go, Pa."

"You ain't much of a swimmer yourself, son." Tom shrugged off Guy's clutching hand, and stepped into the water. He then began to swim, his thin agile arms lifting and falling, his feet kicking. Guy began to tremble. He went into the cold water, which immediately tried to suck him down. He retreated. Despairingly he looked for his father in the welter of green water and sun. Tom was nearing the rock. The youth watched him, panting, half drowned. Tom reached one of the rocks, clung to it, lifted his head. Guy could hear him speaking, over the sound of the river, but what he said Guy did not know. He saw that Tom was trying to edge from one rock to the other, towards the youth, and that he was in trouble himself.

"Oh, God," groaned Guy, aloud. "They'll both drown!"

He fought back his almost complete terror, and threw himself into the water. He was a clumsy swimmer, but he was young and strong. He splashed towards the rocks, fighting the current wildly, feeling it clutching at his body and trying to drag him down. When he could raise his head a little from the water, choking, he saw that his father was apparently exhausted, for he had stopped moving, though he continued to shout encouragingly to the youth. Guy was making little headway, but he struggled on, doggedly. He forgot the youth. There was only his father now. Again he lifted his head from the water.

He was nearer to the rocks. Now the tumbling current hurled him towards them. He tried to tread water, and delayed himself a little. Then he bumped into his father, whose hands were sliding on the brown-green moss. Tom's legs flailed the water, but his hands continued to slip. Guy caught him by the waist in one arm, and threw the other arm about a rock. The current tormented them and tore at them. Guy held his father, gasping and spitting. Tom was strangling, but he yelled, "Get that kid first!"

391

"No," said Guy. His father's body, in his arm, was thin and frail. "I can't save both of you, Pa."

The youth, on the rock six feet from them, gave a loud and hopeless cry. His arms, torn and bleeding, apparently could hold him no longer. He slipped into the water, and his body, bouncing and jumping, rushed near father and son. Guy now had a choice: To release his arm from the rock and seize the youth, or hold up Tom, whose strength was now almost gone. He closed his eyes, and he did not let his father go. He felt something trying to clutch him, and he knew it was the youth's hand. But he would not let his father go.

Then they were alone, desperately alone, holding on to the rocks. Tom did not speak; he was gasping. But his blue eyes looked, in that strange fashion, at his son. Guy spluttered, "We've got to get out of here. Grab my shoulder, Pa. We'll make it back."

Fearfully, he let go of the rock he was clinging to when he felt Tom grasping his shoulder. They went down, once, twice. They came up, choking. The bank seemed leagues away. Foot by frantic foot, Guy struggled towards it, Tom attempting to swim also, and beating the water with his thin legs, and clutching Guy's shoulder in slipping fingers. The bitter current clawed, sucked, at them. It seemed hopeless, and then Guy felt the bottom under his feet. He stumbled. They both fell face down into the water, now blessedly shallow. Guy pushed himself up and stood and practically lifted his father from the water in his arms. Tom's eyes were closed. He appeared dead, the reddish-gray beard dangling and wet beneath his chin.

In a dazed nightmare of thudding heart and numb legs and arms, Guy reached the bank and dragged his father up on the grass. Then he lay beside him, fighting for breath, icily cold and shaking. Finally he sat up. "Pa?"

Tom's eyes were open. He was even trying to smile. He coughed over and over and shuddered. Guy wanted to weep with relief. In fact, he did cry a little, snuffling, and rubbing his nose on his wet arm.

It was a long time before they had the strength to get

up and start for home, nearly a quarter of a mile away. They were too spent to speak. Tom had to stop frequently to breathe. In his dripping clothing he seemed infinitely fragile to his son, who had only enough energy to pat his father's shoulder encouragingly. The hot sun dried them a little, but the way seemed endless.

Guy and the present woman put Tom to bed with hot-water bottles and a large dollop of whiskey. He fell asleep. In the meantime Guy called the local police and told them of the accident. (Later, it was discovered that the youth had been a summer visitor on a nearby farm, a relative from the city. They found his body a week later, far downstream in the shallows.)

But that night of the accident was a nightmare to Guy, as he waited for his father to wake up and speak. It was dark before he did so. He called for Guy, and held out his hand to him, and Guy took it in choked silence.

"Never thought you had it in you, son," said Tom. "You getting so prudent lately."

"Pa."

"Yes, I know you couldn't save both of us. You chose me. Son, that kid had a lot of tomorrows coming to him. Me, I'm in my fifties, and there ain't too many tomorrows for me."

"Pa, you're my father."

"I know. I'm not saying you should've chose different. But, you see what I mean now? Time and the river. It gets us all eventually. So, son, live, live while you have time. You never know when the river will take you."

"And I never did," said Guy, to the silent James, who was waiting. "Now there's no time, either."

James looked at that dark and somber face which did not appear to see him, but only something else.

"While you are alive," said James, "there is always time."

"Not for me," said Guy.

"We make our own reality," said James. "If you believe there is no time for you, then there is no time. But
393

believe that while you are alive you have eternity, and you have it, for your own uses."

Then Guy really saw him. He said, with bitterness, "You're so damned full of platitudes and aphorisms, Jim."

James smiled. "There's a lot of truth in them, old Jerry, a lot of truth. Besides, I invented that platitude myself."

"Cheers," said Guy. He lit a cigarette. He stared through the window at the glittering snow. "Christ," he said. "When did the summer end?" He seemed astonished.

On Monday, James said to Emil, "I am more encouraged than ever, I really am. He keeps remembering things that agonize him, but he's seeing something in them he never saw before. Yes, indeed, I'm quite encouraged."

He told Emil of his encounter with Guy's family, and the conversation. He mentioned having had dinner with Hugh Lippincott and Marian Kleinhorst.

"There's another man who has to make a final decision," he said. "But, don't we all, eventually? We have to make our choice, one way or another. And on that our lives depend."

He added: "And somehow, I feel I must make a choice, too, but I do not know what it is I must choose, if I am to live."

22

When James greeted Guy on Monday, his elation over Emma's pending arrival making his voice light and happy, he found the other man in a sunken mood of mingled rage and heavy somberness. There had been a sharp thaw during the night and now patches of green showed on the lawns of Mountain Valleys. James felt that spring was practically here, though in fact it was many months away. He said, to Guy's averted face, *"Diffugere nives, redeunt iam gramina campis/Arboribusque comae!"*

"And what the hell's that?" Guy asked. He was seated
394

near the window again but the draperies had not been drawn against a warmer sun. He looked at James with dark disfavor.

"Oh, Horace. It means: 'The snows have scattered and fled; already the grass comes again in the fields and the leaves on the trees.' A happy thought. So long as we live the grass comes again to the fields—and spring to a man's soul. Now, don't tell me that I am speaking clichés again. I know I am. They're not substitutes for thought. They *are* thought. Somebody thought them and spoke and wrote them, and millions of other people felt the truth of them and echoed them."

"My father was full of aphorisms, platitudes, and clichés, just like you, Jimmy. I still think they are escapes from the necessity of thinking and speaking your own thoughts, your original thoughts."

James beamed. "But one is thinking, really, on finding aptness in an aphorism, a cliché, and a platitude. The recognition of aptness is using your imagination. Well."

Guy was silent, but it was not the old silence of hopeless despair and near madness. It was gloomy, of course, but it was alive. This silence had resentment in it and hard glumness. Guy, by inference, was actually thinking, and no longer in flight against thought. James's elation grew. Guy said, "I wish you'd get the hell out of here, Jimmy. Oh, I'm sure I should be grateful, or something, but for what? You're making me wretched, with all your damned talk."

"Good. Better to be actively wretched—it means you're seeing what you ought to see—than to be dead in your mind, and unresponsive." He paused, then added, shaking his head, "I, too, have been running away but I don't know from what, yet, so I am in a worse state than you. At least you know what you face. I do not." His face changed, and Guy saw it, and for the first time he felt a faint throb of interest in his friend.

"You've never had real trouble in your life, Jimmy, or a real problem."

"Perhaps that's the trouble. I am less experienced than
395

you. I could always rationalize, and dismiss, uncomfortable emotions, or fatalistically accept them, and put them out of my mind. So, you see, I've been running away, too, while all the time I should have been facing it with candor and understanding."

Guy was silent. James thought vividly of Emma, and he said, "I used to write to you about Emma Godwin, Lady Emma, my dearest friend. Now she is coming to America on Friday, so that we can do a little sightseeing in your vast country. And elsewhere, too. We've not had a long holiday in years. And I hope, this time, that I will get her to marry me."

"What for?"

James laughed. "That's what Emma says, too. Yet, again, why not?"

Guy shifted in his chair, and James saw that his thoughts were no longer in the room.

"Why not?" asked Guy, in his surly voice, and he gave Beth Turner his surly smile. "Why wouldn't you marry me if I were free to marry you?"

The time was three years ago. It was the spring of the year and two of Beth's cows had freshened, and two little heifers had been delivered. Beth and the boy she employed to help with the chores had just come in with milk pails, and a warm violet light lay over the earth and the distant mountains, and the blessed tranquillity of renewed and joyful life. Guy could hear the melancholy but musical tinkling of a cow bell and the evening-pure clamor of birds' voices. It was so still, so drowned in peace. A single great white star was rising in the west, effulgent and calm, brightening in a sky of heliotrope. The windows were open, and Guy could smell the innocent carnality of the risen earth, and feel the secret pulsing. The softest breeze moved the white curtains at the windows, and a low red fire rustled on the hearth. Guy had just arrived. Beth came into the room in her overalls, rubbing her hands together. She started when she saw Guy, and then her smile became lambent as usual. She said, "Well! If I'd known you were coming today I'd have something better to feed you than cold meat loaf from yesterday."

She came to him, as he stood in the center of the room, and she gave him her usual ardent kiss, then laid her head on his shoulder. He clasped his hands on her upper arms, then moved them to her slender back. She sighed. "You haven't been here for a week." She felt him withdraw a little—as usual. He let his arms fall. She knew that he resented—still—any suggestion that she might have a claim on him, and that he denied a total commitment. That was always why, on leaving, he gave her no positive information as to when he would arrive again, if ever. Yet she knew that he loved her and that it was this love that he feared, and so it inspired his covert hostility. But the hostility subtly increased the more he loved her and relied upon her for his frequent escapes from a life he was finding more and more intolerable. She knew he was being torn by two antagonistic drives, the first to materialistic power and excessive prudence and "responsibility," and the second to an intense yearning for what Burke had called "the unbought graces of life."

She suspected his mother's influence of the first, his father's of the second. He often quoted both with irascibility and open contempt, yet he could not escape them.

So she moved away from him briskly this evening, pretending she had not noticed his withdrawal, and she said, "I must clean up and change."

"You smell of the barnyard," he said, and threw his coat and hat on a chair.

"And you smell of dry dust," she answered. She picked up the hat and coat and put them away.

He gave his reluctant laugh. "It could be. I spent the whole day in the banks."

She brought him a drink, and he sat down near the fire. He looked very tired and aloof. She touched his cheek lightly, in sympathy. Spontaneous gestures were alien to him. He feared them also. So he moved his head when she touched him, and, as always, she was saddened.

Whistling, she left the room to change into a cotton frock and when she returned she found him asleep. She sat down near him and studied him with the acute eyes of complete love. Lines of weariness were driven into his cheeks and on his forehead and about his mouth. His dark face appeared depressed and lonely. She touched his shoe, and sighed. She drank her own drink slowly, watching him. Was it her imagination that he had grown thinner recently? Later, after he had had another drink or two, and had enjoyed his dinner, she would wait for his confidences. She knew he trusted her. She never pressed him to confide in her, so he did not feel harried. Earlier, a year ago, he would speak, sometimes, of his family and always in a neutral tone, without open complaint or impatience or criticism. He no longer did this. He did not, any longer, speak of his wife or his children. She knew why. He was feeling an angry guilt because of his liaison with her. He would sleep with her but often would not even kiss her good night. She suspected that there were faceless women in Cranston and other cities to whom he would resort without guilt. He did not, lately, tell her that he loved her, which she found significant and sometimes gratifying.

Suddenly Beth felt rebellion.

She had known and loved this man for two years, and her love for him was now so complete and abandoned that it often caused her fear and dread. What was to become of her, Beth Turner? What did she, at heart, really want from him? She knew. She wanted him to love her fearlessly and openly, and rejoice in that love. Were he free to marry her, would she marry him? A year ago she would have said no. Now she was not so sure. She derided herself for feeling the "nesting instinct." She knew that his visits gave her joy beyond expressing, and that his absences left her bereft, shaken, lonely and restless. She knew he came to her out of his deep need for love and companionship and tenderness, all of which he fought. But I am a woman, she said to herself, a woman who loves, and I have needs of my own.

He would encourage her to speak of herself and her past experiences, and he would listen with genuine interest and pleasure, and would often laugh. But never, she believed, would he understand her need for a deeper intimacy, that of the spirit and of the mind. Yet, he had this need in himself! The abandon of the heart was unknown to him, or if he felt it perilously close he would stay away from her for at least a week, suddenly reappearing as if he believed he had his own yearnings again under control, and it was safe to be with her.

It was true, she thought, that joy and love must be paid for with pain and anxiety. She wanted to tell him this but knew it would frighten him, for he knew it himself. I have no fear, she thought, and I am only a woman. He is a man: why does he fear? As she thought this she felt a wildly tender pang of compassion for him and her eyes grew full of water. She must resign herself to having what he wanted to give her and ask for no more.

Two years. My God, I only want to help him! I only want, in the full meaning of the word, to lay my heart on his. I want him to tell me of his own terrors, to confide utterly in me. She brushed away the tears on her cheek and looked up to see he was awake and that he was watching her.

"What's the matter, Beth?" he asked, leaning towards her.

"Oh, I don't know. Maybe it's the spring, and springs bring memories." She smiled.

"Of what?"

She was silent a moment. "Memories of wanting what you can never have," she said.

He frowned. "But you seem totally satisfied with your life."

"Do I? In many ways, yes. In other ways, not so obvious, no."

He seemed annoyed at this. She refilled his glass. When she returned from the kitchen he had clasped his hands between his knees and was staring at the fire. He took the glass from her. "What are the less obvious things you want, Beth?"

I don't dare tell you, you darling fool, she thought. It would scare hell out of you. She said, "After all, I am a woman, and men and women can never really communicate with each other, can they?"

He was surprised. "I thought we had absolute communication."

She touched his knee lightly. "Oh, we have, we have!" And smiled bitterly to herself. He looked relieved, but there was a wrinkle of suspicion between his eyes. He began to talk of some new land he had acquired, near the river, and what he intended to do with it. She listened, as always, but she saw that he still watched her suspiciously. After a while, he was more relaxed. He said, "The land I just bought was owned by a young man and his wife. Alex Brannigan. Alex wouldn't sell, yet his land was vital to me. Right in the center of land I already own. I could have built all around that small farm—sixty acres—but it would have destroyed what I wanted to do, to make another new community. Alex and his wife were schoolteachers, and they hated it, as you hated it, Beth. Well, I won't go into intricate details, but they are amateur farmers, city people. They were falling deeper and deeper into debt. Two large loans from the Cranston Savings. The bank was getting alarmed. I'll spare you the details, but I bought up Brannigan's paper. He had a choice, now, but only one. I could foreclose on him, and leave him with nothing, or I could give him what he had paid for the farm originally, his equity, that is."

Beth knew him to be ruthless and exigent, and because she was neither she had often felt admiration for him when he competed inexorably with other builders. But now she felt a shrinking in herself. The Brannigans were no competitors. They were a helpless young couple who had put all they had into their piteous little holdings.

"So," Guy continued, "they took my offer. It amounted to six thousand dollars. They had no other choice. They
400

were failures at farming. They would get only deeper and deeper into debt and then the bank would foreclose and they would have nothing. At least, with me, they got back their equity. They moved out yesterday."

It's only business, thought Beth, and it goes on all the time. Then why did she feel sick and repelled? She said, "Their equity. And nothing else?"

"No." His voice had become cold.

"How about their stock?"

He shrugged. "There wasn't much. They sold it for what it was worth."

"What will they do now?"

He shrugged again. "Beth, I'm not a social worker, I'm not a philanthropic organization. As it is, dealing with me saved them something from the debacle. The bank would have been less merciful, I assure you."

Beth was silent, then she said, out of her own pain, "I can understand. Business is business. But I can't help worrying about those young people."

"Don't be maudlin. That's life. By the way, you don't look very well today."

Her heart jumped with a throb of delight. "I have felt very tired today. Maybe I need sulphur and molasses, the horrible mixture my mother used to force down me when I was a child, in the spring. It was an annual ritual, to help unthicken winter blood, I think it was alleged. I used to recover fast from whatever ailed me, out of sheer fear that I would be dosed again."

He gave his grudging smile. "I went through the same ritual with my own mother, too. I can still taste and smell the damned stuff. But it did have a psychosomatic effect." He studied her closer. "You're very pale, too, and your eyes look heavy."

"Well, I'm tired, Joel's got his schoolwork and can't give me more than two or three hours a day, until the summer. And there's so much to do in the spring, you know. I'm glad I bought that new tractor; it does three times as much as my old one." She yawned. Then suddenly she shivered and her spine was stroked by an icicle. She got up and closed the windows on the darkening earth, then went to find a knitted shawl. He watched her cover herself. Was there actually a gleam of alarm in his eyes? She added, "Joel's older brother is going to lend me a hand, too, beginning tomorrow. Though we seem to have a minor depression, or what is called a recession, now, it is very hard to get competent help." A wave of exhaustion flooded her body, to her dismay.

"I know. They all want jobs that are 'creative, imaginative, innovative, self-fulfilling,' as the jargon goes. They live in a dream world of absolute unreality. The humdrum jobs and the routine and monotonous ones don't appeal to these fools. Every little ordinary man or woman now demands something glamorous, I think they call it. Their parents and their teachers taught them that. But they never taught them to work, only to dream. Stupid, weak, dependent. They want to laugh their way through life, wetting their teeth."

"Dreams are good," said Beth. "In their own way they do help relieve the long misery of living. But they shouldn't be mistaken for raw reality." She sighed.

"I never heard you mention 'the long misery of living' before, Beth."

She said, with involuntary sharpness, "I don't tell you everything about me, Guy!"

"I thought you did."

"Then you were mistaken." What was wrong with her? It was the week's long silence; he had not even called her, as he sometimes did when he could not see her for some unspoken reason or another. And she really was very tired, and the icicle had become quite active up and down her spine. It was also the thoughts she had been thinking tonight. She stood up. "Dinner in half an hour or so. I'll get you another drink." Again, the wave of exhaustion rolled over her.

When she went into the kitchen she burst into silent tears. She told herself it was only her menopausal condition; it was making her hysterical. But the sense of bereavement quickened, and the sense of loneliness, the sense of loss. Why had she never previously felt this so keenly? She had come as close to quarreling with Guy as never before. I was actually shrill, she thought, with disgust, and men hate shrill women. But, God, am I supposed to be serene and lighthearted all the time, and complaisant and agreeable? I am only human, after all, but men don't want to think of women as human. Less than human, perhaps, or superhuman. What imbeciles they are, to be sure! They want everything from a woman, and want to give nothing, especially if the woman isn't married to them. I think we women should get together, and force the boys back to the professional whores, who will listen to them for fifty dollars an hour. And forget them at once.

She found herself both sniffling and laughing. The kitchen felt very cold. She put her hands inside the hot oven to warm them. When she carried the food to the table she was more cheerful, though she was developing a headache.

Guy ate almost in silence; he was in a heavily dour mood. What was wrong with Beth, tonight? She was usually highly joyful when he visited her. Tonight she had appeared cool, and her voice had been edged. When he had dropped his arms from her back she had not taken his hands as she always did. There was a sudden hollowness in him, and a deeper apprehension. This annoyed him. Was she thinking about the Brannigans? Now he was affronted. It was unlike the realistic Beth to be maudlin and sentimental. Perhaps he wouldn't stay the night with her, if she persisted in this mood.

It caused Beth considerable effort to pretend to be lighthearted at the table. For all through the dinner she was feeling an ominous physical malaise. She was rarely if ever ill. But once or twice, at the table, she had an almost uncontrollable desire to vomit. Her flesh had begun to ripple with coldness and the pain in her head had become an unbearable throbbing. Extremely tidy, she decided not to wash the dishes tonight or clean up the kitchen. She longed, inexpressibly, for bed, a warm bed. Her whole body had begun to ache, as if every bone were broken.

403

When she stood up to take the used dishes from the table, she swayed. But Guy, gloomier than ever, was looking through the newspaper. He did not even glance at her, and this made her want to cry.

In the kitchen, she was overpowered by weakness. The cold had gone. It had been replaced by fire. She sat down at the table and put her face in her hands. She simply did not have the strength to move. From far away she heard Guy's voice, distantly imperative. She lifted her pounding head. He had on his overcoat, and his hat was in his hand.

"I said, Beth, that I must go home. And not bother you tonight." The look in his eyes was condemning, and resentful. She tried to get up, in despair. He was leaving her. Leaving her, leaving her. He enlarged before her eyes, and it was like looking at a distorted image through water. He was turning away. Her voice came in a croak. "Don't—don't—"

"Don't what, Beth?" He had turned to her again, frowning. She rested her hands on the table, stiffened her elbows, and forced herself to her feet. But her head was made of iron, and it fell on her chest. He came to her and took her by the shoulders. She looked up at him, but he was advancing and retreating, becoming tiny one second, a giant the next.

From some far space she heard him exclaiming, "My God, Beth, you're sick!"

She whispered, out of a throat that was full of pain and soreness, "Does that matter to you, Guy? Did I ever matter to you?" There was a furnace in her chest now.

She felt herself being lifted, and there was a darkness all about her. She felt the bed under her body. She was shivering and burning all at the same time. She began to retch. Someone was undressing her hastily, pulling on her nightgown. She felt a faint curiosity. Who was with her? Then the blankets were drawn over her; the lighted lamp beat red as blood against her closed eyes.

Guy's first impulse was to call his own doctor, but

prudence prevailed. Even in his real terror for Beth he could be prudent. So after he had put her to bed he ran to the telephone and called the local Medical Registry for a physician nearer the farm than Cranston. Didn't she have a doctor of her own? But Beth had never mentioned him. It was doubtful she had a doctor anyway. Panting and sweating, Guy went back to the bedroom. His heart was banging in his ears with fear. He looked down at the sick and now unconscious woman and he cried aloud, "Beth, Beth! I'm here, Beth." She stirred faintly once, then subsided. Her cheeks were like flame; she was breathing noisily. How could a woman get this sick so soon? Guy took the burning hands; they moved restlessly in his. Beth began to moan hoarsely. Her loosened red hair streamed over the white pillows. Her face had changed, become ghastly and remote. He said, "Beth, Beth," and he grew more frantic and he trembled. If Beth—died—he could not live. He put his head on the pillow next to hers and he began to utter, over and over, frenzied endearments he had never said before. He took her fluttering hands and held them tightly, calling her name desperately. He heard the clock chime ten. Where was the damned doctor? He got up and ran to the window, staring out at the soft silent night. He returned to the bed.

His mind whirled tumultuously. He had never felt such terror before, not this sick and shouting terror, no, not even when he had rescued his father from the river. He had not felt this terror during the war, with the guns bellowing scarlet lightning so very close. He had only one anguished thought: If Beth died from what ailed her he would die also. He kissed the flaming cheeks, kissed the pallid mouth. God, she was on fire! Her breathing was strident and harsh. He felt sick to death himself. He went into the bathroom and dipped a towel in cold water, and laid it on Beth's forehead. She was muttering something, but he could not understand her. The lamplight shone peacefully, and a night bird called outside. A cow lowed, a pig squealed. Guy cursed them, incoherently.

It was nearly eleven before the doctor came. Guy's

knees wobbled as he ran to the door to let the man in. "Dr. Farmer? Mrs. Turner, a friend, in the bedroom here. She's very sick."

The doctor, a young man with a keen smooth face and brown hair and eyes and a competent air, looked at him curiously. Now, where had he seen this big and frenzied man before? Or a photograph of him? "Mr. Turner?" he asked, tentatively, as he took off his coat.

"No," said Guy. "In here, please." The doctor took up his bag and tried to keep from smiling. "A friend." Now, where had he seen this man before?

He did not even smile inwardly when he examined Beth. He said, tersely. "The flu. And pneumonia. It strikes fast. A lot of it around lately. She belongs in the hospital. I'll call an ambulance at once. She's a very sick lady."

"But, she won't die?" Guy's eyes were glittering and distended. The doctor said, "I hope not. But she's got to go to the hospital at once. Where's the telephone?" The doctor followed Guy into the kitchen, began to murmur into the mouthpiece. "Emergency," he said.

The world was like an ax blow in Guy's belly. Dazed and shaking, blinking his eyes to clear them of a sick mist, Guy watched the doctor give Beth an injection. "She won't die?" he pleaded again, and again the doctor replied that he hoped not. "But this is very serious." They stood and watched Beth; she was starting to stop her restless movements on the bed. But her loud and anguished breathing was increasing in intensity. Once she opened her eyes and Guy bent over her and said, "Beth?" He saw the distant emptiness of her eyes, the lack of recognition, the grave withdrawal. She closed her eyes. Guy took her hand and held it fiercely. Now he himself was muttering her name over and over, pleadingly. He forgot the doctor. He and Beth were alone, fighting a terrible enemy together.

The doctor studied him musingly, the big head with the black hair tumbled with a little white, the strong dark face, the hard mouth, the aquiline nose, the great shoulders, the expensive clothes. The poor bastard was almost
406

out of his mind. Now, where? Then the doctor suddenly knew. Guy Jerald, the famous land developer and builder. Married, wasn't he? Yes, his wife's picture often appeared in the newspapers over a story of her charities and activities and social affairs. Mrs. Turner? The name was familiar. Yes. She owned this small farm. Not a young and pretty woman, but striking, even if she was almost moribund and disheveled and the long red hair was dark with sweat. The doctor was intrigued. His narrow nose twitched. He said to Guy, "I think you'd better have a drink, a big one, sir."

But all the power of Guy's formidable mind was concentrated on Beth, holding her back from death, holding her hand with such strength that his knuckles paled. Beth, Beth! he shouted in himself, you can't leave me, Beth! You must never leave me, Beth! If Beth died his life would be like a desert with a lost and broken fountain, waterless in the gray silence. He began to stroke Beth's unconscious cheek. She opened her eyes. Was there a fleeting recognition there? Was she trying to smile? Had she heard him? Guy could not hold back a dry sob of panic and horror. "Beth?" he said aloud. But her eyes had closed again. He needed to relieve himself, badly, as he had so needed on that frightful day when he had learned that his father was dying. Stumbling, he ran into the bathroom. He crashed into the door. Then he was savagely nauseated. His vomit was tearing at his throat like a wild dog. He heard the siren of the ambulance, and stumbled back to the bedroom again.

They wrapped Beth in a number of gray woolen blankets and covered her head. They lifted her on the stretcher, then one of the attendants said politely, "Mister, we're taking her out now. You'd better let go her hand." He glared at them with confused hate. The doctor took his arm and held him back, and gasping, he watched them carry Beth out of the room. The doctor put a glass of whiskey in his hand, and Guy stared at it confusedly. "Better drink it," said the doctor. Guy put the glass to his lips, took a sip, retched, then drank the liquor swiftly.

"I think we ought to have a specialist," said Dr. Farmer. "Anyone you'd like me to call?"

"I don't know—no, I don't know any. You'd better do it. A private room, too, of course. Nurses. Anything—anything—"

The doctor went to the kitchen to call. Guy's trembling almost made him fall as he looked at the empty bed. Would Beth ever lie there again, and he with her? The terror increased to the point of voluptuousness.

Her mood tonight. She was ill, and he had been offended at something she had said. What was it? Christ, what did it matter? He had been on the point of leaving. What would have happened to her then? She would have died here, alone. He cursed himself, hated himself. Why hadn't he seen at once? But no, he had been offended, and he was going to leave her. Just as he had been offended with his father, and had neglected him, and had not seen at all. His self-hatred became an agony. When the doctor returned he commented to himself that Mr. Guy Jerald looked as though he had gone insane.

"Better wait until morning before you see Mrs. Turner," said Dr. Farmer, intrigued. "They'll be busy with her all night; you'd just be in the way."

Guy came briefly to himself. Prudence. They'd know him there, in the hospital. Prudence. He said, "Yes. I'll—call—in the morning. I'll visit her, of course. A friend, a very good friend. I bought some land from her."

He saw the doctor's face, condemning, suddenly antagonistic.

"Yes," said Dr. Farmer. "I'll go to the hospital tonight. Where can I reach you, sir, in case of an emergency?"

The cold caution quickened in Guy. "I'll call you. Every day. I'll call the hospital." The doctor shrugged, put on his coat and hat, and went away. Why, that son of a bitch, he thought. That poor woman might not make it, and he was already protecting himself! But all the big businessmen did that. Nothing must be permitted to rumple up their cautious lives. Their safe powerful lives.

But the doctor was pleasantly surprised, the next morning, to hear that Mr. Jerald—Mr. Jerald!—was already in Mrs. Turner's room, and that nurses had been ordered for the patient. He had said he was an old good friend of Mrs. Turner's, and that nothing must be spared to help her recover. Well, well, thought the doctor. He began to plan how to protect the name of this most important man, and to stifle any gossip which might arise, as it probably would. Still, what was more natural than a friend aiding a friend? The doctor chuckled.

Beth was under oxygen for three days, and on several occasions she nearly died. And Guy came every morning and every evening, and stayed for at least an hour, sitting silent and motionless beside the bed, his eyes fixed on the sick woman.

On the fourth day Beth became conscious. Guy was with her when this happened. She opened her eyes, in that light, airy, and sun-filled room, and looked at him in astonishment. She tried to say his name, but she was too weak. He bent over her, and when he saw that the nurse had her back to him, he quickly kissed Beth on her poor parched mouth. She smiled and sighed. He held her hand.

"You're in the hospital, Beth," he said. "You've been very sick." Her head moved in a feeble assent on the pillow. Her dry cool fingers wound themselves about his. She looked at him and her sunken eyes, in their dark shadows, were filled with love and contentment. Her hair had been braided into long red plaits. Her slender body was now very thin. Her skin was more transparent than ever, and revealed the delicate purple veins under it. She lay languidly, like one who had been rescued from death.

A week later Guy was alone with her. She could speak more now, but he would not let her. He said to her, "Beth, if I were free, would you marry me?"

She smiled, then gravely looked at him, long and thoughtfully. She wanted to say, "Yes, of course." But she knew she must not do this. Guy had far to go. The time was not now. So she said, "No." He said, "Why wouldn't you marry me if I were free?" And did not want an answer.

He patted her cheek, and smiled. Was he relieved? Beth smiled in return, sighed, and closed her eyes and fell asleep. But never again was she to doubt his love for her, and this knowledge hastened her recovery. From that time on she knew him more clearly and more intimately than ever before.

Guy looked at James, as they sat together in the suite. "I should have done it then, three years ago. I shouldn't have waited. Three more years. But—I was afraid. I had too many—commitments." His face expressed contempt for himself. "I could have saved both of us so much."

James knew he was speaking of Beth Turner, and he was exultant.

"Oh, we all have regrets, some of them horrible, Jerry. We're blessed if we have time to rectify our mistakes."

"Platitudes again," said Guy. "You don't know about commitments, Jim. You never had any."

James's face became almost somber. He said, after a moment, "I'm afraid you are right, old boy, too right. Now, I'm going to make a commitment. Two, in fact. One I know, the other I don't know. Yet. But I will." He thought of Emma.

"Remind me to applaud when the time comes, Jim." The surliness had returned to Guy's voice. "Now run away and play with your toys. I've got some thinking to do."

"And I, too," said James. "The trouble is that most of us don't start to think until it's too late. Yes, a cliché again. But what was it Spinoza said? We are twice guilty if we feel remorse. I think he meant that we should not do anything to cause us severe guilt for to feel guilt, after the act, is indeed to be twice guilty. Once committed, we should stop feeling remorseful, and go on with the business of living, understanding that guilt can be crippling, if we allow ourselves to feel it, after accomplishing what started the guilt in the first place."

"I don't think you have any morals, Jim."

410

"Perhaps true. And aren't I fortunate?"

"Nor any sense of duty and responsibility."

James said, "You are quite right. Of course. Again, aren't I fortunate?"

He took himself off, laughing. When he reported to Emil, Emil congratulated him. "Don't praise me," said James. "I didn't do a damned thing. He did it himself. As we all have to do."

23

That night James dreamt of his father again. His father appeared young and vital and his passionate blue eyes regarded his son reproachfully. They seemed to be in the library of the house in London; his father was in his favorite brown leather chair, which rocked under his great weight. James was filled with happiness that his father was alive and that his death must have been only a dream. He himself was a youth, and strong, in the dream.

He heard what his father said now; he heard it in full —precise, unbending, commanding. He listened. He shrank at the indictment. He had an impulse of weakness, of denial, of self-absolution. But his father's voice continued implacably. When he was silent, waiting, James said, "Yes, Dada. I will. I promise you." And he was inundated with fear; but also with resolution. My pleasant and guarded life, he thought, looking at his father. La dolce vita. The careful and tolerant and smiling life which he had lived since the war. Loftily removed from the struggle, living only for the immediate: That was a most awful indictment. To be amused when terror engulfed the world: That was to be accursed. If a man's life had any meaning at all it was to fight evil. Even if he died in the battle, he had truly lived. But the amused and disengaged, watching the battlefield from a safe and comfortable distance, were not alive at all. What had John Donne

411

said? "Never send to know for whom the bell tolls; it tolls for thee."

James awoke in the darkness. Never had he felt so alive, so clear, so clarified of vision, and yet so quaking. At heart, he thought, all men are cowards when their ease is threatened, their fortunes, their cozy ruts, the safe life they have made for themselves. They might not be completely enamored of that life, but it was all they knew and they trembled at the thought of abandoning it for the cold and violent winds of engagement. But if a man was not engaged in living he slumbered in a warm tomb, where voices were only memories of past pleasures, and hopes for more pleasures to come, with no burnings of the heart, no pain, no clash of arms, no untidiness. The "order" they spoke of was not of law. It was a plea not to be disturbed, not to be involved. In short, they were really saying, "Let me die comfortably, after my comfortable life."

He thought of the aristocrats and nobility of France, during the French Revolution—the first Communist Revolution, the appearance of the first Jacobins, who were later to control and terrorize the people in every country. The aristocracy, the whole urbane class of patricians and civilized men, had not only not fought against the monstrous enemies of their country but they had laughed—laughed! —at the earlier dreadful signs of the cannibal conspiracy. They went in their prison-worn finery to the guillotine, not contemptuous or stern or in prayer, but coquettishly, giggling in the tumbrils, as to a festival. They were dying, but not as men, but as silly women who chattered of amours and perfumes. Ten years before, they might have saved France, and in saving her would have saved future generations from the Socialist disease, from the red terror of spiritual, moral, and economic collapse of all the world. Their girlish laughter foretold the slavery of men. Their twittering witticisms in the carts which bore them to their death were not only depraved and shameful, but mocked the agony which was to come.

They had had swords; they had had allies; they had
412

had power. But they were too slothful, too pleasure-loving, too detached, to utilize these. They had refused to believe. They had lacked the imperative to be men, to be warriors.

I, at least, know and believe, thought James, in the darkness of his bedroom. But I have been like those Frenchmen also. I did not, at any time in England, or anywhere else in fact, raise my voice against *l'ennemi sur la gauche* (the enemy on the Left). I have been only a spectator at the ruin and the chaos. I preferred, with casual mirth and cynicism, to merely observe the destruction of my country. I shrugged. I was more than half convinced that there was nothing I could do, of myself. I wished to believe that. Yet, evil is never invulnerable. It flees in the face of strong and resolute men—armed men.

It is time for me to leave my downy crevice in the rock of the shaking world. It is time for me to take up arms against the universal horror. I may die for it, but it is a better death than the life I have been living, among the millions who have lived it with me.

By voice, by pen, by any other means, I will fight. What is it that the men who founded America had said, in the fullness of their true manhood? "We mutually pledge to each other our lives, our fortunes, our sacred honor." Yes.

He knew Emma would understand. But—had she not always understood and he had not heard? He recalled conversations with her. He had suggested flight, and she had not agreed. For, in reality, there was no place any longer, on the whole earth, to where a man could flee. There was not a handful of free soil remaining. There were only brave men, men like himself, he hoped, to confront the beast which was slinking, with death in its maw, in every area of this beleaguered planet. Perhaps it was too late. But one could only try, please God.

At last the malaise left him, for he knew what he must do, and he felt like a youth who had been rescued from age, exhilarated and revived: He knew now what his father had meant, long ago, and perhaps, even now. The son must not be less than the heroic father who had fought

413

his own fight against evil. It is possible that he had won, even in the gas chambers of Fascistic Communism. There is no death for the noble spirit.

His half-conceived book, *The Decline of Western Morale,* leaped from his brain as Pallas Athene had leapt from the brow of Zeus. No more psychiatric books, for many psychiatrists had played a huge and terrible part in the corruption of men's minds, from Russia, from Bismarckian Germany, from England, and now in America. They had attacked the very walls of rationality, and had breached them to admit madness. For only in madness could the disease flourish and survive. Sanity could destroy it.

There was only one choice now: To stand as men or kneel as slaves.

He had chosen. He experienced joy.

"You seem very refreshed this morning," said Emil Grassner, as they drove to Mountain Valleys.

"I had a dream. No, it was reality," said James. He told his friend. Emil listened with a severe face. He nodded, over and over. "But what the hell can I do?" he asked.

"Think of it constantly. It is the most important thing in the world for yourself, your children, your grandchildren, for the whole world. It will come to you as it came to me."

He had called at the desk. But there was not as yet any word from Emma. He was now wildly impatient for her arrival, and to see her courageous face.

"I forgot to tell you," said Emil. "I read in the newspaper last night that the thief who had attacked you has been listed as a 'juvenile offender,' and has been relegated to the warm arms and love and compassionate tears of social workers. As he had been relegated before. After his 'rehabilitation' in some soft nest, he will be released to attack again, and then probably kill."

"We have the same thing in England. It is part of the modern conspiracy. Alas, that we have no Ciceros."

414

Emil smiled. "But you intend to be one, don't you?"

"I can only try, mate." He added, "As soon as I can get Jerry out of his own sweet nest, I will go to war."

It had begun to snow again, a gentle patient snow, a snow immune from men's madness, men's bloody chaotic thoughts, men's lust for power and murder. The only evil in the world was man. "I regret," said James, "that I wasn't born a lion, or some other innocent animal. At least they don't kill, except for necessary food. And they never go insane."

James found Guy slowly pacing his sitting room, his head bent, his face dark with thought. When he saw James he said, "Are you here again, Jim?"

"Yes, and I will stay until you make up your damned mind."

Guy turned on him and his eyes glared. "About what?"

"You know only too well. Hurry up, Jerry. I have work to do." He sat down. He told Guy of his dream. Guy had begun to pace again. Then he stopped, his back to James. He was lighting a cigarette. James knew he did not want his friend to see his face. He stood there, smoking, for long minutes. Then he said, with scorn, "Heroics."

"What this world needs, Jerry, is a few heroes."

Guy moved to his chair and sat down. He smoked slowly, looking into space.

"What this world needs, Jerry, is a few heroes," said Tom. "And we ain't got any now."

"You're always ridiculing that war in Europe, Pa."

"As everybody should."

Guy was seventeen and he was already resenting his father, afraid to face the wisdom the older man spoke. Tom said, "In my way I was just a little hero. Face to face with a very powerful organization, the Bureau of Internal Revenue, which is very busy lately, gathering up all the cash it can, in a fever, so we can go to war, too. And help bring America into the circle of Fascistic Communism."

"But you haven't any money, you never make money."

415

"What do they care about that? They just want it. Let me tell you."

It had been a summer day, a month ago, full of bees and flowers and the conversation of birds. The distant mountains were a soft lavender against a radiating sky pulsing with sun. Tom had just finished inspecting his burgeoning corn, and harrowing the rows. He sat on the steps of his old house, smoking his pipe, drinking a cold glass of beer. He was content. His current woman was a friendly and dimpled wench, who never stopped talking and giggling. But she was amiable, and a practical cook, and Tom asked no more of a woman.

He heard a car coming up his narrow private road and he turned his head. It was a new car, and gleaming. A visitor. But he rarely had visitors. Idly he watched a youngish man detach himself from the interior of the car. He took out a white handkerchief and wiped his sweating face. It was a hot day. Now Tom was curious. The man was fairly young and had a tight humorless face, and he wore a city summer suit of brown gabardine and his shoes shone from merciless polishing. He closed the car door and sent his narrow eyes slowly over the land, as if measuring every acre. He looked at his car. It was dusty, and he was displeased. He came towards the house and Tom.

"Hello," said Tom. "Who are you, son, and what do you want?"

The man carried a briefcase. He also produced a card, which he gave to Tom. Tom squinted at it. He stroked his beard. "What can I do for you, Mr. Henderson?"

"It's about your taxes, Mr. Jerald."

"Now, is it? I pay my land taxes, and it breaks me. But I pay them. Real patriotic, ain't I?

The man refused to smile. He stood before Tom, and Tom, with amusement, saw that he was trying to look very formidable. "I'm not impressed," Tom said, and laughed.

"By what, sir?"

"By you, and what you represent. Sit down, boy, and have a glass of cold beer and try to be human and not one of those fucking tax gatherers whom the good Lord hated above all other evildoers. I believe He forgave one. when the bastard repented. But he had to repent first. Doing any penance lately, Mr. Henderson?"

"I'm doing my duty, Mr. Jerald."

"Are you?"

"We have to have money for the running of the government, and for social services."

"Never cared about either, son. I suppose you don't know, but this country became strong and rich, the envy of the world, its currency backed by gold, before we ever had a federal income tax. Now our money ain't worth more than wiping your ass with it. Nineteen thirteen. So the Sixteenth Amendment was passed, so we could engage ourselves in Europe's war. The first one. And I suppose you're scraping the barrel now to finance getting into this one." Tom shook his head and pulled his beard and grinned. "I'm not going to be part of it. I got a conscience, I have."

The man sighed loud and disgustedly. "Your taxes," he said.

"I don't believe in 'em."

"There's a penalty for not paying them, Mr. Jerald."

"So I heard. And where the hell is the spirit of American men now? Seems to me this country was founded by brave men who refused to pay taxes. They established a free nation. We need some more Boston Tea Parties, and we'd have 'em if American men, these days, weren't so scared of the damned government that at the mention of you they shit in their pants. Well, sir, I'm not scared. I'm an American. And my pants are sanitary, which is more than most men can say these days."

The man's face became very pale and much tighter. He put on his glasses. He stood and opened his briefcase. He brought out a sheaf of papers and studied them, frowning a white frown. Tom watched him, lightly humming a bawdy song.

"You file, each year, a tax return, Mr. Jerald."

"So I do. That's the stupid law, ain't it, and I'm a law-abiding citizen of this great You-Ess-Ay."

The man's thin face became grimmer. "Last year you reported no profit on this big farm. Nine hundred acres. You alleged you had an income of only eight hundred dollars, with expenses and real estate taxes of five hundred dollars."

"Correct."

"So you netted only three hundred dollars."

"Correct, again. Seems to me I heard that in view of my income I didn't need to file any return at all. Correct?"

"And you have only six hundred dollars in the bank. You say."

"And I said it right. By the way, ain't there a law or something which says I have the right of privacy?"

"If you aren't a felon, Mr. Jerald."

"Oh, I'm a felon, all right, according to my neighbors. But ain't been arrested yet. I know the Chief of Police. All of my crimes are minor and happy ones, such as loving women. Or have you got a law outlawing that too? Shouldn't wonder." Tom stood up, and spat in the man's vicinity, and laughed. "Sorry, son. When I see fellas like you my mouth sort of drools, like a cat seeing a rat."

"Insults won't get you anywhere, Mr. Jerald."

"I wasn't insulting you. I just spoke the truth, and the truth is something bureaucrats can't tolerate. What made you get into this foul business, anyway? Ain't you ashamed of yourself? Couldn't you find an honest job?"

The man was breathing loudly and his thin cheeks flushed scarlet. He said, "This is a big farm. Are you trying to say you don't make any profits on it?"

"I'm not 'trying to say.' I'm saying it."

"Why don't you make a profit?"

"Simple. I like the way I live, and I don't like to pay taxes. If I worked very hard I'd have no fun, which is the only thing worth living for. And I'd have to pay taxes, and my conscience as an American prohibits that. Sure, for defending our country, it's worth it. Lincoln had a federal income tax, but after the War between the States

418

the U. S. Supreme Court declared such a tax was unconstitutional. Right. The matter came up time after time, and the Court, every time, said it was unconstitutional. Still is, in spite of that amendment. Then came the Spanish-American War, and war taxes, and for the last time, unfortunately, a federal tax was said to be against the Constitution. By the Court. Or, don't you know your history, son?"

"Mr. Jerald, let's not be facetious."

"Well, well," said Tom, with admiration, "a real educated fella. You never can tell, can you?"

The harsh scarlet deepened on the man's face. He looked again at his papers. "You list only one employee, a Miss Grace Schultz."

"Correct. She's my housekeeper and helps with the chores. Not a lot of them. And my son, who's seventeen, helps out every weekend, and in the summer, and I don't pay him anything."

"You haven't been withholding income tax on Miss Schultz's income."

"What? On eight dollars a week, which is all I can afford to pay? She don't get enough money to pay taxes. I pay her Social Security, though, you'll see."

"Eight dollars a week?"

"Right. She ain't really worth that, but I'm a generous fella."

"And you're letting this land just lie, without cultivating all of it?"

"True. Just cultivate enough to keep me in fruit and vegetables and raise corn and hay for the stock."

"If you cultivated it you'd make a lot of money."

"Which I don't need or want. And, I'd be paying taxes."

"You've listed Miss Schultz as housekeeper-assistant."

"And fifty percent of that eight dollars a week is tax-deductible, as a farm employee. That is, if I needed tax deductions, which I don't."

"Mr. Jerald, I don't believe a word you've told me. Now, there's a matter of net worth. You're subjected to that."

419

Tom chuckled. "I paid a dollar an acre for this farm, and it's still worth only nine hundred dollars. I pay taxes on the land. I listed the taxes. Still ain't worth more than nine hundred dollars. Make a net worth of that, son."

"Nine hundred dollars, for all this?"

"That's all."

"No other source of income?"

"No." Tom was enjoying himself.

"We'll send someone out to appraise this farm."

Tom stopped smiling. "No, you won't. I know the law, too. And that reminds me. You're trespassing. I never asked you to come. I didn't invite you. So haul ass out of here before you get a dose of lead poisoning."

"Are you trying to threaten me?"

"No, I'm not trying to. I just am."

"That's a crime."

"So's your trespassing. We're even! Now, get out of here. I've had my fun with you."

Mr. Henderson backed away and put the tax returns in his briefcase. He said, in an ominous voice, "You'll be hearing from us."

"I hope not. Can't stand the sight of you. Now, get out. Come again, and they'll haul you away in a meat wagon."

Tom had finished his story. When Guy could stop laughing, he said, "Did they arrest you, or something?"

"No. When a bureaucrat comes up against an American —I mean an American—not the simpering slobs they call men now—he runs. He just can't stand the sight of a man. But there are fewer men in America now than ever. So, we got an oppressive government. That's the price we pay for our sins. Oh, they did some snooping around, I heard. But it came to nothing. Kind of regretted it. Wanted to blow that fella's belly out with my shotgun, for trespassing. Chief of Police mentioned something about 'threatening.' I said I never showed that fella a gun. And I got a license for the gun I have. To shoot rabbits. All farmers have guns. Wonder why they don't start using them, as they did at Bunker Hill."

" 'The shot heard round the world.' "

Tom sighed. "You'll hear shots all right, son. But they won't be for freedom. They'll be to enslave mankind, and maybe that's all it's worth now."

James was watching Guy closely. Then to his great astonishment and pleasure he saw that Guy was not only smiling, but laughing. It was a rough laugh, and reluctant, but it was surely a laugh.

"My father was right," he said. "There aren't any heroes anymore. And, God, do we need them now!"

"I thought you didn't like 'heroics.' "

"I don't. I just like heroes. My father was one, a genuine one."

"So was my own father."

"I'm no hero," said Guy.

"Neither was I. Until today."

"Congratulations. You're too fat to be a hero, Jim."

"And you're too thin."

They actually shook hands. And Guy laughed again.

That night James said to Emil, "I think a few more days will do it."

"If he doesn't have a relapse."

"Yes, he might. Let's hope not. He's just about made up his mind, tenuously though. He's rocking back and forth. A little more time. I wish I knew what it was that made him laugh today."

James called at the desk for any word from Emma, but there was none. Tomorrow would be Wednesday. She was probably home now, packing. At nine o'clock James, with increasing impatience, called her. Simon, the chef, answered.

"Sir James?" His voice was suddenly cautious and careful. "Yes. Her ladyship, you know, is in Torquay."

It was the elderly man's tone of voice which alerted James, and not his words. His heart began its painful throbbing.

"But she is supposed to be in America on Friday, Simon."

"Yes, indeed. I know, Sir James. She'll probably be home tomorrow."

"To pack?"

The man hesitated. Then he said, "Yes, to pack, Sir James. She did say she would be away for a long time."

When he had completed the call James sat down abruptly on his bed. He found he was breathing hard and too fast, and there was a sudden sharp pain in his chest. He tried to calm himself. Simon had assured him that Lady Emma would be in America Friday. Why, then, was he so agitated? "It's just that I want and need her so desperately," he said. "Desperately."

He reassured himself by saying aloud, "Friday. I only have to wait for Friday. On Thursday, she promised me she'd call to tell me her flight number."

But when he went to bed he could not sleep.

24

The next morning, at breakfast, Emil looked at James with gloom. "Bad news, I'm afraid. Our friend has gone back into the silences—a pseudo-catatonic state. He showed as much response to his nurse, and food, as a statue seated in his chair. I got the impression from the later nurse that you seemed to have precipitated this new crisis." Emil's eyes were sharp.

"Not true," said James, dismayed. "We even laughed together and shook hands when we parted. I heard that he was showing some appetite. We joked with each other —yes, joked. I was very encouraged and started to plan on leaving in a few days at the most."

"Then," said Emil, "in some way he brought this on himself. He's in retreat, I surmise, a deliberate retreat, because he understood where he was being led and he's not up to it yet, or he wants more time. I'd advise you not to visit him today. He's got to get his breath."

"Will you see him, Emil?"

422

"I'll look in on him, and decide if he needs more medication. But I won't question him or talk to him." He stood up, then seeing how downcast James was, he pressed the other man's shoulder. "I half expected this, you'll remember. He was coming along too fast. A man doesn't descend so low as he did and then snap out of it in two or three weeks, remember. It takes much more time."

James, by himself, ordered more coffee. He began to read the morning newspaper Emil had left behind for him. He saw, through the tall windows of the room, that it was snowing again, determined and silent, and the air was dark gray. It was a cold disheartening winter day and though the big old-fashioned room was very warm James shivered, as a nameless premonition came prowling through his mind. He could not focus on the depressed foreboding and did not know what had provoked it. In forty-eight hours Emma would be here, he reminded himself. Though even his closest friends thought of him as a healthily cheerful man, stable and always self-disciplined, never emotional or volatile and never out of perfect control over himself, he was secretly fanciful at times, and he felt high peaks and low depths more strongly than other men. Manic-depressive, he had laughingly diagnosed himself. He was now at low ebb and sickeningly despondent. He had felt this way before meeting Emil at breakfast, but it was not because of Guy Jerald, he knew. It was that mistily vague conversation with old Simon, Emma's chef. He reminded himself that he had slept badly, and that he had been frightened to the very heart, though he did not know what had affrighted him. Emma would be here on Friday. On Thursday she would tell him her flight number, BOAC, and the time of her arrival. He would hear from her tomorrow at the latest. Again he shivered. What would he do with himself today? He did not feel inclined to take a walk. He had ordered some new books, all murder mysteries, to which he was addicted. After all, he would think, some of the best writing of today was done by writers of mystery and suspense novels. They were clear-cut, interesting, exciting, absorbing, with few

423

if any signs of the universal malaise. They had more insight into human nature than the modern straight novel. So he would inspect the new delivery and rest and enjoy himself, if he could, in some suspenseful novel, and would drink quietly, alone, until it was time to receive Hugh Lippincott and Mrs. Kleinhorst and take them to dinner.

He followed this schedule with determination. After lunch, he felt sleepy, and went back to his room for a nap. After all, he had slept very little last night. He awoke about five, discovered it was very dark outside and that the gentle snow had turned into a blizzard. The window ledges were heaped with snow and the glass vibrated in the storm. His guests and he would have dinner here to-night. He thought of Beth Turner. He called her at her house and when her warm voice answered him some of his amorphous misery lifted. He invited her to dine with him tonight, in the company of new friends, and she happily consented. He felt certain that she would enjoy the company of himself and Mrs. Kleinhorst, if not Hugh's company. He delicately neglected mentioning names, because he was somewhat apprehensive about her acceptance had she known. After all, the encounter with Guy's family had not been a pleasant occasion for her.

He took a nice hot bath, and reclined in the water, read more of the book he had started, and smoked his cigar. He began to feel soothed and drowsy again. In a little while he reluctantly left the tub, and shaved and dressed. It was now seven o'clock and his guests would be here in half an hour. He went down to the dining room to reserve a table and inspect the evening menu. Knockwurst and pickled hot cabbage, or fried chicken, or roast beef, or calves' liver. Very provincial and hearty, and satisfying. Nothing sophisticated or continental, thank God. He reserved another table in the bar. He went to the lobby to wait for his guests. Beth was the first to arrive, her cheeks rosy from the cold, her tawny eyes shining like a girl's. "I was feeling very blue, James," she said. "Thank you for calling me." Her hand was warm in his and he gave her a smiling look of deep affection. She was wearing, tonight, an obviously new dress of brownish-gold soft wool and she wore a gold chain about her long white throat, and the gold and diamond bracelet and gold earrings. Her red hair was braided about her small head, which was regal.

He took her into the bar, which was already filled with residents of the Old House and their guests of the evening. He found his table. He was very pleased with her. It was nonsense to say a man could not love more than one woman at a time. He loved three, in different ways, Emma, Beth, and Marian Kleinhorst, and they were grande dames and worthy of a man's devotion.

"I'm having two other guests," he told Beth, after he had ordered their drinks. "Hugh Lippincott and his friend, a Mrs. Kleinhorst."

Beth's face changed. "I don't think Mr. Lippincott likes me, James."

"Of course he likes you. He paid you several compliments after you had left."

"Did he—guess?"

James shrugged. "Possibly. But he's not one of those slyly sniggering men. After all, Mrs. Kleinhorst is his dearest—friend, and he needs such a woman. He wants to divorce his wife, but it seems that Marian won't marry him."

Beth became interested. "Why not?"

"I think it has something to do with old Jerry, who castigated him for a lack of 'duty and responsibility,' and he seemed to disapprove of Hugh's relationship with Marian."

Beth colored a little. "Yet he—I—"

"I know. That's part of his bad trouble. Ambivalent. I imagine he disapproves of himself, too." James laughed gently.

Beth shook her head, and in silence sipped at her drink. The subdued light in this wood-paneled barroom, with its brown leather chairs, made Beth appear young and too vulnerable.

She said at last, "Guy is a very strange man. We've known each other for almost five years, yet I never know, when he visits me, what his mood will be that night. There were times when I thought he hated me, though he never told me why."

"His conscience, I believe," said James. "Now, I have no conscience, thank God." They laughed together. Then James said, "I did not see him today. Emil Grassner advised against it. It appears that old Jerry had had a bad night. Now, don't be alarmed. We expect these setbacks during the process of regaining mental health. And I think he is steadily coming to some final decision in spite of himself. Final. When he does he will be completely well."

Beth said in a low voice, "Whether or not that includes me doesn't matter so much anymore. I only want him to have some peace of mind. If his peace of mind demands his never coming to see me again, I think I could stand it. I know I could. I only want his happiness."

Hugh and Marian arrived, and James rose to meet them. Hugh's blond face was surprised, as he shook Beth's hand, but his smile was kind and thoughtful. As for the women, they were at once *en rapport*. Beth studied Marian with admiration, the slender aristocratic face, the pale gilt hair, the lovely silvery eyes. Marian was swathed in an abundance of dark mink, and her dress was an elegant black silk and her jewels flashed at ear, throat, and wrist. An open fireplace sparkled and cracked on the black marble hearth, and Marian looked about with appreciation. "How charming," she said. "I've never been here before. It reminds me of some old Austrian inn on the Gross Glockner, in the winter. Helmut and I—it was one of our favorite places." Sadness touched her sensitive face. She said to Beth, "My husband. He was—killed—after the war. At Nuremberg. He was a soldier."

Beth understood. She lightly touched Marian's hand with sympathy, and in love Hugh touched Marian's hand. He said to James, "What does a man do when the woman he wants to marry says no."

"He thanks her," said James. The two women laughed aloud but Hugh looked blank for a few moments. He said, "You're a great help, Jim."

426

"I'm in somewhat of the same situation myself," said James. "My friend, Lady Emma Godwin, refuses to marry me, too. She is afraid that if we marry, and one of us dies, the sorrow will be too much for the one living. She imagines that death, if we are not married, will be less terrible for the one remaining. She is wrong, of course."

"Women," said Hugh, waving his hand. "Marian, as you know, is afraid that if she marries me I will come to hate her for my having given up my whole life's work. I can't follow a woman's reasoning, but then no man can."

"You men are not so simple," said Beth. "You are very complex characters, much more so than are women. Compared with Guy I am as clear as brook water and as uncomplicated."

"I never could understand him," said Hugh. "He's closemouthed and surly, and we never particularly liked each other. Now I'm sorry for him."

The guests were enthusiastic about the dinner, and James enjoyed it also. He was not feeling so despondent now in this kind company. He looked frequently at the two women, admiring them, loving them both. Emma would delight in them, and they in her. He began to talk about Emma and her imminent arrival, and Beth and Marian listened with affection. "I think Emma will come around to marrying me when she arrives. At least, I hope so."

Finally, he turned to Hugh. "I think," he said, "that when Jerry completely recovers he will feel more generous towards you. I don't know why, but I am almost sure. In that event, there'll be no obstacles, I hope, between you and Marian." Marian gazed at him and there was a bright moisture in her eyes.

"You're more sure than I am," said Hugh, almost sullenly. "I know Guy too well. Obstinate, unbending, like the laws of the Medes and the Persians. You don't change, in your middle years, into something entirely new and different."

"I've seen that happen," said James.

Hugh sighed. "I never could understand why he married

427

my sister. It's incongruous. She's 'faultily faultless, icily regular, splendidly null.' Even if Lucy is my sister I can honestly say I never met a more stupid woman. If she ever had an original thought it would crack her alleged mind like the mirror of the Lady of Shalott. Oh, she's attractive, all right, but Guy's too wary and cold a man to marry a woman just for appearance. And he didn't marry her for money, or to advance himself in any way. He didn't need her at all."

"As I told you before, I think, she must have been surrogate for another woman. There was a girl in Germany. I never saw her but he described her to me once, and it sounded as if she resembled your sister, Lucy. Most people would never guess that Jerry was vulnerable, perhaps even sentimental in hidden ways, but he is. When I knew him, as lads together, a livelier lad you'd never find, and full of passion and vitality, and hope. It's all under that façade of his, still. I've seen it burst out these three weeks, at intervals—the old Jerry. Vital. Furiously ardent —and full of pain. In all these years, didn't you get glimpses yourself?"

"No," said Hugh, promptly. "Except when he was raising hell with somebody, often me. No wildness; just rage. No passion; just fury. Dogmatic when it came to destroying someone's hopes. Then he really had a good time." Hugh's voice was bitter. "If he couldn't enjoy living, then no one else had a right to that enjoyment, either. A brighter woman than Lucy would have divorced him long ago, but she's so stupid that she probably thinks all men are like Guy, more or less, and should be endured, as a nice wife. When she would complain sweetly about him she never blamed the things he really was, incredibly bad-tempered, ruthless, grim. A tyrant. She only blamed him because he wasn't demonstrative with his children, and didn't 'adore' them as she did. Never for his brutal insults to her even before relatives or guests, never for his open contempt for her, never for lacking tolerance for her shallow feelings or silly remarks. She was always avid for money, and what life she had to give was for her children.

428

She never saw them for what they were. She thought that every hour that Guy wasn't working should be 'devoted to the family.' She never stopped talking about that. In fact Lucy seldom stops talking. She's more like a poster than a woman, a pretty but two-dimensional lithograph. Advertising Jell-O."

"But, he's been faithful to her—in his 'fashion.' "

"Yes, and isn't that insane?"

"Quite."

Hugh looked at Beth, whom he had come to admire and appreciate. How could a woman like this stand his rude brother-in-law, his violent and somber nature, his puritanical inconsistencies? She was either a saint or a fool. But no one could understand a woman in love, especially not a woman who loved a man who was not lovable in the least, or even endurable. Aside from her sensual mouth she looked serenely contained, of a piece, and sensible. Her clothing might be inexpensive but Hugh sensed that this was not because of poverty but of choice. Unlike his sister, Beth was a lady, as was Marian.

Hugh looked at James. "I've heard that my nephew, Bill, has been consulting some lawyers in Philadelphia, about his father. He'd surely love to consign Guy to some far-distant little institution, burying him alive and then forgetting him. There seems more to his hate for Guy than just a desire to take over, and I know what it is, I think." He thought of Guy's savage beating of his son after the raping episode. His hysterical sister had told him.

He said, "Old Guy had better snap out of this very soon or we'll be in an unpleasant situation. Bill can't do much harm because I am there. But he'll try."

"I have every hope, Hugh, that Jerry will come out of it."

The guests left because the storm was increasing and James went upstairs to his books and his bed. He looked at his watch. In less than forty-eight hours Emma would be here, and he smiled tenderly. That night he slept. He had never been happier, for he would have the woman he loved, and he would begin his new life. He felt buoyant, excited and renewed.

The next morning when he met Emil at breakfast Emil said, "We've had the worst storm in anybody's memory. It went on all night, and it will be a day before even the Interstate will be completely open. It's still snowing and blowing, you'll notice. I called Mountain Valleys before I came down for breakfast. Guy is still in that catatonic state, but he seems less unaware. I think he's deliberately cultivating it, to avoid our efforts in his behalf. Well, anyway, we can't go out there today."

"Well, I don't entirely regret that. I'm expecting an overseas call, which will arrive at any time today, and I want to be here to receive it. Then I must go at once to New York to meet Emma's plane." He looked anxiously at the snow. "Will the airport here be open?"

"We try to keep it open even when the roads are clogged, for Cranston is as attached to Philadelphia and Pittsburgh as a placenta is attached to the wall of the uterus. We're more dependent than we like on those cities. I listened to the weather reports before I came down. The snow is slowing down. So, when Lady Emma comes to New York on her way here our airport will be ready to receive her. As for your going to New York early tomorrow, or even tonight, your chances are good."

When Emil had left to see some patients in the Cranston Memorial Hospital, James could hardly keep his excited anticipation under control. He informed the desk that he was not leaving the hotel that day, but would be in either his room, the dining room, or the lobby, and that he was expecting an important call. At noon, he was trembling with impatience. At two o'clock he was almost wild, for there had been no word from Emma. He took to pacing. What could have gone wrong? He calculated the time. In England, it was night, seven o'clock or more. James called the Plaza Hotel in New York and reserved three rooms for himself, Emma, and Emma's maid, Susan. They would stay overnight in the city, for Emma would be tired. The next day they would come to Cranston. He looked at his watch. Only half past two. Then, unable to endure the tension any longer, he called Emma's house. But there was no answer. His heart began to thump. He tried to reassure himself. Thursday was Simon's day off. But Emma should be packing, with Susan helping her.

Now he began to sweat. His whole body was shaking. He bathed his face with cold water, and, rare for him, he swallowed a tranquilizer. He went down to the lobby. The elderly clerk saw him from a distance, and smiled and beckoned to him. Emil ran as swiftly as a youth to the desk. The elderly clerk beamed on him. "We tried to call you, Sir James, but the telephone was in use." He paused, then said with his own excitement, "The lady, her ladyship, is in her suite. She—"

"Lady Emma is here!" James almost shouted in his incredulity and joy. "In this hotel? Here now?"

"Yes, sir. She seemed tired, so went to the suite. You'll find her there—" But James was already racing for the elevator, gasping, his face ruddy and slight. Why hadn't she called him from New York? Or from the London airport? Or from anywhere? Why this secrecy? The elevator crawled. It stopped. People got in and out and James almost screamed in his impatience. After a long, long while it reached his floor and he ran out and galloped down the hall to Emma's suite.

The door was open. He ran into the living room shouting, "Emma, Emma, where are you, Emma?"

She came from her bedroom and ran into his arms and he held her as if he would never let her go again, and kissed that dearest face over and over, and almost cried with his joy and love. He heard his own exclamations of rapture and adoration. He held her off to look at her, his eyes wet, his mouth shaking. And she clung to him, held his face in her hands and kissed his eyes, his lips, his chin, and her own eyes were wet.

"But why, Emma, didn't you let me know?"

She took his hand and kissed it. He could feel her trembling. "It's a long story, love. A long story." How incredibly wonderful it was to hear her rich voice. But her glowing olive complexion was sallow, and no longer vibrant. She shivered a little. He took her back in his arms, smoothed her hair, stroked her cheek. "I've been almost out of my mind," he said. "I was going frantic. Why didn't you let me know so I could meet you in New York? How could you have been so cruel to me?"

She gently removed herself from his arms. There were tears on her cheeks. "And where's Sue?" he demanded, as he placed Emma in a chair.

She looked up at him and he saw something he had never seen there before. Terror. He recognized it at once, and at once a thick cold fist struck him in his vital center.

"I came alone, love, because I wanted to be alone with you." She reached out and took his hand. "Alone with you, with no interference. My bags are here. I was just unpacking." She scrutinized him with close attention, and smiled. "Jimmy, you are fatter than ever, you big pig. Oh, Jimmy, how I love you! Love you, love you!"

He drew a chair close to hers, caught her hands and held them tightly. "Very well, Emma, tell me." He saw that she was considerably thinner than she had been almost a month ago. That splendid body was still splendid, but it had dwindled to a certain extent. He saw that her lips were dry and blistered, as if she had been exposed to a heavy frost. Her smile was less gay and raffish, though it was evident she was trying to conceal this. The little streaks of white in her chestnut hair had widened. She had aged. Again he saw the terror in her eyes. The hands he held were slighter, and too hot. A huge pain shrank his chest, and then his temples. He felt he was smothering. "Emma, tell me."

She said, "Have you whiskey, Jim? I'd appreciate a drink, a very large drink."

He stared at her and did not know how white his own face was. He was a physician as well as a psychiatrist. Emma was ill. Her vividness had dulled. Some vital virtue had left her. He caught her chin and minutely examined her face. He saw what had to be seen, and a vast dark
432

coldness came to him. When he stood up his legs were so weakened that he almost fell. He filled a glass with whiskey, and poured water into another glass. He could feel her watching him, and now he knew she was afraid for him. She took the glass and drank deeply, unusual for Emma. She coughed, choked, gave him the empty glass, and smiled that awful new smile of hers. He sat down again. He said, "Emma, stop torturing me. Tell me."

"I didn't want to tell you over the telephone, Jimmy. I wanted to be with you." Her voice broke. "In fact, I was going to write you, to tell you I must never see you again. That it was all over."

He thought he was impervious to shock. Now he knew what terrible shock was, numbing, crushing, making one shudder, turning one's body to wood.

"Never to see me again? Why, Emma?"

"To spare you. You see, I've known for over a week. I was going away before you returned. Somewhere on the Continent where you'd never find me."

Her voice had become faint and dim. When he could not move or speak she reached for his hand, pressed it to her cheek; it was very cold and tremulous. His hand was limp in her own. He was breathing the slow ponderous breaths of shock, of almost mortal shock.

"But I'm a coward, Jimmy, love. A nasty weak coward. I couldn't do it. I couldn't write you a chilly letter saying it was all over, and that we must never see each other again. I even thought of inventing a new lover—to spare you. But, when it came to the sticking point, I couldn't. I couldn't do that to you, Jimmy, though it would have been the best for you. You would suffer a little while, then you would forget me, and perhaps come to hate me. I'd have been more content with that—if I hadn't been such a coward."

His eyes were glaring, stunned, at her. There were drops like tears falling from his forehead. She closed her eyes and said, very quietly, "You see, Jimmy, I'm dying."

"Dying," he repeated, stupefied. The word was unreal,

but it was like the rattle of dead bones, bones irretrievably dead.

She was groaning as she spoke. "I should not have been such a coward. I should have removed myself from your life, as I originally intended. I was going to hide, to die alone, happy that you'd never guess. It was all arranged."

He could not speak. She said, "I've been in New York for three days, Jimmy. I went to the Sloan-Kettering Institute. I wanted to get a final opinion. After all, there are so few competent neurologists in England now. When I went to the Institute, it was to see your old friend Dr. Norton, who left England five years ago. Dr. Norton. He saw you in New York this time. And—when he confirmed— what Dr. Brandall on Harley Street had already told me— he said I must tell you. I refused. He has given me until tomorrow to tell you myself, to show you— If I haven't told you by then he is going to call you."

"Tell me what, Emma?" His voice was weak and stifled.

"That I am dying. Jimmy! Don't look at me like that! I can't bear it!"

He could not have stopped her, for he was too prostrated. She went to her bedroom and brought back a large heavy folder. She put it on his knees. Then she sank beside him on the floor, and laid her head against his thigh. He stared at the thick folder, and his breath wheezed in and out of his lungs with a long moaning. For the first time since his father had been killed he experienced total anguish.

Everything shimmered and wavered before him as through a heavy veil of rain. The squeezing agony in his chest and temples increased. He fumbled with the folder. X rays, sheafs of typewritten copy, doctors' signatures, the smell of dry soulless paper. His fingers felt thick and useless, like fingers carved of stone.

Emma was saying, "My headaches, over the past two months or so. My increasingly bad vision. My oculist sent me to Dr. Brandall on Harley Street. For examination."

But James already knew. He fumbled for his glasses. He fumbled at the papers. He held up the X rays to lamplight.

434

But he had already guessed. "Oh, Jimmy, don't breathe like that!" Emma cried. She was pushing something in his hand and he felt the smoothness of glass. She guided the glass to his lips and he drank in mindless obedience. A fire exploded in his paralyzed middle. He struggled for breath. He felt death in himself, and closed his eyes for a moment.

At last he was able to focus on the swimming papers. So great was his shock that he began to mouth the frightful words to himself. Emma had cancer of the brain. He could read only slowly, feebly, but he read it all. The oculist's report. Headaches, nausea, vomiting, choked disks—increased intracranial pressure. Patient referred to Dr. William Brandall, neurologist. Infiltrating glioma. Angiograms. Scanners. Technetium. EEGs. Pressure on brain had caused it to move five millimeters. The cancer had crawled like the silent crab it was, in the frail tissues. It had not yet destroyed the vision nor induced paralysis. Surgery was recommended, though, said Dr. Norton's report, it would probably only increase life expectancy to a year or less, but would possibly induce immediate vision loss and paralysis. In short, Lady Emma Godwin was doomed either to instant blindness and helplessness, through surgery, or to a quicker death without the operation, and the possibility of retaining her vision and mobility to the very last. Demerol was recommended for the present pain, and morphine tablets for the inevitable final agony.

James carefully read page after page of reports, slowly, weakly but thoroughly. He had studied neurology also. He knew exactly what all this meant for Emma. He had to blink his eyes frequently to clear away the dark mist from them. There was Dr. Norton's report, from the Sloan-Kettering Institute, not only confirming what Dr. Brandall had reported, but even more pessimistic. Patient refused surgery, Dr. Brandall wrote, and it was evident, in his most conservative innuendos, that he agreed with Emma even if reluctantly. X ray after X ray. Angiograms, more reports, detailed. Prognosis: negative. The patient, without surgery, had a life expectancy of three to four months, at the most. Chemotherapy was not recommended.

Slowly, painfully, precisely, James gathered everything together and with a dazed frown put them back into the folder. Then he dropped his hands on his knees and stared into the distance, his chest heaving, his broad full face the color of the gray sky outside. He was facing a loss he could not endure. There was an imperative for him to lie down, for all his muscles had become liquid and unable to support his body properly. He closed his eyes and wished for death. An excruciating pain was twisting in his temples. He was near collapse.

Sluggishly, as through viscid mud, he fought to return. Slowly, his anguished eyes sought and found Emma. She was seated near him and her fascinating simian face was calm and smiling. She said, "Jimmy, we've had twenty blissful years, almost unmarred, which is more than the rest of the world can say. We've been blessed. We've given to each other, completely. We've had joy and health and tenderness and devotion. It is enough, it is more than enough. But we forgot that there is the great inevitable: death. It was bound to happen, sooner or later. It is something we cannot escape. If I had children I would teach them, as soon as they could toddle, that death waits for them and no one knows how soon it will come. So enjoy the present and not strain after tomorrow. It might never come.

"Jimmy, love, this is a beautiful world. I want to see as much of it as I can, for the next several months. I want to fill my mind and my heart with the beauty and majesty. I want to have the memory of glory, in the last hours. For you see, that glory is from everlasting to everlasting. And, Jimmy, we'll meet again, just as we met this time. Of this I'm sure."

She held his hands tightly. She was the comforter, he the comforted. But he could only look at that beloved face with the great brave eyes for all they were wet, at the smile which was not forced but open and expectant. Then he

436

said, "We must be married immediately." She could hardly hear him.

"No, Jimmy," and she kissed his hand. "I couldn't do that to you. When the time—comes—I want to be alone, somewhere. Alone. I don't want you to see; I don't want you to remember the final time. I want you to remember only what we have had and be comforted by the memory, and hopeful. I—I couldn't stand you to be there, Jimmy, when I die."

"Emma, I couldn't stand it, I can't stand the thought of it even now, if I weren't there. I want the right to be there, as your husband."

She sighed. "Jimmy, you've always had the right."

But ponderously he shook his head. It was like the headshaking of a dying bull in its last agonies. "No, I haven't, Emma. True"—and he gasped for breath—"we've seen each other at least three times a week. But there was always separation, I to my way and work, you to yours. I want to be with you every night, Emma, beside you. I'm a physician, too, if you'll remember. I want to watch you, all through the night, and most of the day, too. I want to be there when you need help; I want us to be one, Emma."

"We always were one, from the time we met—"

"But this is different. How could I be parted from you for a single night, a single day? Waiting for the terrible news. Unable to live—until the next time I saw you. And, frightened always, that you might slip away from me, as you intended, to die—alone. No, Emma."

She gave a pathetic little laugh. "Jimmy, you've become conventional!" But she knew what he meant.

"Marriage gives me the right to be closer to you, Emma, and I need that closeness, if I am to survive. I have the need to share, constantly."

"But, it will be so awful for you, Jimmy."

"Not as awful as if we weren't married."

She went on her knees to him and pulled his hands against her breast. Now her own face was anguished. "I'm a coward, Jimmy. Promise me this: That you won't let me suffer too much. Too long."

437

For a long, long moment they stared fixedly into each other's eyes. It was an endless moment. They were bared to the soul, completely, as never before had they been bared, not even in the most intimate and joyful hours.

Then James said, steadily and clearly, "I promise."

She laid her head on his knee. He began to stroke that bright chestnut hair and thin cheek. The tears ran down his own cheeks without a sound. But Emma did not cry. She was tired, frightened, undone, terrified. She fell asleep against him, and, sitting there, she slept more peacefully than she had done for several weeks. Occasionally, like a child, she sighed deeply, yet peacefully.

His numb mind was beginning to accept the appalling inevitable. It shrank, it whimpered, it tried to deny, it tried to say that there was hope when there was no hope. He faced the liar fully, the tortured liar skittering about in his skull, looking for escape, when there was no escape from the inexorable. Nothing could be done to save Emma. He thought of what Socrates had said when he had wept for his dead son and a friend had said, "Why do you weep? Nothing can bring him back." Socrates had replied, "That is why I weep."

James said to himself, with agonized bitterness: Why do we try to forget death, when we all begin to die the moment we are conceived? He had been no more realistic than the weakest and most timorous of men. He sat for a long time, unwilling to disturb the exhausted woman in her sleep. He could hear the murmur of traffic, the sound of horns outside, and the battering wind pounding against the windows. He could hear the hiss of the snow. The day darkened.

Face to face with the death of all that matters to a man, he knew the sadness of humanity, the sadness of living, the unbearable pain, the black resignation. The hopelessness of joy. He had known this professionally; now he knew it as a man, naked, alone, no more and no less than the most abject creature. The companionship of happiness was a fleeting and superficial thing. But the companionship of sorrow made mankind one, bound together, heart
438

to heart, understanding to understanding. For the first time he felt compassion for all that lived, whether good or bad, whether foolish or wise, whether dull or brilliant, whether happy or unhappy, whether beautiful or ugly, whether young or old. This was more than the happy knew. The brotherhood of grief was complete.

Emma stirred. He forced his shaking legs to lift him. He took Emma in his arms and then into her bedroom. He laid her down on the bed. He looked heavily and slowly about the large room, with its old-fashioned and weighty furniture of dark red mahogany, all extremely polished. It was very Victorian, and genuinely so. The white lace curtains were stiff and immaculate, under draperies of deep yellow velvet. It seemed quieter here and more restful. James took off Emma's shoes, and he drew the quilt over her. Her head on the pillow looked as if it had fallen from profound weariness. He lay down beside her and held her hand, and then she turned, murmuring, and lay closely at his side, his hand in hers.

He began to weep involuntarily, but there was no comfort in weeping. Finally, when he could endure no more, he fell asleep beside the dearest thing in the world to him.

No matter the cost to him he would not let Emma suffer the final crucifying agonies. He swore a grim promise to himself before he slept.

25

When he awoke in the gray dimness he saw that Emma, beside him, was leaning on her elbow and watching him. "Hello, ducks," he said, and his voice was uncertain and hoarse. She bent her head to kiss him. Though the light was faint he saw the old raffish glint in her eyes. "Emma," he said.

"Dear old fat bald Jimmy, I love you," she answered. Briskly, she threw back her hair. Sometime during his long unconsciousness, she had removed her traveling frock, and she was lying only in her rosy slip, her deep breasts spilling creamily against the silk. At some time she had recovered that remarkable stamina of hers, which met life steadfastly and unafraid. "Jimmy," she said, and her voice was strong, "we are going to think of only one thing, the lovely spots we are going to visit all over the world, the highways, the byways, in slow comfort, seeing everything. We are going to make this a holiday to remember, never to forget. We are going to laugh and sing, and dance; we are going to be complete fools. In short, we are going to have fun."

"After we are married, ducks."

She rolled up her eyes in mock despair. "Very well. After we are married. But I warn you, you may regret it." She lay down and nestled against him, holding him in her arms like a mother. "Now, tell me again," she whispered, "that you love me."

A little later she said to him, "I will marry you only if you promise me something. I want us not to speak of this—thing—all the time. Sometimes, perhaps, but not constantly. It's there. It won't go away. But we must not stare at it all the time, as if at a basilisk. We have living to do, together."

"I promise," he said. The dull grinding pain in him could not be denied. "But we must not pretend to each other that it has gone away. That's childish, stupid, and only makes matters worse." After this hour he could understand why men and women, frenzied, could couple in streets red with blood, in noxious alleys, in fetid rooms, under the very shadows of guillotines and the rope and murder and holocausts. It was their instinctive affirmation of life, celebration of life, that made them make their life-giving gesture in the very face of death. He did not know precisely why they had done it, nor why he had just completed the same act. Was it defiance? Was it bravado? No. It was something primally profound, a primal knowledge that life did not end in obliteration, and that death was only a beginning. His training, his awareness, wished to dispute that, but his instinct only affirmed it.
440

He knew what lay before Emma, and for himself, and he knew his would be the greatest suffering. For him there would be no anodyne as there would be for Emma in drugs. She would not suffer mentally as he would suffer. Her torment would be physical, and there were always palliatives. But what palliatives were there for the living as they watched the beloved one slowly and agonizingly die? Emma, who was stronger than he, had accepted. But he could not accept. He could only pretend, as much as possible in order to spare her, that he had admitted the inevitable into his consciousness and had adjusted to it.

When Emma, somewhat rested, had gone into her bathroom to bathe and dress, he lay there in the rumpled bed and let the waves of complete pain roll over him. What would he do without Emma? How could he exist? She had been his emotional life for over twenty years. She had been more than his mistress. She had been his friend, his most trusted friend, his absolute confidante. He forgot all his philosophies, his easy acceptances, his rationalizations, in the knowledge that he could do nothing for Emma, who had done so much for him. To another man in his present situation he would have said, "We are men, and men are superior to circumstance. Yes, you'll bleed awhile and feel prostrated and believe that life is over. But it is not. Time does go on, a very wise platitude to remember, and one day you'll have the courage to face life again, to live again. It seems impossible for you to believe it, but I can tell you it is true."

He did not believe it. When Emma died, he would not continue living. A great sense of relief came to him then, a reprieve. Death was better than life without Emma. When she came out of the bathroom, steamy and pink of lip, she said, "What, you slug! Are you still in bed? Get up. I demand sustenance, and very shortly." Her voice was the same round and hearty one he so dearly loved.

Love had given her strength and tranquillity, and there was no sign of the terror he had first seen in her eyes. He recalled that she had cried only a little, far less than he had cried. He felt ashamed. She playfully took his hand

441

and said, "Up, up with you, Jimmy! And get dressed. Where are you taking me to dinner?"

His voice was dry and cracked to his own ears. "There's a storm, ducks. We'll dine in this inn. Plain heavy food, not the delectable delicacies Simon concocts."

"That's good. There were delicious odors in the lobby when I came in. I could do with something very fattening and forbidden in these health-conscious days. Do they have passable wines?"

"Not really. But excellent beer."

"I prefer it. At heart, I am a rough proletarian with a prole's greedy appetite. Up with you." She pulled at his hand and he sat up, feeling feeble and old. "Jimmy, you're a disgrace. You've gained over ten pounds." She bent and kissed the top of his big bald head and ruffled the red-gray curls which fringed it. "Oh, Jimmy, I'm happy, happy I am here with you. That's all that matters, isn't it? 'This is the day which the Lord has made. Rejoice in it, and be glad.' One of your favorite quotations. Now I know what it means."

He knew that she was not trying to be speciously brave. She was too gallant a woman for that. No matter what frightfulnesses life had had for her, and would have soon again, she would stand victorious over the most terrible of enemies. She had done it before. Once more he was ashamed, for she was braver than he.

He slowly dressed. His hands trembled as the hands of the very old and ill tremble. She sat near him. "Oh, Jimmy," she said, "we are going to have such a glorious time!"

"When we are married, Emma."

"Oh, dear, how you harp. When we are married, then. It seems you don't like living in sin, do you?"

He tried to laugh. It was no use. She stood up to give him a tender kiss, to pet his cheek. He caught her to him and held her fiercely, saying silently to himself: Oh, God, God, God! She murmured, "I know, I know, I know." Then she gently disengaged herself. "Tell me more about the friends you have made here, about whom you wrote
442

me." When he could not speak, she said, "Don't make it harder for me, love."

His voice broke. "Forgive me, Emma." He took her hands, her dear hands, and kissed the palms, and when he looked up at her she was smiling brightly.

"Wasn't there some kind lady to console you while you were here alone, Jimmy?"

He thought of Beth Turner. "I consoled a lady."

"Oh, you dog. I can't trust you out of my sight. Was the lady in need of consolation?"

"Very."

"Then I am glad that she had you for that time." Was she pleading with him to be courageous? He knew she was. He said, "Would you like to meet Emil Grassner tonight?"

She hesitated, then apparently decided it would be best for James. She nodded. "You like him so much, don't you? I want to meet such a man, and thank him."

He thought. Then he said, "I'll go to his room and ask him to join us." He wanted to be alone with Emil when he told him of this monstrous thing which had entered his life. Before Emma could suggest the telephone he went from the suite and down to Emil's quarters.

Emil was surprised, but pleased, to see him. But his smile went away when he saw the haggardness on James's face, the mortal pain in his eyes. "Come in," he said, subdued. James fell into a chair. Emil surveyed him, then went for whiskey. "That bad, eh? Drink this. I heard Lady Emma had arrived earlier."

So James told him, his voice tightly held and monotonous. He looked into his glass, as he spoke. Between sentences he sipped the whiskey. The storm screamed outside and seemed a counterpoint to the desperate narrative. Emil listened, asking no questions, not speaking. When James had finished, Emil still remained silent, and looked only at his friend. There was really nothing to say. Words of comfort would only enlarge this pain, or only tend to make it trivial, only mock it. But there was enormous comfort, to James, in Emil's silence, the acceptance of horror, this understanding. Emil lit his pipe. He

443

refilled James's glass. He prepared a drink for himself. Then he went to the window and looked out at the storm for a long time.

"Hell," he said at last, and some of the renewed anguish subsided in the stricken man. "God damn," said Emil.

"Yes," said James.

They went down to meet Emma in the warm well-lighted lobby. The old chandeliers glittered and swung a little. Emma was waiting for them, in a gown James particularly admired. It was a crimson velvet, very revealing of her fine figure, and there were rubies at her throat and at her ears. Emil's first thought was: What a splendid woman. And a noble one. She was gracious and charming to Emil, but she knew James had already told him. She said, "I want to thank you for being so kind to this old dog of mine. He wrote me about you, Dr. Grassner."

"Emil," said Emil.

"Yes. Well. Emil." She smiled at him and he saw all her charm.

He said, "The food here isn't what you're accustomed to, my lady."

"Good. I often cook for Jimmy, when I can chase Simon, my chef, out of the kitchen, which is a hard thing to do. We both have plebeian appetites. I made kidney-and-steak pie for this rascal, rarebit, kippered herrings, and toad-in-the-hole. It reminds him of Eton." Emil was fascinated by her rich laughing voice. "He's very sentimental about Eton, even including the strapping, Emil."

There was nothing in her demeanor, her voice, her eyes, which told Emil anything about her present suffering. He decided she was not in the least afraid. When she glanced at James her expression was one of absolute love, amused love, tender love. A lucky man, thought Emil. But Emil had seen the dilation of her pupils. Demerol, he suspected. She was not one to whimper at torture; she would not resort to the final drugs until the last, for she wished to be alive and aware. Emil knew all this, instinctively.

They enjoyed their dinner, or at least Emil and Emma

did. James found that food choked him. He listened to the conversation of the others. Emma was relating some of her risible, and ribald, anecdotes to Emil, and he was laughing, sincerely. People looked at her from other tables, and found her enchanting, and smiled with pleasure.

Emil thought of his dead wife. She had been this gallant, too, when she faced death. But it had been a quick death, and a comparatively easy one, and Emil, for the first time, was grateful.

Emma said, "Jimmy insists on us getting married, almost immediately, Emil."

"An excellent idea, Emma."

"I'm not so certain. I think I read once that marriage is a romance in which the hero dies in the first chapter."

She looked about the big red, white, and gilt dining room, the old room. She said, "I think this is wonderful. So many of the great ancient hotels are being destroyed these days, in the name of 'progress.' Progress to what? Uglitude. Very efficient, but very barren and cold, the newer hotels. People are sick of 'progress.' They want something substantial, solid, soothing, and it can only be found in the established old, the secure, the pleasant, rooms enfolding and warm and full of tradition. It is a strange thing, but it is not the young who are destroying the old landmarks, the old ways, the old strengths. It is the elderly, the middle-aged. Perhaps they think destruction is really living, and that by destroying the old they spuriously extend their own lives. How very sad."

But white lines of pain and fatigue were coming out about her lively eyes and Emil glanced at his watch and said, "I'm sorry, but I have a very complicated case I must attend to tomorrow. James? Will you go out to Mountain Valleys with me tomorrow, as usual?"

No, James wanted to say. I don't want to leave Emma. But Emma was looking at him with a smile, and he said to her, "Old Jerry, you know. I think he is coming along a bit."

She nodded and smiled, as if relieved at his answer.

445

"And I will unpack, and read. I am really quite tired. The 'jet lag,' you know. Dear me, I wish we had all the fine old liners we once had. So luxurious. So restful. You arrived from your journey rejuvenated. Now even the liners rush, and congratulate themselves when they can cut off an hour or two from their last run."

"We live in a very sterile age," said Emil. "All the color has gone out of the world, all the happy denials, all the joyousness. And that's a bad omen."

When James and Emma were alone she spoke with enthusiasm of Emil. "He is so placid, in a way, so content. That means he has endured a lot. Those who have known sorrow rarely appear sad."

" 'I laugh that I might not weep,' " James said.

"Oh, you and your sententious platitudes, Jimmy. Let's go to bed."

He slept little that night, with Emma at his side. Once or twice in her uneasy drugged sleep she moaned and moved her hands in a gesture of pain. He listened to the shouting of the wind, the lonely winds of midnight, and it seemed to him that he had come to the end of his life.

26

"Man is a symbol-making animal," Tom had once said to his son. "He invents symbols by which he lives, or they are given to him. It is almost impossible for him to see his life clearly and in whole without illusions or delusions, once he accepts symbols in place of reality. He comes into this world symbol-free, but he is not permitted to live in that pristine state. Perhaps he can't live without symbols, which, to him, make sense of a senseless existence, a senseless universe. Yet, in their way, some symbols do have a certain beauty, even if they are illusionary. Poetry, for instance, is pure symbolism, and so, in most ways, is all art. The cross is not only a symbol of Christianity; it symbolizes life and death, resurrection, faith. In short, symbols are code words."

He pointed his pipe at the young Guy. "You're full of symbols, son. You use the code words 'duty,' 'responsibility.' By that, you mean grim self-sacrifice, self-denial, meaningless work, absence of joy and contentment. You use the code and you don't know what it means. Maybe your ma's black and cruel symbolism did impress it on you. I tried to teach you different. Me? I think I'm pretty free of symbols and codes. Took me a time to get rid of them, and live. I did it, though, and that's why I love living, and love love, and enjoy every minute I am alive—with no code at all." He laughed. "Maybe symbols are a substitute for living in its full sense. They don't demand that you think. You just have to accept, and that's easier than using your mind." He paused. "Maybe I'm not making myself clear."

"You're not," said Guy, seventeen years old. His father shrugged. "Who can? We use the same words but they're not in the same context."

Guy was remembering this now, this wild stormy winter day. He was alone. Emil Grassner thought that his retreat was a protection against thinking things through, but in truth Guy was facing fully what he now knew he must face, once and for all. But what his ultimate choice would be, he did not as yet understand, or did not want to understand. The choices were, for the first time, clear and ruthless and there could be no compromise. Once chosen, they were inexorable.

He was seeing his life in whole, and he was full of pain. He did not ask himself: Where did I go wrong? He knew now; yet, could he have taken a different way? If he had taken that would he now, in this year of his life, be regretting it? He was not sure. No life was free of regret, of wondering, of conjecturing. He only knew that six months ago he had found his barely tolerable life intolerable. Up to almost recently he had endured it, accepted it, as inevitable and cast in stone. He had told himself he had a better life than most men, a more successful one, even if there was no joy in it. (Joy was the babbling of children.) What more, he had asked himself, could a man ask than health and wealth and success, and the freedom these bring? He now knew he had not been free at all. He had only been afraid.

Beth had never advised him what to do. She had never criticized except to say that he had never reached his potential. She had listened with the deep sympathy and understanding of love. She had silently consoled, and with compassion unspoken. He had talked with her only as he had once talked with his father, without restraint, without judiciousness, without false words—code words. She knew, he saw now, that he was frightened by what he had made of his life, but even more frightened at the thought of abandoning it for something he had always wanted. There was, in a way, safety in fear. It kept a man's feet on the ground—on the way others thought he should go. No, he thought, I've done with lying. I chose the way myself and there is no one to blame, not even poor Ma, though I've been blaming her for years.

He could even admire his mother now. Though he had forced luxury on her—no, let's tell the truth—she had not been "forced." She had liked it, had reveled in it. She felt it was a reward for her virtuous life, for had she not been taught that material rewards were God's gifts to just men? A man of misfortune, she had been taught from childhood, was a man of whom God disapproved. She could point to excerpts in the Bible to justify this belief, but she never saw the context. A Job was not a man whose faith was being tested. He was a man who had offended God, though she was not certain how or why. The subtleties of the testing, of the battle between God and Lucifer for a man's soul, were beyond her comprehension. Job had been relieved of his afflictions, she believed, when he was "born again."

So, she had been reasonably happy in her condition. Yet, she had retained her boardinghouse to the very last, though she no longer lived there. However, she visited it almost daily, to be sure that the "manager," an elderly woman, "was doing things right and that the rents were collected on time." Lucy had been mortified, Guy amusedly disgusted. But on this stormy day of his life he felt a profound and smiling admiration for his mother. She had lived without hypocrisy in her grim fashion. She had lived in accordance with her beliefs, however arduous they were, however life-denying, however stringent. Tom himself had never accused her of hypocrisy. In her way, then, she had been an entirely honest woman. That she had distorted another soul, had denigrated its struggle for freedom, she had not known. Her way was her way; she saw no reason to doubt its verity not only for herself but for others also. If they departed from what she believed was truth and righteousness she condemned them, not out of meanness but out of conviction.

In her strange fashion she had been free, free as Tom had been free. They had chosen their lives, and had had great satisfaction in them. But he had been less strong, and so was suffering.

Even now, though, the thought of poverty horrified him. It always had, since he had been sixteen. A poor man was a poor miserable creature. That much he had accepted from his mother's teachings. He had not seen the wholeness of his mother's reasoning, which for herself was valid. That it was not valid for others she had not known. Nor did I, he said to himself bitterly.

Up to a few months ago he had compromised with life, had been reasonably happy when with Beth. She was his surcease, his consolation, his refuge. He had been able to endure Lucy's vapidity to some extent; at least, she had no longer irritated him to the furious hatred he had felt for her so long. He had learned not to think of his children, to goad himself with his bitter resentment. Through Beth, he had learned a cold

449

tolerance, a complete indifference. He suppressed all his emotions concerning them. He did not know that he had merely buried an abscess until it had burst forth one summer day four months ago, in all its fetidness, all its stench, all its putrid agony.

He had been in his offices in Cranston when one of his secretaries came in to tell him, with distaste, that "an old, old man" was asking to see him. A shabby old man, she said, "but nice and clean." A senior citizen. His name was Sam Kurtz. "Sam Kurtz?" Guy repeated, frowning. "I don't know——" Then he stopped. But surely it wasn't Sam Kurtz, of the sawmills, who had married—— Sal? If Sam were alive he would be almost eighty! It could not be the same Sam. Guy sat at his desk while his secretary waited, and he was filled with memories so sharp and clear that they might have been only in the immediate past. He had not thought of Sam and Sal for many years; he had never wanted to see them again, but why, he did not know, except they reminded him of a drab life, of uselessness, of hopelessness, of animal acceptance of their poor lives, of meagerness, of mediocrity.

Guy hesitated, then he said, "Well, send him in." He sat back in his chair and he was again a youth, determined that his life would not be one of meanness, of ugly survival only. He waited for the old contempt, for the old repudiation. They did not come. He rubbed his forehead. He was feeling his middle age, he thought, its tiredness, its bone-weariness, its dissatisfactions. But he had not been in the best of health these months. He was subject to nightmares, to obscure pains, to acute restlessness, to suppressed despair, to a sensation of being trapped. Only when with Beth did he feel vital, and even this vitality was beginning to diminish, for when he left Beth now it was not with the old renewed strength and fortitude. He hated to leave her, as he had never hated leaving before. He felt, when leaving her, that he was leaving life and courage and color, and was returning to what was—loathsome? Yes, loathsome.

450

He heard a door open and close, and opened his eyes with a start. He looked at the very old man facing him, a bent thin old man with thin white hair and a face carved out of a brown stone. Only the brown eyes were bright and clear. The old man stood before the desk and the two men looked at each other. Neither smiled. Sam's expression was stern and remote. He said, "Well, Guy."

Guy stood up. "Sam?" he said, almost incredulous.

"The same. I won't take up your time." His voice was tremulous yet had a certain strength to it. "I brought something for you." He fumbled with a brown bag and his trembling fingers began to withdraw something. It was a battered black notebook, small and creased. He laid it on the desk. "That's all. Sal wanted you to have it, when she died."

"Sal?" said Guy. He felt sick and curiously stricken. "Sal's dead?"

Sam had been turning away. Now he looked at Guy steadfastly. "Don't we all die? Yes. It was her time. No sickness. She just—died. She had a stroke in her sleep. Healthy to the last, my Sal. And I guess I'll soon be going to her. Can't wait." The steadfast regard did not change, or waver. Was there condemnation in it, or contempt? Contempt!

"I'm sorry, Sam," said Guy. His voice was dull.

"Sorry for what? She had a good life, Sal. Always did. Better than most. Happy to the last. Always singing. Always working. Never was a woman like Sal. When I had the cancer, she wouldn't let me die. She made me live. Doctors said I couldn't live, after the operation, twenty years ago. But she made me live. Kind of a miracle. Laughed me out of it, you could say. They made me retire. Made me sick. What's a man without work? He ain't anything. So, even if I did have a good pension, and the savings, I got me a job. Night watchman in a little plant. Sal made me do it. That's when I started to get better. Useful. Now I got a little land in the country. Raise chickens and vegetables. Useful."

Guy's mind repeated: Useful. But, he thought through a sharp pain in his head, I'm not useful. Perhaps I never was. He shook his head, trying to rid himself of the pain. He was again startled when he saw that Sam was still there. He had forgotten him. He was dazed, as if something had moved, shifted, had become fluid and was running away, and he was sick and undone.

"Well," said Sam. He pointed to the notebook. "Your dad—he gave that to Sal. Full of his writing. It was hers. But she wanted you to have it, after she was dead. She died a month ago." There was no sorrow in that old voice, only love and tenderness, and the crumpled brown face smiled slightly. "Pretty place, in St. Anthony's Cemetery. Got two graves."

"Is there something I can do for you, Sam?" asked Guy.

The old man stared at him, as if amazed. The clear brown eyes became keen and thoughtful, studying, understanding. "For me? No, sir. Not for me! But you sure look like you could do something for yourself, boy. You sure could, looks like. Sal knew it all the time, though you never came to see us. She'd say, 'I love that boy like my own flesh and blood, and I'm sick about him.' Never told me why. Women are funny. Maybe they see things we don't. I do now, though. Goodbye."

"Sam," said Guy, and held out his hand. But the old man went through the door and was gone.

Guy sat down heavily. He had not felt remorse for many years, or regret. He felt them now, aching, acrid, sad. He suddenly knew that he had not avoided Sam and Sal because of their obscurity, because of the "meaningness" of their satisfied lives. He had avoided them because he was afraid! Afraid of their perspicacity, their lucid understanding, their affection for him. He was afraid they might speak of his father. He had avoided thinking of Tom for decades, until these last weeks when the memories had come on him like flashing lightning which revealed everything. His useless life. His meaningless life. His arid life. His tormented life. The lightning had shown him a desert in which there was only one oasis: Beth. And

452

he had fled the oasis—in fear again, fear that the water would revive him and make him think.

He picked up the notebook and opened it. It was full of Tom's writing, now faded and browned, sharp small writing like engravings. Most were quotations, meticulously recorded, and with love. Guy had heard many of them, spoken in Tom's voice long ago. Some were his own meditations, acidly humorous or sad. Some were crude poems. Tom had never told his son that he wrote poetry. Why?

I am a stranger here. I always was.
I have troubled the world with my footsteps
And found no place to be comforted. As a child
I said to Heaven, "Is this my home?"
And He did not answer. I found no peace,
No warm roof, no laughing fire, no loving hands,
No language I ever learned to speak. I can
Only make mute gestures, and in the mist
Which surrounds me I can only grope,
Crying, "Are You there?"
I am answered always in a foreign tongue
Which eludes me. In Your Heart, O God,
Shall I find my place? You have not answered yet.
But then, You are known to speak only in centuries.
Remember, God, I live only in days,
And with days You have cursed man. With the hours
You have counted his bones, as the Egyptians,
In their games, threw down their painted sticks.
Are we Your merriment, Father? Or Your affliction?

You answered on Calvary.

Guy's hands pressed down the book and he shut his eyes. I never knew, he thought. I believed my father laughed and sang and joked his life away—yet here is the evidence of his human despair. He had thought his father a complete agnostic if not an atheist. Yet here was the fumbling evidence of his secret pain, his secret love. He
453

had thought Tom satisfied with his life, completely satisfied with his hours and his days, and Sal. But here was the evidence that he, too, was a stranger in a strange land, questioning, hoping, desolate, speaking but not understood, asking but never answered. "You answered on Calvary." Was that the last mute cry of a dying man who really had no hope?

I never knew, thought Guy, I never knew my father. I never knew anyone else, perhaps not even Beth. I never knew myself.

"We go brawling and kicking to our death, we who have never lived."

Guy thought: I believed he had gone to his death with humor and courage. I did not know that he fought in himself. What in hell did I ever know? I saw only faces. I never saw the man.

"If you have no bravery in the face of life, die like a whimpering child."

His father had been brave; he had more than courage. He had not smilingly succumbed to life. He had challenged it, and had lived. But I never lived, thought Guy. I once did, in dreams, I think. But I forgot the dream.

"Live your life, for it is all you have. Live it wrongly, live it painfully, live it angrily. But, live it."

I never lived. It is now too late.

Another short crude poem:

There is no sin except not loving.
A life without love is like a life
Without wine and sun, without laughter.
Love wildly, love strongly, love with will,
And deny those who would deny you.

Beth, thought Guy. And he left his office and drove to the little farm.

It was a hot and rainy summer early evening, and though it was not yet five o'clock it was dark with gathering storm. Lightning flickered through the hills like glittering swords lancing into flesh and surly thunder answered far off in dusky boiling clouds. Blasts of wind made the heavy car waver; ditches chattered with water. Trees creaked uneasily, their wet leaves dancing in the headlights. The air was heavy and seething with heat. Guy was driving too fast—his usual way—for he felt that he could not wait to see Beth and to tell her of the day's encounter with Sam Kurtz. Once or twice the clouds were torn apart and the colorless sun floated for a moment or two in the billowing rack, only to be submerged again. The raw fierce light blinded Guy for an instant.

What should he tell Beth? She would understand, of course, but all at once he knew her understanding would not comfort him. The air conditioning in the car blew in his face but could not cool him. He could hear his heart pounding in his chest irregularly and he vaguely wondered if he were about to have a heart attack. He had seen Beth yesterday. It was not his way, lately, to see her too often, for a reason he was afraid to acknowledge. "God, I'm tired," he muttered aloud, and had a thought to turn about and return to his house. But the thought suddenly appalled him. His empty house, where he had never really lived; his wife, whom he tolerated but whose voice he could not endure: What was there for him? What had ever been there? He came to a crossroads and almost turned into it. It led to what had once been his father's farm, and now, too, there was nothing there for him. What had made him instinctively try to turn there, before he came to his senses and continued on his way to Beth's house? He only knew a sense of profound loss, of rootlessness, of something vanished, some consolation denied, some refuge demolished. He ached with grief and with an obscure rage. His father's notebook pressed into his side like a living hand. In a few years he would be sixty.

> Tell me, where all past years are,
> Or who cleft the Devil's foot.

What had he done with his life? He had worked, and he had made money. But something vital had eluded him.

455

No, he had eluded it himself. It had not run from him; he had run from it. He knew, all at once, that Beth more than suspected this also. He could see her eyes clearly, thoughtful and conjecturing, as if she waited for him to tell her something. Over and over he had said to her, these past five years, defiantly, challenging, "We all have dreams when we are young, but we compromise with reality—don't we?" She had never replied, but had only gazed at him sadly—waiting. God damn it, waiting for what? He felt a rush of anger against her, a hostility. But he was on the way to see her. He slowed down and again almost turned the car about. If only he could drink as other men drank, and fall into a stupor. But try as he often did liquor unnerved him in large quantities, made his flesh creep, his head ache.

Damn Sam Kurtz for coming to see him after all these years! Sam had uncovered a noxious cistern, a sewer. The lost years. But every man has his lost years—doesn't he? Looking back at them, he reminded himself that duty, responsibility, stability, were the mark of a man and not a dreaming fool who dreamed impossible dreams in his youth. A man does not live for himself alone. ("It's your life, kiddo.") Once again Guy felt bitterness against his father and forgot what he had read in the notebook. No man's life is his own, despite what Tom had said over many years. Unless he was insane, unbalanced, he understood that he must compromise, adjust, substitute performance for aimless fantasies. A man could not live in a civilized fashion, in a civilized society, unless he conformed, in a great measure, to its mores. Otherwise he was an outlaw, a fool. Wasn't he? Unless he was satisfied with nothing—but who, except one who would have nothing to do with the world and its incessant demands—could be satisfied with nothing and be contented to live in a beggarly milieu? He had argued this with his father years before, and Tom had replied, "Who says you have to be contented with nothing? 'In the devil's booth all things are sold—each ounce of dross costs its ounce of gold.' I chose my life and I'm reasonably happy with it.
456

But that don't mean you have to live the life I live, or anyone else's life. You've just got to sort out what you really want out of living, and it's your choice, always your choice."

Circumstances, thought Guy tonight, make your choices. Fear makes your choices. He was startled by his own thought, and denied it angrily. I'm losing my mind, he said to himself.

Through the shimmering rain he came upon Beth's house, drove up her driveway, got out of the car, and ran through the downpour to the door. It was unlocked, as usual, as if waiting for him. A glare of sun came out briefly, and showed the barn and its lighted lantern and a youth working there, milking the cows, and whistling. Beth's dog, a nondescript but amiable brute, rushed out barking and wagging its tail at the familiar car. The lightning and the thunder prowled closer and the thick dark rain increased.

The pleasant living room was empty though lamps were lighted. Beth was in the kitchen; Guy could hear her humming and the rattle of pans. He discovered that he was out of breath, though the run from the car had been short. He shook the drops of rain from his shoulders; they left wet stains on the light fabric. "Beth!" he called, and did not know that his voice was not only commanding but enraged.

Her humming stopped. She was startled; she came from the kitchen, wiping her hands on her white apron. "Why, Guy," she said, her face at once luminous at the sight of him, "I didn't expect you tonight." She came to him and put her arms about his neck and kissed him soundly and with delight. He pulled her to him, breathing rapidly, but he did not kiss her. She moved a little back from him and studied his face, which was deeply flushed.

"What's wrong?" she asked, in alarm.

"What the hell could be wrong?" His voice was hard and rough. "I just thought I'd like to see you, that's all."

But she continued to study him with gravity. Those amber eyes darkened subtly as if with pain. "I'm so happy
457

you came," she said, gently. "Let me get you a drink. I have only some braised short ribs tonight."

"The hell with food. I'm not hungry. Yes, get me a drink. I'm tired."

He fell into a chair and stared sullenly in front of him, in obvious resentment. He rubbed his flushed forehead and winced. He yawned abruptly. She was accustomed to his moods, but never before had he seemed so desperate, so lonely, so hagridden. He had aged these past few months, had become very thin and very nervous, as if he could not rest. The gray at his temples had widened. All at once Beth was frightened. He was in this room with her, yet he was not here at all. He was wandering frenziedly about, far from her. The room was hot, yet Beth felt chilled. She smoothed her blue cotton frock and apron, then silently went to the kitchen for whiskey. She found that her hands were trembling. There was such a lack of sound from the living room, yet a tenseness hovered there, waited, like a storm. There was no creaking from the chair, no snap of a lighter to light a cigarette. The only sound was the approaching thunder. The house might have been empty except for herself. She prepared the drink and took it into the other room. Guy was sitting as she had left him, staring sightlessly before him, but the muscles of his face were clenched. He looked very ill, very alone. Beth put the glass in his hand. He did not thank her, as usual. It was as if she were not there. He raised the glass to his lips and did not sip the whiskey. He drank it all in one gulp.

"Do you want to tell me, darling?" Beth asked. He lifted his black eyes and there was a sort of furious rage in them.

"Tell you what, for God's sake?"

Unlike any other woman, Beth did not press him, asked nothing more. She merely sat down near him and put her hands on her knees. The room simmered with the rich fragrance of braised meat and onions. The rain was increasing; it lashed at the windows in gusts. Guy suddenly glanced at Beth, and his black eyes were sunken yet full of lighted wrath.

"What's the matter with you?" he demanded. "You sit there as if at a wake, or a funeral."

Beth smiled faintly; she forced herself to smile. "I've had a hot busy day," she replied, careful to keep her voice light. "I've been preserving quinces."

He shrugged as though disgusted with her. "What trivial things you find to do," he remarked. He held out his empty glass to her and she took it.

"Preparing for winter isn't trivial, Guy. It does come, you know."

He muttered something profane. She went to the kitchen and refilled his glass. Her heart was beating fast with renewed alarm, and a new fear for him. Something was tearing at him, some rage, some helpless repudiation. When he was in a bad mood—and the bad moods were increasing lately—she was no longer frightened that he was tired of her. His moods had nothing to do with her herself. But they had never been as tumultuous as this present mood. Never before had his face been so darkly flushed, so clenched, nor his eyes so ferocious, so denying. She brought the freshened glass back to him. He made a gesture as if to refuse it, then snatched it from her.

"You're like all other women," he said in that newly rough tone. "You want an explanation for everything, no matter how unimportant. I've had a rugged day today. Damn it, that's all."

"Very well," she said, and felt some anger of her own, yet it was at once followed by an aching compassion. "The air is very humid, and the storm is getting worse."

"Is it?" he asked, in a sneering voice. "I didn't notice. Oh, I forgot. You're afraid of summer storms, aren't you? Like any other silly woman."

She could not help saying, "If you'd ever seen cattle killed by lightning, or a farmhouse set on fire by it, or a tree shattered, you'd be afraid of storms, too."

"Oh, shit," he said. "I've lived on a farm. I know all about it. Let me alone, will you?"

459

He looked at her as at any enemy. She could not bear that look. She silently rose and went back into the kitchen. She wanted to cry. He was very ill. His hand had shook as he had taken the glass from her. He was losing control of himself, very rapidly. She had never seen him so close to collapse as she did now. True, he had sometimes been gloomy and evidently distraught, and lately he had appeared extremely restless and besieged on several occasions, but never so totally near the edge as tonight. What had happened today to reduce him to this deep and disordered inner turbulence? This lack of command over himself? He had very often been cruelly rude to her when beset, but never such rudeness as tonight. He had usually apologized. He had not apologized now.

There was a vivid red flash against the kitchen windows and then such a blast of thunder that the glass rattled. Beth put her hands over her ears. That had been very near, very dangerous. The rain and wind roared against the windows. Joel came into the kitchen, drenched. "Hey, that was a near thing, Miz Turner," he said. "Think it struck something close by."

Beth tried to smile at him. He said, "See Mr. Jerald's here tonight."

"Yes," said Beth. "Want a slice of raspberry pie, Joel, and some milk?"

He accepted with a youth's pleasure. He sat down at the scrubbed kitchen table. He had taken off the farm boots and was in his socks, white and clean. Beth looked at him fondly. There were times when she wished she had a son like Joel, but only at rare intervals. His artless farm boy's face was rosy, his gray eyes clear and wide, his blond hair wet. Life would never be very confusing to this direct youth, who knew what he wanted. He wanted land of his own. He did not know that Beth had left her small farm to him in her will. There were times, lately, because of Guy's growing savage moods and verbal abuse, when she had even thought of giving the farm to Joel and going away, perhaps forever.

She was startled when she saw Guy on the threshold of
460

the kitchen, standing in the doorway. Joel started to smile at him, then, seeing Guy's face, he colored, began to eat the pie very rapidly.

"I never see you here without you feeding your face," said Guy, in an ugly voice. "Do you ever stop eating?"

"Guy!" said Beth, outraged. But Joel stood up with young dignity and said, "Thanks, Miz Turner. See you tomorrow." He opened the back door and disappeared in the thunderous darkness.

Guy looked at Beth formidably. "Why do you cater to that brat?" he asked. "He's as stupid as a cow."

"Guy," she said. "You're not yourself. You have always been so kind to Joel, and you know he's not stupid. He knows what he wants—"

It was as if lightning had ignited him. He was infuriated. "And I don't, eh?" He flung his empty glass from him and it crashed on the floor and broke. For a long moment they both stared at the shards. "God damn," said Guy, slowly and loudly, and he turned and went back into the living room.

Beth stood in the kitchen and she trembled with terror. Never had he been like this before in all the years she had known him. She went into the other room. Guy was standing near a window, his hands in his trouser pockets, and he was looking at the storm. Feeling her presence, he swung about and faced her and she saw the repudiating and terrible hatred and despair in his eyes.

"I'm not coming here anymore," he said, and it was the voice of a hating stranger. "You upset me."

Beth felt an enormous sickness and hollowness in her breast, an awful sorrow and desolation. He continued to stare at her and she felt ugly and repulsive and drab, and old. The room and the man shook before her. But she said, quietly enough, "Very well, Guy. It's your choice."

"Choice, choice, choice!" he shouted at her. "What the hell do you know about choices, you and your bovine contentment? You're as stupid and as shallow as my father was—you and your choices!"

So, thought Beth, that's it. There was a new stir of anger in her, and a sudden coldness. She said, "At least we had the courage to live our lives."

"And, I never did! That's what you mean, isn't it?" He struck a table with his fist and the lamp on it jumped.

She drew a deep breath. "Yes, that's what I mean, Guy. I've watched you for years, and I know what's tearing you apart. I've watched you killing yourself. No, please. Let me finish. I can't bear it any longer, watching you die day by day. I can't live under these circumstances."

"You're an idiot! I wonder what the hell I ever saw in you. A superficial woman, pretending to be intelligent and wise! You haven't the brains to think rationally—"

"Guy!" her voice rose, for all she said to herself: It's over, finally and irretrievably over. "I don't make any pretense at all, about anything. I know one thing for certain: You hate your life. You don't hate me. You hate yourself. I know what you've always wanted. You wanted to be a doctor, a medical researcher. But you didn't have the courage to make the right choice. You didn't have the courage to live."

To her horror he reached out and struck her violently across the mouth. She fell back, holding her face, in which something had exploded. Then she stood, dropping her hand, confronting him fearlessly.

For an instant or two he looked aghast; he even looked at the hand which had struck her. Then the dusky red of rage returned to his face and his eyes leapt with black light at her.

"You'd have liked that, wouldn't you?" He almost yelled. "You'd have loved a weak poor man, wouldn't you? A man as worthless as any father! Yes, I bet you would have! The hell you would, damn you! You'd never even have looked at me! You love what I represent—"

"And what do you represent, Guy Jerald?"

"Money! And there never was a frigging woman who didn't love money, and the smell of it! I know all about you, you see. Would you have fucked me if I had been a

462

poor farmer, a mortgage-ridden farmer? Yes, I bet you would at that. Any port in a storm, I suppose!"

Her voice was very still. "Don't talk to me like that, Guy. I'm not your wife, thank God. Or do you dare talk to Lucy like that? I suppose not. She has a brother to defend her. She has money. She is your wife, your property, the mother of your children, and you think she deserves your respect, and I do not." Her breast rose and fell with a rage equal to his, and for a moment he was taken aback. The room was loud with their heavy breathing. Beth did not know that a trickle of blood was running from her mouth, but Guy saw it and something changed in his infuriated face. It was a peculiar change.

"Go back to your wife, Guy," said Beth, in a pent quiet voice. "Go back to your money, your easy life, your comfortable life. Go back to what you hate, what you've always hated. You made your choice long ago, so now live with it. And never come here again, until you want to live."

She put her hand to her agonized cheek and did not know of the quiet anguish in her face, and her brave expression. Her tawny eyes were brilliant with pain, but also with resolution.

"Don't worry," he said. "I won't come here again. I promise you that! I'm sick of your foolishness; I'm sick of you and what you represent. We've had our fun, such as it was. I'm sick of your imbecile conversation, your prattle of 'choices.' You're always babbling like that. It's you who have never lived, not I. You're only a silly goddamned middle-aged woman, and I'm ashamed I ever had anything to do with you. My whores have more sense than you have." He threw the words at her as if they were stones.

Thunder shook the house and lightning lit up every window and the wind screamed in the chimney. The clock chimed half past six, and it was a sad and dolorous sound, and to Beth it was the end of everything.

"Go home, Guy," she said. "Your wife is probably

463

waiting dinner for you. Your wife, Guy." She could not help the childish words. "Remember? You have a wife."

"Yes, thank God," he said, in a hoarse and brutal voice. "She never pretended to have intelligence. She accepts me as I am."

Beth went to the door and opened it and stood by it, her face white as death but her eyes gleaming in the lamplight. "Goodbye," she said.

He stood very still and looked at her and now his expression was strange and imploring. Then he walked past her into the stormy night. She closed the door quietly after him.

Her grief and sorrow were too dreadful for tears. She stood in the middle of the room and she trembled as if covered by ice. "Guy, Guy," she whispered, and the desolation spread all about her like a tangible presence. "Oh, Guy."

It was a long time before she could move. She was shivering and broken. When she sat down near a table she felt as if she was dying. Then she saw the notebook he had inadvertently left, his father's notebook. With cold hands she picked it up and read it.

Then she said aloud, "I see. I see. Now I understand. Oh, Guy." She put her head down on the table and cried until she could cry no more.

He had driven off into the wild summer storm, and he tried to kill himself.

27

Guy put his elbows on his knees and his head in his hands. He was remembering it all. He was remembering the stunned shame, the wounded humiliation, on Beth's face, on that summer night. Never had he talked before to other women, not even the cheapest of them, in such a voice and in such words. But he had shouted at Beth like that, Beth who had loved him and cherished him and had wanted only his peace of mind, who had suffered with him and consoled him and laughed with him and slept in his arms, and had given him what no other woman had ever given him: complete companionship and sympathy and tenderness. "Each man kills the thing he loves." He had "killed" Beth and her love. He hated himself with violence; he writhed in his chair. He wanted to beg Beth's forgiveness—but how could a woman so injured forgive him? Even the most profound love has its limits. Even in her pain she had not answered him as she should have done, with contempt and disgust. But Beth was a gentlewoman, and she would not descend to foulness as he had descended.

He knew that his "accident" had been reported in the newspapers, and no doubt it had also been reported that he was now in Mountain Valleys. So Beth knew. She had not written him, had not given him any indication that she was concerned for him. It was only just. He had killed the thing he had loved, in the most terrible fashion possible, and Beth would never permit him to see her again. It was over. It was asking too much for understanding. He had been abusive to Beth before, over the past year, when his oppressive life had become intolerable, that is, he had become sometimes insulting and extremely impatient with her, leaving her abruptly and shaking off her hands and glaring at her meanly. She had forgiven him when he had returned, days later, without warning. But she could not forgive this. She was a great lady, and great ladies did not forgive such savage attacks, such cruel derision, such filthy accusations.

But how could he live without her, she who had made his life one of meaning again, or at least had shown him the way to have meaning? She was no slave; she had probably suffered, but she was too intrepid to be devastated for long. He had no reason to live without her, but she had her steadfast reasons in herself to endure and survive. Once she had mentioned that she was leaving her farm to Joel; she had probably already done that and had

465

left, and he would never find her again. She would make sure of that.

He had experienced anguish before, but those occasions could not compare with this. Once she had affectionately said, "You are your own worst enemy, Guy." Now he knew that he had always been his worst enemy, and that no one had corrupted or perverted him or injured him—except himself. He had known men who had endured the worst of living, evil childhoods, undeserved injuries from friends, betrayals from those trusted, deaths of those dearest, under awful circumstances—they had shown little if any anger, and only sadness. They had not directed their pain upon others, as he had done. Because they were strong, because they accepted things most appalling with bravery.

I am not brave, I don't even have courage, he thought. Do I have the courage to go on without Beth? I only know that what has been my life mustn't be my life any longer. I owe that to Beth at least. Perhaps, someday—but there would be no "someday" for him and Beth. She had gone from him as irretrievably as to her grave.

I must go on, even if I don't want to. Again, I owe that to Beth, to be a man. I owe nothing to my wife and children; I gave them as much as it was possible for me to give, and they have no rights any longer insofar as I am concerned. My father and Beth were right: It is my life. I must do something with it. I owe that to them. I owe them that duty, that gratitude for their love.

As they drove to Mountain Valleys, Emil glanced sideways at James Meyer with compassion. James had aged. His ruddiness had disappeared. He had a closed distraught expression; he was sunken in himself and his dreadful sorrow. Love, thought Emil, caused more suffering than it was worth—perhaps. Only once had James spoken in the last fifteen minutes. He had said, in a dull voice, "How long does it take to get married in Pennsylvania, Emil?" Emil had replied, "I will arrange it."
466

A little later Emil said, "That thug who attacked you, James—I knew he would be coddled and 'loved' and let out on probation. Well, last night he killed a woman he was trying to rob, on the street. The weeping judge will probably sentence him to a year in jail, one of our nice new country clubs. It's a strange thing. If a desperate man tries to hide a little of the money he has so painfully earned, from the tax gatherer, no ferocity is as fierce as the government's, no wrath more vicious, so murderous. In Cranston, six months ago, a small businessman, who had worked hard and austerely all his life, 'failed' to report eight thousand dollars in income for 1975. He was fined five thousand dollars and sent to prison for two years. You see, to our present governments, no decent life is sacred, only the lives of the incompetent, the criminal, the malingerers, the thieves, the murderers, the unproductive, the parasites, the killers of a civilized society. But Money is everything to our governments now, money to support the worthless, the misfits, the outlaws. And so honorable people must be robbed of their last pennies to do this 'compassionate' job of their governments. But, it's probably our fault. A strong and courageous people don't have to stand that state of affairs. They have might. When they put up with it, it is their own fault. It's time for a revolt."

James said in a distant voice, "But where is manhood in the world today? We all cower and slaver before our governments, instead of taking up arms against its cruelties and tyranny. We could stop all this monstrous thing in twenty-four hours, if we had any bravery at all. A bureaucrat is a cowardly snarling dog who can be set to run with a hard kick in his arse. But, it's an old story. It was the bureaucrats and their mendicant misfits who murdered the Roman Empire, and it will happen again."

"I never thought," said Emil, "that my country would ever adopt Marxism, but she did. Now we are a covert Marxist country."

"So is England, only more so," said James. He seemed to arouse himself a little from his deep lethargy of grief.

467

He seemed to be thinking. "I've been talking to Emma. She says I am needed, that I must go on—in spite of anything. That I must start to fight for my country. I couldn't care less—as of now."

"But you will," said Emil. "You will."

James uttered something that was between a blasphemous expletive and a groan.

"You can't do anything else," said Emil. "It is your life, James."

"But what if your bloody life becomes meaningless?"

"It's never meaningless, James. No life is meaningless, unless we make it so."

"As our friend in Mountain Valleys has made his life meaningless," said James, with the first bitterness he had ever expressed against Guy Jerald.

"Yes. Quite true. But he did it himself. He had a choice. I am sure. But he didn't make the right choice, or perhaps, he never made a clear choice at all."

"He just drifted into it, eh?"

Emil paused. "Or he was probably afraid of something."

James said, "Just as I have been afraid, afraid to abandon my urbane comfortable life, my smiling cynical life, my satisfied life, for—"

Emil waited, but James did not go on. After a while he said, as if to himself, "My father made his clear choice. But then, he was a man." He did not know it, but Emil saw it: A tear touched his lower lashes. How many of the helpless had his father rescued? There was no way of knowing. He had only given his life for them. Was that ridiculous, or was it the noblest thing a man could do?

It was a very dismal and depressing day—gray sky, gray snow, gray wind, gray air. James felt it all through his flesh. He thought of what Emma had told him this morning. "Love, you have your life to live, and it will be a fine life, worthy of you. Don't tell me you can't go on without me. I will always be with you. I couldn't bear it if I thought you would give up in despair. Remember me, but with love and laughter and contentment. Anything else would be an insult to me. All those wonderful years! We were blessed. Now, you must go on with the work you must do, for your sake and mine." She had smiled at him tenderly, with the old raffish glint in her eyes. "Otherwise, I'll haunt you. This is a time for warriors, love." She had kissed him. "Before you go, let's make love again. I can't have enough of you, you basket." She smacked his bare buttocks soundly, and he had yelped and laughed.

Women like Emma and Beth and Marian gave not only faith to their men but bravery also. They tied their kerchiefs on a man's lance and sent him off to battle. Emma, Emma, thought James, and he shivered in the warmth of the car. He must never break down before her again, and cause her more pain. He must pretend to be courageous, and he was enough of a psychiatrist to know that the posture a man frequently struck often could become second nature, and natural. For her sake he must try to be what she believed he was: a man like his father. In time he might believe it. But as of now there was such a hollowness in him, filled with cries.

When James and Emil parted in the corridor of Mountain Valleys, Emil noticed, with a little perturbation, that James wore a grim set expression, purposeful and forbidding, and he wondered why. He looked like a man deeply vengeful, even formidable. They had agreed to meet for lunch; Emil watched James march very fast down the corridor to Guy's suite, and he scratched his ear. I wouldn't like to be the target of whatever he's got in mind, he thought.

James flung open the door of the suite, curtly dismissed the nurse, then stood, staring at Guy, who was seated at a table and not in his usual wing chair. But James, in his emotional state, did not notice that the table was covered with sheets of paper on which much had been written. He stood, breathing heavily, near the door and did not sit in his chair near the fraudulent fire. With an enormous effort he clenched his fists at his sides and reminded himself that he was a psychiatrist and psychiatrists did not display personal disarray to patients, particularly ones in Guy's hazardous condition. So he breathed out hard, and said in an ominous voice, "Well."

Guy started to rise from his chair, then, seeing James's face, he sat down again, obviously shaken. His black eyes widened. He said, "Jim." James turned from him and stared at the fire and his back was the back of a bull. His voice was low but pent as he said, "Damn you, you are as sane as I am, and you know it, but you are crouching there like a beaten misunderstood dog who has been battered half to death by unfeeling monsters! You've spent months pitying yourself, feeling a victim of fucking injustice, while all the time you were the bloody unjust one! Let me tell you something"—and he swung on Guy again —"this is the last time I am going to waste hours and breath on you, Jerry. I'm finished! I've had it. You make me ill."

He tore his chair from near the fire and flung himself into it. Be quiet, said his physician's inner voice, and he answered as soundlessly: The hell I will! He said aloud, "I've met many a man like you, Jerry, who shat up his life and then tried to end it, blaming not himself, but others, for the mess he has made on the carpet. Yes, you've had your rough spots; who hasn't? But we cleaned up the spots ourselves. What do you know of the life of anyone else? Have you ever wondered? Have you ever had pity? Have you ever realized that we are all caught in the same human predicament of despair, loneliness, mental and physical suffering, anguish, hopelessness, abandon- ment—with little joy to compensate? I know you for what you are—a driven man. But you are the driver! No one harnessed you to the cart. You did. You married a fool of a woman—yes, she is a fool!—but no one forced you into that marriage. Instead of ridding yourself of her earlier you stayed with her. Why?

"Oh, I know the stupid reply you'd tell me, if you'd ever open your mouth long enough to give a reasonable answer! You'd say, 'duty, responsibility.' Catchwords, the words of a man who tries to explain his irrational con-

470

duct—which was motivated only by cowardice! Have you ever thought of what you did to your wife when you did not set her free to marry a man of her own kind, a foolish man as mindless as herself? Don't look at me like that, damn you! Do you think she is happy being married to a man who was always a stranger to her, an incomprehensible stranger, who did not behave as she believed a man should behave—conforming and loving, a mere servant to his family, as most of you American men are? You revolted against her demands; I admit her demands were as demeaning and crass as are the demands of many women. You knew those demands were demeaning and crass, but you put up with them! Why? Duty again, responsibility? Do you think a man who abrogates his sacred duty to himself, his responsibility to himself as a full human soul, is admirable? No, he is a liar and a coward! I have an inkling about you now, Jerry. Your wife was a surrogate for someone else, and then when you realized that, you did not admit that you had defrauded her. No, indeed. You treated her with contempt and hatred. You didn't let her go in peace to make her own life as she wanted it. The worst and cruelest thing a man can do to a woman is to hate her—then sleep with her and remain in the same house with her. *That* is degrading both to the woman and to the man, the worst degradation."

He had to stop for breath. He did not know that his condemning, even his hating, face was ghastly and quivering with his own inner torment. Guy sat in silence, looking at him as a man looks at a judge.

"Oh, God," James groaned. "Oh, my God." He had done the most unpardonable thing a psychiatrist can do to a patient: He had projected his own anguish on another human being. But he could not help it. He was only a man after all. The last few days had broken him completely, he who had vowed that nothing would ever break him, that he was above the witless and doltish lack of discipline of lesser men. Emma, Emma, he thought with a deeper inward groaning. Oh, Emma, I really can't stand it! His heart was thumping like a drum whose skin has been too

471

tightly drawn. Its beat was erratic and infinitely painful. For Emma's sake he had tried for resignation and thought he had achieved it. But he was not resigned at all.

Guy was looking at him strangely and something stirred in him—pity. Guy saw how distraught his friend was, how deep in his extremity, though he did not know why. He saw only the torture. Jim—always affable, always controlled, always understanding, always urbane, always humorous and in command—something had struck him down and was killing him. He said, "Jim?" But James did not hear him in the blackness of his own travail, where he lay, writhing.

James's voice was choked when he could speak. "Your children. I've met them, have studied them. They are children of your loins, but they are not really your children, and never were. But how many children are really the offspring of their parents? A father should have compassion on his children, that he ever begot them. I think God has more pity for us than condemnation—for aren't we His creatures, for whom He must bear the guilt? What did you expect of the strangers you casually begot? Perfection? Understanding? Gratitude? Love? It is wiser to look to a mongrel dog for these than to your children!

"Pity your children that they were born! Teach them what you can—if they will listen. Treat them with mercy, for they, too, will suffer in the common pit of misery in which we all live. But never condemn them for being what they are; you don't know the mysteries of inheritance. Who does? Your children were a disappointment to you. Perhaps your father was disappointed in you, too."

Guy's face changed, but James did not see it. "Be kind to your children," he said. "But once you have brought them to manhood let them go. Don't hate them. Yes, I know that you dislike your children or at the very least are indifferent to them. But pity them for our common human predicament. Your children may have the usual human malice and ingratitude, stupidity and trend to evil. We all have. Their lives are their own, as yours is your own. Years of fatherhood may be wasted, but even in that

472

waste we learn something about ourselves, or we should. We should learn tolerance even during dismissal, and hope for the best."

The gray snow and wind rumbled at the windows but there was silence in that charged room. It was James who was the unseeing one now, and Guy the seeing. One was stunned almost to the dying point; the other had begun to live, and Guy, all at once, knew this was so but why it was so he did not understand.

James, in his agony, had begun to pace the room, as a man paces who has been stricken by an unbearable and twisting pain, and can find no surcease. He said, in that strained unnaturally high voice, "I've learned something about your father, from your own ramblings after you came out of your damned trances. He pitied you, didn't he? You probably saddened him, but he did not blame you, or anyone else. He knew you had to find your own way, as we all must do. No one can find it for us except ourselves. If your children are intolerable to you, perhaps they found you intolerable also, for you were the stranger, the rebel, the strong one, and they have no strangeness, are not rebellious, and have no strength. I saw that for myself. You should have chosen a better mother for them, a woman more like yourself. That was your crime against your children—marrying their mother. What did you expect of that misbegotten marriage? Children of your own heart? If you did, then you are a worse fool than your wife, whom I pity. The kindest thing you can do for your children, now, I think, is to forget them or remember them with some commiseration and lenience. They will learn, and you can be sure of that! One day they might even become your friends, if you mercifully forgive them! But never indulge the folly of blaming yourself for what they are, though by your marriage you condemned them to that. To feel guilty is to be twice cursed."

He turned his throbbing and exhausted face on Guy, and it was a face Guy was never to forget. James said, "We'll probably not meet again. But, in your way, you have taught me something, though that was not your

473

intention. You taught me to confront myself, though you could not teach yourself that! You brought me face to face with myself; you taught me that I was as self-indulgent as you are, and just as craven, and that it was time for me to be a man and do what I must do. So, perhaps, all the time I have spent with you was not a waste at all. It was an awakening, wretched though it was, almost unbearable though it was. What I must face now—it may be easier for what you have taught me."

"Jim," said Guy, but again the agonized man did not hear him.

"I couldn't teach you to be a man. But you taught me!"

He looked savagely at Guy, and did not see that aware expression, that acutely understanding expression. He saw an obdurate one, a sullen and denying one, and suddenly he could not stand it. He ran at his friend and struck him furiously, backhand, across his face, crying out aloud in his increasing extremity of despair and grief. "Oh, damn you, damn you, you stupid bastard! You have the greatest thing a man can expect of life, the only glorious thing, the love of a noble woman! And what have you done to that woman, you wretched swine! I've seen her; I've talked with her; I have heard her voice and the love in it —for you! She did for you what few women can do for a man: Teach him how to truly be a man, how to truly live! Was it too much for you? So too much that you tried to kill yourself? Ran from her?"

He did not see Guy jump to his feet; he only saw that they were facing each other, their breathing tumultuous in the room.

Guy exclaimed, "Beth!"

James shouted, "Yes, Beth! The woman you don't deserve, never will deserve! Beth Turner, who came here regularly to ask about you." He wanted to add, in his turbulent pain, "The woman who came to me for consolation, as to a surrogate, the loving woman." But he caught himself in time. It would be a monstrous thing to do to that woman, who had wept in his arms in her own anguish. He sorely wanted to do that thing, to alleviate his
474

torture and make his friend share it with him, if only out of male jealousy. But he recoiled from that natural human desire.

"Beth—she has come here, to find out about me?" James did not see the sudden brilliant joy on the other man's face, the elation, the overwhelming passion.

"Yes, yes! That she did, but why, God only knows. Only another woman could understand such pardon, such devotion, little as they are deserved."

"Beth!" cried Guy, and he struck his palms together.

But James's suffering was now too much for him to tolerate. He collapsed down into the very wing chair which Guy had abandoned. He put his hands over his face and moaned over and over, rocking himself back and forth. Tears spurted through his fingers. He had lost all control of himself. He was now just another man prostrated by hopeless grief, by a loss too terrible to be endured. He had consoled others; he could not console himself.

His voice came from behind his hands in paroxysms, as if his throat was being torn from him in bleeding fragments. "No, no, you aren't worthy to have that woman. At least I've loved Emma and have returned her love. At least I've appreciated her, have never said one vicious word to her. The loveliest woman. I can't ever condemn myself for coldness to her, for lack of consideration, for hardness of heart, for cruelty. No, never. I—I— Oh, my God! I—I can't stand it! How can I stand it, that I must lose her soon, and watch her die? Lost forever. The only thing I love. Watch her die, in the worst pain imaginable. No—I won't let her go through that! No, no. Oh, Emma, my love, my love. Take my life, but live. Emma, you mustn't leave me—I—I— Emma."

He rocked more wildly on the chair and the tears poured through his fingers and his whole body was convulsed. All the suppressed rebellion, all the suppressed agony, of the last days burst from him in a flood, uncontrollable, devastated. Blackness, streaked with scarlet, ran behind his eyelids and pain roiled his heart. He heard nothing but the scream of his own suffering, both mental and physical.

475

It was a long time before he could quiet himself, before his own torment numbed him. Then he became aware that Guy was kneeling beside him, that his head was on Guy's shoulder, that Guy's arm was about him in comforting, that Guy was wiping his eyes with a brother's consolation. He lay in profound exhaustion in Guy's arms and he closed his swollen eyes in a child's desperate relaxation.

Only Guy heard the door open to show an astounded Emil Grassner on the threshold of the room. Emil stared, then understood, and his face was contorted with sympathy and his individual pain.

Guy said, "Let him rest, Emil. Then, I'm going home, today, to Beth." He held out his hand to the psychiatrist and Emil came to him and took that hand and he put his other hand on James's shoulder, in blessed silence and pity and affection, the soundless mutual affection which only men can know for each other in distress. It had no need for words.

28

Beth sat by her fire this gloomy day and stared sightlessly at the frost which glittered on her windows. Her eyes swelled with tears which endlessly dropped on the green wool of her frock, and her hands were clasped together on her knees. Her face was calm, however, and full of resolution.

She had come to the end of waiting. She knew it was the end and though the pain was there so also was her strength. Emil's last message to her had informed her that Guy was now completely rational and that he had come to his own hour of decision. He had not spoken of her to the psychiatrist at any time, nor of his decision, Emil had regretfully told her. She should have patience.

"No," she said aloud, "I have reached the end of patience."

476

She considered Guy's apparent decision. Whether or not that included her, she did not know. He had, without doubt, decided that she had no more part of his life or that he expected her to continue as before. "No," she said again. "It can't be as it was. For my sake. I owe that to myself, if I am going to continue living. To drift along again is beyond my courage and my endurance. I have my life to live, and it is my own. Certainly I will suffer, but I won't let it go on so long that it destroys me. That would be a crime against myself and a crime against life. I am a breathing human being, and nothing is ever lost. I have had over five years of uneasy happiness. Yes, they were uneasy, I admit that at last."

She would sell the farm to Joel on long terms, to be given to him on her death. She would find another place in this world to live, this most beautiful world. Only she could make it a desert to exist in, and she had never lived in a desert and would never live in it. There were too many fertile places, too many seas and mountains and vast glowing plains. She was not young, in her body, but she felt that in her soul she would never be old. The final separation in mind and flesh from what she had known these considerable years would be agonizing, she knew, but when were separations ever happy? Somewhere there was a place for her, uniquely her own, where she would find peace and contentment and no hopeless waiting any longer. Somewhere there might be another man to love, but it would be a man who was composed and of a piece, who could give her, if not rapture and total joy, then serenity and tranquillity. She had known too many men, and was too sophisticated, to believe that the death of one love meant the death of all love. No one could live fully without love, and love she would have. She was no callow woman or young girl. If one were deprived for all time of wine, there was good sound water; if excitement and leaping joy were lost, then they could be replaced by contentment and a measure of placidity and service. The evening of life was as beautiful as the morning, and far richer, for it had fulfilled itself. The moon was as lovely as the sun and it held more mystery. It had a majestic silence.

Perhaps there would be for her a man like James Meyer, a good kind man who could be trusted, a gentle man in whose arms she would sleep in peace, knowing he would be there tomorrow, and without caprice, who would trust her as she trusted him. It had come to her that she had never completely trusted Guy Jerald. She had understood him too well for that.

Of course, she reflected, the improbable might occur: Guy would return to her, his twisted life resolved, and with his own resolution. For an instant her heart beat faster and then she sternly repressed the sudden surge of emotion. If that impossible thing happened to her there would still be that change in her. Could she, however deep her love, be happy with a man without absolute trust? Was love possible, indeed, without trust, without the giving of one's whole self? Yes, it was possible, but it was a love that would always be shadowed in some tarnished way, tarnished with a dim mistrust.

She asked herself: Am I looking for perfection when I know only too well there is no perfection? No, I am not looking for that. I only want to give completely of myself, as I want a man to give completely of himself to me. That doesn't necessarily involve total trust; it involves—or does it?—a compromise. Am I strong enough to live the rest of my life in compromise? I don't know.

She had almost immediately forgiven Guy for that dreadful night of shame and degradation. She had told herself, until just recently, that she had understood in all the ramifications of understanding. But she would never forget. She had too much pride. Even if Guy became trustworthy, there would always be that remembrance, like a warted toad in a clear polished pond within a forest. For there would be fear, which was part of mistrust. He was too changeable, and though changefulness had its own certain excitement it was too disturbing. The world was disturbing enough without bringing that turmoil onto one's hearthstone.

478

She did not intend to vegetate in some backwoods of life, but she did intend to keep the eye of the storm over her as long as possible during the rest of her life. Middle age had its own ripeness and the maturity of golden wheat and tasseled corn. She would rejoice in the storms, revel in them, and then sit at her own fireside when the storms were over. Middle age brought the knowledge that nothing remains, nothing is eternal, and the fury of one day brought the calm of tomorrow. Without fury there could be no following calm; without calm there could be no thunderous fury. Youth saw only one shallow aspect, one fugitive facet, to life. But middle age knew that life had infinite variety, and every variety was a wonder in itself.

With a sad and loving smile she thought again of James Meyer. By this time his Emma had joined him. He would not leave the city without informing her. She envied Emma who had such a man; he had told her that she resembled that Emma in mind and spirit. I should like to meet her, Beth thought. James was to be trusted, and he was solid and assured, but never would he grow fat in spirit and retreat from living. He could be hurt, but he would endure and still feel zest and eagerness for the next day. Perhaps, somewhere, there was a man for her like this, who rejoiced in the blissfulness of good food and good sleep and laughter and surety, who could love without giving pain, or, at least, not too much of it. Had Guy ever truly loved her? She wondered.

She heard her dog's rollicking bark, which increased in sound as he rushed nearer the house. Was some visitor arriving, for her who rarely had a visitor? She stood up, put aside the book on her knee, turned on another lamp. Then her heart gave an incredulous and gasping leap. That hard running footstep on the packed snow: Only Guy ran like that when he could not wait to see her. "Oh, no!" she exclaimed, and tried to move, but she was trembling, and she locked her hands together and stared at the door. It opened. For an instant she closed her eyes; her heart was rushing so fast that it was choking her. She opened her

479

eyes again. Yes, it was Guy, it was surely Guy! She uttered a strange strangled cry and then her face lit up as if a searchlight was pouring its fullness upon it. Her eyes became huge and enormously brilliant. Her mouth flushed red and quivered.

"Beth!" he shouted, and came towards her, hatless, his heavy coat flaring out behind him.

"Guy," she said in a faint voice. She saw him fully now in the lamplight. He had always been lean, but now he was emaciated. The strong rectangular face she had known had aged, had become lined with suffering. The black eyes were as bright as ever, but they were sunken. His dark color was not vibrant now; it was merely sallow. Her mouth opened on a moan of compassion and love.

He came towards her, smiling widely, and breathless, and he held out his arms to her. He expected her to turn into them as always she did, crying out in the dear and remembered way. But to his bewilderment and sensation of absolute coldness he saw that she was paling, and that though she smiled there was a kind of sternness of her features, an unfamiliar withdrawal. He stopped. "Beth?" he said. "I've come home, to you. Beth?"

She came to him slowly, walking in some sort of feeble slow way, and then she was in his arms and her head was on his shoulder, hidden. He felt the quickened breath heaving against the ribs of her slender body. She did not put her arms about his neck as always. They hung limply at her sides. But he felt her tears on his neck, the hot slow tears. He put her from him gently, and looked down into her face, the shut wet eyes, the pale mouth. It was Beth, the Beth he loved, and yet it was not Beth. He held the upper part of her arms strongly, and a terrible fear came to him.

"Beth?" he said. "I'm here, I've come home to you."

"Have you?" she said, in so dim a voice that he could hardly hear her. But he heard. He held her arms tighter and the fear was almost overpowering. He said, "Can you forgive me, my darling?"

"Yes. I forgave you. Almost at once." She did not add,
480

"But I can never forget." She did add, in that unfamiliar voice, "I read your father's notebook. I understood, then."

She felt the growing chill of his fingers through the wool of her frock. She remembered that he had been very ill, almost mortally so, these past months. She reproached herself distractedly. With the remembered gentleness she slowly removed his coat. "Come, and sit by the fire, and tell me all about it—my darling."

But he stared at her speechlessly for several moments. Then he said, "Is there something wrong, Beth?"

"No," she answered. She did not say, "But I have changed, and I am not the woman you ran from." She tried to smile. Her face was very strained. She took his arm and led him to his old chair by the fire. He let her lead him but he continued to stare at her. He sat down as obediently as a child. He took her hand. He held it to his cheek, then kissed it. He heard himself stammering idiotically. "They lent me a car today—the sanitarium. I'm discharged. Emil Grassner. He knows you. He told me all about it—your visits. I didn't know. I had to—I came as fast as I could." He was staring up at her pleadingly, and this was a Guy she had never known before.

"Yes," she said. "I want to know everything." She struggled to become normal, made herself smile. "I have a roast loin of pork and baked yams and applesauce." Her tone was mischievous, if labored. "Or, is your wife expecting you for dinner?"

"You haven't kissed me," he said, like a complaining young boy.

"And you haven't kissed me, either," she replied.

Then she dropped on her knees beside him and laid her head against his chest and wept. He stroked the fine red hair, which was limper than he remembered; he stroked the white cheek, which was drawn and thinner. She did not cling to him. She just lay against him, crying soundlessly. But he was no longer afraid; the terrible crushing fear had left him. She still loved him.

481

"Do you still love me, Beth?" His voice was hoarse and unsure.

"Yes. Oh, yes. Always."

He took her face in his hands and kissed her as he had never kissed her before, slowly, gently, as James had kissed her. It was not the old kiss of passion, rough and demanding, but it was the sincerest kiss she had ever had from him. Her lips were still under his, then they began involuntarily to move and they kissed long and deeply and with a greater tenderness than before, a greater knowledge. Her salt tears ran into his mouth. He held her head closer to him, and now the grasp was a little fierce. Then again he held her off and looked at her earnestly and she saw something in his eyes that had changed also. The impatient light was not there. But there was something deeper, something stronger yet softer, and they were shining with moisture.

"I've come back from hell," he said, with a simplicity alien to him.

"I know, my dear, I know."

"I must tell you about it." He stroked her wet cheek. "Your nose is running. Here." He wiped her nose with his own handkerchief. Then all at once they were laughing at the Bathos which could attend even the most tragic moments, laughing helplessly together, Beth rocking on her knees and he in his chair.

"Get us something to drink," he said at last, wiping his own eyes, and he spoke with much of his old command, and to her amazement she rejoiced at it. She ran into her kitchen, and she stood there for a few moments, looking about her, trembling, feeling a bursting of joy in her heart that was almost unendurable. "I can't believe it, I can't believe it!" she whispered. She was dazed and weak, but with such happiness, a happiness she had never experienced before. The house was empty no longer; it was filled to its very rafters. She heard Guy poking at the fire and she squeezed her radiant eyes shut, and almost cried out aloud in her ecstasy. She was young as she had never been young. But it was
482

not peace she felt; it was far more than that. It was life, vivid, shaking, victorious, exultant, and she wanted to dance.

Guy had turned on her record player and was listening to the record she had left there. "One fine day, he will return, he will return!" She did not find it banal, embarrassing. She found it a fulfilled promise, without the ominousness of its context. For that night, she forgot all that she had been thinking before Guy had come to her. But it was firmly lodged in her soul like a drop of hard cold lead in seething red wine. The day darkened and she did not see it.

As they drank their drinks in the comforting warmth of the fire Guy spoke of James and what his friend had done for him, and Beth nodded, her face soft and wistful, and she said repeatedly, "I know. He claimed nothing, but I knew he was helping you and that only he could help you. I tried—and failed."

Guy touched her hands. "You were too close to me. I couldn't see the truth because your dear face got in the way. It all seemed to depend on what I felt for you—it's impossible to explain. It was subjective. I had the thought that if I refused to do what you thought I should do, you would turn away from me—"

"Like some silly, pouting woman who had been frustrated? Guy!"

"Well, yes, I was stupid. I was using you to keep me from seeing the truth about my life and myself. I forced myself to believe that you had given me an ultimatum." He smiled. "And I am no man for ultimatums, especially from a woman. I forgot the hundreds of times I had just about asked for your advice—and you had refused to give it, telling me that what I chose was my own decision and no one else's. You see how cowardly I was?"

"We're all cowards in one way or another," said Beth. "Never in the world would I try to force a man to make a choice—nor would I ever be guilty of destroying a man's marriage. No one can destroy a good sound

483

marriage; it takes the combatants." She smiled again, and again that new expression was on her face. He looked at her earnestly, and with some trepidation.

He had not as yet told her of James's tragedy. For these hours, at least, he would not speak, afraid of spoiling this deep rapport between them. He only said, "Jim is getting married to Lady Emma tomorrow. He wants us to be witnesses."

"Of course we shall." Her voice was full of happiness. "I do so want to meet his Emma. He told me often of her—when we met." She had her own reticences. Knowing Guy too well, she would never tell him of that gentle and warming encounter in her house, not even that James had ever been here. She had no urge to "confess," for she felt no guilt and only a sweet memory of consolation and surcease from pain. But Guy would not understand. Beneath this new facade of reason and enlightenment still lurked the rigorous man, and in many ways, she was glad of it. A submissive attitude on his part would have been abhorrent to her. Part of his appeal for her was his innate strength. She had seen him weep, and knew that only a strong man can weep. She knew that later—in his pursuit of what he had chosen—he would be just as rigorous, and she desired that above anything else. Moreover, she had learned that emotionally men were frail and very sensitive creatures, far more so than women. It was that frailty and sensitivity which made so many of them towering geniuses, which enhanced their masculinity. Only the weak were afraid of emotion, vulnerability, and display of their own humanity. She kissed his hand and sighed. God did give women one advantage, she thought: We can understand men but they can never understand us, and perhaps that is for the best.

But, what had he chosen? She said, "No matter what you have decided, my darling, I will always be here." (Not entirely, she added to herself. I will never be broken again. I, too, have learned. I will bend, but I will not break.)
484

"My decision? I thought you already knew that!"

"You give me credit for too much intuition."

He jumped up like a youth, but she saw the evidences of his long illness. It would be months before he had recovered. She saw the exhaustion on his dark lean face. He went to his coat in the closet and brought out a sheaf of letters, and he laid them on her lap. "I am mailing them tomorrow. I want you to read them first."

She gazed at him with thoughtful trouble. "Are you sure you want me to see these? I see one is addressed to your—wife—one each to your son and daughter, and one to Mr. Lippincott, whom I met, as you know."

"I brought them to you because I want you to see them. It will save much talk and explanations, and I hate both." He touched her cheek. "You always did talk too much. You're as bad as Jimmy."

She smiled and lifted the unsealed flaps and read the letters. Her heart swam with elation and with joy. Yet each had asked only for the presence of the others four days from now. However, he did inform his wife that he was not returning to his house but would send for necessary clothing. Still, what was the decision? "These tell me nothing," she said.

"Oh, my God!" he said, with his old impatience. "Do I have to write books for you? These announce the finale, for Christ's sake, Beth! I intend to tell my wife that I am divorcing her in New York State, that she may keep the house I bought and paid for and which I hate now, and I am telling my children that they are in their young middle age and they neither need nor will they get any more consideration, or money, from me. As for Hugh, I am going to right a wrong I did him, out of my contemptible self-righteousness." He threw up his hands. "I thought this was all explicit to you, Beth!"

"I am not a mind reader," she said. "Dear as you are to me, your masculine mind is too complicated for a simple woman to follow." Again she looked at him earnestly. "Are you certain, absolutely certain, you want to do all this?"

"Christ," he muttered again. "Must I spell it out like a teacher?"

"I'm afraid so."

In rapid and impatient speech he told her. "And, in addition, Emil is going to find some small and sound college, accredited, where I can do what I always wanted to do—become a doctor, so I can pursue cancer research. I thought we'd talked this all over months, years ago!"

She laughed and shook her head. "No, we didn't. Oh, you hinted, but I knew you weren't sure. Your business, the banks. I gather you intend to throw them all over? This is a momentous decision."

"I certainly don't intend to give up the business. I will remain in control, make the major decisions. I have good managers. As for the banks—they are going to be Hugh's. He put up with me for years; he deserves some reward. I stood in the way of his marrying Marian Kleinhorst, by threats—it seems incredible to me now— how like my mother I am in many ways—and because Marian would not marry him, for fear of destroying him by depriving him of his damned life's work. He can have the fucking banks."

"Guy."

"Well, all right, but you can be damned obtuse when you want to be, Beth. All right, I'll remember your delicacy after this, unless you annoy me too much, which I suspect will be regularly. You're not as gentle and yielding as you pretend to be with me, my girl, and I am sure you intend to take your revenge for those years of submission."

She laughed outright, she was so full of jubilation. "I'll try," she said. "We are going to have a very spirited—" She caught herself. He grinned at her.

"Marriage? Are you proposing to me, woman?"

"I wouldn't dream of it.

His face became somber. "All those years—wasted— when we could have been happy together."

"Oh, Guy. Nothing is wasted. If you had moved prematurely you would always have looked back, wondering, conjecturing, if you had done the right thing. Now you are sure. You are sure?"

"More sure of this than I was ever sure of anything before."

He rubbed his chin. He had not shaved today, as yet. "It comes to me that I was never really sure of one damned thing I ever did, until now. Now, I am free."

She gazed at him steadily and knew that he had spoken the truth. He had always been confident in her presence, but she had known that he had not been confident at all, and was only justifying himself, or seeking reassurance.

He was smiling and shaking his head. "You and my father, and old Jimmy. You are all of a piece. I don't know whether to thank God for all of you, or to howl at Him."

"Thank you," she said. "Either way, it's a compliment. Now, do stop rubbing your chin; yes, you have quite a beard. Go into the bathroom and shave while I put the dinner on. Oh, what a beautiful day this is!" Though it had been, in the beginning, the most dismal. The clouds had briefly parted; the sunset light was already on the hills. Beth gave him another drink. She had never heard him hum before, but he was humming when he took the glass into the bathroom. It was the dearest sound to her, that hoarse humming, and it told her all that she wanted to know. He was not realizing his weariness yet, though he would, and she was ready for it. She savored this new peace, this tremendous joy, this anticipation, this hope. Her man had come home. It was a turbulent homecoming, and it would always be turbulent, for which she was grateful now.

In the bathroom, Guy removed his coat and looked about the small clean room with pleasure. Only in his father's house had he felt this calmness, this emcompassing pleasure. He took out his shaving kit from the cupboard where it had always been, and opened it.

Then he stopped, freezing.

Among the blades and razors and tubes and bottles there was a strange and challenging thing: a gold cuff link in the shape of a six-pointed star, with a ruby, like blood, in the center. The Star of David. A Jewish symbol. He took it in his hand and stared blindly through the window, where the evening light was a silver glaze on the hills.

At first he was numb, and then like a murderous tide rage rushed in on him, primeval rage, the lust to kill of a male animal whose woman-territory had been invaded by another male. He clenched his hands—one of which held the Star—on the edge of the basin. Jimmy. And Beth. Jimmy had been here; why hadn't Beth told him in all these hours? Jimmy had used his kit, Jimmy, his friend! A man does not shave in a woman's house unless he has stayed with her overnight—and slept in her bed, before the morning. Beth had not told him. Jimmy had not told him. He recalled, in fiery and flashing detail, James's denunciation of his treatment of Beth, and there had been more than noble indignation in those denunciations, those crying adjectives of affection for a woman who was not his, those broken cries. There had been more than pity in those agitated condemnations—there had been tenderness and remembrance.

"God, God," he muttered, and the points of the Star in his clenched fist seemed to bite maliciously into his palm. His rage increased until it was a blinding redness before his eyes. In that redness he could see James in his bed, in Beth's arms. The urge to murder was a wild burning in his mind. He moved convulsively. He wanted to rush out to Beth with the damning evidence in his hand, shouting hateful accusations, then taking her by the throat. His hands longed for her throat, they itched and twitched for it. He did not know whom he hated most, James or Beth, for this ugly deception while they ostensibly mourned for him. Mourned for him, the damned frigging hypocrites! Perhaps they had even laughed at him—

He shuddered with his raw and primitive hatred, his

488

jealousy, his rage and affront. He had felt this way only once before, when he had killed the Russian soldiers in payment for Marlene's death. His roaring imagination conceived the lewdest and most lascivious pictures of James and Beth together—in his bed. He clenched his knees together and shuddered over and over. His breath was thick and choking in his throat; his heart was screaming in his ears. He felt mortally sick—and the urge to kill became stronger. In a moment, when he had his strength back, he would go to her and—

He looked at the Star, the blameless Star. So he was in love with his Emma, was he? Yet he could take Beth as lightly as he would take a whore, and she had taken him as lightly as a whore would take a man. Beth, who claimed to love him, had forgotten him long enough to caper with another man, in lust and abandonment! He knew the passion of which Beth was capable. That she could feel that passion for someone not himself was intolerable to him. He leaned against the basin, out of very weakness, out of the weakness that only strong emotion can provoke. There was a taste of blood in his mouth. He did not know that he had savagely bitten his tongue.

How carefully Beth had avoided telling him even that James had been in this house! Meeting him at the hospital, yes. Meeting him with Hugh Lippincott and Marian Kleinhorst, yes. Eating lunches, dinners with him, yes. But not this foul and unconscionable thing. The inexorable evidence was in his hand. He remembered, now. He had seen both cuff links on James's shirt once, in the sanitarium. They had blazed at him in the lamplight, enormously increased. He had never seen them again. Did the bastard ever wonder where he had lost it?

"I'll kill—kill—kill—"

Did the bitch know that this—thing—was in the shaving kit? Had she left it there to mock him, to laugh at him, to confront him with her vileness, her concupiscence? Had they both knowingly agreed to leave it there, so that they could shout their laughter at him to his face? All his

489

gorge, his male pride, his outrage, struck him over and over like meaty fists, bent on destroying him. His whole body ran with an ice-cold sweat. When had they committed this crime, this heinous crime, against him? That bastard, that whore?

And all this time, these weeks, he had been struggling to decide, to go home to her! What had they plotted against him? What could be the plot? Emma was dying—there was no doubt in Guy's mind that Beth knew also, though he did not know how. Was Beth planning to marry that fucking Jew when he was free to marry her? More fool she. He heard himself laughing low and hoarsely, and with gleeful hate and almost insane wrath.

He turned to the closet to look for more evidence of their perfidy, more shameful evidence. If James had slept here, then he had used Guy's clothing. He had used his pajamas. Even in his madness Guy did not think that this had been a plotted thing, an arranged thing. It had been spontaneous, like most crimes. He fumbled through the clothes, examining, in particular, his pajamas. Was there a crease here, a smear there? No, Beth was too fastidious. But one set of pajamas was out of place, as if hastily returned.

It was this search that finally almost sobered him, made his flesh flush with red heat. He drew a deep and shivering breath. It was evidence of his complete turn of mind that made him start thinking, and thinking clearly. James's agony that morning had been more than sincere. It had been devastating, prostrating. Still, a man can deeply love one woman, then turn to another for a moment's variety. He knew himself well enough to realize that, he knew his whole sex. But Beth. Against all evidence, she was a loving woman, and she loved him, and loving women did not betray their men no matter their desire. That aspect of womanhood had always astonished him. That female constancy had been a wonder, a derision, a pathetic thing, to him. Beth, out of some terrible need, some awful hunger, had
490

succumbed to seduction. Now it was only James he hated, this violator of his bed, this invader of his male territory.

What had been her need? Mere lust? He knew that was not so. True, she had gone to bed with him the very night of the day they had met. But surely out of love, as she always said. Beth was no liar. Beth was no light woman. James, in a moment of suffering, had been a surrogate— For me, he said to himself. For me. But James had taken advantage of this sorrow, this weakness. He must kill James, not Beth. But he would never see Beth again.

What stupidity had he been thinking these last days? He had been more than willing to throw up a life's work— for a weak and stupid woman. His family, his property, his place in the world, for which he had worked so hard. For a woman, only a woman.

Then a cold and steely light flooded into his mind. No. For myself. For myself only. Memories of the past five years rushed in on him, of more than five years, of more than twenty, thirty years. He had not had a truly happy day since he had returned from the Army—until he had met Beth. Still, Beth had been only the precipitant of what he now knew must have eventually have frothed over. He saw himself with absolute clarity now. He could not blame Beth for what had happened to him, as once he might have done, and had really done. He recalled that terrible night when he had left her, to kill himself. He saw her stricken face again, her wounded face, her proud face. No, he could not blame Beth for the fury and the illness which had been his life. He could blame no one but himself. And from that pit of despair Beth had rescued him.

James had destroyed it all. Beth was blameless.

His thoughts turned brutally on James. But all at once the fever and rage in him began to subside. He knew James too well. James might have had his whores all his adult life, but James was no casual seducer, no contemptuous womanizer, no exploiter of women. Once, long ago, he had said to Guy, "A man who exploits a woman, so much

491

more defenseless than himself, so much more vulnerable, so much more piteous, is worse than a murderer." It was as if James stood in this cramped little space of toilet, washbasin, and tub with him, and was repeating his words in stern tones, not righteously, but with absolute conviction and belief. "A man who victimizes a woman is lower than the lowest dog. At least dogs have morality, which no man really has."

No. James had not seduced Beth, nor she him. They had come together out of some dreadful need—both of them. For whom was Beth the surrogate? Lady Emma Godwin, of course, the dying and fascinating woman of whom James had so often written, so often spoken. James, at that infamous time, had not known that Emma was dying. But today, in his tears, he had mentioned that he had "known" something was wrong with Emma for over two weeks. He had known in his vitals, if not objectively. But even before that, he had said with shaking wonder and grief, even before he had left England his physician's mind had subtly warned him.

Beth and James had come together out of their mutual and unbearable need.

Even a year ago Guy would not have understood it, would have been scornful about it. Now he understood, now he was not derisive. A deep pity came to him for both of those he thought had violated his life, the deepest compassion he had ever known. It was alien to him, strange to him, so unfamiliar that it dazzled his mind. It shook him to the heart. Beth had not betrayed him; James had not betrayed him. In coming together they had affirmed their love for another man, another woman, and that love had been strengthened, not weakened. It was not lust but love which had brought them together.

It was more evidence that his ruthless nature had changed to such extent that he could say aloud, "God have mercy on all of us. In a way, I am the one to blame, not my darling, not my friend. I deserted Beth. And James stayed with me, to help me, when he must have been in a sweat to return to his Emma."

492

Guy had cried only three times in his adult life, once when he had heard about Marlene, once when his father had died, and tonight, earlier. He cried again.

"Guy?" There was a knock on the door. "Is there something wrong?"

He could hardly speak. "No, dear, nothing wrong. I'll be out in a minute."

She laughed. "I thought you had fallen in, you're so thin."

He looked at himself in the little mirror. It was a changed face he saw there, but one infinitely stronger.

He said, "No, I've fallen—out."

He had one foolish impulse, to walk out with James's cuff link in his hand and nobly say, "I found this. I understand."

Instead, he wrapped the cuff link in a piece of toilet paper, threw it in the bowl, and flushed it away. He said to himself: The hell with spoiling my happiness tonight. I am going to tell my poor Beth about Emma. Poor women.

29

Lucy Jerald called her brother, Hugh Lippincott. At first he could not hear her clearly through her whimpering and gasping. He had never liked his sister, who, apart from being a fool, was also tearful a great part of the time, and had been from earliest childhood. She said, "Hugh. I've had a letter from Guy—"

"I know. I did, too. The family conclave day after tomorrow."

"But. It's so confusing. Billy and Marcy got the same letters. I don't seem to grasp it."

"Don't try," said Hugh, kindly. "Might tax your brains."

"What? So confusing. I don't even know where he is."

"I'm sure he knows," said Hugh, who also knew.

"So strange. He sent a truck driver or something, from the country, for all his clothes. All. I wonder why."

"Maybe he's going on a trip."

"Well. Why didn't he tell me, to give me enough time to pack, too?"

"Oh, God," groaned Hugh.

"Never knew he had left the hospital until hours later, when Emil Grassner called. Discharged. I think that's terrible— Discharging a poor, sick, deranged man who needs tender loving care all the time. Billy was arranging—"

"I know what Billy was arranging," said Hugh, grimly. "Maybe that's why Guy has gone with the wind." He chuckled. "And he isn't sick, and never was. He just had had a collapse, and he's over that now."

"I've called all the hotels, here and in Philadelphia. He isn't there. What a thing to do to his wife and family. The children." As usual, she never listened. "Lucy," said Hugh. "Calm down. We'll know everthing on the day after to-morrow."

"The children," said Lucy. "Only a crazy man would act like this."

"Or a sane man."

"What?"

Hugh lost his short patience. "Please listen for once, Lucy. I think I know what Guy has in mind. A divorce. From you."

"What?" said Lucy. Then she shrieked. "A divorce? Why? I don't believe— Why should he want a divorce? I've always been a warm loving wife, faithful and devoted. He never said a word— I don't believe—"

"You can believe it. He never told me, but I know. Lucy, he's sick of you; he's been sick of you from the beginning." Hugh spoke brutally. "I warned you not to, before you married him, but you and Dad were so sure. I don't know how he stood this for so long, until it made him almost crazy."

"The children!" wailed Lucy. "I don't believe— How shall we explain this to the children?"

"The hell with the children," said Hugh, genially. "And they're not children. They're overripe adolescents, and
494

always were. And always will be. Even I, their uncle, can't stand them. They're as attractive as bunions, in body and soul."

"How can you talk that way about the children, Hugh Lippincott?"

"Easy. It comes naturally, after looking at them."

"The money," said Lucy, weeping wildly.

Ah, now we're down to basics, Lucy's basics, thought Hugh.

"Lucy, Guy has more than tripled the original fortune you had when you married him. And he's put you into some very sound investments, besides. You're a very rich lady, thanks to your husband."

"If he—if he—I'd want alimony."

"And I don't think you'll get it."

"But there are the children!"

"Adults in body if not in mind. Marcy's got a rich husband, thanks to the bundle Guy gave her before she got married. Billy's got a private income from his grandmother's, our mother's estate."

"But Marcy's got children of her own! They'll need every penny!"

"Oh, I'm sure if they ever do you'll help them out, Lucy."

He could see her shivering. "I don't know how a man could do this to the children."

"Lucy, if you don't keep your mouth shut about your damned holy 'the children' I'll hang up on you."

"I'm thinking of my dear lovely home, my home."

"I think it's Guy's. He paid for it; you didn't put in a cent, Lucy. I have an idea he will give the damned house to you, and be glad of it. He never liked that house, and I could see it, though he never told me."

"The children are just as confused as I am, the poor darlings. What? Oh, my home. You think he will turn it over to me?"

"Pretty sure."

He heard her sigh in relief. Then she said, and her

voice became unusually sharp. "Is there Another Woman, Hugh?"

"There usually is. But the Other Woman couldn't make headway if the marriage were strong, and yours never was, Lucy. No, I don't know of any Other Woman," and Hugh grinned to himself, thinking of Beth Turner.

"What do you mean, if the marriage were strong? There was nothing ever wrong with it, Hugh Lippincott, until Guy became so sick, the poor man. What are the children to do without a father?"

"How many infants does Guy have? That's interesting."

"Oh, Hugh. I mean Billy and Marcy. What are they to do?"

"What they're always doing. I have clients here, Lucy. Buck up, old girl. You're not losing a husband. You're just releasing a prisoner, and be a good sport about it."

Lucy shrilled, "A prisoner! What do—" But Hugh was already gone. She sat down and cried a little, then opened a drawer in her desk where, in a neat file, were recorded her financial assets. They made very comforting reading. She felt no grief, no real outrage, no sorrow, that her marriage was ended. In fact, there was a measure of relief in her shallow reflections. The house to herself. No bellowing, intransigent, impatient stranger who looked at her with a stranger's eyes and usually concluded the conversation with a weary "Shut up, Lucy, why do you have to flaunt your foolishness?" And Eric Daumbler had recently become a widower and looked at her yearningly when she entered the bank. It was only The Children— But she'd make it up to The Children. Encouraging them, giving them supportive help, maternally guiding them, the poor darlings, in their suffering. They didn't deserve this heartless traumatic injury. They needed their mother. She must remember to send Marcy's older child ten dollars next month on her birthday, as usual.

Lucy went out to lunch.

"I want these few days alone with you," said Guy Jerald to Beth. "We'll go to James's wedding this afternoon, then we'll be alone." His exhausted face was still exhausted, but the tense lines were diminishing.

"If you're taking up permanent residence here, sweetheart, you'll have to help Joel with the chores."

"Oh, I'm a farmer myself."

"And with the dishes."

"Like all women you try to make slaves out of men."

"I'm not your housekeeper, dear."

"But you'll soon be my wife. Thank God for New York State and its sensible divorce laws. Beth, you are sure you won't regret giving up the farm to go with me?"

"I'm not giving up the farm, Guy. Joel is going to run it for me when I am with you in that university town. And we'll use it ourselves in the summer."

"Ah, you're already plotting. Come sit on my knee, dear conspirator. I can't seem to get close enough to you, Beth. As you know, Beth, I will be taking summer courses, to speed things up." His black eyes were alive, full of anticipation. "It'll be a long hard grind, but I'll make it."

"With no regrets?"

"Yes, with the regret that I didn't do this three, four years ago, when I already knew I should. But I was afraid of losing money, then, afraid to break out of my nice cozy nest."

"But you'll still be making money in the building business."

"True." She saw, with amusement, that he had a satisfied look. No matter what happened, a strong man always put money, territory, and power ahead of any woman—that is, if he was a man. The new philosophy of the man-woman relationship degraded a man, emasculated him, corrupted his intrinsic nature, destroyed his natural place as a man among men. The area where he met women should not be confused with the mighty place where he met his peers. One was a predatory forest where he hunted with his male companions. The other was the hearthstone where he rested and built up strength for the next foray. Whoever violated this instinct, built into a man's genes throughout the millennia, violated the very essence of a man, and distorted the normal world of men. Women who believed that they could hunt beside a man, and compete successfully in his own territory, were deluding themselves, and corrupting their instincts. Beth, smiling as she perched on Guy's knee and submitting to his caresses, thought of what her mother had once said: "God created man out of the dust of the earth and breathed the breath of life into his nostrils. But it's nowhere recorded that He did this for women. He used one of Adam's ribs to make a woman—but He never gave her the breath of life to make her a living soul."

"What are you smiling about?" said Guy, with suspicion.

"Nothing, really."

"When a woman wears a smile like that she should be taken to bed."

"In the middle of the day, with an apple pie baking in the oven?"

Guy said, "I concede to the apple pie."

Beth said, "The hell with the pie; I can turn the oven off."

They went to the quiet wedding of James and Emma, in the county courthouse. They, with Emil Grassner, were the only witnesses; the mayor officiated, with some self-important pompousness. He had discreetly notified the newspapers. It was not every day that an English baronet and an English peeress appeared before him for his services. Such a handsome lady, too, with a devilish look in her eyes and a hearty manner, if a rather loud voice. She seemed to be laughing inwardly all the time. The baronet was a gentleman, that was obvious, though he looked a little sick today. But men were always agitated when getting married. There was money here, too. He could smell it. There was a white envelope peering from Emil's pocket. "Dearly Beloved," began the mayor, and Emma squeezed James's hand and winked at him lewdly. She wore a sensible tweed suit and a tweed hat, and looked, James thought, remarkably like Beth Turner though they did not resemble each other physically in the least. There
498

was a certain dauntlessness about them both, a certain intrepid nobility.

Guy had had a sharp twinge at the first meeting between him and James, for the male instinct was still there, possessive and ferocious. Then he cursed himself for a contemptible wretch who should grovel at James's feet and not have had that lust to kill. He saved both of us, thought Guy. He admired Emma, but thought her somewhat ugly. There was no comparison between her and Beth, for, to him, Beth had become the fairest and most desirable of women blooming in his love like the most precious of wines. Beth was tweedily dressed also, and James thought that both she and Emma were county ladies. James had looked at Beth with deep fondness and joy in her happiness, and had kissed her cheek on greeting her. Somewhere he had acquired a red rosebud, and Emma carried a bouquet of yellow roses, gift of Emil Grassner. There was also a smaller bouquet for Beth.

The mayor, a jovial little man as spherical as a pear, insisted on taking them into his office, where he served them a dubious brandy. (The English liked brandy.) The reporters came in with cameras, to James's startled annoyance, and the mayor apologized. "Make it short, boys," he said, sternly, and put himself in the center of the picture. "Let them have their fun," said Emma, who was always tolerant. She gave them her best smile and profile, her face jaunty under the tweed hat. She had decided that Guy was a somewhat dour and humorless man, but extremely masculine and sensual. She approved of him. She had loved Beth on sight, recognizing their unique sisterhood. No doubt Beth was the lady James had comforted, and she was pleased. The poor girl seemed very comforted now. As she sipped at the brandy Beth's hand had crept into Guy's.

Beth carefully kept from her expression every sign that she knew of Emma's malady and her impending death. She had wept in Guy's arms last night, but she had understood Emma even before she had met her. Emma was her own kind. There was no indication on Emma's face of her mortal illness, though she was darkly pale. She joked, somewhat naughtily, with the mayor, who blushed. James was unusually quiet and he kept his eyes fixed on his bride as if no one else was present.

It was seven o'clock when they left the mayor's office, and the snow was flying again and the wind was bitterly nimble. They went to the Old House for the wedding dinner. "We leave tomorrow morning for Nassau," said James. "So, with many regrets, I am afraid this is goodbye."

The word hung in the air poignantly, and no one said, "Oh, not goodbye. We'll meet again." They knew they would not.

But they all got drunk in defiance of the dread and invisible sixth member of the wedding. Guy raised his glass and said, "As my father always toasted: 'To life, to love.' " They returned the toast. Guy said, "This time, my father will dance at my wedding. He promised. He'll be there, the old scoundrel."

30

It was the night before Thanksgiving and Guy wryly thought how appropriate it was for him. He and his wife, Lucy, his children, William and Marcy, and Hugh Lippincott and Louise, were gathered together in the cold, vast and elegant sitting room of his house. The big fire could not warm that atmosphere or render it relaxed and comfortable. With Guy were two of his lawyers from Philadelphia, chill-eyed, alert youngish men with whom he had been consulting all day yesterday. They held dispatch cases on their knees and they had thoroughly studied, in a few minutes, all the members present.

Lucy's first remarks to her husband had been, "Where on earth were you?—so confusing—the children—I called —why did you disappear?—are you still ill?—you look awful, so thin—are you sure you should be out?—it's been a very hard time—the children have been out of their minds—how could you do this to us?—where did we go wrong?—don't you have any feeling for your warm loving family?—the children have been distracted—I haven't slept since you ran away from the hospital—how could they discharge you when you are so sick?—Billy's been running home every weekend to help poor Hugh—I don't know—I don't know—"

Dressed in her favorite blue, she had gone to her husband when he entered his house, her face puckered in a tremulous silent whimper, her absent blue eyes dimly expressing reproach. She had expected a kiss, a muttered apology, but he had gently put her from him as though she were an impertinent and tiresome stranger. Louise had drawn a deep gusty breath, looked at Guy critically and with malice, and had blurted, "Well!" She gave him a view of her wet flaring teeth, and then treated him to a sneer, and a shrug. She had gone to sit beside Lucy with an air of intense sympathy and consolation. Marcy and William sat together. Hugh sat alone, smoking and silent and watchful. He regarded Guy with curiosity. What was the enigmatic bastard up to now? He might look ill but he was very much present.

"We can make this very short," said Guy, standing as if about to depart. "Lucy. I apologize for marrying you. In a way it was a crime against you."

"Oh," said Lucy, and she smiled sweetly and with an air of martyrdom. "I know, dear, it hasn't been the happiest of marriages, though I did try my best. Now we—" (How absurd of Hugh that he should have mentioned "divorce"! Guy did not want a divorce. A little counseling, perhaps, by an expert, should set things right.)

Guy went on, "Yes, it was a crime against you. I didn't love you, not ever. You were only a substitute for someone else, long dead. I thought I had found her again in you."

How darling and sentimental, thought Louise with contempt, and she swished her long-out-of-date ponytail on her black silken shoulders.

501

"So I wronged you, Lucy," said Guy, with gravity. He felt sorry for Lucy, the first sorrow he had felt for her in all that long married life. "I know it's late, but not too late. You still have a life to live, without me—"

"Without you?" quavered Lucy, her mouth opening. "Why?"

"Because I am no good to you, and never was. You have a right to much better, because you were cheated of a real husband. A man like yourself, who would never have troubled you as I did. A man who would have loved your children, as I did not. You see, I speak of 'your' children, not mine. They were always yours."

Marcy, his daughter, glared at him. "You were never a real dad, Daddy. It was always your work before your family."

Guy looked at his daughter thoughtfully. "Now that, Marcy, is pure idiocy. A man's work should always come before his family. He's made that way. If his family comes first, then he has perverted his nature. He is not quite a man, or is a hypocrite. Either way, he has abrogated his instincts and has ruined his life, and his family inevitably is the victim. Thank God I never perverted the masculine nature, nor did I pretend to. I advise you, Marcy, to remember this when dealing with your own husband. Try to make him exclusively a daddy and he will become weak and infirm of will, or will run from you to a woman who will let him be a man."

"As you did," said Louise, with a malevolent grin.

"I'm sure I don't know what all this is about," said Lucy, looking at her son, William, her fat son with the sloping shoulders and loose mouth and avid eyes.

"I'll make it plain," said Guy. "I am going to divorce you, Lucy."

"Divorce!" Lucy shrieked. "Oh, no!"

"Divorce," said Hugh, and he smiled. "Good luck, fella."

"Divorce!" screamed Marcy, shifting her heavy buttocks on her chair and setting her bulky arms to flailing.

"Divorce," said William, significantly, and he glanced

502

at his uncle. "I think this is insane. He shouldn't have been allowed out of the funny farm. He needs conservators. He isn't responsible for what he's saying, or what he wants to do."

"I agree," said Louise. "It's crazy. I think we should have another consultation with Dr. Grassner. This poor man is out of his mind. Why should he want a divorce?"

Guy looked at her long and deliberately. "I want a divorce because I'm sane for the first time in many years. I want out of a marriage I should never have committed in the first place. I want my life."

"And," said Louise, giving him a look of pure malignance, "and you want that old laundress, too. Well. Water seeks its own level. I've told that to poor Lucy many a time. I agreed she shouldn't have married you. But that was long ago. You see, my friend, I've known all about you for a long time. I saw you with that old lady in Philadelphia, with her dyed red hair and her hideous cheap clothes, and her ugly freckled face. On your way to bed with her."

Lucy was weeping. "I don't know about another woman —what woman, Louise?"

"The one we saw at the hospital that Sunday—such a monster. Of course, she's just right for your husband, poor Lucy. Cheap, illiterate, homely, no style, a farm woman. No looks."

Guy said, repressing his rage, "She is a woman. Something you can't say about yourself, Louise. Sorry, Hugh!"

"Don't apologize to me," said Hugh, laughing, and beginning to enjoy himself.

"Where did I fail?" moaned Lucy. "Guy, there isn't anybody else, is there?"

"If there is, it isn't any of your business, Lucy."

"But that's adultery!" cried Lucy, in horror. Guy thought how much inadequate women loved that word. He thought of his mother.

"What does adultery mean to any man?" said Louise, now shooting her husband an evil look. "They're nasty, all of them."

503

"Yes," said Hugh. "We're a nasty race, Louise. And when we marry we commit miscegenation, or something."

"Don't talk to me, Hugh Linnincott, with your filthy innuendos!" his wife shouted. "I know all about you and that Nazi woman, who should be charged as a war criminal! If you don't let her alone I am going to bring charges against her!"

"So," said Hugh, and his fair face flushed with fury. "It was you who wrote that anonymous letter to the governor! I always thought it was."

"I never—" Louise began.

"Yes, you did. No one could have been so vicious and cruel like that but you."

"I can't believe my father was fooling around with another woman," said Marcy. "Why should he? He has a wonderful wife, a wonderful family, a wonderful position, a wonderful lot of money—everything wonderful. Mom's pretty and dutiful and a lady; Billy and I have never done anything wrong to disgrace Daddy. What more does a man want?"

"Marcy, a man wants, and must have, his life. I am not blaming your mother for anything. I am blaming myself that I married her. I am not blaming you, my dear; in your way you've been a good stolid woman, like my mother. I never had my life. Now I am going to have it. No, I blame no one but myself for the mess I made for everyone else, including me. But I have time to rectify this, and this is what I am going to do."

"Lucy," said Louise, "don't let him get a divorce."

"I will," said Guy. "I have all the information. I am establishing residence in New York State, where they now have sane laws about divorce. If Lucy tries to balk me, then I'm afraid I will have to do something drastic against her. She must let me go, in peace."

"To marry that frump," said Louise.

"To live," said Guy. "Louise, this is not any of your business and I advise you to keep quiet, or I will have you removed from this house now."

Louise turned savagely to her husband. "Hugh, are you going to let him talk like this to me?"

"It's his house," said Hugh. "He can order you out if he wants to. Shut up, why don't you, if only for five minutes?"

"You and that Nazi," said Louise. "You'll never get a divorce from me, Hugh Lippincott. I didn't know you loved Fascism that much."

"Alimony," wailed Lucy, who had been sunk in shallow thought. "You'd have to pay me alimony, Guy."

"I don't think so, Lucy. You are a rich woman in your own right."

"But. The children."

"I have given them too much of my life as it is. They're not young any longer. They've had all they're going to get out of me." His dark face was exhausted, but resolute. He looked slowly at his children. "Marcy's husband is well-off. Bill has his own income, and a nice bank account. I am not liable for his upkeep. In June, he will be earning his own way in the banks. If Hugh wants him."

Hugh sat up very straight in his chair. "If *I* want him? They're your banks, Guy."

Guy gave him a long humorous smile. "Not any longer, Hugh. You see, I am turning them completely over to you. Out of justice, out of penance."

Hugh gaped. He tried to speak. He choked. Every eye was on him now. His face swelled, became scarlet. He almost glared at Guy. "Do you—do you—know what you're saying?"

"I do." He gestured at his silent lawyers. "The papers are all in those cases, ready for us both to sign. Good luck, Hugh. Oh, there's just one condition. You divorce Louise."

"Divorce!" yelled Louise, her eyes bulging, her teeth thrust out. "He'll never get a divorce from me!"

Guy folded his arms across his chest. "I think he will. You see, your family's whole fortune is in some difficulties, including those of your precious nieces. The banks bought up most of their paper. Yesterday. It cost me a lot, but it was worth it. Hugh can straighten it all out—if he wants

505

to. If you don't let him get a divorce, he won't be of much help, I can assure you. In fact, he can ruin the whole works for your family. It's up to you, Louise. You're rich, and secure, thanks to Hugh. Perhaps you'd like to bail your family out yourself. It'll cost you everything. You'd better come to mutually agreed terms with Hugh, who should have divorced you years ago. Hugh"—and he turned to his brother-in-law—"I'm sorry. I was a self-righteous bastard to force you to live with this woman, when you wanted out, too."

"Don't mention it, fella," said Hugh, whose blue eyes were sparkling with excitement. His forehead visibly showed sweat. "If it had been earlier I'd have missed this wonderful showdown. You really mean it, Guy?"

"I do mean it."

"It's against the public interest to force a divorce," said William.

"You mean, in a will. I'm not dead yet, Bill, and you no doubt regret it."

"But you're insane. I intend—"

One of the lawyers spoke for the first time. "Mr. Jerald, your accusation is actionable. Your father is more sane than you are."

William subsided for a moment, full of hate. He said, "My poor mother."

"Who is a rich woman," said the lawyer. "Your father intends to release this house fully to her, after the divorce. His house."

"My mother's!" shouted Marcy, throwing her arms about wildly and stamping. "She was born here, it was her father's!"

"The property belongs to anyone who pays for it," said the lawyer. "Your husband paid for it, Mrs. Jerald. It's his."

Lucy looked at Guy, her mouth trembling. "You'll give me the house, Guy?"

"Yes, provided you don't contest the divorce. The papers are here for you, tonight, to sign, consenting, and
506

releasing me from all obligation to you from this day on. Lucy? It is agreed?"

"Don't sign," muttered William, automatically.

Now Hugh spoke, and with authority. "Keep up that advice, Bill, and you won't have any place in the banks." He drew one fast breath after another. He looked at Guy. "My banks?"

"Your banks."

Hugh turned to William. "You've heard. Behave yourself, and all will be well. In fact, encourage your mother to let your father go. If you don't, then I'll move against you myself."

Louise had been stunned, sitting in blinking silence, her teeth hanging out, her eyes bulging almost out of her head, her tanned face pallid. She had been gulping over and over. The news about her family had shocked her. She knew of their predicament but had determined that Hugh, and Guy, would assist. Now it was in jeopardy. Much as she sincerely loved her nieces, the thought of sacrificing her own fortune for them was unendurable. She was terrified. She clutched her hands tightly together, found it almost impossible to swallow. She cried, "It's all blackmail!"

"Sure it is," said her husband, happily. "It's the kind of thing you've been doing for a long time, dearest."

"Damn you, you and that Nazi!"

William had been thinking. It was all very plain to him. Oppose his father, and he'd be looking for a job next June, and he was certain that his uncle would pursue him with vengeance. He turned to his mother and said, "Mom, dear. I think it's all for the best. Don't cry."

Marcy, less intelligent, said, "I disagree. Mom has her rights, and we have our rights, too, as Dad's children."

Hugh said, "Your father, Marcy, gave up his rights twenty-seven years ago. I think he's served enough of the penal sentence. Don't make a fuss. It will be very bad for all of you."

"What about the business?" asked William. "Don't we get a share of it?"

"No," said Guy, feeling more aversion for his son than ever before. "I am maintaining control of the business. I will be back and forth, between here and New York, regularly. Where am I going in New York? None of your business, Bill. I am none of your business, or you of mine, after tonight. Now, shall we begin with the papers?"

They were signed, but not without much weeping, pleading, wailing, and protesting from the women. Now William was solidly aligned with his father and uncle. He had his own future to consider, his own welfare. He was determined to cultivate his uncle assiduously. Lucy said, "And I get all the furniture, too, Guy?"

"You do." He felt quite kindly towards her and kissed her cheek. "You get the cars, too. Except one, for myself, which I am taking tonight." He felt weak and shaken. It was all finished, all done. He had cut the past from himself forever. He had expected more opposition. Thanks to Hugh it had been much easier.

He kissed his daughter, and shook hands with his son. "Good luck," he said, and felt that he was leaving strangers in whom he had not the slightest interest.

"How can you desert us like this, Daddy?" asked Marcy, in tears.

"How can I desert someone I was never with?" he replied. "I did the best I could for you, Marcy, though I never felt you were my children. You were always your mother's. Take care of her, Marcy. She is a rich woman." He saw the gleam of speculation in Marcy's eyes, and was bitterly amused. She knew she would inherit nothing from him. It was all her mother's. I suppose, Guy thought, she is frightened that Lucy might marry again, which would be disastrous for her and Bill. Or, she is wondering how long her mother can live. Children!

Lucy clung to him on parting. Again she whimpered, "The children."

"The hell with them, Lucy. Think of yourself."

When he and Hugh were alone outside the house and in the midst of a whirling blizzard, Guy shook hands with his brother-in-law, who was still dazed.

"Give my love to Marian," he said. "Go to see her tonight."

"On that you can bet," said Hugh, with fervor. "God, Guy. You don't know what you've done for me. It was worth waiting for."

"Sometimes things fall into place, if you wait," said Guy. "Not always, not regularly. But sometimes. Good night."

"God bless," Hugh said, and was amazed he meant it.

31

In March, both Emil Grassner and Guy Jerald received a telegram from Hawaii:

> God mercifully delivered me from my promise to Emma. She died peacefully and painlessly this morning. Am returning with her to England, where I will begin the work I must do, for my father and my wife.
>
> In the dark night of the soul, bright flows the river of God.
>
> Devotedly, James Meyer

ABOUT THE AUTHOR

One of America's most popular and prolific novelists, Taylor Caldwell has "always written"—since she learned to write at the age of four. She began writing novels at nine and by twelve her first novel was submitted to her grandfather, then on the staff of a major Philadelphia publishing house. He dismissed the book, refusing to believe a child could have written it, and advised her father, "Burn it; she'll cause you trouble." Undaunted by this early rejection, Miss Caldwell kept at her writing and went on to publish more than thirty books.

Born in a suburb of Manchester, England, of Scotch-Irish ancestry, Taylor Caldwell came with her family to the United States when she was six years old. She was graduated from the University of Buffalo (Miss Caldwell holds three doctorate degrees), and in 1938 she achieved instant literary fame with the publication of *Dynasty of Death*. Since that time she has written many bestsellers, including *This Side of Innocence, Testimony of Two Men, Captains and the Kings,* and *Glory and the Lightning. On Growing Up Tough* is her autobiography.